Top Dog

TOP DOG

HEROES OF HENDERSON: BOOK 3

Liz Kelly

Published by Kelly Girl Productions
©Copyright 2014 Liz Kelly
Cover design by Tammy Kearly

ISBN: 978-0-9889838-6-1

This book is a work of fiction. The characters, events and places portrayed in this book are products of the author's imagination and are either fictitious or are used fictitiously. Any similarity to real persons, living or dead, is purely coincidental and not intended by the author.

For more information on the author and her works, please see www.LizKellyBooks.com

To

Pat Crain
and
Jeff Carraway
Who inspired the perfect hero.

And to all my Tiara Wearing Besties
This one's for you.

CHAPTER ONE

May

Crain Carraway slipped inside the luxurious bathroom of his Las Vegas suite and shut the door quietly. Even though he couldn't sleep, it seemed that his beautiful bride was out cold after a very lengthy, highly energetic, totally off the charts, roll-me-over-and-do-that-again consummation of their marriage. God, she was something. Something fine looking and brilliant and just as sweet as the cherry on top of his old-fashioned. He couldn't believe she was his. All his. And he couldn't sleep because he wanted the world to know it.

Starting with his parents.

He dialed their number, checking the time on his watch. Dallas was two hours ahead of Vegas and, on a weekday morning, his parents should be up and at 'em. No doubt this would get their day started with a bang.

"Honey Bear!" his momma said in greeting, as if he wasn't thirty-five years old.

"Momma Bear," he said back, playing her game. "Put me on speaker and round up Papa Bear. I have big news."

"Big news?"

"Texas-sized news."

His mother laughed. "Bigger than when you started CC Dallas, Inc.? Lucius," his mother shouted. "Your son has Texas-sized news he wants us to hear together."

2

"May as well grab a bottle of champagne while you're at it, Ma. You're gonna need it," Crain said.

"I'll bet that luxury suite at Cowboys Stadium came through," his father's voice echoed over the phone.

"Even better than that," Crain grinned at himself in the bathroom mirror. "Dad, do you remember that statuesque blonde I pointed out when you stopped in the office a month ago? The one trying to hide all that beauty under those smart-girl glasses?"

"Do I? That pretty, little gal had you drooling like a bluetick coonhound."

Crain chuckled. "Guilty as charged. Well, it took some doing, but I finally got that pretty, little gal to agree to a dinner date. I took her to Nick & Sam's."

"Best steakhouse in Dallas," his dad said.

"And she loved it. In fact, the date went so well she agreed to meet me for drinks at the Ice House the next night. One thing led to another very good night, and although I will admit she was a little bit tipsy when I asked her to accompany me to Las Vegas, I assure you she was completely sober when I asked her to marry me."

"You're engaged?" his mother exclaimed.

"Better than that. We're married."

"Married?" Papa Bear sounded astonished.

"We eloped. Last night. It was just…right. Everything about it was perfect. And I'm sorry you weren't here, but I know you're gonna forgive me when you meet my bride."

"Wha…ah…well of course we'll forgive you," his mother stuttered. "But darlin' boy, this is all so quick. So sudden."

Crain smiled, softening his voice in an effort to soothe his momma. "I know it seems that way, I truly do. But you know I've dated a lot of wonderful women over the years. And every time I figured out what I didn't want, I knew better what I did want. And this one, this one is the complete package. Underneath her bright and engaging business persona, there's a bewitching temptress just as sweet as praline pie. She's the one I've been looking for all my life, Momma. She's the one I want."

"You sound so certain."

"Because I am. I was certain the first time we met, and after date number two, all I could think was 'how fast can I get this girl to the altar?'"

"Any faster and you'd catch up to yesterday," his father said.

"And now I'm burning daylight, so let me get back to my bride," Crain countered.

"Wait," his mother cried. "What's her name? Who are her people?"

"Well, I don't exactly know who her people are, Momma, because I've been solely focused on sweeping her off her feet. But I'll tell you what. Anybody who can raise a woman like her can't be all bad. Now I've got to go and talk my bride into a nice long honeymoon in Hawaii, so if you two don't hear from me for a couple weeks, don't fret. And in the meantime, Momma, you can start planning whatever extravaganza you've got in mind to introduce my bride to *our* people."

"I can tell you one thing," his momma scolded. "It's gonna look a whole lot like a church wedding and a big fat reception. You tell my new daughter-in-law the first thing I plan to do is to take her shopping for a wedding dress. I love you, but I am not particularly happy about this."

"Oh, come on," he goaded. "You know you're a little happy about this."

"I'm very happy you're happy, darlin' boy. But I sure don't like missing my own son's wedding. Now bring that girl home, so I can hug her neck."

"Will do, Momma. Will do. Papa Bear, I am signing off."

"I'll take care of your momma. You go take care of your bride."

"Over and out."

Crain hung up. And then he did what turned out to be about the dumbest thing a man with a Texas A&M degree could do. He took the time to text everybody he knew, telling them he had married the cutest Ole Miss Hotty Toddy ever found in Dallas. Yep, he was one happy groom. Right up until he made his bride a cup of coffee just the way she liked it—with a whole lot of cream and sugar—and carried it into the bedroom.

"Sweetheart," he whispered, until he realized the bed was empty. "Sugar?" he yelled, looking around the room, his eyes coming to rest on the note written with her preferred red Sharpie. "Honey?" he said, moving forward to pick up the note.

Four little words. Four little words Crain Carraway had no idea what to do with. Four little words that left him certain of absolutely nothing.

I'm sorry – cold feet.

CHAPTER TWO

September—Four months later

Tansy Langford blinked her eyes at the handsome couple who stood together holding hands in the center of Evans & Evans Investment, Inc.'s reception area. Sitting at her desk, her brain could not comprehend what the tall, dark, notorious womanizer and the pink-cheeked, curly-haired blonde had just announced.

"You're what?" Tansy shouted at Piper, accusation resonating in her words as she stood and pressed her hands flat on her desk.

Her long-lost childhood friend, Piper Beaumont, had come back to their hometown of Henderson only a few weeks ago on the arm of Tansy's nemesis, Vance Evans. Who, due to an unfortunate series of events, also happened to be the guy now signing her paychecks.

"We're married," Piper said, beaming. She held out her left hand and wiggled her fingers, showing off a three-carat oval flanked by trillion diamonds.

"You can't be…*married*," Tansy insisted.

"Oh, we can," Vance assured her.

"You practically just met."

Piper tried to placate her with a smile. "Tansy, you of all people know I've been in love with Vance since fourth grade."

"Fourth grade. Yes. Then you moved away and haven't seen each other in what? Twenty years? It's been less than eight weeks since you've reunited. That is too quick to responsibly marry someone," Tansy insisted. "*Way* too quick."

"No one's ever accused me of acting responsibly," Vance said with a radiant gleam in his eyes. "Least of all you."

Tansy could tell he was enjoying delivering this news all the more just because it was pissing her off.

"Clearly I'm not talking about *you*," she said, sitting back down at her desk, pulling out a red Sharpie from the group of them sticking out of her Ole Miss mug. "I mean, what are people going to think?" she asked Piper. "Sensible, well-brought-up people *do not* elope after being together for such a short period of time for goodness sake. They get engaged, they meet the families, they plan a wedding, there are parties—"

"Oh, there's gonna be a party," Vance insisted. "And we didn't elope. Our friends and loved ones were right there with us."

Tansy looked up and blinked. She felt her mouth falling open in shock and hurt.

Piper gave her new husband a look and dropped his hand, coming toward Tansy and leaning over the desk. "It wasn't like that," she said quietly. "I was being treated at Raleigh Memorial when Vance proposed. He managed to have the wedding ceremony performed in the hospital within a few hours."

"Why were you in the hospital? Why would you get married in a hospital? Oh my God, are you dying?"

"No. I'm fine," Piper soothed. "But I was severely dehydrated. Because I'm pregnant."

"You're pregnant," Tansy said on a breath, falling into the back of her chair.

"Yes." Piper was clearly elated. "Isn't it fabulous?"

"It's…well, it certainly is a reason to get married quickly," Tansy offered, wondering if she had any Advil in her desk drawer. Or migraine medicine. This was probably a migraine coming on. Vance Evans was going to be a father. Her old friend Piper was finally going to get to be a mommy. And her own life was on hold and yet spiraling out of control all at the same time.

"It happened so fast, there was no time to call you," Piper continued.

Vance feigned a cough, letting Tansy know that she was the last person he'd have called. Tansy rolled her eyes at Vance and then pulled her focus back to Piper as she continued.

"Vance's father and his new bride weren't there of course. We called Hale and Genevra in Europe after the ceremony to tell them. They've decide to cut their honeymoon short to come home and celebrate with us. Once they're back, we'll plan a big reception, and you'll be the first one on the list."

Vance coughed again. Piper threw him an "enough" look over her shoulder and then smiled down at Tansy. "You'll be the first name on *my* list."

Tansy stared up into Piper's happy face, those round pink cheeks promising adorable babies for the object of her scorn. "He doesn't deserve you."

"Now that's the first thing we agree on," Vance said, sneaking his arms around his wife's tiny waist.

"I don't deserve Piper," he said with more sincerity than Tansy thought him capable. "You and I see eye to eye on that. But I love her. I always have. Nobody means more to me. Nobody. So hear me when I say I'll make her a good husband, Tansy, because I mean that more than my words can convey. And right now, in this judgmental and gossipy town where we all went through fourth grade together, Piper is gonna need you on her side. For all those reasons you listed and more. I may not care what anybody thinks, but Piper does. So please, don't take your disdain for me out on her. She needs a friend, and even though my gratitude probably means nothing to you, I'm offering it anyway."

Vance Evans was holding out an olive branch. And here Tansy thought the marriage announcement was a surprise. She stood up, reached over her desk and hugged Piper. "If you're happy, then I'm happy," she offered. "It's just…you know, sudden."

"Yes," Piper agreed with a laugh, "and we certainly didn't plan it this way. But since we both couldn't be happier about the baby, we're just rolling with it. Really. Everyone will talk behind our backs and our poor little precious bundle—"

"Vance, Jr." Vance interjected.

"Yes." Piper agreed, grinning up at the man before settling her gaze back on Tansy, "*Vance, Jr.* will always be the reason people around here say, 'They had to get married'. But whatever. I'm sure the news of Hale and Genevra's pregnancy will raise even more eyebrows since Vance, Jr. is destined to have an uncle or aunt his same age."

"Wait." Tansy looked up at Vance. "Your father and Genevra are expecting?" Tansy had just attended their wedding not a month ago. How could they already be expecting? And at their age? Seriously, she needed some migraine medicine.

"It isn't common knowledge, but it's a good bet Genevra will be showing when she returns from their honeymoon," Vance said. "And since there is going to be *growing* evidence to support the fact that my father and I can't keep it in our pants, this town is going to have its fill of gossip pretty darn quick."

Tansy didn't realize she was tapping her red Sharpie repeatedly against her desk until Piper's hand reached out and stopped it.

"Oh. Sorry." She put the pen back right before she burst out laughing. She couldn't help it. Her situation. Their situation. All of it was verging on the ridiculous.

Piper and Vance joined in immediately, their laughter escalating into out-and-out howling as they made jokes about what Henderson's faithful were going to say when they heard the news that both Hale Evans and his son, Vance, had knocked up women before they had the decency to marry them. And then they laughed harder because they'd just reduced it all down to a laughing matter.

Their laughter was so infectious that Davis Williams had ventured out of his office to find out what was going on. True to his nickname, "Pinks" wore a pink button-down shirt tucked into a very businesslike and expensive light gray pair of pants. His infamous needlepoint belt was now saved for his more casual wear. Instead, he sported a fashionable cordovan leather belt and a trendy pair of cordovan shoes. His hair, the color of Tansy's cream-laden morning coffee, was stylishly cut. Her eyes ran over him as she continued to laugh and it occurred to Tansy that Pinks had definitely upped his game.

Davis, a recent graduate from NC State University, was smart. Smart enough to sell himself into a nonexistent summer internship with the newly founded Evans & Evans Investments, Inc. Essentially, he was hired to be Vance's right arm, though he'd quickly managed to make himself so invaluable to the entire Evans family that they offered him one of the many guest rooms in their mansion. He was bright and he was young—way young—and his gold eyes glistened with mirth. Always. At the moment, his grin went from ear to ear as he witnessed their insanity.

"It's gotta be a cold day in Hell if Tansy and Vance are laughing together," he said to Piper. "Most of the time they are laughing at the other's expense."

"Yes, well," Piper said over her merriment, "let's hope this is a new beginning. I feel a little responsible since their vendetta started because Vance refused my advances at an eighth-grade dance—"

"I was mistakenly distracted by dollar signs and didn't recognize you," Vance interjected.

"Just an endearing part of our past," she said soothingly. "But since you and Tansy are now working together for E&E, *and* for Team Henderson, it would be nice if you'd wipe the slate clean and make a fresh start. For Pinks' and my sake," she added with a nod to Davis.

"I'm sure Brooks wouldn't mind having the peace made either." Vance winked at Tansy.

"Maybe," she offered with a forced grin. The man signed her paychecks. What else was she going to do?

Frankly, she'd bet good money that Brooks Bennett, Golden Boy of Henderson and shoo-in for mayor, couldn't care less if their *vendetta*, as Piper called it, lasted forever. Oh, Brooks had cared a lot about it back when she and Brooks were dating, but at present, Brooks was too caught up in his darling little *Lolly*. The same Lolly who was now Vance's stepsister since her mother just married Hale Evans. Which, Tansy realized, now made Lolly DuVal

Piper's sorta-kinda sister-in-law. *Wow*, Tansy thought. She was being pushed so far out of Piper's friends and family circle it wasn't even funny. She did need to wipe the slate clean. Or come clean. Or something...

Ugh.

She opened her desk drawer looking for a painkiller.

"Okay," Vance said. "I've got to go. One more patrol and tomorrow I'm officially handing in my badge." He kissed Piper and gave her butt an affectionate squeeze. "You can find your way home?"

"I can."

"Pinks, you'll take care of my girl—my wife," he corrected, "until I get home?"

"I don't need a babysitter," Piper insisted. "Besides, your grandmother will be there."

"Pinks," Vance shouted over his shoulder.

"I'm on it," Davis said.

Piper let out a long sigh as Vance left the building. "I married a control freak, didn't I?"

Davis shrugged. "He loves you. You were in the hospital for four days. You're carrying his child, and frankly, with his history of his mother running out on him, I'm surprised he's letting you out of his sight at all. Give him some time."

Tansy saw it in Piper's face. She was so in love with the man she would give him all the time he needed.

Double ugh.

Piper turned to Tansy. "I want you to come to Vance's retirement party at the police station tomorrow. It's a surprise. They're going to have a cake for Vance, and toast his future here at Evans & Evans, that sort of thing."

"Vance won't want me there," Tansy insisted.

"I don't know. It might be right up your alley." Pinks grinned. "It'll probably turn into some kind of a roast, knowing his 'not much of a cop' reputation."

"Please come," Piper pleaded. "It will help with the fresh start, and truly, Tansy, you're the only one who remembers me in this town. I'm going to need support when everybody starts whispering about the out-of-town, gold-digging blonde who trapped Vance Evans into marrying her."

"No one is going to say that."

"Everyone is going to say that."

Starting with Tansy's own mother, Tansy thought glumly.

Tansy's mother, Garland Langford, was nothing if not the pillar of decorum in the town of Henderson. Never making a wrong move in society because her every move was calculated. It was why Tansy's nerves were wound tighter than rope these days. Her mother did no wrong and expected her daughters to follow in her footsteps.

Yeah. And I blew that one sky-high. And now she was scrambling to contain the damage before anyone was the wiser.

The Langford name was well respected in Henderson and where her momma may chastise her daughters for gossiping unkindly at the dinner table, she was sure that her mother's circle of friends would have a heyday over both Evans men, father and son, having shotgun weddings within weeks of one another.

And poor, sweet Piper would be eaten alive by those vultures if Tansy couldn't find a way to convince her mother to take the lead and come out in defense of Piper and Vance.

Garland Langford had the power to squelch the nasty backlash of any gossip in this town. A word or two from Garland could turn any breach of propriety into a non-issue or blow it sky high. No one would dare besmirch something Garland Langford deemed acceptable. And no one would question her censorship either. Tansy's mother was her generation's Evie Jackson in this town. And even Evie seemed to be stepping aside, letting Garland lead the way of Henderson society these days.

Which meant that Tansy may be able to use her influence with her mother to help out her sweet friend, Piper. But it also meant that she herself was in deep, deep doo-doo.

CHAPTER THREE

As soon as Piper left the office, Tansy turned an accusing eye on Pinks. "You knew about this wedding."

"Of course I did. And you would have too, if you'd ever taken me up on my offers for drinks after work. I mean, what the hell is up with that, Yacht Club?"

"Why do you insist on calling me that?" she snapped.

"You're kidding, right? Are there no mirrors over there at Mommy and Daddy's?"

Tansy grimaced at the reminder that she'd moved back in with her parents. She wanted to snap out a quick retort about him living with his employers, but the words dried up in her mouth as she took a good long look down her navy and white striped boatneck top with its three-quarter length sleeves. It was tucked into a pair of smart, red Bermuda shorts. On her feet, she had red sling-back, peep-toe Sperry Top-Siders with a cork heel, and at her waist sat a thin red belt with gold nautical knots for the clasp. She felt her earlobes. Yep—gold nautical knots there as well.

Good freaking grief.

"So were *you* at the wedding? In the hospital?" she asked.

"Who do you think pulled it all together?"

Tansy sighed, looking Davis right in the eye. "Of course you did." Man, she felt defeated at every turn when it came to him. "You're Vance's right-hand man. Who else could have possibly arranged…whatever it was you managed to arrange. You're the

Robin to his Batman, the Tonto to his Lone Ranger. He says jump through a hoop, and you dive through a dozen."

"Pretty much," he agreed.

"Well…" She turned away, unable to look him in the eye when she admitted, "Whatever he's paying you, it's not enough."

"We're in negotiations."

Her head popped up at that. Davis' overly confident but totally disarming I'm-all-that-and-a-bag-of-chips grin spread clear across his face.

Oh, no. No-no-no-no-no. This could not be happening.

"What do you mean, negotiations?" She whispered the words in hope of stemming her panic. "You *can't* be in negotiations," she said a little louder. "You've got that other job lined up. That big deal, big bucks, moving-back-to-Baltimore job."

"Is that why you keep refusing to have drinks with me? Because I'm leaving?"

"I refuse to have drinks with you because we don't like each other."

"Oh, come on," Davis cajoled. "There's a conference table right down the hall that begs to differ."

Tansy closed her eyes and took in a long breath. "Davis," she ground out, her voice low and serious. "We agreed *never* to discuss that unfortunate night."

"You mean the one where I had you every which way but loose? That night?" He moved forward, barging into her personal space. "The one where I collected my cherished souvenir of a navy blue bra and a tiny little lace thong? Is that the one? And why exactly is that night—the night I can't get out of my head, the night I've been reliving over and over in my mind—a taboo subject? I've been racking my brain over that for weeks. Why, Miss Langford, are you so dead set against admitting that we'd developed a crazy amount of sexual tension that exploded all over the conference room?"

"Because it wasn't sexual tension," she protested. "It was just… tension. Basic, regular, my-life-is-out-of-control-and-I-don't-know-how-to-handle-it tension. And I'm sorry that it exploded all over you. I really am."

"Well, I'm not. I'm not at all. I mean you certainly aren't any picnic, and I generally don't go for the biggest bitch in the room, but hell, we had a good time, and I, for one, wouldn't mind a repeat performance."

"Of course you wouldn't, because you're practically a teenager and your hormones are out of control."

"And as such, my youthful vigor is a perfect match for your thirty-year-old sexual peak."

Tansy gasped, horrified. "I am *not* thirty years old."

"You are in another month."

"How do you know—" Tansy stopped herself. No good could come from the direction they were heading. She reeled herself in and redirected. "Davis, that job up North has got to be starting soon," she said as calmly as she could.

"You want to get rid of me, is that it? Huh. It all makes perfect sense now," he said, wandering his way around the foyer, speaking like he was some damn lawyer arguing in front of a jury. "I mean, how else are you *ever* gonna be the shining star around here? I get it." He looked over at her as if he understood her better than she understood herself. "With me out of your way, you'll finally be able to achieve your lifelong dream of becoming Employee of the Month."

"Oh my God you're such an a—" She snapped her mouth shut.

"Why do you do that?"

"Do what?"

"Stop yourself from cussing?"

"I cuss."

"Yes. Yes, you do. But you don't like that you do, do you?"

"What are you talking about?"

"You're…interesting, Miss Langford."

God, she hated when he did that. Raise his chin and look down at her like he wasn't six years her junior.

"When the *hell* are you leaving?" she asked, letting all the exasperation she felt fill in the spaces of that question.

"I'm not. I'm staying."

Tansy's mouth hung open, her eyes blinking rapidly. Her brain refused to process this information. "What do you mean, you're staying? You can't...*stay*." *Oh Lord, no. There was no way he could stay.* "You're a summer intern for God's sake," she cried. "And it's the middle of September. You've overstayed your welcome, *Pinks*. Yankee, go home, and all that. Time to get the heck out of North Carolina."

Pinks laughed. "Ah, Tansy. As if anyone could ever get enough of North Carolina."

She certainly could. She certainly *did*. And she had *loved* being away from North Carolina. In fact, she had loved who she was away from Henderson, out from underneath her parents' *strong suggestions*. And boy, she'd been regretting her hasty and impromptu move back home since about thirty minutes after she'd arrived.

Big, big mistake.

But she was Garland Langford's daughter, after all, and as such Tansy knew exactly what was expected of her. And more importantly what was not. *And holy shit*—think of the devil and in she'll walk, Tansy thought as the front door to E&E opened and her beautiful mother, along with her invisible broomstick, walked on through.

Pinks was no stranger to wealth or beautiful women. Had he been, spending the last couple of months living on the Evans estate encountering Genevra, and Vance's grandmother Emelina, on a daily basis would have certainly cured him of it. But he still did a double take when Garland Langford walked in.

Tansy and her mother didn't look exactly alike, but they were both striking. Both tall, streaky blondes. Mrs. Langford's figure was a good bit slighter than her daughter's, and Tansy wore her hair a lot longer.

But if Tansy dressed like she was a member of a yacht club, her mother dressed like she owned the biggest yacht in the place.

Her hair, her makeup, the jewels, the knit suit, all not-so-subtle indications to Garland Langford's station in life. She was enchanting and poised when Tansy introduced him as Davis Williams, adeptly asking him polite first-time-meeting questions. He was feeling quite enamored until he was abruptly dismissed.

"Davis, I'd like to speak with my daughter now," she said. The indication clear she wanted him gone from the room.

Which totally pissed him off.

This was a place of business for God's sake. He was tempted to blurt out something like, "Perhaps you'd like to do that during her lunch hour, you wicked bitch," but he thought better of it, especially when he noted the annoyance all over Tansy's face. For once, her annoyance wasn't directed at him.

So he moved down the hall but stopped inside the first office, Hale's office, and didn't feel one iota of guilt eavesdropping on the conversation between the beautiful bitch and her dangerous offspring.

"Mother. That was a little abrupt, don't you think?"

Damn right it was, Pinks thought.

"Darling, time is money, as I'm sure Hale Evans knows. The way that man has begun to flaunt his wealth and his lust for that DuVal woman, he certainly isn't going to want to hear that you and that young man are cavorting during office hours."

"Cavorting? There is no cavorting going on between Davis and me."

Bullshit. There had been cavorting. In fact, he was eager for a little more cavorting.

"No? He seemed quite smitten with you—"

Smitten. I'm far from smitten. Pinks rolled his eyes.

"—and although this isn't the primary reason I came in to talk with you, I understand that the DuVal woman's child has gone back to college."

"Mother. For goodness sake you were at 'the DuVal woman's' wedding. And the two of you have lived in the same town your entire lives. I think you know her name is Genevra and her daughter's name is Lolly. And Lolly didn't go back to college. She went back to finish her graduate degree."

Well, now. Tansy defending Lolly. This is something new.

"Whatever, darling. They're simply N.O.C.D."

"N.O.C.D?"

"Not Our Class, Dear. Which is why you will certainly be doing the Bennetts a favor by using this opportunity to insert yourself back into Brooks Bennett's life. Now that *Lolly* has gone back to school."

"You cannot be serious."

"I'm dead serious. How else do you plan to get the love of your life back?"

"Mother. Trust me. You have no idea who the love of my life is."

Hmm.

"Of course it's Brooks. And I've just heard from a reputable source that he's finally ready to run against Mayor Stevens in the next election. Now, his parents will want you on his arm for that. That has always been the plan. Certainly, the DuVal girl is not First Lady material. It's obvious Brooks is using her to make you jealous. To make you pay for running out on him just as he was ready to propose. I told you that was not your finest hour."

"Yes, Mother. You've told me and told me. And life has moved on. Brooks has moved on. I have moved on, and now it's time that you and Daddy move on too."

"And leave you here working for Hale Evans and his randy son? You and I both know your ambition goes well beyond…this. You certainly have the brains and savvy, not to mention the credentials, to run Henderson all on your own. Wasn't that the plan? Get the local sports star elected while you run everything behind the scenes? You really don't need Brooks to do it, though I wouldn't recommend running against the man. Lord knows no one could win against him, and you'll just come off looking like a scorned woman or a dyke."

"A what?"

A what? Pinks covered his mouth.

"Well, of course. If you ran against Brooks, you'd just come off looking like a man-hater at the very least and a lesbian at the worst."

Pinks heard Tansy choke out a startled laugh. "You've got to be kidding."

"Indeed I'm not. You know how conservative Henderson is. And I know better than anyone how they think. I hear what they say around here."

"Because you're the one who's saying it," Tansy shouted. "You're the *voice* of Henderson."

"And who better? Your grandparents were model citizens for years. Your father and I have done our best to carry on in their footsteps and have increased our family's social standing. We've raised two beautiful daughters who have worn the Langford name with dignity. Although, really darling, no one understood your need to run off and spend last year traipsing around Dallas. Fortunately, the town just chalked that up to the impetuousness of youth. And, frankly, compared to Lolly's cousin, Molly DuVal, and all her wild antics, well…no harm done."

"Mother. Can you hear yourself talk?"

"All I'm trying to say is that you and Brooks made a brilliant team. He the brawn and you the brain. And now that Lolly is out of the way, you may want to…dress up a bit. You have a plethora of designer suits hanging in your closet. I know you're simply the receptionist here, but darling, please, show a little pride. You look like you're dressed for a pleasure cruise instead of a day at the office."

Pinks had to cover his mouth not to burst out laughing.

"I'm not simply a receptionist, Mother. I'm the office manager, and they told me to dress casually. We all dress casually," Tansy insisted, sounding a little desperate as she went on to explain. "E&E isn't the kind of business where people usually walk in off the street. Hale travels the country conducting business and occasionally has meetings here. Although, if Brooks does run for mayor, I imagine this will become his campaign headquarters since Vance is claiming to be his campaign manager."

"Perfect. You'll start wearing your suits and let the campaign bring the two of you back together."

"If I wore those suits, I'd look just like you, and the town of Henderson would be scared to death."

"Henderson loves me."

"Henderson fears you. We all fear you. Now, what exactly did you come in here for?"

"Fine. Just…consider what I've said, and we'll leave it at that. For now. So," Garland Langford went on, smoothly shifting gears, "I'm sure you've received your invitation to the Ole Miss 100th Homecoming celebration where they are honoring all past homecoming queens. You must attend."

"Aww." Tansy's voice got all soft and warm, which sent warning bells off in Pinks. *Tansy was never, ever soft or warm.* "I'm guessing you're picturing a mother–daughter trip. The two of us going back to Ole Miss arm in arm, wearing our matching tiaras." Tansy's voice actually lit up in excitement then. "And I bet a few of my designer suits would be perfect for the occasion."

"Absolutely."

"Dream on, Mother."

Yep. Back to mean ol' Tansy.

"Elizabeth Tansy Langford, this is not up for discussion. You're going," Garland insisted. "You and I are going together, and we're going to have fun. You, me, and your sister, who has not been returning my calls."

"Mother. You go. You have fun. All your old cronies will be there, I'm sure. You can all take Scarlett and her friends out to dinner. Let her be the one you show off. I'm certain that out of all the returning homecoming queens, you will be the fairest of all. But the tiara and sash are your thing. I'm perfectly happy to pass the torch to the new, much younger queen."

"You loved competing in those pageants."

"*You* loved that I competed in those pageants."

"You were so good at them."

"I was good at them because you are my mother. You are the one who was good at them, Miss North Carolina."

"Winning felt good."

"It always does."

"Tansy. Please. Come with me to see your sister at Ole Miss. Wear your tiara and sash one more time. For me. They're playin' Texas Tech. We'll have a catered tailgate at The Grove. Tell me a football weekend back at your alma mater doesn't sound like fun. We'll get Daddy to charter a plane. Fly right into Oxford. Easy peasy."

"Do not ask Daddy to charter a plane."

"You can't get there from here unless you do. So you're going then?"

"Mother."

"Tansy, please. Indulge me, darling. I'm your mother."

There was a big sigh and a long pause.

"Mother…I personally do not want to do this. But I do need a favor, for a friend, so I'm willing to bargain this trip to Ole Miss with you in exchange for your cooperation."

"Lovely. What can I do? Make a donation? Wrap up a gift basket for a raffle?"

"Nothing so easy. What I'm asking for is going to take a considerable amount of your power and ingenuity. Not to mention an abundance of self-discipline, because it is no doubt going to go against your sanctimonious nature. You're probably going to hate it."

"What in the world is it?"

"I can't give you any details until I have your word that you'll use your powers for good instead of evil."

"Stop being so dramatic and tell me, who, exactly, this concerns?"

"Not until you promise to do as I ask. This is a good news/bad news thing, Mother. The good news is that you'll have the pleasure of breaking the hottest scoop in Henderson since Molly DuVal ran off with Vance. The bad news is that instead of *indulging in* the gossip, you will be directing it. You are going to make it sound like this is the most natural and charming thing to happen in Henderson in years. *You* are going to personally endorse what I'm about to tell you. To everyone. Especially your holier-than-thou syndicate."

"Well, my goodness. Just how bad is this?"

"It isn't *bad*, at all. It's really rather wonderful. But it is juicy. Very, very juicy."

Pinks heard Tansy's voice reeling her mother in.

"And, as you mentioned earlier, the town of Henderson is very conservative. So, a kind word about the situation and the people involved will make a big difference coming from you. You and Evie Jackson have the power to give this situation the proper spin."

"And it involves a friend of yours."

"It does."

"Someone I know?"

"Yes, and you used to be very friendly with her parents."

"And you'll come to Ole Miss with me, wearing your tiara, your sash, and *a smile*, correct?"

"I will be in your debt for the entire nightmare of a weekend."

"Oh, Tansy. Stop saying that. It's going to be such fun."

"Do we have a deal?"

"Of course we do, darling. I'm happy to throw a little kindness around if it's going to help your friend."

"Four of my friends. You're going to help *four* of my friends, Mother. You're going to use all the power you hold in this town to help Hale Evans, his N.O.C.D wife, Genevra, his randy son, Vance, as well as my childhood friend, Piper Beaumont."

CHAPTER FOUR

At eleven o'clock that night, Brooks Bennett and Vance Evans were in their squad car following a slow-moving pickup truck as it drifted over the centerline. The driver corrected by pulling sharply to the right, putting the pickup back in the center of the lane. Eventually, the truck began drifting toward the right, running off the side of the country thoroughfare before being brought back on track. The officers watched the scenario repeat three times before they decided to turn on the siren and pull the driver over.

Brooks turned to Vance. "You want to do the honors? Last chance you're probably gonna get."

"Your generosity overwhelms, but I've got a sneaking suspicion that truck belongs to Finn McIntyre, one of the sophomores we want to move up to varsity this year. The fact that he's out here driving under the influence is not making me happy."

True enough, it was Finn McIntyre who stumbled out of the truck and headed to meet Brooks and Vance as they approached. Vance shined his flashlight in the eyes of the tall, lanky teen, bringing him to a stop.

Finn shielded his eyes and said, "I know what this looks like. I do. But I swear it's not what you think."

Able to see the boy well enough in the combination of moonlight and headlights, Vance turned his flashlight off and pocketed it. Besides, he knew the kid.

"Finn. You been drinkin'?"

"No sir. I haven't had a thing. Not one beer."

"Then what the hell is going on? That truck of yours was all over the road."

"I know. And I'm sorry about that," he said, stepping closer and lowering his voice. "But Ashley McCauley asked me to give her a ride home from the rugby game in Oxford, and she won't keep her damn hands to herself."

Vance blinked a couple times and then rubbed a hand over his mouth. "Where she puttin' her hand exactly?"

"On my knee. I keep swatting it off, but she's relentless. Which is why I had to drive so damn slow. Because it's distracting."

"I understand," Vance said, eyeing Brooks and trying his damnedest not to smile. "Why don't you show Officer Bennett how well you can walk a straight line while I have a talk with Miss McCauley."

Finn's exasperated "Good luck with that" made a grin break out on Vance's face. As he walked toward the truck, the driver's door swung open, and a very pretty, very much-older-than-Finn vision of feminine youth leaned out with her long hair hanging down to one side and the top of her dress barely concealing her lovely cleavage. Vance took a moment to mentally stand in Finn's inexperienced shoes and knew exactly why he'd been so distracted.

Poor kid. Didn't know dumb luck when he found it.

"Miss McCauley," Vance said.

"Coach Evans."

"You tryin' to get young Finn into trouble?"

"No sir. He offered me a ride home from Oxford, and we were taking the scenic route."

"On a school night?"

"Professional day for the teachers tomorrow. No school."

"Ah. Well then. What's your curfew?"

"I don't have a curfew. My parents trust me."

Foolish, foolish people.

"Then they're probably trusting you to keep buckled up and your hands to yourself when one of my ballplayers is kind enough to give you a ride home."

She smirked.

Lordy, lordy. Finn certainly did have his hands full.

"You care to tell me why a girl like you is catching a ride with a lowly sophomore?"

"Finn's nice. And cute. And *tall*." She said the word tall like it was a unique and highly desirable attribute.

Vance cleared his throat. "And he's doing his best to get you home safe. So slide on over into the passenger side if you will." Vance came forward and watched her follow his directions. "Now put on that seatbelt, nice and tight. Good. Now, while the ignition is on, you are going to stay buckled up and snug against that door over there. No more distracting my player until he pulls up into your father's drive. Then…" he said, giving her a wink, figuring Finn needed to learn how to handle aggressive women at some point, "you can cut yourself loose."

Yes, the boy needed experience. Vance just didn't want him getting any of it while he was driving.

He stepped back from the truck and patted Finn on the back when he walked by to climb in. "Be safe," he said to the two of them and then stood back and watched as Finn drove off.

"Kid's got his hands full," Brooks said.

"And no idea what to do with it," Vance agreed.

When Vance arrived home after midnight, he found his new bride wide awake in his father's enormous gourmet kitchen. She motioned him over to where she sat perched on one of the tall stools at the island counter. Her fork was poised over an enormous pie, and at the very edge of her lower lip, there was a tiny bit of cherry filling.

"I know what you're thinking," she said.

Vance would have bet good money she had no clue what he was thinking.

"But it's not the pregnancy causing me to chow down in the middle of the night. It's this piecrust." She shook her head, as if she couldn't figure something out. "Grab a fork," she ordered, pointing in the direction of the cutlery drawer. "Take a bite, and tell me what you think."

The bite Vance happened to be interested in didn't have anything to do with pie. But she was so engrossed in her thoughts as she stared down in wonder at the pastry, it got him thinkin' about something other than licking that cherry stuff off her lip.

He watched her take another bite.

She didn't speak, just chewed, and when he sat there continuing to watch her, she motioned that he should get his fork into the pie and join her. Quickly.

She waited as he dug up a large chunk of the double-crust pie and slid it into his mouth. He wasn't hungry, didn't particularly like fruit pies all that much, so he wasn't sure what he'd be able to offer—

"Holy piecrust," he said with his mouth full. His eyes spread wide open as he looked between Piper and the enormous dessert. "I'm no expert on pie," he confessed, "but that is damn good." He dug his fork back in and took another bite.

Piper followed his lead, shaking her head like she couldn't figure something out.

"What?" Vance asked around a mouth full of cherry.

"It's the same recipe my mother perfected years ago. Only it has never tasted like this."

"It's delicious."

"I know. It's better than ever. I don't even know how to describe the difference, it's just…crispier? Could that be it?"

Vance shook his head, not having a clue but definitely interested in more. He stuck his fork back into the enormous plate.

Piper started touching the sides of the pie plate, running her fingers around the fluted rim, and then lower, around the glazed green color of the ceramic. When he finally got his fork out of her way, she carefully picked up the heavy pottery and looked at the bottom.

"Who's Molly?" she asked.

"Who's Molly what?" he responded, waiting for her to put the pie down so he could get back at it.

She looked at him like he was a dumbshit, pulling the pie against her chest not letting him have any more until he answered her question. "Who is Molly DuVal? I'm assuming she's one of Genevra's nieces, but which one? Why didn't I meet her at the wedding?"

Vance took the pie plate out of her hands and set it back on the counter. "Why do you want to know about Molly DuVal?" he asked, going back to the pie with his fork.

"Because it appears she made this as a wedding gift for your father and Genevra. It has her name on the bottom with a lovely inscription."

"Nice."

When he didn't say more, his darling little wife reached over and halted his fork from making contact with his mouth.

"Who is Molly?"

"She's...you know, like you said. One of Genevra's kazillion nieces."

"I want to meet her."

"That's not necessary. I'm sure Genevra is going to write a beautiful thank-you note."

"I'm sure she will. But I want to know about the pie plate. Find out if she indeed made it and how."

"It's a pie plate. I mean, it's definitely a big-ass pie plate, more the size of a large pizza but it's still...you know, just another pie plate."

"It's not just another pie plate, Vance. That's what I've been trying to tell you. It's taken my perfect piecrust and made it *better*. And why the hell are you making this so difficult?"

Vance sighed as he dropped his fork and faced the first turning point in his marriage. He hadn't thought it would come so soon.

Apparently, there was going to be no honeymoon period for him. He looked at Piper's bright blue eyes and all those blond curls and put his hands on her cheeks, pulling her face to his, kissing her lips one last time before the shit hit the fan.

"The truth is I would prefer that you and Molly never meet," he said against her lips. "I know that's probably not possible, but if you had any idea how hard I worked to keep the two of you apart at the wedding, you would be cutting me a little slack now."

"I don't understand," she said, shaking her head loose from his grip. "Why wouldn't you want me to meet—Oh!" *Yep, his wife was a smart one.* "There's history there," she guessed.

"You could say that."

"How much history?"

"Enough."

Piper quirked a brow high. Really high. "Enough that you don't want me to meet her?"

"Enough that I don't want the two of you cuddling up together and discussing the size of my—"

Piper's hand came over his mouth and shut his stupid self up.

"Vance. If I throw a stone anywhere between here and Raleigh, I'm gonna hit some woman who can attest to the size of your... anatomy." She glanced briefly at his lap. "However, the only size I want to discuss with Molly is the size of this pie plate. It not only makes one mighty gorgeous dessert, but there's something about this type of pottery that is performing miracles with my crust."

Vance kissed her hand. "Fine."

"Fine?"

"Yes." He picked up his fork again. "Fine. Talk to her. I'll set it up. Just keep the discussion to pottery and..."

"And what?" she prompted.

"Ask her to make us one of these. I didn't realize how much I like pie."

CHAPTER FIVE

The next afternoon, Tansy walked into Henderson's police headquarters just as Chief Carl Lumblad started heaping accolades on Vance. The two of them were standing at the back of the room facing a crowd of some forty people gathered around an enormous sheet cake. Tansy joined the crowd, and in a rare moment of goodwill toward Vance, she thought it was a shame they hadn't waited for Hale and Genevra to return from their honeymoon so Vance's father could be here.

Of course, when you weren't much of a cop, handing in your badge probably wasn't much of a big deal. Although listening to the Chief, she was surprised to learn that Vance had been the one who'd initiated the Bicycle Squad several years back and that he was the best shot on the force. However, when Brooks took the floor, he pointed out that being the best shot on the force didn't do them any good since Vance refused to carry a gun.

There was laughter and fun poking, especially when the tally of how many days Vance had actually worked for the HPD over the past seven years was announced. Vance insisted the number was total bullshit, reminding everyone he was their high school's championship-winning baseball coach along with his other various jobs.

And then Tansy watched Vance get serious, saying that he did want to share with those in attendance that he was now not only a partner in E&E Investments with his father, but that he was also a happily married man. Shock, surprise, and a round of applause erupted as Vance pulled Piper from the crowd and introduced her as his wife and long-time girlfriend. Which was a bit of a stretch Tansy thought, but served the rest of his announcement well as Vance went on to tell them all that he was also going to be a father.

Piper simply beamed, looking all of seven days pregnant as excitement and congratulations sprung up around them. There was no missing the love in her eyes as she gazed adoringly at her new husband.

Tansy's stomach churned in envy as she remembered a time not long ago when she'd gazed up at someone just like that. But she'd managed to botch that up big time.

She started gnawing on a fingernail.

Vance eventually held up his hand to quiet the crowd, saying he had one more announcement to make. The room hushed in expectation. He asked Brooks to join him front and center, and then Vance told everyone that his top business priority was to get Brooks Bennett elected Mayor of Henderson.

The cheers were deafening, the place crazy with the news. It took long minutes to get everyone quiet enough so Brooks could be heard when he tried to speak.

"Thank you," he said. "I appreciate your support, and I'm sure this isn't coming as a huge surprise."

"You're the Golden Boy," somebody shouted. "It's about time."

It was obvious that comment got to him because Brooks had to clear his throat and look down as he shuffled his feet a moment before going on. "Well, I'll tell you this. I am blessed," he said, looking up. "This town has blessed me in ways I have a hard time putting into words. And I'm grateful. I love this town and all the people in it. But to be honest…I'm afraid Henderson is dying."

Tansy held her breath, because you could have heard a pin drop. This was not the rousing campaign speech everyone expected.

"I believe if we can't find a way to open our minds to new ideas, bring more businesses into our community, and stop the mass exodus of young people, our town is going to shrivel up and die. That's why Vance and Hale Evans, myself, and several others like Josh McCourt over at the high school and Davis Williams right there," he said, pointing toward Pinks, "have formed a committee to brainstorm ways of bringing economic growth to Henderson.

"Now in conjunction with that, something we'd like to see come from the Henderson Police Department is an initiative called Henderson Helping Henderson, or H-Cubed, if you will. We hope to get the cooperation of Mayor Stevens' office, the school board, the library, and our city council to help us instill and promote it.

"The idea is simple. One Henderson citizen helping another. Spontaneously or intentionally. We're not talking about soup kitchens and charity, 'cause we've got that. We're talkin' about driving our senior citizens to doctor appointments, maybe taking them out to lunch. We're talkin' about picking up trash when you see it, helping a pregnant woman carry groceries to her car, teaching a kid how to ride a two-wheeler.

"If you like to paint, offer to teach someone whose house is peeling. If you don't mind mowing grass, look down your street and see whose grass needs it. If you like to tinker with tools, walk around your street and fix a mailbox, or offer to fix your neighbor's leaky faucet. You see somebody new moving into your neighborhood—offer to grab something off the truck and carry it into the house for them. If you like to cook, consider teaching a group of high school seniors heading off to college how to save a little money by feeding themselves. If you like to read, volunteer at the library or better yet, find someone who needs to learn and teach them how. Henderson Helping Henderson is about cooperation. It's about sharing your time and talent in a way that you enjoy. It's about fostering pride in our neighborhoods, and our business district.

"If we polish the neighborhoods as well as our citizen's hearts, Henderson will become a shiny new draw in North Carolina for businesses, families, and economic growth. And that will enhance the quality of life for all of us.

"So, please, as you enjoy Vance's very big cake, made by his beautiful bride, Piper, take a look at our logo for Henderson Helping Henderson and share your ideas on how best to spread the word."

Brooks stepped out of the limelight to a round of applause and the hum of conversation and movement. Tansy stood still, thinking she'd been involved in the brainstorming meeting when the idea of H^3 was just a nugget. Obviously, Brooks and his posse had fleshed it out over the past several weeks.

Without her.

And didn't that sting? She'd been totally unaware they were rolling out the initiative today. She'd figured it was something Brooks was going to do when he became mayor. But it seemed Brooks wasn't willing to wait another fourteen months to start improving Henderson. He and Vance obviously felt an urgency to get started, and getting people on board was nothing short of paving his way to the mayor's office. It was brilliant. Although Tansy knew that was the last reason Brooks had done it.

"Well, this is a surprise," Vance said as he approached her.

Tansy couldn't help it. It hurt that she'd been dismissed from the so-called committee. So she defaulted back into the super-bitch role she'd adopted to handle Vance all these years.

"I'm here for Piper," she said, sticking her nose up at his offered slice of cake even though it looked sinfully delicious.

"Annnnnd I appreciate that," Vance said, setting down the cake. There was a bit of silence before he ventured further. "Pinks has decided to join E&E as a full-time employee and stay on here in Henderson."

"I'd heard a rumor. And I'm not particularly surprised since the two of you are soul mates and all."

"Yes, well," Vance said with a smile and a shake of his head, "The Ninja is certainly handy to have around. He's smarter than Brooks and I put together, and when you give him a job, it gets done. However, I'm not unaware of the, ah…tension between you and my man."

"I don't know what you're talking about."

"Really? Well, let me remind you about the night Pinks and The Outlaw played their rock-and-roll set at The Situation, and you turned out to be their biggest groupie. And then I found you sprawled all over your desk the next morning—"

"I wasn't sprawled."

"Would you like me to pull up the picture I took of you on my phone? The one where you're passed out with only two buttons left on your shirt, your skirt on backwards—"

"Enough. Your point?"

"I didn't like you messin' with my boy back then, but that night did seem to soothe the tension the two of you had generated in the office. Now that we're all going to be working together, you and Pinks are free to, you know, hook up. Whatever. As long as you can continue to work together, I don't care. But know this. My allegiance is to Pinks. This thing between you two blows up, you're out."

Tansy notched her chin up and gave Vance a look she hoped conveyed the words "drop dead." "While that comes as no surprise," she said, "trust me when I say there is nothing between Davis and me."

"Bullshit."

"Let me rephrase that. There will *never again* be anything between Davis and me."

"And why is that, huh? Please tell me you're not thinking of making another play for Brooks, because my allegiance to Pinks falls way short of my allegiance to Brooks and Lolly."

"Oh, please."

Vance lifted a brow. "July third ring a bell?"

Tansy held up her hand. "Stop. Just stop. You have no idea what was going on back then, and I promise you have no clue what's happening with me now, so just stop. I'm over Brooks and I don't want Pinks, okay? And that is all my *employer* needs to know."

She tried to turn and walk away but Vance grabbed her elbow. "I'm not trying to be an asshole, Tansy. Truly. If you want to date Pinks, I'm just letting you know it's fine by me. The poor kid has been panting at your heels ever since you two got it on in the conference room."

"Vance," she pleaded.

"Look, you asked my father for a job, and I've just married one of your friends. Seems we are destined to see a lot of each other. It might take some time to step out of our old habit of slinging sarcasm back and forth, but for the sake of Piper, my father, Brooks' campaign, and the future of E&E, I'm willing to try."

"Okay."

"Okay, what?"

"Okay, okay. I'll stop hurling insults. It's just that," she said, plastering on a brilliant smile, "you make it so easy."

"Christ. You are a piece of work, you know that?"

"I know," Tansy said contritely. "You bring out the worst in me. I'll work on it. I need this job."

"I know you do, which is why I didn't shove your fanny out the door the moment I heard my father hired you."

"Well, thank you for that. And I wouldn't mind being a part of Team Henderson, you know. I liked that brainstorming session. I thought…"

"You thought what?"

"I thought…rather, I hoped I'd contributed."

"You did. You are. Why would you think you're off the team?"

She shrugged, tossing her chin toward Brooks. "Henderson Helping Henderson."

Vance waved a dismissive hand. "Bah. Brooks just pulled all that shit out of his ass. We decided to run with it while we were on duty last night. It's good though, right?"

It was the first time Tansy ever remembered Vance Evans caring about what she thought. So she extended her own olive branch.

"It's good." She nodded. "It's real good."

CHAPTER SIX

Dallas, Texas

Crain Carraway leaned his desk chair back and threw a rubber ball toward the ceiling, over and over, playing catch with himself as he searched for a way to settle the anger and frustration churning up his insides. The new document he received this morning was the only thing that sat on his desk. The only thing he could think about. The only thing he'd been thinking about in one way or another for the past four months.

The sound of his executive assistant's voice came over the intercom. "North Carolina on the line again."

He caught the ball and abruptly leaned over his desk. He was planning to shout that the hillbillies of North Carolina obviously didn't understand the meaning of the word "no" when his office door flew open and his beloved momma walked through like she was on a mission from God. From her expression, Crain didn't have to guess what the mission was about, so he whispered closely to the intercom "Tell North Carolina to hold."

"Momma Bear," he said in his most jovial voice, as if he didn't have a care in the world. He stood and moved around his desk to embrace his momma in a big ol' hug. "To what do I owe this extraordinary pleasure? Come in, come in. Have seat," he said, smiling like life couldn't get any better. "How do you like this new leather couch?" He pushed her down into it. "And this Whatchamacallit table. That's new too, I think."

His mother, Melinda Carraway, was the kindest, most gentle woman he knew. People thought she'd led a charmed life, but he knew different. He knew she'd spent the better part of half her life exasperated, frustrated, and overwhelmed. He knew that better than anyone because he and his ADHD, along with his somewhat dyslexic brain, had been the cause. Or at least most of it. His brother, Cash, was no picnic either. And it was Crain's daily intention to make it up to her whenever he could.

Unfortunately, he was at a loss about how to placate her now.

"Honey Bear," she said, using the endearment without any of the usual joy behind it. "It's time to tell your momma what the hell is going on."

Whoa. His momma never cussed. Never. It almost made him chuckle. "Momma, I've told you and Daddy. There's nothin' for you two to fret about. I know this is all a bit unorthodox, but it's going to work out. You'll see. Trust me on this."

"Crain, I've been known to be a foolish woman at times, but trust me when I say that right now you are not foolin' me or anybody else. Now, what the hell happened to your bride?"

If I only knew the answer to that.

"Ma, I told you. We took that month-long honeymoon, and then Elizabeth headed back to her hometown to tie up some loose ends. She's askin' me to be patient, and I've agreed. Now I'm askin' you for the same courtesy.

"Mr. Carraway, North Carolina is still holding," came his assistant's voice over the intercom.

Crain jumped up. "Ma, I'm sorry, but I've got to take this. I've been working on a big deal with some people in North Carolina and I've got to ta—"

"Why the hell do you want to do business outside of Texas?"

He didn't. He was definitely not interested in doing business outside of Texas. He just needed to get his mother out of his office. To fend her off with whatever he could.

"Aw, Ma, now you've used the H-E-double-L word three times in the last minute and a half," he said as he began to usher her out of his office. "Sounds like you need a trip out to Aunt Gem's to put your feet up and share a bottle of wine. I'm sure she'd love to see you. Help soothe whatever's ailing you."

"My sister is the one who told me to march in here and demand some answers. This whole 'married in Vegas and then lose your bride' thing has her as twitchy as it has me. Darlin' boy, please, tell your mother what is going on."

Crain leaned over and kissed her cheek. "All in good time, Ma. All in good time. Now I've really got to go."

His momma turned away without another word. Without so much as a goodbye or a fare-thee-well. Which caused the anger in him to bubble up and boil over. He knew one thing for sure in that moment. When he did find his runaway bride—and he would—the first thing he was going to do was strangle her with his bare hands.

Crain took the call from North Carolina, listening without enthusiasm until the mention of a lake and unbuildable land happened into the conversation.

His great grandpappy had been the key engineer responsible for filling up swampland and making it something a fellow named Walt Disney could build upon. Crain loved that story. More than all those roller coasters and fantastic exhibits at Disney World, Crain loved watching the story about a man with a dream and the engineers who helped him achieve it.

Now, Crain was no engineer. But he did mirror Walt Disney a bit when it came to the big idea. What Crain brought to the conference table was vision. His vision, especially if it had anything to do with sports, was what made him the big bucks. And as he listened, it occurred to him that was exactly what North Carolina was looking for. A vision. A big idea. Something exciting.

He almost smiled when he heard his momma's voice echo in his head. "Why would you want to do business outside of Texas?" Well, he didn't. To him there was only Dallas and West Texas. Outside of that, there were only a whole lot of wannabes. But he'd been holding people he loved at arm's length for a good four months now, and their collective patience had run thin. He desperately needed an excuse to be out of the office the next time his momma, his daddy, or any number of his friends walked in here demanding to get to the bottom of the "lost bride" scandal.

So he agreed to a meeting in some rinky-dink town in godforsaken North Carolina and prayed the distraction lasted at least as long as it took his private investigator to finally find his wife.

CHAPTER SEVEN

By lunchtime Friday, Tansy begrudgingly admitted she was getting a teensy bit excited about heading back to Ole Miss for the weekend. She wasn't about to tell her mother that, but a few quick emails to some of her college friends had rallied the troops, and now she was looking forward to seeing them.

Her sister, Scarlett, a senior at Ole Miss who'd been dodging her mother's calls—simply because—picked up Tansy's call on the first ring and laughingly gave her grief about agreeing to once again be their mother's show pony.

Tansy countered by offering to let Scarlett wear her tiara during the Party at the Grove so she wouldn't feel so bad about never making the Homecoming Court.

When their laughter subsided over how absurd the whole "Gathering of the Queens" was, they started laughing even harder about their poor father, who had to accompany his wife and daughter to Ole Miss and pretend he gave a damn about The Rebels. They were all certainly in for a round of Rye Langford's relentless "Why would anybody in their right mind want to go out of state to college when they lived in North Carolina?" now that he had to foot the bill, once again, flying them all to and from Oxford, Mississippi.

It will be fun, Tansy thought. Getting out of Henderson. Being Tansy the co-ed for a weekend. Then she'd come back and…well, why ruin her mood.

She was about to stroll down the hall and look for Pinks to tell him she planned to leave early and to find out how Genevra and Hale's homecoming went last night when he suddenly emerged into the reception area with a big grin.

"You look happy," she said.

"That's because your big, bad, Golden-boy Brooks is finally going to have to bow down to this lowly Ninja. I have single-handedly managed to get the Top Dog CEO he's been after to agree to meet with us. He's flying in Monday and has promised us the entire day. You'll be here, right? Back from Ole Miss?"

"We're flying back Sunday."

"Great. Make sure you wear a dress."

"How 'bout a business suit?"

"Mmm, that's not really the look I had in mind. I was thinking of something…friendly. Something that, ah, really shows off your legs. Because if all goes to plan, you'll be the one giving our Top Dog a walking tour of the center of town."

"Shocking that you and your Mad Men sensibilities are planning to pimp me out."

"I told you on day one it was your job to sit there and look pretty."

"Right. Look pretty, order lunch, and bake up a batch of Famous Amos cookies when required."

Pinks looked pointedly at the dreaded cookie machine sitting on top of her credenza still in the same pristine condition it had arrived in. When his golden-brown eyes looked back at her, they clearly indicated she'd not been doing her job.

"Look Ninja-boy," she said while poking him in the chest. "Vance may have promoted you from Summer Intern to Official Sidekick and Lackey, but you are still not the boss of me."

"Look, I'm kidding you."

She threw him a "yeah, right" glance.

"I'm sort of kidding you," he confessed. "Vance, Brooks, and I will be driving this guy around in the mud all morning. He's gonna need a break from that and our ugly mugs at some point. It certainly couldn't hurt to have a pretty blonde, born and raised in Henderson, walk him around our little downtown area. It would also serve to give Vance, Brooks, and me a chance to converse about our strategy for the afternoon.

"Besides, there's a good chance the two of you might actually have some things in common, which could help us develop a rapport with this guy."

"What things?"

"Well, he's from— Oh, shit." Davis' face went white. From shock or fear, Tansy couldn't say, but she followed his line of vision out the large picture window of E&E Investments to a white BMW sedan with out-of-state plates parked across the street.

A middle aged, sharply dressed couple emerged from the car. The man, medium height with a stocky but athletic build, had hair the exact color of Davis', but what really gave him away was the gorgeous pink shirt he was wearing with his handsome suit pants. Tansy watched as he opened the back door of the car and retrieved his suit jacket, putting it on before holding out a hand to the woman as he helped her cross the street toward them. The woman, a petite honey-blond, wore a pale pink suit similar to one Tansy's mother owned.

"Ah, let me guess. Mr. and Mrs. Pinks?" Tansy joked.

"Do me a favor and stall them while I get Hale on the line." Davis was already dialing his phone. "Vance and Brooks too. I'm going to need reinforcements," he said as he took off back down the hall.

"What the…? Davis!" But he was gone.

Tansy had overheard enough conversations to know that Davis' parents weren't happy with his continued delay in returning to Baltimore. But it was evident he hadn't expected them to show up in Henderson.

She quickly stepped behind her desk, pulling out a hand mirror to check her teeth and lipstick. Then she pinched her cheeks, all the while feeling Davis' panic rise up inside her own chest.

E&E Investments needed Davis. She hated to admit it, but he'd proved himself invaluable. In his five years at State, Pinks had double majored in Finance and Economics and earned his MBA. He was exactly what Brooks and Vance needed to help redirect Henderson. He was just as equipped to weigh in on the rest of E&E's business dealings as well. He'd proven his worth, and as office manager, she'd seen the hefty contract Hale and Vance had recently offered him to stay. Tansy bet he'd have done it for peanuts because he liked it here. He liked being the unsung hero, the jack-of-all-trades, and as much as the two of them were constantly trying to one up each other in their bosses' eyes, she knew he liked her as well. Liked her a little too well. But that was her problem.

Tansy sent up a silent prayer that both Hale and Vance were able to get here fast. For Davis' sake. Because honestly, for her it'd be best if his parents threw a sack over Davis' head, wrestled him into their big trunk, and drove north.

The little bell jingled as the front door opened. Tansy stood up to greet Davis' parents, pretending she hadn't seen them coming and wasn't aware of who they were. "Hello," she said in greeting. "I'm Tansy Langford. Welcome to Evans & Evans Investments. How can I help you?"

Mr. Pinks offered her a smile. Yep, there was Davis in another twenty years. "I'm Arthur Davis Williams, the Third," he said without the least bit of pretentiousness—which was really a feat when you added "the Third" to any given name. "And this is my wife, Sabina."

Tansy offered Mr. Williams her hand. "Nice to meet you," she said, then made a point to nod toward his wife. She wasn't smiling.

"I believe our son, Davis, works here. We thought we'd surprise him with a visit."

"Oh, you're Davis' parents," she gushed. "Of course, Mr. and Mrs. Williams. It sure is a pleasure to meet you both," Tansy said, pouring on her best southern charm. "And it certainly is obvious where Davis gets his good looks," she went on, her head spinning with the words "stall them." "I understand you're from Maryland."

"That's right," Arthur responded. "The Baltimore area. We're big Os fans," he said, jingling the change in his pocket. "I understand baseball is the major sport around here."

"Why in Henderson, yes. We're known for our championship-winning high school teams lately. In fact, Vance Evans, one of the owners of E&E, was not only on the original state championship team at Henderson High, but is presently the reigning state championship coach. Ah!" she said, relief evident in her overzealous introduction. "In fact, here he comes now."

Tansy was never so glad to see Vance Evans come through the door. Her anxiety didn't necessarily lessen as Vance came in, hair on fire, but she at least felt like Pinks was gaining reinforcements. "Vance. These are Pinks'—I mean—Davis' parents. Mr. and Mrs. Arthur Davis Williams, the Third."

"So glad to meet you," Vance said, breathless, as he shook their hands. "The Ninja—I mean—Pi—Davis," he finally spat out, "has become an indispensable asset around here. We're doing our best to convince him to stay." Vance made a grand show of looking at his watch. "I believe right now, he's in a client meeting with my father. So, how 'bout I show you around our little town and then take you to lunch while you wait for him to finish up. Tansy, if you'll call the Club, and let them know we're coming. And when Hale and Davis get back, just send them right over."

"Happy to—" she said, just as the front door jingled open and her mother walked in.

Everyone in the crowded foyer turned to stare at Garland Langford and immediately stopped talking. Not because Tansy's mother happened to be wearing the same beautiful suit as Mrs. Pinks—no, Tansy was sure no one was going to notice that. They were staring because on top of her mother's beautifully coifed hair sat a very large, sparkly tiara. In addition, and probably more alarming, draping from slender shoulder to tiny hip was her Ole Miss Homecoming Queen sash.

"Vance," Garland cooed, not bothering to apologize for appearing in public like an overgrown Barbie doll. "I understand congratulations are in order," she said as she came forward and grabbed him by both of his upper arms. "Piper Beaumont is simply one of my favorite people, and Evie Jackson and I couldn't be more delighted to hear that the two of you have married. What a coup for

Henderson that you plan to settle here and raise your children. You know we need children to keep this town flourishing, so I hope the two of you will get on that quickly."

The Williams might not have seen the wink she gave Vance, but Tansy sure didn't miss it. Though she had to give her mother credit. She was doing the job she'd promised she'd do and then some.

"Now who do we have here?" Garland asked, clapping her hands and turning a gracious smile toward Pinks' parents.

Vance did the honors. "Garland Langford, I'd like to introduce you to Mr. and Mrs. Arthur Davis Williams, the Third. Of Baltimore," he added.

"Oh, Baltimore," Garland said slyly, like it should be kept a secret. "Hard crabs, Berger Cookies, and Schmidt's Blue Ribbon Bread. Not to mention those scrumptious Rheb's candies. My, my, my, I've never tasted so many delicacies in one place. Put me in that gorgeous ballpark on a hot summer night and hand me a Natty Boh, am I right?"

Vance and Tansy stared at each other, wondering if her mother was speaking in tongues. But whatever she was saying, Arthur Williams understood and practically melted at her feet—apparently in shock that someone from Henderson, North Carolina would have such an understanding of his beloved hometown.

Vance, who made his fortune by taking advantage of an opportunity when he saw one, asked Garland to join him and the Williams for lunch at the Club.

"Oh, don't you know I would just love to," her mother gushed, moving over to speak directly to Mrs. Pinks. "But my daughter Tansy and I are flying out this afternoon to our alma mater. It's the 100th Homecoming anniversary you see, and this silly little get-up I have on is simply a prop for our trip. I just stopped in to show Tansy, but I don't want to take up any more of your time."

It was then that the front door burst open with a harried-looking Hale buttoning his suit jacket and combing his hands through his gorgeous black head of hair. Tansy sighed internally. There would certainly be no God if Vance Evans ended up looking as devastatingly handsome as his father did at the age of fifty-two.

"Well, hello," he said to the room at large. His smile and his demeanor immediately added to the jovial atmosphere Garland had created. "I'm Hale Evans," he said, hand out toward Mr. Williams. "And you must be Davis' father. Why don't the two of us head on back to the conference room and have a little chat."

"Not so fast," Arthur said. "I'd like to introduce you to Davis' mother, Sabina."

"Of course," Hale said. "My humblest apologies, Mrs. Williams."

"Nonsense," Sabina cooed. "It is certainly a delight to meet the man behind my son's enthusiasm."

Tansy noticed that Mrs. Pinks' enthusiasm had skyrocketed now that she'd laid eyes on Hale.

"And we were enjoying the company of Miss Garland over here," Davis' father went on. "In fact, your boy Vance has offered to take us all to lunch. Isn't that right?"

Vance nodded, looking very happy with the way things were going. "Indeed it is," he said. "Tansy will send Davis over as soon as he's available."

"I thought he was with you," Arthur addressed Hale.

"Yes, but when I heard you were here, I was eager to meet you, so I came running. I left Davis to wrap things up. Give the boy a little practice, you know. He's good, but he's green. Fresh out of school and all that. He needs hands-on experience, and he's not going to get that anywhere else like he's getting it here."

Tansy's mother looked over at her pointedly and snickered.

What the…?

Tansy watched as Garland leaned into Pinks' mother and made a quiet comment that looked treacherously like, "I think your son has a thing for my daughter."

OMG, Mom.

And in walked Pinks. The man of the hour. The man christened Davis Williams, but better known around these parts as Pinks or The Ninja. Because he tended to dress like an Easter egg and had a double black belt in karate of all things. He'd been in town only two months and was the youngest and least experienced of his peers, but he practically ran the place.

Tansy realized then that if Mr. and Mrs. Williams did decide to kidnap Davis and toss him in their trunk, he'd find his way back before sunrise the next morning. Davis was now a Hendersonian. And it occurred to her that if Brooks ever got tired of being mayor, Davis would happily step in and take his place.

The reception room kept getting smaller as the crowd before her kept getting louder. Davis acted as if he couldn't be happier that his parents had driven five hours south to surprise him. He proudly reintroduced Hale and Vance and then took his parents on a tour of the office. Tansy watched her mother follow along down the hallway, leaving Tansy alone with Vance and Hale. Tansy couldn't help it. She burst into a fit of nervous giggles.

"Holy shit," Vance whispered to his father, angst and worry clearly written all over his face.

"I think it's going well," Hale said. "Let's just stay calm, take them to lunch, and sell the hell out of E&E and what we can do for Davis' career."

"You do realize Mr. Williams' best friend is a big muckety-muck in the financial firm Davis was supposed to be working for, right? He probably thinks this reflects poorly on him and is here to talk Davis out of staying."

"Like I said. We're going to do our job. Sell E&E to Mr. Williams so well that he's going to be grateful we are taking a chance on his wet-behind-the-ears son. Trust me. We've got this."

"I don't have this," Vance confessed over wide eyes, shaking his head no. "I'm too invested. As Brooks' campaign manager, I need The Ninja. I need Pinks. He's my right arm."

"Call Harry at the Club. Make sure he's working, and tell him to bring the magic. Then call Piper—oh, and ask Genevra to meet us there too. And your grandmother. If anyone can seal the deal, it's the Big Em. We'll present a family front. Show them that Davis is being well looked after on the personal side too." Hale slapped Vance on the back. "Trust me. We've got this."

Vance nodded a couple times and then pulled out his phone and started dialing.

"How can I help?" Tansy asked Hale.

"Come to lunch. We'll just lock up and show the Williamses how important Davis is to us."

Tansy smiled. That wasn't at all what she'd expected.

CHAPTER EIGHT

Pinks stood at the side of the tarmac watching Crain Carraway descend from his private jet. There was no CC Dallas company logo across the side of the plane, and since there didn't appear to be an entourage following him down the steps, Pinks was surprised at the size of the aircraft. Until he realized that this particular CEO happened to be at least six and a half feet tall. Legroom and all that.

If Dallas, Texas was going to send a representative from their city who wasn't George W. or a Dallas Cowboy's cheerleader, this is the guy they'd most want to send. Big and fit, sharply dressed, wearing cowboy boots that didn't look at all ridiculous with his business attire, Crain Carraway walked across the tarmac in a pair of shades Pinks thought Vance might kill for. There was a taupe-colored cowboy hat dangling in his hand, and Pinks was well aware that putting the thing on his head would not detract from but somehow add to his persona.

No nonsense, straight up, dealmaker.

As previously discussed, Brooks took the lead, reaching his hand out to Crain as the man approached.

"Mr. Carraway. I'm Brooks Bennett."

"Pleased to meetcha."

"This is Vance Evans."

"Howdy."

"And this is Davis Williams, better known as Pinks."

"Pinks?" Crain asked, shaking his hand, looking him hard in the eye.

"Correct," Davis responded. "Welcome to North Carolina."

"Gentlemen," Crain directed. "I'm wheels up in twelve hours and the clock is ticking. Let's get this show on the road."

All business, Pinks noted. Just like he was on the phone.

The four of them piled into Vance's new Land Rover, letting the guest of honor ride shotgun. Pinks reached over the front seat and handed Crain a map of the mid-Atlantic states, where he'd circled Baltimore, D.C, Richmond, Raleigh, Durham, and Greensboro. Henderson was starred. Then he handed him a local map of Henderson and the surrounding area, pointing out the high school, parks, country club, the main business district, the layout of the neighborhoods, both low income and high, neighboring Oxford, and how the fingers of the lake in many places were just muddy unusable messes. He'd drawn circles and marked them with numbers explaining the sites they'd be heading to in order. Then he sat back and let Brooks do the talking.

"I've never been to Dallas, Mr. Carraway—"

"Call me Crain."

"Crain," Brooks said with a head bob as Vance drove them away from the executive airport. "I know enough about Dallas to know that it's everything Henderson is not. Henderson is small, rural, and dying. Now we aren't tryin' to be Dallas, that's not why you're here."

"I'm here because you need a big idea. And you think that big idea is a minor league baseball team along with a minor league stadium. Something to bring interest to the area, jobs to your town. You want a minor league team because baseball is your *thing*. It's what put you and Mr. Evans here on the map. And you want it to do the same for Henderson." Crain looked over his shoulder at Brooks. "How'm I doin' so far?"

There was dead silence.

Pinks could have told him that he was no doubt pissing Henderson's next mayor and his campaign manager off. Pinks happened to agree with CC's assessment of the situation. He just didn't have the balls to put it out there like that. So he chimed in trying to defuse the situation before Vance pulled over and tossed the cowboy out on his ass.

"The minor league stadium is one idea we're looking at," Pinks said. "Because we like sports, America likes sports, and the three of us and the towns of Henderson and Oxford, are sports enthusiasts. Just like yourself," Pinks added. *Two could play at this game.* "If your parents hadn't sent you to that snooty sports-first high school you attended, you might never have gotten into Texas A&M, where you played on three varsity teams, a feat unheard of in this day and age of specialized sports. And having had that experience, plus the notoriety, you now get to run around Texas as CEO of Crain Carraway Dallas, Inc. giving advice to every wannabe sports-first school and training facility that can afford your time. Baseball may not have put you on the map, Mr. Carraway, but football and basketball sure did. Although I'm pretty sure not one of your teams won a state championship, or the equivalent of a College World Series."

Vance coughed into his hand.

Crain turned around as best he could, first eyeing up Vance who was obviously reigning in his mirth and then hooking eyes with Brooks and finally Pinks. "Who the hell are you again?"

"Davis Williams, a.k.a Pinks or The Ninja. Take your pick."

"And you work for?"

Pinks pointed toward Vance. "Evans & Evans Investments, Inc."

"How much is he payin' you?"

When Pinks simply sat there, Crain said, "Whatever it is, I'll double it. Right here, right now. Damn pink ninja," he muttered as he turned around. "Is it too early for a beer in these parts?" he asked the car at large. "Because I just got my ass handed to me by the one I misjudged as a pipsqueak."

Laughter broke the ice.

"I think I'll just shut the hell up and listen for a while. Brooks, my apologies. Please, proceed."

A camaraderie grew steadily over the next three hours. Crain listened to Brooks, listened to Vance. Kept pretty quiet, just like he promised. After site number three, he started asking about the climate and yearly temperatures. Finally, Pinks couldn't help but ask, "You have any thoughts?"

"I've got some ideas," Crain said.

Next they drove him through Oxford, explaining about the amount of land the former tobacco-growing community encompassed. Explaining about the rivalries between the two towns, both friendly and not so friendly. They told Crain they had an Oxford insider on their team, just in case they needed to sell an idea to the powers that be over there.

After surveying the fourth site, they got back into the truck and Vance asked Crain, "Any thoughts?"

"I've got some ideas," Crain repeated.

While they drove on to site number five, Crain asked some personal questions, with most of them directed at Brooks and Vance. He threw in a couple for Pinks, though Pinks could tell he was just trying not to leave him out. Pinks could have told him not to worry—he was learning a lot about his employer and the town's Golden Boy by listening to the answers.

Pinks was also learning a lot about Mr. Carraway. The guy was big and bouncy. Was moving pretty much all the time. In comparison, Brooks—who was also a big guy—sat still, quiet, easy.

Crain Carraway didn't seem…easy.

Crain had started playing with a small rubber ball he'd pulled from his pocket at the first destination. And, even though this tour of potential sites could have been conducted with a look out of the Land Rover's windows, in every case Crain asked to stop and get out. Pinks got the feeling he needed to stretch his legs, stomp around the ground, and bounce that ball a bit as if that somehow grounded him or helped him think.

As they piled back into the SUV after the same routine at location number five, Brooks gave voice to what the rest of them were thinking.

"I hope like hell there's something goin' on in that head of yours."

"I've got some ideas," Crain said once again.

"Care to embellish?" Brooks coaxed.

"Is everything always this green here in September?"

A little taken aback, Brooks said, "Of course. Aren't things green in Dallas?"

"Where there are irrigation systems, yes. The outskirts and West Texas, no. It's hot and dry and parched. I like your tall trees, the rolling hills. Texas is flat for the most part. Is this a good sample of what the East Coast looks like?"

"Don't get out of Texas much?" Vance asked.

Crain leveled a stare at Vance. "Why would I want to leave Texas?"

"I don't know? Travel? See the sights? Trees?"

"Went to Vegas once."

"That right? Win or lose?"

"Thought I'd won. Big."

"How's that?"

Crain waved him off. "Y'all ever hear of a feller named Nick Bollettieri?" he said as Vance drove them toward town.

"Tennis guy?" Vance asked.

"That's him. Runs a tennis school in Florida."

Quiet fell over the interior of the Rover. Crain was a bit more fidgety than usual, crossing his leg, tapping his shoe, shifting around again. Pinks couldn't tell if he was thinking or just trying to choose his words carefully.

"I can tell y'all are hogtied to the idea of a fancy baseball stadium, and you've certainly got the land for it. I'm not fixin' to sit here and squash that dream. Because if you do end up going in that direction, I can certainly put you in touch with a few teams who'd be interested and companies who might help sponsor it all. However, I will tell you it'd be more practical to start with something smaller."

"Okay," Brooks said. "Whatcha got in mind?"

"You say this town loves sports. Well, the idea that's been squawking around in my brain is to make Henderson the sports capital of North Carolina."

Brooks laughed. "Oh, is that all?"

"Now hear me out. This is an idea that starts small but has unlimited growth potential."

"Growth potential is definitely what we're after," Vance said.

"Nick Bollettieri started a boarding school for tennis players back in the seventies. With the sports craze in this country, that little tennis school has developed into somethin' called IMG Academy. They train and educate near 13,000 athletes each year. Their grounds cover some 400 acres. Every varsity sport you can think of." He turned and looked over at Pinks. "A helluva sports-first school, don'tcha think?"

"Indeed," Pinks said as he pulled out his phone and Googled IMG Academy.

"What do you think about building a sports facility that's used all year round? One you could add on to as you grow? Something where building a stadium eventually pays for itself and gets used continuously, not just during baseball season. One with potential to jump-start your economy fairly quickly."

"You talkin' about a sports academy? A prep school?" Brooks asked.

"A boarding school focused on training athletes. Not just in their chosen sport, or sports. But training them physically and mentally. Y'all are close enough to those damn college basketball teams that have busted my bracket a time or two. All those coaches would love to recruit from a school like this."

"Basketball?"

"Basketball, baseball, tennis, golf. You start with those four because you've got clout with that World Series win and want to use it. I see a country club or two on this map. They've got tennis courts and golf courses already built, which you could arrange to use until you can afford to build out the academy's facilities. There are more sports trainers, coaches, medics, psychologist, and nutritionists coming out of colleges with degrees than there are jobs. You'll provide jobs for those and get them cheap to start. Make it mandatory that they teach an academic subject. Start your advertising for students in those major cities you circled on this map, plus make an intensive push across North Carolina. Hit the middle schools, the elementary schools, the little leagues, etc. All the while you build your state-of-the-art training facility first, because that's what's gonna reel them in. Then you build your school and dormitories at the same time you build your fields. You hire locally as much as you can, get the whole area behind the project."

"We're going to need investors for something like that," Vance said.

"Right. Investors, sponsors, that's where I come in. That's what I do. I make connections. My people will investigate companies that have something to do with sports—from sports drinks to sports equipment, from suppliers of turf to the equipment you'll need to maintain that turf. We'll put a list together of companies who are actively looking for ways to put their brand out in a positive, youth-centered way. Then you three go in and sell it."

Crain continued, "You can offer the name of the academy to the biggest contributor. We'll set up meetings with say, Under Armour. See if we can get them to buy into the idea. Make it the Under Armour Varsity Academy or something. Hell, you got me out of Texas. It's not going to be hard to sell an idea like this to a company who is gonna want all of the next generation's top athletes used to wearing their logo."

"A school that teaches the art of competition," Vance said. "I wanna be, like principal of the damn thing. No, no. Maybe the athletic director. Or…I don't know, maybe just the damn baseball coach. What I do know is that I would have wanted to go to school there. So, yeah, I want in."

"We need a couple big names in tennis and golf to get it off the ground," Pinks said. "What we really need is a meeting with this Mr. Bollettieri. It says here that he's in his eighties but still training and coaching and hitting the gym every day."

"Forget him," Crain insisted. "You don't want to be the next Bollettieri. You want to create your own brand. That's where I come in. My staff can quickly interview their graduates. Find out what they do right and where they fall short. Then we'll survey some of the key trainers and coaches across the country today and develop a better model," Crain insisted. "Because Winters in Florida trump winters in North Carolina, but y'all are far more centrally located on the East Coast."

"I like this idea," Brooks said. "I really do. I like the potential for expansion. I like the possibilities of summer sports camps, using the grounds and dormitories. The idea of hosting tournaments in Henderson all year long. I like the thought of needing more bars, restaurants, shopping, and hotels for people who'd come and watch them, not to mention those participating. As a town, we'd focus on sports, and it'd give us a reason to build up the business district selling goods and services that cater to sports enthusiasts. And frankly, the idea of Henderson becoming the sports capital of North Carolina is a bigger dream than I've had the guts to envision."

"Lacrosse."

Brooks looked over at Pinks. "Oh God, here we go."

"Ya gotta have lacrosse. Come on!"

"Give it a rest. Please."

"The pink ninja is right," Crain said. "Hottest growing sport in Texas right now. It's ugly, but it's the truth."

"What the hell do y'all have against lacrosse? It's like ice hockey—only better."

"Ice hockey is big right now," Vance said. "Maybe we should think about building an ice rink."

"Lacrosse," Pinks insisted. "We hire The Outlaw after he graduates from Princeton. With his Ivy League degree, he oughta be able to teach somethin' while he's coaching."

"We are not letting The Outlaw anywhere near a bunch of high school girls," Brooks insisted.

"Oh, yeah. Forgot about his penchant for the young ones. Yeah, once we get this school up and running, he may not be allowed to come back."

That caused Vance to grin. "You hungry?" he asked Crain.

"I could eat."

"Good. We thought we'd head back to the office and introduce you to Tansy. She's the office manager at E&E and our token female on the Henderson Economic Stimulus committee. Not that we don't value women and their opinions," Vance wanted to make clear, "but we've just been flyin' by the seat of our pants as we get this thing rolling. Anyway, as a born and bred Hendersonian, Tansy will be able to give you the two-dollar walking tour of our business district, which will give your legs about a ten-minute stretch while we have lunch brought into the conference room. You don't mind a working lunch, do you?"

"Time is money. I'm in."

"Great," Vance said as he pulled parallel to the curb in front of E&E Investments.

The men exited, four heavy doors slamming at different intervals. Pinks trailed behind Vance and Brooks up the short set of stairs and held the door open for Crain, following him through as Vance began to introduce Tansy.

"Tansy Langford, this is our consultant, Crain Carraway," Vance was saying as Pinks watched her start to stand. "Crain, this is—"

"One mean, self-centered bitch," Crain growled.

"Well, now." Vance grinned in surprised glee. "I see the two of you have already met."

CHAPTER NINE

Tansy-schmansy.

Crain didn't know what these jackasses were tryin' to pull. Because it didn't take him more than two seconds to recognize the woman standing before him. After all, he'd been searching for her for a good four months.

He may have looked her up and down because she was dressed like she was heading to the beach and her glasses were nowhere to be found. But her hair was down, just like she wore it when she'd promised to forsake all others. Yep. No doubt about it. This was his one true love, a.k.a. Cold Feet.

"Elizabeth," he said, stepping in front of Vance and the rest of them. "What the hell is going on here?" he ground out, because honest to God, he didn't get it. If this was some kind of a joke she'd been playin', he really didn't get it.

"Elizabeth?" Pinks questioned. "This is Tansy. Tansy Langford."

That got Crain's back up good and straight. He threw a glare over his shoulder. *Really? The pink ninja wanted to argue with him about this?*

"I think I know my own damn wife when I see her," he growled.

"Wife?" Pinks spouted.

"Wife?" Brooks choked.

From the corner of his eye, Crain noticed Vance's eyes were wide open and intently focused on the situation. He also noticed that Elizabeth was saying nothin'. But from her alarmed expression, it was pretty damn obvious she hadn't expected him to come through that door.

"What do you mean, 'wife'?" Pinks asked.

"Wife! Wife. You know, as in…wife." Crain insisted, not bothering to keep looking at the jackasses but locking his gaze on those sultry deep hazel eyes.

"She can't be your *wife*," Pinks argued. "She's…Tansy."

"You can call her by any name you want," Crain said, turning slowly, the entirety of four months of vexation about to rain down on the pipsqueak. "But it won't change the fact that she's my wife. My bride."

"I don't understand," Brooks said. "Tansy, is this true?"

"It's not true," Pinks scoffed.

"Tell them," Crain insisted, eyeing his beloved.

"It can't be true," Pinks insisted.

"And why the hell is that?" Crain shouted, turning his irritation on The Pink One again. "Huh?"

"Because," Pinks confessed, throwing his hand out toward Crain's bride, "the two of us—"

"Davis." Tansy cut in.

When Crain realized Pinky Boy was the one she'd shut up, he looked at him and squinted. "Just how many names do you go by?"

The kid didn't answer. Couldn't answer. Because his mouth was hanging open and his sole focus was Elizabeth. *His* Elizabeth.

Things started to go real quiet in Crain's head, that hyper-focus ability of his kicking in. The kid was dumbfounded. And worse. And Brooks saw it too, because Crain noticed the man's jaw was clenched tight as he looked between Pinks and Elizabeth.

Pinks and Elizabeth.

That's when Vance stepped in, looking directly at Elizabeth, eyebrows raised and a shit-eatin' grin on his face as he said, "Mrs. Carraway, I presume?"

Crain saw the fight fall out of her then. Saw her gaze drop to her desk, saw her shoulders crater as her body dropped heavily into her chair. Every protective reflex he had shoved its way to the surface.

In a quieter, gentler voice he asked, "How 'bout you fellas give us a minute?"

"Sure," Vance said with a pat on his back. "Gentlemen, let's give the Carraways a chance to reunite."

Crain noticed Brooks' rigid expression as he stared at Elizabeth a few seconds before nodding and moving off. The pink ninja seemed determined not to move until Vance grabbed him by the back of the neck and pushed him out the front door behind Brooks.

"We will be right outside if either of you need anything," Vance said, looking pointedly at Elizabeth.

But she didn't see that. Because when Crain looked back at her, she had her face in her hands and her shoulders were shaking.

Aww, Judas Priest. Crain sighed, his heart melting at the sight. He took a step forward, promising himself he'd get to the strangling later.

"Sweetheart," he said as he moved behind the desk and crouched down in front of her. His arms had a mind of their own, and they pulled her to him, her arms finding their way around his neck, and her tears landing on his shoulder.

"I'm sorry," she sobbed. "I'm so, so sorry."

She wasn't sorry. She wasn't sorry at all, and he knew it. She'd sent him annulment papers for Pete's sake. He wanted to strangle her for what she'd put him and his family through. He really did. So he pulled her out of that chair, wrapped one arm around her waist, and dragged her up against him. With his other hand, he gripped the back of her neck and then…

Then…

He kissed the shit out of her.

CHAPTER TEN

When Pinks took up a stance looking in E&E's big plate glass window, Vance had to drag his ass down the street.

"They need privacy."

"That's not his wife," Pinks said.

"You don't know that."

"Of course I know that. He doesn't even know her name."

"She can't be his wife," Brooks chimed in, moving down the street with them.

Vance turned and faced the two of them, wondering why the hell it was taking them both so long to catch on.

"Her name is Elizabeth. Pinks, you may not know that, but Brooks, you damn well do. We called her E.T for an entire year once we found out those were her initials."

"So? That still doesn't explain how she can be married to a guy we just dragged in off the street."

"Did we? Did we just drag him in off the street? How the hell did we get his name, anyway? I'm sure I've never heard of CC Dallas before now. Oh, and by the way, in case you knuckleheads forgot, Dallas happens to be the city where Tansy lived for a good nine months."

"Yeah, but she's been back since…June or something. If she'd gotten married, we would have known about it," Brooks said.

"I'm not disagreeing that the past ten minutes didn't come straight out of the Twilight Zone. I'm just suggesting we stop arguing with the man about whom he thinks his wife is. Because if I can take your focus off the tall blonde in there for just one moment and bring it back to the business we've been discussing all morning, you might remember we actually need this guy."

"We don't need this guy," Pinks said. "He gave us an idea—and we can run with it. Put his big Texas ass back on his big Texas plane and say so long."

"Vance is right," Brooks chimed in, coming to reason. "We need the guy. We do. We need his connections. And why the hell are you even upset?" Brooks asked Pinks, pulling himself up to his full height. "Huh? Why the hell do you care if Tansy's somebody's wife?"

"Back off, Golden Boy. Lolly's not gonna wanna hear how upset you were at the news. She thinks you and Tansy are through."

"We are through," Brooks shouted. "But the fact that Carraway is claimin' they're married is a bit of a jolt, don't you think? I mean, were they married when she got back to town and tried to bust up Lolly and me? This doesn't make any sense."

"You can say that again," Pinks said.

"Oh, shit," Vance said, his eyes narrowing in on a red Lexus one block down. "Tansy's mother. You'd think if she knew her daughter was married to someone like CC, the rest of the town would too. I'm guessing Tansy's mother might be in the dark on this, just like us. In any case, probably not a good time to chance it." He patted Brooks on the back. "Time to pull out that Golden Boy charm and stall her. I'll…I'll go alert Tansy."

Vance moved quickly, pulling the door to E&E open with purpose so the little tinkling bells would chime as quickly and loudly as possible.

Wasted effort. He had to take two steps in and glance around the little corner before he found Crain Carraway, Dallas tycoon, lip locked with Elizabeth Tansy Langford, apparently also known in some parts as Mrs. Carraway.

He cleared his throat loudly.

When that didn't work, he yelled, "Tansy. Your mother is outside."

That got her attention. That got both their attention. But while Tansy looked over at Vance, horrified, Crain just kept looking at his…whatever.

"Perfect," Crain said, smoothing the hair from her face. "It's about damn time I meet my mother-in-law." He pulled away and started running fingers through his hair and tuckin' his shirt in like he was all about making a good impression.

Fool.

"Vance," Tansy begged with a desperation Vance had never heard before. "Please get him out of here."

It took him a second to choose. To choose whether to let the inevitable unfold right in front of him or to spare the woman who'd been a thorn in his side for years.

Goddamn it. Perfect Piper was wearing off on him.

"Come on, Tex, we don't want this rodeo of yours to turn into a bloody Alamo." Vance said, holding out an arm.

"More like the Apocalypse," Tansy said.

But Crain didn't seem to be paying either of them any mind. He just kept prettying himself up.

"Crain," Tansy said as she reached out and touched his shoulder. "Please. My mother…she's fragile."

"About as fragile as a locomotive at full speed," Vance said. "Trust me, Tex, this is one momma bear you don't want to wrestle with. Now, I can see there's plenty going on here, but I'd suggest you give the two of you a chance to straighten it out before getting the likes of Garland Langford involved."

When Crain said nothing, Vance shouted. "Are you hearing me?"

"I hear you. Loud and clear. I just don't like it," Crain said, picking up his hat and hitting the side of his thigh.

He looked over at Tansy.

"North Carolina?" he said, his face all squinched up like he couldn't believe it. "You're from North Carolina? Not Dallas? Not even Mississippi?"

Tansy shook her head, apology written all over her face.

"*North* Carolina," he reiterated. "Well, you sure fooled me. I've been looking for one Elizabeth Langford all over Dallas. Then all over Texas. Then Mississippi, figuring you'd gone to Ole Miss and maybe that's where you were from."

"Crain—"

"Save it," he said, putting his hat on his head. "I don't much care about meetin' your momma after all." He turned back and stared at her. "And I'll sign your damn papers. *Tansy*." He looked over at Vance. "You got a back way out of here?"

Vance pointed down the hall and felt the overwhelming vibration of hurt and loss as he followed the man from the room.

CHAPTER ELEVEN

Crain appreciated the silence as they drove. He looked out the passenger side window, not seeing a damn thing. His brain was stuck in idle, except for his visual cortex, which kept replaying pictures of his Elizabeth over and over…few of them jelling with this North Carolina Tansy.

North Carolina.

"How did I get here?" he asked the car at large.

"Pardon?"

"How the hell did I get to Henderson?"

When there was no response, Crain turned in his seat and faced them all. "You called me. Asked me to come out and give you a consultation. How did that happen?"

"It was my father," Vance said, clearing his throat. "He, ah… says he found your business card in the office. Googled your company. He saw you had a hand in several small stadium structures and thought it might be something Brooks would want to look into."

"That's right. Hale sent me an email with your website," Brooks said. "I didn't bother to ask how he knew about CC Dallas. I just ran with it."

"So Elizabeth—Tansy," Crain corrected himself, "didn't mention me? She didn't suggest you call?"

"Not to my knowledge," Brooks said.

More silence.

Vance pulled the Land Rover into a parking lot in front of a long white building with black shutters and a pretty, little porch.

"What's this?"

"Henderson Country Club," Vance said.

"Do they serve whiskey?"

"All day long."

Crain exited the truck feeling a whole lot like he'd been sucker punched. None of this made sense. How could he have not known she was from North Carolina? As they walked toward the front doors, he grabbed Vance's arm, pulling him around to a stop. "I gotta be crazy lettin' you talk me into leavin' that office. Do you know how long I've been tryin' to track her down? I need answers."

Vance motioned for Brooks and Pinks to go ahead inside. "Look," he said quietly. "You're gonna get your answers. But this is Henderson, not Dallas. Somethin' goes down here and the whole town knows about it in less than an hour. And your *mother-in-law* prides herself on her social standing in this town. Believe me when I say that no good would have come from forcing the issue back there."

Crain started to protest, but Vance held up a hand.

"I saw the way you kissed her, okay? I saw it. With my own damn eyes. So trust me. I know where you're at. And maybe you didn't know you were bluffing when you told her you'd sign whatever papers, but you were. Because you don't kiss a woman like that and then just walk away."

Crain couldn't deny it. He didn't even try.

"Now the good news is it was obvious that Tansy was giving just as good as she got. So, I did you a favor. Bought you some time. You've found her. She knows you've found her. She's got no place to run off to. This is her home. Whatever happens next, it's all up to you. The ball is in your court."

Crain stood there, digesting all of what Vance had to say.

"You're gonna need some patience and a game plan."

"Patience is not my strong suit," he admitted.

"I hear ya. I get it. But since you've waited this long, there's no reason you have to go busting in, acting like a bull in a china shop. No harm in lettin' the woman stew a bit while you simmer down."

Crain saw his point. "Yeah. Okay." He pulled out his phone and started dialing. "Go on in. I'm just going to release the plane."

"Probably a good idea."

"You got a Ritz Carlton around here?"

"Yeah," Vance laughed. "It's called the Evans Estate. Luckily, I know the proprietor and can get you a room."

When Crain entered the building, Vance stood at the top of a short flight of stairs talking to a young waiter. As he joined them, Vance made the introduction. "This is Harry. Harry's a fixer. He's going to put us in the card room so we can have some privacy to put our heads together and fix this."

"Lead the way," Crain said, falling in behind.

The room was paneled in dark wood, looked very old school, and held several square tables surrounded by comfortable club chairs on rollers. They chose the table closest to the windows and gave Crain the seat with a full-on view of the golf course. A flurry of activity ensued, saving him from having to comment as waiters laid the table with a white cloth, napkins, silverware, and water goblets. Harry entered carrying in a silver tray, drawing Crain's eye to the bottle of twelve-year-old tequila that sat on it. The exact brand he'd been drinking the night he'd asked Elizabeth to accompany him to Vegas.

Fitting.

"Mr. Carraway. There are times when a simple shot of tequila is worth its weight in gold. If I may start you off with one of these," Harry said, placing a shot glass in front of Crain. "Then I'll be back in a moment with that old-fashioned you really want."

What the…?

Crain's head snapped up. "Are you sayin' you can take one look at me and know my drink?"

"I've kind of got a knack for that." Harry filled Crain's shot glass.

"Is that right? What are they paying you, Harry? Because I'll double it."

"Hey. Hey. Simmer down there, Tex," said Vance. "Stop trying to buy up the place. You can't have Pinks, and you can't have Harry."

"Not everything can be solved by throwing money at it," Harry said, leaving the bottle in the center of the table and closing the doors behind him.

"If only it were that easy," Crain said. He picked up his shot. "To one hell of a morning."

They drank, slammed the glasses on the table, and then Vance got to laughing.

"As much as I'd like to get down to business…" he paused as he reached in and grabbed the bottle, "after we all witnessed whatever the hell that was back there," he said, refilling Crain's glass and then his own, "you've got to explain how the hell it's possible that you are married to Henderson's own Tansy Langford."

Crain grunted and twirled the shot glass on the table a few times before he picked it up and downed it. "Gentlemen," he said, sitting back, staring into the eyes of the men around him, "if I knew the answer to that, I would tell you. But up until twenty minutes ago, I thought I'd hitched my wagon to a woman named Elizabeth whose hometown was Dallas."

Pinks picked up the bottle and refilled his own glass.

"And I guess it doesn't speak much for me as a businessman that I didn't take the time to vet my bride properly before I hustled her down the aisle. I was just…certain that she was the one."

"Was she working for you?" Brooks asked.

"No. No, I was working for her."

"How's that exactly?"

"CC Dallas was hired by The George W. Bush Presidential Library and Museum. They're wantin' to keep the place current. You know, change things up on a regular basis. Keep the visitors pouring in. Elizabeth was the liaison between the library and my staff members who were running surveys and scouting out ideas. I'd seen her in our office regularly for about a month before I got up the nerve to ask her out."

"You're the effing CC in CC Dallas. How hard could it possibly be to ask a woman out?" Pinks spouted.

"Gol, I don't know. I wasn't thinkin' like that. Frankly, I just liked lookin' at her for starters. She was the prettiest thing I'd ever seen. I mean, you've gotta admit, there's somethin' about those pricey little suits she wears that remind you more of a beauty queen than a ball buster. And those cute little glasses."

"Glasses?" Pinks said.

"Yeah, you know. Those smart-girl glasses she wears. Drives me wild."

"Suits?" Brooks asked.

"Oh, come on. The suits, and the way she winds her hair up and tries to make herself look like a damn librarian?"

"Huh-uh. Nope. Doesn't sound like Tansy," Vance said. "Tansy's more like…like—"

"Yacht club."

"Pardon?"

"She only wears navy and white, occasionally red. Even her bikini is nautical. Navy and gold," Pinks offered.

Something about The Pink One was starting to irritate Crain. He turned his head and asked, "You've seen her in a bikini?"

"Ah, yeah. Right here at the Club."

"And at the pool party," Brooks added.

"Oh yeah, the pool party," Pinks agreed.

Crain started looking between Pinks and Brooks. Then Vance chimed in. "You know I've never really thought about it, but you're right. She does wear a lot of navy and white. My God, it's like Piper with her yellow."

"I've been tellin' you," Pinks said.

"Y'all spend a lot of time lookin' at my bride, do ya?" Crain pulled at the damn bottle again, wondering where the hell Harry was with his old-fashioned.

"Well," Pinks said cautiously, "we do work together."

"Ya do, do ya? You work with her at the pool? While she's wearing her bikini?"

Vance cut in. "Crain, this is a small town. Brooks and I've known Tansy since we were kids.

"How 'bout The Pink Ninja? Huh? How long has he known Eliza—Tansy?"

"Well, Pinks and Tansy have a very…ah, close working relationship," Vance offered. "They both came on board with E&E this summer when we officially opened our doors."

Crain swung his head around toward Vance. "So Elizabeth has been here all summer."

"She came back…" Vance hesitated, looking over at Brooks, "I'd say somewhere around mid-May."

Brooks leaned into the table across from Crain. "When exactly did the two of you get married?" he asked.

Crain looked at the tequila bottle. *What the hell?* He poured himself another shot and downed it. Then he ran his hands through his hair.

"May twelfth. After working together for a month and then two quick dates, we eloped. In Vegas. I'd asked her to accompany me out there for a conference, but in the back of my mind I was probably hoping we'd throw caution to the wind and just tie the knot. And we did."

"So what happened?"

"The next morning I came out of the bathroom, and she'd left me a note. Said she got cold feet. I figured she was spooked because it had all happened so fast. I left a message on her phone tellin' her I'd wait in our suite out there, hopin' she'd come back. But after two days of no show, and realizing that her phone was no longer in service, I flew back to Dallas and went to her place. The doorman hadn't seen her. Her neighbors hadn't heard anything. I convinced the police we needed to get in and make sure she wasn't lying on the floor unconscious or anything. When we did, all her personal stuff was gone. The only thing left was her rental agreement for the furniture."

"Man, what the hell did you do?" Brooks asked.

"I hired a private investigator to find her. What do you think I did?"

"No. No. What did you do to make her run off after spending one night in your bed?"

Crain pulled back and blinked. "Exactly what are you implying?"

"I'm implying that you might be some sort of kinky bastard who forced Tansy to do something she wasn't comfortable with. That's what I'm implying."

Crain looked to his right at Vance. Then looked to his left at Pinks. "Gentlemen," he said as he stood up. "If you'll excuse us, Mr. Bennett and I are gonna take this conversation outside."

"Nobody is taking anything outside," Vance said, holding on to Crain's shoulder, wanting him to sit down.

"It's a fair question," The Pink One chimed in. "You're a good-looking guy, you're made of money, and the woman spends one night with you and runs?"

"Enough," Vance warned Pinks.

"I'm just asking the man a question," Pinks growled back.

Harry came in with his drink then, followed by two waiters bearing large platters of Texas-sized burgers and a whole lot of fries. This time the growling came from Crain's stomach as he got a whiff of red meat and bacon. He sat down and put his napkin in his lap.

The moment Harry put his drink on the table, Crain upended it and handed the glass back. "Refill, if you don't mind. I'm not driving."

"Coming right up."

Crain stared at his plate, reliving his wedding night for the thousandth time. Hell, he couldn't blame them for asking the same damn questions he'd asked himself a dozen times. What happened to spook her? What happened that caused her to run?

He shook his head, reaching for the ketchup. "I get it. It looks bad," he admitted. "If I was standin' in your boots, I'd be asking the same thing." He shook some ketchup over his fries and then screwed the top back on the bottle and set it down.

"But I love her." He looked up from his plate. "I probably have since the first time I saw her standing in the office. She's just so… sweet, you know?"

He saw it then. Brooks' eyes flashing over toward Vance.

"What?" he asked.

"Nothing," Brooks said.

"Aww, c'mon fellas. I'm pouring my heart out here and—" he looked right and left. "Hold on now. You don't think she's sweet."

Pinks eyed him over his burger. "Ah—no. No, that's not a word we'd use to describe Tansy."

"That's not a word anybody would use to describe Tansy." Vance added with a laugh.

"You gotta be kiddin' me. Brooks," he asked, pointing across the table, "you think she's sweet, don'tcha?"

Brooks smiled after wiping his mouth with his napkin. "There is a gentler side to Tansy than she hands out to these two," he said, indicating Pinks and Vance. "But sweet? No. Even I don't think she's particularly sweet."

"In fact," Vance said, holding a French fry in his direction, "your first assessment of Tansy was right on the money."

"What do you mean?"

"What did you call her? Back there at the office."

"A mean, self-centered bitch," Pinks supplied around a mouth full of burger.

"Yeah. That's it. That's the Tansy we know."

Crain sat back and wondered who the hell these fools were talkin' about. His Elizabeth was the kindest, gentlest, sweetest woman he'd ever had the pleasure to know. She settled him. She was the only one who could.

"And those suits and glasses you mentioned," Pinks said. "Never seen 'em."

"What?"

"Face it, Crain. You're in love with a woman who doesn't exist." Vance said.

"She sure as hell existed in Dallas."

"It's starting to sound like our Tansy is your Elizabeth's evil twin. And if that's the case, you dodged a bullet, my friend."

They all laughed.

"I'm glad y'all are finding this so amusing. I really am. But my beloved momma is tearing her hair out over this mess, and she doesn't deserve that. In fact, the only reason I took this meeting is because I had to get out of town. I could not look that woman in the eye and tell her one more lie."

"So your parents don't know what happened?"

"Hell, I don't even know what happened. I made up a story about a long honeymoon, figuring I'd find Elizabeth and ease her concerns before too much time went by. I sure didn't want to taint my parents' opinion about their daughter-in-law by letting them know she'd run out on me. But then one week turned into six, and I'm in deep making stuff up about dying grandparents and whatnot, knowing damn well I wasn't foolin' anybody."

"Well, now you've found her," Vance stated. "You took the meeting and found Tans—Elizabeth. So…what's your end game?"

"My end game?"

"Yeah. What are you going to do now?"

"Well, first I'm going to strangle her," he said before munching down on one of his fries. "And then if one of y'all manages to pull me off while she's still breathing, I'm gonna hook her up to a lie detector and ask the woman a few questions."

"Sounds fair," Brooks said.

"I wouldn't mind being around for that," Pinks agreed.

Vance spoke directly to him. "You are not the first man in these parts to want to strangle Elizabeth Tansy Langford."

"Is that right? Well, tell me. What has this Tansy done to y'all that would make *you* want to strangle her?"

"Other than the fact that she and I haven't seen eye to eye since eighth grade…" Vance said, "I can't think of a thing. But this isn't about *us*," he said to the table at large with great emphasis. "This is about you and your *wife*," he stressed again. "And if I could just redirect for a moment, there's still the small issue of turning Henderson into the Sports Capital of North Carolina. As to that, under the circumstances, I'm hoping CC Dallas is now willing to extend E&E Investments their Friends and Family discount."

CHAPTER TWELVE

Molly DuVal and Piper Beaumont Evans stood smiling at each other across the enormous island in the center of Hale Evans' gourmet kitchen.

"What?" Genevra asked as her gaze swung between her niece Molly and her new daughter-in-law, Piper. "What's going on here? I thought the two of you had never met."

"We haven't," Molly said, almost near to giggling.

Piper shook her head too, biting down on her bottom lip, seemingly unable to speak.

"I don't get it," Genevra said. "The two of you look like you've swallowed canaries." She started to laugh simply because the two young women were obviously about to burst at the seams.

"It's Vance," Molly said.

"He's given us strict instructions not to discuss anything…um, having to do with him or his anatomy," Piper said, bursting into a broad smile.

"Oh. Oh!" Genevra's eyes widened. "Because you two…you both… ah, I see."

"So, you know, this is awkward," Molly said, "but hilariously so, and at the same time, exactly what he deserves."

The girls couldn't take their eyes off one another.

Assessing the situation, Genevra went over and carefully pulled at the pocket doors that shut the kitchen off from the rest of the house. Then she came over and got in between Molly and Piper.

"Emelina is taking a nap," she said quietly, "and Hale is working in his study with the doors shut and the music on. Whatever is said in this kitchen stays in this kitchen. Are we agreed?"

Molly and Piper nodded at one another, each of them smiling from ear to ear. "You first," Piper said.

"I stole his virginity," Molly confessed.

"You what?" Genevra covered her ears, horrified.

"Oh, Aunt Gen, please. Like you're the Virgin Mary."

"I beg your pardon," she tried to say, but ended up needing to put a hand over her own mouth to stem her laughter so no one would come in and disrupt the conversation.

"When was that?" Piper asked Molly, eyes glistening and eager.

"Back in high school. He thought he was all that, and I was tired of hearing about it. So I dragged him into my parents' basement late one night and showed him he had no idea what the hell he was talking about."

"You did not!" Genevra said.

"What's said in the kitchen stays in the kitchen," Molly threatened her aunt. "And yes, of course I did. He was Vance Evans for God's sake, and I needed to get my hands on that body."

"It's a great body," Piper said. "Have you seen him with his shirt off lately? He's got these bulging biceps that I just want to sink my teeth into. Said he's been lifting weights with his team for the past year. Me likey."

"Dear Lord," Genevra said.

"I'm just saying my husband has awesome biceps and abs. Oh! And his back." Piper looked at Molly. "You should see his back."

"He is one fine specimen," Molly agreed. "But I'm over it. I only have eyes for my Josh now."

"Well, good. I mean I certainly am not trying to tempt you. It's just that...well, I've been dying to talk to somebody about his body. I just—I just can't get over it."

Molly laughed. "He would make a fabulous nude model. No doubt about that. Did you know he and his body tempted me to run off for a weekend with him while I was engaged to someone else?"

"No!"

"It's true," Genevra chimed in.

"I thought it would be…you know, one last fling before I got married," Molly said. "One last romp with good ol' Vance before I marched down the aisle. Unfortunately, it didn't occur to me that everything I do ends up on the front page of the damn newspaper around here. That's why I've had to lay low in Raleigh all these years."

"Because of Vance?"

"Because of Vance."

"You're not going to believe this," Piper said. "But he broke up my engagement too. About five years ago."

"You're kidding."

"Swear to God. Only, obviously, that ended up okay."

Molly held up her hands. "For me, too. Or else I'd be Evie Jackson's granddaughter-in-law, and Lord knows I could never have lived up to her standards without wanting to self-medicate."

"Who knew we had so much in common?" Piper asked. "And now that we've broken the ice about as much as we possibly can, let's talk about your miraculous Big Pie Plate."

Piper reached over and cradled the enormous green ceramic plate against her chest. The thing was over fourteen inches in diameter and had three-inch sides. Piper's fingers drifted around the fluted edge and stroked the Evans crest Molly had inscribed on the inside.

"There's only one like it," Molly said. "I knew Aunt Gen loved to cook, and I wanted it to stand out among the many wedding gifts."

"And it has," Genevra assured her. She leaned over and gave her niece a hug. "I've loved it since the moment Hale and I unwrapped it. Hale especially loved the family crest in the center. But while I was on my honeymoon, Piper, who is a passionate baker, discovered something rather amazing."

"Did you bake in it?" Piper asked Molly.

"I don't bake edible things. I bake artwork."

"Gotcha. It's just that your Big Pie Plate took my perfect piecrust and made it even better."

"Good. That's good." Molly said.

"No. You don't understand," Piper tried to explain. "My crust, on its own, could win awards. Your pie plate took it to a whole new level. Genevra and I have been baking in it nonstop for the past four days. *Everything* we bake in it comes out better."

"I'm glad to hear it."

"Molly. Pay attention. If you can replicate this pie plate exactly, if you can create additional Big Pie Plates that make my crust do what this one does every single time, well, then I could help you become one rich lady."

"You've got to be kidding."

"I'm not kidding. At all. To the point where I can't sleep at night thinking about what I'm going to bake next in this Big Pie Plate. To the point I worry it's somehow a *magic* pie plate, and you won't be able to make another one that does what this one does. And then I'll have to resort to stealing this one from my fabulous mother-in-law. Whom I love! To the point where I have spent a good number of hours working on a business plan for the sale and marketing of your Big Pie Plate."

Molly blinked a few times and then looked over and spoke directly to Genevra. "Is she for real? Because I don't know her, and I'm not sure what to think of all this."

"Can you replicate the pie plate? Make it just like this one?" Genevra asked.

"I don't see why not. I use the same pottery mix for all my original pieces. It's a recipe I came up with to hold the color."

"That recipe of, of pottery mix. Is it yours exclusively?" Piper asked.

"Sure. I have it written down on a piece of paper, but basically I've used it so many times I have it in my head."

"Okay. You're gonna want to get a patent for that formula. You're gonna want to keep that piece of paper in a safe from now on. And under no circumstances are you to share your Big Pie Plate recipe with anyone."

"You just got a little scary."

"I'm a lawyer."

"Ah. Okay then."

"There's something different about the way your pie plate conducts heat. We've tried pies, cakes, puddings, egg dishes, sticky buns, rolls." Piper ticked off the items on her fingers. "The list goes on and on. Every single recipe we've created in your Big Pie Plate has turned out better than ever before. It has got to have something to do with your pottery. Maybe the size of it. I don't know."

"Okay." Molly tapped her chin thoughtfully. "Let's experiment. Because it could be a lot of things. From the paint pigment to the specific glaze to the stars being aligned just right when I threw this one in the kiln. Let's see if I can create another one that gives you the same results before you lose any more sleep or start talking about patents, safes, and making me a rich woman. Which I'm not at all opposed to, by the way."

CHAPTER THIRTEEN

The anxiety Tansy was feeling as she headed to the office early the next morning was incalculable.

Because *nothing* had happened. Nothing.

Crain hadn't come back to the office after her mother left. Neither had Vance or Davis. The only correspondence she'd had with anyone was a text from Hale telling her to lock up when she was ready to go home.

So she did.

And then sat in dread all night at her parents' place anticipating Crain showing up on their doorstep and introducing himself as her husband.

She was a wreck.

And when she crawled between the sheets last night and closed her eyes, exhausted from the fear, the shock, and the crazy emotional turmoil, she immediately thought about that kiss.

That kiss.

The one where Crain had pulled her to him, intent on corporal punishment she was sure. Instead, he'd held her so securely in his big, strong arms against his big, broad chest it made her five-foot-ten-inch self feel more like tiny Piper Beaumont. And then his mouth, that big, happy, handsome mouth of his just crushed down on top of hers. And that was when her insides scrambled up and her brain passed out. Lord, she hadn't been kissed like that ever.

Ever.

Not even by Crain himself on their wedding night when it was just the two of them in their own little bubble of a world, and everything was perfect. Not even then did Crain kiss her as well, as long, and as thoroughly as he'd done in the office that afternoon.

Oh, he'd done plenty of other things long and thoroughly on their wedding night.

At first, Crain had seemed a little tentative, sort of overwhelmed by her having agreed to be his bride. So she took him in her hands…literally…and started their foray into matrimony slowly… and in a very…submissive…position.

Crain seemed to appreciate her efforts even though he wasn't quite able to respond with the English language—or even his version of it in his Texas vernacular. But there was no doubt of his enjoyment. Of the pleasure she'd given and he'd received. Because when he'd pulled her up from the floor with his big muscular arms strapping her skimpily clad torso against his naked chest, his heart beat frantically against her bosom while he took the time to catch his breath. The sound that spread from deep inside him was something between a purr and a growl. The meaning perfectly clear. She'd unleashed his primitive desires. The ones he'd apparently been keeping in check ever since she'd caught his fancy. Because up until that point, he'd been the perfect gentleman. Up until that point, he hadn't so much as sworn in front of her.

"Damn it, woman," he panted into her hair. "That was more—way more—than I'd bargained for." He backed up and practically collapsed onto the bed. His nude body glistening, all sculpted angles and lines in contrast to the soft bedding he sat on. When she tried to follow, he held out his hand and said, "Wait." So she stood before him, watching his eyes zero in on her mouth. She saw him swallow, the faint protrusion of his Adam's apple bobbing up and back. Then his gaze began a slow journey south, to her chin, her neck, and down to her chest. When his eyes rested there, his longing became palpable, transferring between them and causing a surge of sexual awareness inside her chest, a flash of heat seeping out to the rest of her body, causing everything to drip hot and molten. Her nipples puckered under his scrutiny, her breathing became labored.

She felt terribly conspicuous standing before him in nothing but a little bit of satin and lace while his eyes studied all the gown revealed. He, as nude and as magnificent as Michelangelo's David, seemed content to let her stare back at him. Perhaps he wasn't even aware, so intent on what was standing just out of his reach.

Eventually, his gaze struggled past her bosom, settling further down at the juncture of her thighs hidden behind the short nightgown she wore. His fingers twitched, and she imagined him touching her where his eyes remained transfixed.

Crain cleared his throat. "Come here," he said roughly. The sound of his voice sent tingles up her spine. He held out his hand, and she took it, stepping to him. His hands traveled up to the straps of her gown. His fingers found their way underneath them and pulled them over her shoulders and further down. When she tried to pull her arms up and out, he captured her forearms in his hands and stilled her movements. "My turn," he said, his gaze back on her eyes, his expression earnest. After a few heartbeats, his attention went back to the straps, sliding them further down, letting the lace and silk bodice roll down her breasts, all the way to her waist and elbows, trapping her arms at her sides within the confines of the fabric. Crain's hands slid over the rest of her silky nightgown and around to her backside, pulling her closer.

She stumbled a half step, moving between his spread thighs. Her breasts fell right where he no doubt wanted them, so close to his mouth she could feel his breath upon them. His big, strong hands, famous for palming a basketball and catching a football in mid-flight, skidded up her ribcage, capturing her breasts in a decidedly firm grip.

She wanted to weep with pleasure. Crain wasn't gentle, but he certainly was not rough. She could feel the tip of every one of his fingers as he explored. His thumbs swiped across her nipples, making them even more sensitive. When he brought his mouth to one, she watched the top of his head until her eyes fluttered closed, and she focused solely on the sensations he was creating throughout her body.

The man was a genius.

Lust pooled at her core. Desire building steadily as Crain teased her with his mouth and hands. She'd never been terribly vocal in the throes of passion, but he had her whimpering fast enough. She tried to move her hands into his hair to pull him closer, but they were still trapped by her sides. Her pelvis rocked of its own accord, dividing her attention between the finesse of his hands on her breasts and the awakening rhythms down lower. She started to shimmy, moving the blue silk down, but it gathered at her hips and wrists. When she tried to pull a wrist free, Crain's big hand stopped her, holding her where she was.

When she settled, he relaxed his grip, sliding his palm soothingly over her hip and around to the back of her thigh. His mouth and one hand continued to make love to her breast, while his other hand moved lower, fingertips scraping over her naked leg, teasing the soft skin at the back of her knee, kneading her calf muscle. Finally, he flattened his hand over her calf. His long fingers wrapped around the inside of her leg and made the slow, steady ascent up, sneaking underneath her nightgown and cupping her bare behind.

That had her going up on her toes, and Crain groaned in appreciation.

His hand dropped lower and pulled her knee up to the bed, to the outside of his big, muscular thigh. She was straddling his leg, one foot still on the floor, one knee tucked into the bedding when his hand stole between her legs and laid purchase to everything that had gathered in need and want of his touch. Nerve endings taut, she let out a tiny shriek that Crain paid no mind. His fingers stroked while his mouth continued to feast. She scrambled to free her hands and gripped his shoulders for stability.

She climbed onto his lap, straddling his thighs. He pushed at the nightgown, then shifted gears and drew it all up in one clumped mass over her head and tossed it to the floor. Before she knew what was happening, she was flat on her back, bare from head to toe, her knees caught around his hips. Crain was smiling down at her, looking his fill.

"What have I gone and gotten myself into?" he teased, searching her face. His grin was as broad as she'd ever seen it. "Behind closed doors, you take off those smart-girl glasses and reveal Wonder Woman. No more complacent about following orders in the bedroom than you are in the office. I believe I have met my match," he said, grinning like it was his best night ever. And that's when he took himself in hand and—

The jingling sound as Tansy pushed open the front door of E&E dragged her back to reality. She shook her head from the reverie. She couldn't afford to let her mind wander again—like it had last night—on and on, ad infinitum, when she'd dissected that kiss. What it meant. How it felt. How it made her feel.

How she *responded*.

Lord knew she'd started seconded guessing herself twenty minutes after she'd scurried out of that Las Vegas suite. But never more so than she had yesterday when she was back in Crain's arms.

She sighed over the bitter mess she'd made of things. Felt deep sadness that there was no way to fix it. She expected to be hit with the blow of finding the signed annulment papers sitting on her desk this morning. It would certainly serve her right.

But when she turned the little corner into the alcove where her desk sat, what was waiting for her was far worse.

Pinks.

A stiff, irritated Pinks with his eyes narrowed and his jaw tense. He didn't resemble the Super-Hero-in-Training Tansy knew him to be. The man before her had aged ten years and turned into a mastermind arch villain overnight. His voice was cold and menacing, escalating as he spoke.

"So…I had an affair with a married *woman?*"

Crap. This was her fault.

"No. No, of course not," she soothed.

"Oh, thank God." Visible relief flowed throughout his body, as the tension he held released. He crumbled into her chair. The twenty-three-year-old kid returned. "I knew he was mistaken.

I mean, you're my—our—Tansy. You couldn't possibly be his Elizabeth."

Double crap. She bit her lip.

"What? He is mistaken, right?"

Her head bounced from side to side. *Crap, crap, crap.*

"So you *are* Elizabeth. *His* Elizabeth?" Davis asked.

"I'm not *his*. I'm just…me."

"So…you didn't get married in Vegas," he stated.

She waggled her head again.

"You *did* get married in Vegas."

Once again with the head jiggle.

"Tansy, stop fucking with me. Did I screw a married woman or not?"

Well, didn't that just put it out there.

"No," she whispered. "At least, I didn't think so at the time. I wouldn't have done that to you. Or me. Or Crain." That was the truth. But the sorrow that memory triggered threatened to overwhelm her. She blinked it back, wanting to spare Pinks. From the look in his eyes, she'd hurt him enough already. So she tried to make light of it all in an attempt to spare his feelings.

"Davis, it wasn't a *real* wedding for goodness sake. I mean it was Vegas, after all. We'd had a few too many drinks, got all hot and bothered, and it just…sounded like a good idea at the time."

"So you were buzzed…" Davis' eyes narrowed. "Hot and bothered…" He stood slowly. "And instead of just giving him a roll on the conference table like you did me, you married the guy?"

The supervillain was back.

"I was caught up in the moment," she defended. "Crain was down on one knee, and this adorable little wedding chapel was right down the street. So…I did what people *do* in Vegas. I…I threw caution to the wind. Sue me."

"Are you crazy? Throwing caution to the wind means going all-in at the poker table, not getting married."

"A lot you know. You can't take two steps in Vegas without running into a bride. But it's not like the wedding actually *counted*," she insisted. "We'd only had two dates, and I was practically engaged to Brooks at the time. There was no white dress, no bridesmaids, my father didn't walk me down the aisle, so—basically—no wedding."

"Were there vows exchanged?"

She swallowed.

"Were official documents signed?"

Crap.

"Was there a consummation of this not-real wedding?"

When she couldn't answer on the grounds she might incriminate herself, Pinks yelled, "Jesus, Tansy!"

"I know, I know," she moaned. "But you have to understand. Dallas was like another world, okay? Here I'd spent my entire life in Henderson where everybody knows who I am. Where I can't make one false move or my mother will hear about it in five minutes, and then I'll really hear about it for the rest of my life.

"And then suddenly, I'm in Dallas. Dallas! Where there are wine bars and restaurants, and services of all kinds. Where I can finally get a decent manicure and bikini wax, and I realize that no one knows me, so I could even get a *Brazilian* if I want too. And that's when it hit me. I can finally be me. Me—not Rye Langford's first born, not my mother's pageant pony, not even Brooks Bennett's girl. Just me.

"So, yeah. I *was* Elizabeth in Dallas. I had a job I loved. I actually got to meet with President and Mrs. Bush. It was all so big and exciting and Crain—well," she sighed, "Crain Carraway was everything good about Dallas all rolled up into one tall, handsome, slow-talking package. And he liked me. The Elizabeth me. Not because I was tall enough, or from the right family, or was the right age, he just—you know—liked *me*."

She drew in a deep breath and finally looked Pinks in the eye.

"He said I was sweet," she whispered.

She could see the fight go out of Pinks as he sat back down.

"I got caught up in the new town, the new job, and eventually in a new man. I didn't stop to think about my parents or Brooks. I was just thinking about me and the adventure I was having—until I woke up married. And that's when I panicked and ran back home."

"And what? Two months later you thought it might be a good idea to drag me into your nightmare?"

"Pinks—"

"I'm serious. Of all the irresponsible, foolish, selfish— Sleeping with a married woman was not on my bucket list," he shouted.

"Oh, please. You were hot to have me since that first day we met."

"Listen, Yacht Club. I may have been hot to have you, but you were just as hot to be had. And I'm guessing by the way you started dodging me at every turn you figured out pretty quick that two wrongs didn't make a right?"

Boy, did he hit that nail on the head.

"Davis," she said quietly, trying to settle them both down. Because this wasn't his fault—not at all. And she needed to own it, at least with him.

"You're right," she finally admitted. "It was irresponsible. I couldn't handle my new life, so I ran back to my old one and tried to rewind everything just as fast as I could. I spent all of an hour hiring a Dallas lawyer to handle the annulment and simply assumed Crain would sign the papers immediately. I honestly considered it a fait accompli. Then I went into complete denial and pretended that the wedding never happened. From time to time, I had an acquaintance in Raleigh check the post office box I'd rented there. The call came in that day you and Jesse James debuted your band at The Situation. A large, fat envelope had arrived from a law firm in Dallas. I didn't ask her to open it. I just assumed Crain had finally signed the papers. I assumed the marriage was officially dissolved."

"And it wasn't?"

She shook her head no. "The day after our little…ah, get together, I drove to Raleigh and picked them up. But instead of his signature at the bottom, Crain, who never uses foul language, had written in red Sharpie across every page that he'd sign the damn papers if I ever got the courage to hand them to him in person. So yeah—no annulment had me back pedaling fast. I was pretty horrified about what I'd inadvertently done, and frankly, I never wanted you to know. Because…"

"Because what?" he snapped.

"Because if you knew, then I'd have to own it. All of it. And I desperately didn't want to have to do that."

"Did you honestly think that none of this was ever going to come out?"

"I had hoped. I mean, at that point, you were a summer intern. Come Labor Day, I'd never see you again, and you wouldn't be the wiser. But September comes and you're still here, and there was no way after our one-night stand that I had the courage to face Crain in person. So I called the lawyer and had him send the papers to Crain all over again."

"What'd he do to you?"

"What'd who do to me?"

"Crain. I mean if he was everything good about Dallas rolled up into one big, handsome package," Pinks exaggerated, "explain to me what happened between the time he got down on one knee and when you wrote out the Dear John letter. Because it sounds to me like he tried some really kinky shit in bed that made you bolt."

"No. God, no. It wasn't anything like that," she sighed. "He… he just…"

"He just what?"

"He just…called his mother."

Pinks stared at the beautiful blonde before him, trying hard to wrap his head around what she was saying. Tansy Langford had been a mean pit bull of a woman since the day the two of them had knocked heads moving furniture into this office. That had started a battle of wills where she'd gone toe-to-toe with him holding her own on every occasion. She was sharp, quick-witted, and had the tongue of a viper, and maybe what he'd mistaken for sexual tension had just been…tension.

Still, he couldn't see Tansy ever agreeing to marry someone just because she was tipsy or happened to be in Vegas. So something had happened. And he was going to get to the bottom of it, come hell or high water.

"He called his mother," he repeated.

"Right."

"And that caused you to bolt?"

"Right."

"I'm not following."

Tansy finally dropped the tote bag she'd had slung over her shoulder and sat down on her desk. She was facing away from him, so Davis got up and came around so he could read her expression as she talked.

"Crain's big," she said, "and he's loud. So even though he'd closed himself off in the bathroom to phone his parents the next morning, their conversation woke me up. He was so happy, telling them that we'd married that at first I just smiled. I reveled in it, to be honest. In fact, I got out of bed planning to join him in the bathroom so I could be a part of the conversation. As I pulled on a robe, I heard him describing me, and it was wonderful to see myself through his eyes. Though I was tempted to laugh out loud when he said I was as sweet as praline pie. Talk about love being blind."

"You're…sweet."

"Oh, bullshit. You know I'm not sweet."

Pinks granted her a small smile.

"I was about to push through the bathroom door and join him, when his tone changed. Just a little, but I could tell his mother had started to ask him some tough questions. Like who my people are, and why we rushed into marriage. And as I listened, it became more and more apparent that she wasn't at all happy that she'd been left out of the wedding.

"It wasn't until that moment that I gave any thought to my own parents' reaction to the news. I realized Crain was going to want me to call them, and just the thought of it set off a panic attack. I couldn't get myself out of there fast enough."

"Yacht Club, on the brink of turning thirty, and after living in another city for the better part of a year, you leave the poor guy because you're worried about what your *parents* would think?"

"You were certainly worried about your parents last Friday when they showed up here to drag your Yankee butt back home."

"How many times do I have to tell you that *Maryland* is the Mason-Dixon Line. So stop with the Yankee bullshit. And I'm twenty-three and fresh out of school, so don't go tossing all of your failure-to-launch, secretly married crap on me."

Tansy jumped off the desk and got right in his face.

"Davis. You have seen my mother in action. She's had my wedding planned for ages. Just the thought of telling her I'd eloped—" she cringed, "I—I couldn't face it. And, if I was going to marry anyone, it was supposed to be Brooks. After two years of dating Brooks, how was I supposed to tell him, them, this town, that I'd thrown over their Golden Boy for some foreigner after only two dates?"

"Brooks seems to have bounced back just fine," he sneered.

"Well, my parents haven't. Once Brooks made the mistake of mentioning running for mayor, that was it. In their heads, our nuptials were set in stone. My parents want their daughter to be the First Lady of Henderson. Not a shameless hussy who ran off to Vegas and married some 'white trash with cash' from Dallas."

"Wow." Davis' eyes went wide. "Is that how you see Crain Carraway?"

"No. Of course, that's not how *I* see him, but that's exactly how my parents will see him. Or at least my mother. And Crain is too kind, too generous, and too precious to be subjected to the likes of my mother."

"Precious? If you consider him precious, why are you trying so hard to divorce him?"

"Because I'm just like her," she cried. Her eyes welled up with tears as she admitted, "I'm a mean, angry bitch, and he thinks I'm as sweet as praline pie."

The last thing any part of him wanted to do was grant this woman comfort. But Pinks couldn't help himself. "You might be a mean, angry bitch at times, but you are not your mother."

"That's kind of you to say," she mumbled, meaning it, which was sort of funny. She must have realized it too, because she looked up and gave him a forlorn smile. "My bitchy side sort of turns you on, doesn't it?"

Yes. "Maybe. I don't know. There are times when you drive me plenty crazy, I know that. I also know this situation is not something I'm comfortable with."

"I know. 'Cause you're a Super-Hero-In-Training. You're one of the good guys." She shrugged her shoulder and scooted around her desk. "It'll all be behind us soon enough," she sighed. "Crain Carraway marched out of my life yesterday plenty resigned. Said he'd sign the papers. So…it's done."

Apparently, the woman wasn't as smart as he gave her credit for.

"Yacht Club," Pinks said. "Don't kid yourself. This thing you've gotten yourself tangled up in. It's far from done."

CHAPTER FOURTEEN

Pinks hadn't explained himself. He rolled right into Super-Hero-In-Training mode, saying he'd already spent too much time this morning on the impossible task of trying to clean up her messy love life, and now he needed to get to work.

Oh, please.

The one thing he did do before heading back to his office was to write the words *IMG Academy* on her notepad and suggest she become an expert on the subject STAT. Like he was a doctor. STAT.

Well, S.H.I.T.

Super-Hero-In-Training, she thought. Yes, he was totally a S.H.I.T.

But she was grateful he'd given her something other than her so-called messy love life to focus on for a moment, so she pulled out her computer and got lost in the research. She didn't know how much time went by before a hot cup of coffee slid into her line of sight.

"Something to warm up those cold feet," came the spine-tingling timbre of his voice, smooth and slow.

Stunned, she glanced up. There'd been no tinkling bells indicating Crain Carraway had come through the front door. She'd heard no footsteps, no heels from his fancy boots. And yet there he stood, gorgeous and larger than life just on the other side of her desk, shimmering before her like a mirage, and a whole lot like her wildest dream. He was decked out in a custom-made suit jacket. She knew the fabric would feel like butter under her fingers. He wore it over a pair of expensive jeans. His collared shirt was left tieless and opened at the neck. The angular edges of his jaw were clean-shaven, his hair gelled just right. And those yummy dark-chocolate-colored eyes were holding her captive.

She was too overcome to speak.

"I had a cup just like that, with lots of cream and sugar. Fixin' to serve it to you in bed. That's when I found your note. Cold Feet."

"Crain…" she breathed. How could she handle him like this? Standing there all sexy and being so…Crain. It was much easier yesterday when he was yelling at her or pulling her into his arms. "You're still here."

"Where d'you reckon I'd be?"

"Dallas. I reckoned you'd be in Dallas." She heard herself fall into his patent way of talking. "When you ran out of here yesterday, it sounded like you couldn't get back there fast enough."

"You mean when *you* ran me out of here. Can't say I've ever been somebody's dirty little secret before, and I can guaran-darn-tee ya that's not how I saw this playin' out when I asked you to be my bride."

She saw his shoulders bunch, heard the change he jiggled in his pants pocket. Without thinking, Tansy opened the top drawer of her desk, pulled out a pencil and handed it to Crain. He took it, speaking all the while, and began twisting the thing back and forth through his fingers.

"But no, darlin', I can't hightail it back to Dallas because there's nothin' back there that can answer my questions and give me satisfaction. And I aim to be satisfied. So in case you haven't caught on yet, let me spell this one out for you, plain and simple. Your chickens have finally come home to roost."

Uh-oh.

"And what kind of a name is *Tansy* anyway?" He tapped the eraser end of the pencil on the desk.

A spout of disbelief burst from her lips. "That's your question? What kind of a name is Tansy?"

"Well, it doesn't suit you, *Elizabeth*."

"I'm not Elizabeth."

"Maybe not here," he said, looking around, tapping the pencil against his other hand, "in this hovel of an office, acting like you're somebody's secretary, wearing Daisy Dukes and flip-flops."

"I beg your pardon."

"Aww, honey," he said, sticking the pencil up behind his ear. "I'm not sayin' your long, tan legs sticking out from underneath that tiny little Island Girl skirt doesn't make me want to tie you up to a mast and go all Captain Hook on your shapely little backside. But it's not much of a look for a serious businesswoman."

Pinks. And the Yacht Club thing. She was going to kill him.

"This is Henderson, not Dallas," she defended, reaching into her purse and handing him a stick of gum.

"That's right," he said as took the gum and slid the paper covering off before unwrapping the foil. "Henderson. Where there's no Presidential Library for you to preside over. I thought you loved that job," he said. And the look on his face implied only too clearly, "And I thought you loved me too."

"I did," she said. "You know I did," she whispered.

"What I know right now wouldn't fill up Granny B's thimble," he groused, folding the stick of gum into accordion pleats.

"Crain," she sighed.

"What?" he snapped.

At her loss for words, he continued to speak.

"Seems someone left my business card around here," he said, pointing his index finger about the office. He took that moment to chomp down on the gum. Tansy didn't have to look at his hands to know they were now going all origami on the foil wrapper. "E&E Investments liked that I had a part in some of the minor league ballparks." His voice dropped as close to a whisper as Crain ever got. "Was it you, Cold Feet? Did you leave my card around here on purpose, so they'd call me? So I could find you?"

The hope in his voice matched what was resonating in his eyes as he stared at her from across the desk.

She wished she could tell him it was true. But she'd led him down enough false paths already. She shook her head. "Not on purpose, no."

"I see." That's when he handed her the mini bird he'd created with his oversized fingers and pulled a rubber ball out of his pocket to start working it between both of his big strong hands. "So even though there's been a piss-poor private investigator lookin' for you all over Texas for the past three months, I just happen to run into you here. Like this is some big cosmic coincidence."

"I'm sure it's no coincidence. I'm just not sure how it's not a coincidence. Crain, where did you stay last night?"

"Stayed out at the Evans' spread. Mighty hospitable of them, wouldn't you say? Puttin' me up like that when I have kin in this town unwilling to take me in?"

"At the Evans' place?" *Dear Lord.* "With Hale and Genevra? Do they…know?"

"Well, since I had dinner with them last night and shared breakfast with them this morning, yeah, I think they know."

"Not that you stayed there. Do they know about…" She waved a hand between the two of them.

His eyes narrowed dangerously. "You can't even say it, can you? You can't say that you and I are hitched."

"Shhh." She threw his dangerous look right back at him. "Because we are not *hitched*—not really," she whispered as harshly as she could.

"I have a marriage certificate that begs to differ." He didn't follow her lead on the whisper thing. In fact, he was using a voice as big as Texas itself at the moment.

"Crain, please. Do you have any idea what this town is going to do if they find out we're married?"

"Celebrate?"

"No! They're going to go batshit crazy. They will form committees. Throw teas. Hold church picnics just so they can discuss it, analyze it, revel in it, hold it all up for scrutiny, and then rehash it again the next day. On and on and on. Now do you want that?"

"Hell, I'm forming the first committee."

"Stop it. I'm serious. This is serious. This is my life."

"Your life?" he bellowed. "What about my life? Do you have any idea of the hell you've put me through? Not to mention my parents, my grandparents, my aunts, uncles, cousins, my *brother*, even my employees? Imagine for a second that you were actually excited you'd married me. That you were so happy you had finally found the perfect mate that you wanted the world to know. So you called everybody you cared about. *Everybody.* And told them."

"Oh, Crain."

"Don't tell *me* how serious this is. My reputation is on the line. Not just with my entire family but with my friends as well. In fact, my business is on the line."

"Your business doesn't have anything to do with our fly-by-night marriage."

"The company name is Crain Carraway Dallas," he insisted. "If Crain Carraway is simple enough to lose his bride within the first twenty-four hours of matrimony, how the hell is he smart enough to fix anyone else's problems?"

"So that's why you stayed in Henderson overnight? For your business?"

Crain staggered back like he couldn't believe she hadn't been following. "I'm *here* because there's no peace in *Dallas.* If it's not my mother coming in for a daily grilling, it's one of my buddies trying to conduct an intervention. They all think I'm insane. They think I hallucinated Elizabeth Langford and frankly," he took a pointed look up and down her frame, "I'm starting to think so too. I'm *here* because the Pink Pipsqueak is like a damn dog with a bone, and I finally realized that if I just gave in and came to godforsaken North Carolina to meet with him, at least I'd be out of the hot seat in Dallas for a time."

He punctuated his words by throwing his rubber ball across the room, where it bounced wildly and ended up rolling under the couch across from her desk.

Tansy didn't think too much about her actions. She was pulling a Wet One from her tote and crossing the room before she even realized it. She got down on her knees and reached under the couch, feeling around. In the end, she laid flat out on the floor so she could peek under and locate the ball to bring it out. She took the time to dust it off with the Wet One before using the cloth on her hands and arms as she stood. When she turned to hand the ball back to Crain, she was shocked at his expression.

"What?" she asked, holding out the ball, perplexed.

"See," he accused. "You *are* Elizabeth." He circled her wrist and plucked the red rubber from her grasp with his other hand.

"When you're right, you're right." Vance's voice came from behind. "Tansy would never get down on her knees and clean my balls."

"You're disgusting," Tansy snapped. Then she dismissed Vance like he didn't exist. "Crain," she sighed, noticing how large his hand was wrapped around hers. And how much she didn't mind him holding on to it. "How long are you planning to stay?"

"Sugar," he drawled, his thumb soothing over the tender spot on her wrist. "I mentioned your chickens, didn't I? I'm *stayin'* until I'm good and ready to leave. I'm *stayin'* until I'm satisfied."

Those delicious eyes of his held only happiness as they wrapped her up in their warmth. Like he had planned every moment that had come before and was right where he wanted to be. And she felt the pull of it now, just as she'd felt it when he'd suggested an impromptu wedding. His eyes, his touch, were a power of persuasion she'd never known before. She was putty around Crain. She was something—someone—he could mold into what he wanted and bend to his will.

"I'll be damned," Vance said in awe. "I believe I've just seen you do the impossible Carraway. All those sharp edges just melted right off of our Tansy and transformed her into your Elizabeth. I've got to hand it to you, man. Those are some mad lady-killer skills you've got there."

"Shove it, Evans," Tansy said, pulling her hand out of Crain's grasp and turning away from his crazy powers of persuasion.

"Oops. Tansy's back," Vance said. "Just as well, as CC Dallas and the Evans & Evans team need to get down to business. Already lost a half day on this Elizabeth nonsense. Seriously, Tansy, are you gonna claim the poor guy or not? Because he's refusing to give us the Friends and Family discount until you admit he's your husband. Which means I now have a stake in all these shenanigans. So you know what I'd like to see happen at lunchtime? I'd like this mythical Elizabeth to show up and take our new business partner on a walking tour of Henderson's town center. You think you can locate her somewhere underneath all of that ball-busting exterior?"

Tansy narrowed her gaze and shot Vance a killer look. Walking Crain around town, out in the open where anyone could see the two of them together, was the last thing she needed. What she needed was to get him out of Henderson fast. She definitely didn't need Vance trying to play matchmaker so he could save his firm some money. "May I speak with you privately, please?" she asked Vance.

"No. No, you may not."

The bell jingled as the front door opened and all heads turned toward Brooks as his tall, lanky body came through the door and up the short set of stairs. The radiant grin the folks of Henderson counted on from their Golden Boy was not present. In fact, when Brooks saw the three of them standing there, his features drew taut and his lips thinned into a single line. He may have given up a short nod to Crain, but when his gaze landed on Tansy his expression was grim. He passed by them with nothing more than a "Let's get started" and vanished down the hallway.

"What's got your pitcher's panties in a twist?" Crain asked Vance as they stared down the hall after him.

Vance shrugged. "My guess is that Tansy has some splainin' to do."

"And why is that?" Crain growled, turning a sharp eye on her.

Tansy blinked a few times, feeling like a deer in the headlights. She'd been worried about keeping the unfortunate one-nighter with Pinks from Crain. She hadn't even considered how Crain was going to feel about her being practically engaged to Brooks at the time of their impromptu wedding. Not to mention the insanity that ensued after she ran home trying to rewind the whole of it. She definitely needed to get Crain out of town.

Vance came to her rescue by wrapping a hand around Crain's shoulder and pushing him after Brooks. "All in good time, my friend. All in good time."

Tansy stared after the two of them, watching Crain look back at her twice before being led into the conference room.

Crain, insisting her chickens had come home to roost, summed it all right up, didn't he? Because although Crain wasn't aware of her relationship with either Brooks or Pinks, and Brooks wasn't aware of her one-night stand with his new girlfriend's ex, three out of the four men sitting in that conference room definitely had carnal knowledge of her and a legitimate bone to pick.

The other one held every one of those scandalous secrets in his hands.

She needed to be nicer to Vance. And that thought was like the proverbial straw.

She went in search of Advil.

CHAPTER FIFTEEN

Tansy managed to swallow the Advil just before the bells over the front door of E&E jingled again. She was seated at her desk when the couple who looked as if they should be on the cover of *People* magazine walked in and bestowed their brilliant smiles on her.

Genevra DuVal Evans, newly married and just starting to show, looked radiant standing beside her dashing husband, Hale. The two of them seemed to be in a constant state of love. The kind of love that Tansy had felt for about twelve hours surrounding her marriage to Crain. Maybe in some places people would have rolled their eyes at the Evanses' obvious happiness, but not here in Henderson. This town had felt the deep pain of suffering these two battled individually years ago, so Henderson was elated to see two of their kindest citizens finally find one another and start their own love story.

Tansy might find it hard to be genuinely happy for Piper and Vance as newlyweds, but she couldn't help but jump on the bandwagon for Vance's father and his new bride. They sure looked good together.

"Mr. and Mrs. Evans," she said in greeting, standing at her desk as they approached.

"Hale, please, Tansy. And that's the last time I'm going to remind you," he said with a smile.

"Hale, then," she acquiesced.

"And Genevra," Mrs. Evans piped in. "Since your friend Piper is much more like a friend than a daughter-in-law to me, I hope the two of us will become friends as well."

Lolly, Genevra's daughter, who also happened to be Brooks' new squeeze, was gonna hate this. "I look forward to our blossoming friendship," Tansy replied with true gusto.

"We…um…had the pleasure of meeting Crain Carraway last night," Hale ventured.

Uh-oh.

"I thought it might be…well, advantageous for you and my beautiful bride to have a conversation."

Tansy looked over at Genevra and received an empathetic smile. The curvy brunette who looked half her age stepped forward and whispered, "Since scandal is my middle name, I will likely make a very good ally."

"Oh. Ah. Okay…" Tansy stuttered. Clearly, they were privy to the secret Tansy had been desperately trying to undo for the past four months. She felt the blood rush to her cheeks as she wondered what they must think of her. She felt tears sting her eyes as she wondered just how many other people already knew. She felt her stomach turn as she wondered how long it was going to be before her mother found out.

She needed to get Crain out of town. Fast.

"It's okay," Hale said with an understanding smile and a soft touch to her shoulder. "Crain seems like good people. He swore us to secrecy. He wants what's best for you in this."

"He said that?" she asked.

"Not in so many words," Genevra offered. "But it was clear. Very clear."

"Whoever crosses you, crosses him," Hale said. "And trust me. As much as we see the benefits of making CC Dallas a business partner, we sure see the ramifications of getting on his bad side. We do not want him and his vast connections gunning for E&E. Now, having said all that, I'm late for my meeting. If you ladies will excuse me?"

Tansy nodded as Hale leaned over and kissed his new wife on the cheek and then he and his serious good looks moved down the hall to the conference room where a lot of boisterous comments over him showing up late could be heard.

"He loves all that," Genevra said.

"All what?"

"Being kidded by the young guys. Being a part of that group. With Vance especially. And being part of their efforts for Henderson. Hale feels guilty he didn't start an initiative like this years ago."

"No one thought about it years ago," Tansy said. "It's amazing Vance bothers to think about it now."

"He loves Brooks. It's important to Brooks. At least that's how Piper explains it."

"This town has always been important to Brooks," Tansy said.

"But not to you?"

"Would you like to sit?" Tansy asked. "I'd suggest we adjourn to a coffee shop, but…"

"Henderson doesn't have that kind of coffee shop."

"The nearest Starbucks is 21.2 miles away," Tansy sighed.

"We need a good coffee shop. Lolly and her friends live on the fancy coffees they can get in Raleigh. If we want our young people to return after college, we need to bring in the things they've gotten used to elsewhere."

Tansy pulled out one of her red Sharpies from the Ole Miss mug on her desk and took up her ever-present notepad, flipping the pages over containing her notes on IMG Academy. When she saw Genevra dragging over a big armchair, she went to help.

"I'm guessing you're aware of my not-so-secret secret," Genevra said, letting Tansy shuffle over the chair while she rubbed her little belly. "I only say that because your mother has gone out of her way to be kind to Hale and me. Which has somehow endeared Evie Jackson and her ilk to us as well. All of them are heavily implying, you know how they do, that our little announcement will be well-received socialite news instead of plain ol' tawdry gossip. Piper suspects you've had a hand in that. And if you have, I want you to know that I'm grateful. Grateful enough to return the favor any way I can."

"So Crain told you about us." Tansy sat behind her desk, unscrewing a bottle of water she retrieved out of the small refrigerator and slid it over to Genevra.

"Crain was kind enough to extend us his confidence since Vance and Davis already knew about your Vegas wedding. He figured it was our due since we were putting him up. At least that's how he said it. I think Vance had suggested we could keep our mouths shut and maybe even help with the situation. I assure you that is our intention. But I figured you might need a friend to help you get through all of this. Piper is still in the dark. But Vance told her to come see you today. I think he wants you to be the one to tell her, and I encourage you to do so. Having friends standing solidly in your corner if this news breaks will be helpful. Now talk to me, sweet girl. Why in the world aren't you claiming that big Texan as your own and shouting it from the rooftops?"

Tansy sat back and gave a brief laugh. Even through all the angst she felt at the suggestion of her mother finding out about her elopement, she completely understood where Genevra was coming from. Why in the world wasn't she claiming Crain as her own and shouting it from the rooftops?

"Because…," she started hesitantly, "too much water has flowed under the bridge. I made the poor choice of marrying Crain on the fly, completely disregarding how my parents would feel about it. Then I compounded it by making a second poor choice to run away and pretend it never happened. And you don't even want to know about the poor choices I continued to make once I got back to town. My parents…they'd eventually forgive me for eloping. At some point. Probably. But Crain, he married a woman named Elizabeth, whom he loves. But she doesn't actually exist. He has no idea who I really am. What I've done since I ran out on him—and those things will break his heart. Of this, I'm sure. Because if he'd done them to me, my heart would surely be broken. So, trust me, the kindest thing I can do for Crain right now is to convince him to sign the annulment papers."

"I disagree. I think the kindest thing you can do right now is to tell him the truth. He doesn't understand why you left him. He thinks it's his fault."

"It wasn't his fault. He's…you know, perfect. He's Crain. He's big and happy and always upbeat. He'd walk into his office back in Dallas dripping charisma with his big 'Mornin', y'all' as he entered, and his 'Y'all have a good night now' as he left. He treated everyone—everyone—like they were important. And I believe they genuinely were to him. If he was talking to you, you had his complete attention, whether you were the janitor or his second-in-command. Crain is patient and kind. He understands in the core of his being that nothing ever goes wrong enough that it can't get back on track. So when mistakes are made, he rolls with the flow and trusts it will all get figured out."

"So maybe he'd roll with you while all this gets figured out?"

"He would. He's planning to. I can see it in his eyes. He's determined to have me as his wife. Because he thinks I'm Elizabeth. Unfortunately, I know the truth. I know I'm only just Tansy."

The front door opened with the tinkling bells again, and this time Josh McCourt, legendary geeky computer science teacher turned exalted assistant football coach overnight, raced in like his hair was on fire. Behind him, he dragged a well-endowed strawberry blonde in a tight green dress who was laughing at his antics.

"Okay—okay, I'm here," she laughed.

Oh, Lord. Molly DuVal. Back in Henderson.

As soon as Molly saw Tansy, she stopped grinning and stared at her with a considerable lack of enthusiasm.

"Well, look who's here," Genevra sang, standing up and greeting the couple with hugs and kisses. "What brings y'all to Hale's place of business?"

"I've been summoned," Josh said with a grin. "Brooks asked me to join the meeting when I had a free period over at school. So if you ladies don't mind, I'm just going to go on in, as I only have about fifty minutes before I need to get back." He leaned over and put a kiss on Molly's lips before he headed down the hallway.

"Molly, do you know Tansy Langford?" Genevra inquired.

"Tansy," Molly said, arms folded over her chest.

"Molly," Tansy responded with an equal amount of enthusiasm. Dead silence.

"Oh dear, what am I missing?" Genevra asked as Tansy and Molly continued to stare each other down.

"Tansy was in the class ahead of me, Aunt Gen. She was the bee-yooty queen." The way Molly said it made it sound like a dirty word.

"And you were *involved* with the jocks. *All* of the jocks, as I recall," Tansy retorted.

"Ah, I see," said Genevra. "High school is like that. Even I remember. And, Tansy, being that you were a beauty queen's daughter, and Molly, since you were wild Jim DuVal's offspring, I'm sure both of you can see from a more mature perspective how the two of you naturally fell into those roles in high school. But that need not define the two of you now. Correct?"

Molly rolled her eyes at her aunt and sighed. Then she stuck out her hand as if to start their encounter over. "I'll cry uncle. You're still a little too bee-yootiful, but I'm moving back to Henderson soon and need all the friends I can get," she said candidly.

Tansy took a longer pause before she grasped Molly's hand. "I guess I can forgive you for having way more fun in high school," she said with a small grin.

"I did," Molly chuckled. "I had more fun. But I got thrown out of town, so…there's that."

"There is that," Tansy agreed. "But since you've lived elsewhere, and your boyfriend is apparently part of Team Henderson, maybe you'd like to help Genevra and me make a list of what this town needs from a woman's perspective. You want to pull up a chair and help?"

"I do," Molly said excitedly. "We need an art supply store," she said, dragging over the other armchair from across the room. "And an adult book store," she said sitting down and tossing her hair over her shoulder.

"What?" Molly asked once she was settled, looking up to find Tansy and Genevra staring at her.

"You want an adult book store in Henderson? Like, one of those sex shops?" Tansy asked, pen halted over the pad of paper.

"Where else are you going to get your vibrators and the lubricant for them?" Molly asked as if this was a ridiculous line of questioning. "My goodness, if you want the college girls to move back home, you need to give them what they want. And trust me, I've got about a dozen cousins and they all want vibrators." Suddenly Molly seemed to remember her aunt was sitting right next to her. "Aunt Gen, Circle of Trust and all that, right? You aren't going back to my dad or my uncles squealing, are you?"

"No, no," Genevra assured her. "This will not be a topic of conversation, ever. Oh my Lord, no."

"Good." Molly returned her attention back to Tansy and her list. "Write it down," she insisted. "I'm telling you what Henderson needs, and I'm not pulling punches. An art gallery, shoe stores, gift shops, coffee cafés, a wine shop, a Target, for God's sake. More restaurants, a spa, better salons…and most importantly, a decent place for people in their twenties to live. I can't be moving back in with my parents, can I? I mean, where are you living now?"

"With my parents," Tansy said sheepishly. "I refuse to live in those downtrodden apartments at the edge of town."

"That's where Josh is, because there's nowhere else to be. So, first of all, that needs to be addressed. You want young people to live and work here, you've got to house them."

"We could use a more luxurious hotel as well," Tansy said, thinking of Crain having to stay at the Evans'. "Which would provide us someplace other than Henderson Country Club to hold events."

The women on the other side of her desk kept talking, and Tansy kept jotting down their ideas. But internally, she sighed heavily, feeling like the job of bringing Henderson into the twenty-first century was too overwhelming to think about. It'd be easier just to leave with Crain and head back to Dallas. Dallas had everything all ready and waiting for her.

Of course, she'd have to tell her parents she was married.

And then face Crain's disgruntled kin back in Texas.

Yeah. Not happening.

Suddenly, transforming Henderson seemed a whole lot more doable.

CHAPTER SIXTEEN

Crain sat in the meeting, letting the rest of them hash it all out. He was just the presenter, after all. The next step was discussion and decision. He didn't have anything to do with that. In fact, this is where he would normally make his exit and tell them to call him in Dallas if they wanted his help moving forward. But as much as he was aching to get back to his beloved home state, he knew he was as hogtied to Henderson right now as Brooks was to the idea of a minor league stadium.

Because of Elizabeth.

Tansy.

Elizabeth.

The damn woman who was ruling his life.

The businessman in him knew he ought to just let her go. Just sign her damn papers and walk away. Tell his family he'd made a mistake, lick his wounds, and find a new long-legged filly to comfort him at night. There were plenty of pretty ones left in Dallas.

But he didn't want just any pretty filly. He wanted pretty Elizabeth. Sweet, sultry Elizabeth. He even kinda wanted this North Carolina Tansy. Hell, as he'd stood over her watchin' that tiny skirt of hers crawl up the backs of those shapely thighs as she'd laid herself flat on the hardwood floor searching for his rubber ball, his dick grew hot and his brain bounced back to their wedding night. Fast.

He'd started thinking about her and those thighs dressed up in the new lingerie she'd bought right before their short, cut-to-the-chase ceremony. A little satiny number done up in navy blue and lace, tied up over her shoulders with nothin' but thread, as best he could tell. He wanted to grab her the moment she came out of the bathroom in their suite, his Mrs. Carraway, and run his hands over every inch of that satin, finally touching all those curves his eyes had been feasting on for a good long month.

Instead, he was paralyzed. Overcome with emotion. Seeing her standing there—his. So he watched as she pulled down the bedding, bending over and giving him one helluva peep show while she folded the covers down just right, so inviting, and then stood right there, smiling across the room at him, holding out her hand.

"Are we gonna do this or what?" she said, causing him to chuckle. It was one of the reasons he loved her so hard. She saw through his big "I can conquer all" exterior, noticed where he was—what he needed—and then said or did the perfect thing to draw him out of his paralysis.

"Damn right," he responded. "Never had to marry a girl to get her in bed before," he joked, coming forward and taking her hand, pulling her body up against his. "But I'm sure glad you put your foot down, Mrs. Carraway, because this ol' boy needs a wife."

"As if," she said between his kisses. "You didn't have to bring me to Vegas, and you didn't have to marry me," she said, going all soft as he stroked her cheek. "But I'm glad you did, Crain."

Staring into her hazel eyes, Crain saw it. The truth. Her love—shining back at him—reflecting his own. Relief flowed, anxiety fled, and his body started gearing up for a long night's worth of sweet southern lovin'. He'd found his mate, the very one he'd been searching for.

"I love you," she said softly. "I know it's fast. But I do, Crain. I love you. Now stop all your fretting and make me yours."

"Finally," he sighed against her lips as his hand slid from her back to her fanny. "You're my best day ever, woman," he told her as he rubbed his palm over her plump, little ass.

She smiled against his lips. "I like being your best day." She started to unbutton his shirt, but then he felt a change. He felt her pull in somehow, make herself a little smaller. He bent his knees to look into her eyes.

"Sweetheart?"

Her words were whispered toward his chest, all soft and vulnerable. "I'm just a little concerned about being your best night ever."

Crain almost choked on his disbelief.

He pulled her to him, one hand on the back of her head and one arm around her waist. "Sweet Elizabeth," he said against her ear. "This—you standing here in this room, wearing this naughty little nighty—*is* my best night ever. You let me worry about the details, ya hear? That's my job, and I'm going to take it very seriously."

His hand slipped the tiny strap from one shoulder, letting his fingers trail along the soft skin just above the plunging lace neckline. He pushed back her hair to kiss the side of her neck and then whispered his intent.

"I am gonna make this good. Very, very good for the both of us. You can either guide me along however you choose, or let me figure this gorgeous body of yours out all on my own."

His hand drifted down to a satin-covered breast, and he felt heaven against his palm for the first time.

"Praise Jesus," he groaned.

"What?" she whispered against his neck, her talented little fingers renewing their efforts to undress him.

He cupped her breast through the material and cradled its softness in his hand. His thumb drifted across her nipple, back and forth, bringing it to life. "I swear to God, they look so beautiful in your clothes, I was worried they might be fake."

"Fake?"

He pulled away from her, not releasing her breast, but just giving himself enough room so he could look at her face while he told her the truth. "You know Dallas. There's far more fake than real. And fake is fake, and these are—" His other hand joined in, taking hold of her other beautiful breast and squeezed gently—"wonderful."

Her expression had her looking a bit smug and proud.

Well, she had every damn right to be smug. And proud. Truth be told, he held off asking her out for a good couple of weeks because he was certain she had fake tits. He liked tits. He was a boobs man by all accounts. And he and his dumb luck had stumbled into a woman who not only knew how to soothe his ruffled feathers, but had big, fabulous, soft, full tits to boot. Tits he now had access to on a regular basis.

He felt the button on his pants give way and those slender fingers of hers grabbing hold of his zipper.

Yeah—that might be a bad idea.

He clasped a hand over hers. "Sweetheart," he said sucking in a sharp breath. Oh man—this wasn't any better. If she tried to pull her hand down and out, he was going to blow. "Darlin' Elizabeth," he gasped. He had to take a few deep breaths before he could go on. "I may be thirty-five, and this is definitely not my first rodeo, but you touch me there and our first time is gonna be over before it starts. So please, darlin' girl, just…just…let me do the touchin' right now. Okay?"

Then he stood there and watched her do it. Watched his woman bite her bottom lip trying to hide a sexy little smirk as she purposely slid her hand out of his grasp and ran it slowly down the front of his britches.

It was the single greatest moment of his life.

Until the beautiful blonde with the very real tits held on to his thighs and slowly knelt down on the floor in front of him.

"Sweet Jesus," he whispered as he went ahead and unzipped his own pants.

He couldn't watch. Hadn't even let himself fantasize about what was happening now. Never allowed his mind to explore the possibility of his sweet, beautiful Elizabeth willingly putting her mouth on him. Hadn't even attempted to imagine what it would feel like. The exquisite torture.

"Crain?"

A bright white exploded behind his eyes. His mind went skyward, and his lower body started to move. His fingers snaked their way into her hair—

"Crain?"

"What?" he shouted. The sound of his own voice pulled him back to the present, to the conference room in E&E. To the four men seated around him, all of them staring at him like he'd just shot a load in front of them. If it wasn't for the raging boner still in his pants, he'd be worried.

"Sorry," he said. "Day dreamin'. What'd I miss?"

"Day dreaming?" Brooks accused.

"Whatcha day dreamin' about there, Tex?" Vance asked, his shit-eatin' grin beggin' for a whoopin'. At least his father, Hale, had the decency to smile down at the paperwork in front of him. The new guy, Josh-the-brainiac, was looking around perplexed, and it did not escape Crain's notice that The Pink One was glaring at him while the Golden Boy just seemed irritated.

Well, excuse me, Crain thought. One night with my wife and then Bam! Four months of purgatory. Now I'm sitting here wasting precious time with this crazy bunch of yahoos while Elizabeth is just ten paces outside the damn door.

Last night Vance told him to be patient, to let it all play out. He'd told him to bide his time and insert himself slowly into Elizabeth's hometown. And last night it seemed like a sound idea. But at the moment, he was finding it near impossible to sit here and pretend to care about whatever the hell was going on at this table while his long-lost bride was within his grasp.

"Y'all got a question for me, or you just gonna sit there and gloat over my untenable situation?"

"What situation?" Josh asked.

"Seems our token Texan has a past with Miss Langford," Hale said.

"A past, present, and future, if I've got anything to say about it. But that doesn't leave this room, ya hear?" After he got a serious nod from Josh, he went on. "Right now, for all intents and purposes, that woman and I just met. Which is complete bullshit, but bullshit I'm willing to wallow around in for the time being." He glanced at his watch. "At least for the next few minutes. Now where are we?"

"We are in Henderson," Brooks insisted. "Miss *Langford's* hometown. My hometown. We are brainstorming big ideas like the sports academy, minor league baseball, a lakeside resort, incentivizing big business relocations—I swear to God we have got to get Lewis Kampmueller to move his damn business down here."

"Who's Lewis Kampmueller?"

"Our buddy," Brooks said, pointing between himself and Vance. "He's into technology. His KampApps gaming and app company is doing very well. We're stockholders."

"He grow up here?"

"Yep."

"So call him. If you can't get him to relocate KampApps, maybe you can get him to sponsor a portion of the academy. He might be interested in having his name on the 'School of Technology', or at least donate the scoreboards and technological equipment needed to run the games. Surely you can twist his arm into something."

"You are dead set on this academy, aren't you?" Brooks said.

"I'm not dead set on anything. But North Carolina has nine other minor league baseball teams already. So, yeah, I like the idea. And—okay, I'm just going to put it out there. I'd like to see it set up to accommodate stellar athletes who struggle with dyslexia. I'd like a program built into the overall academy that caters specifically to dyslexic students. Teachers who specialize in learning disabilities. Smaller class sizes for those athletes. Because those kids fall through the cracks in a lot of schools, and if they don't, they're expending a whole lot of unnecessary energy trying not to."

"You speaking from experience there, Tex?" Vance asked.

"You know it. My fancy 'sports first' school, as The Pink One likes to put it, hired on some tutors who knew how to reteach me in the afternoon what I was already supposed to have learned during classes that morning. But that was because of my size and my speed. I was an asset to the athletic department. Otherwise, I would have been asked not to come back. So, going on to Texas A&M would have been out of the question, and CC Dallas would have only ever been a pipe dream. This is a subject near and dear to my heart, you might say. And I've had it in my mind to start a school like I'm describing at some point. Just haven't gotten around to it yet."

"You thinking of becoming an investor in Henderson?" Vance asked.

"Trust me. At the moment, I'm heavily invested in Henderson."

"Emotionally. You're heavily invested emotionally. I'm talking financially. If we agree to build this academy, are you agreeing to be a partner? With real money?"

"Possibly. Depending."

"Depending on how things work out with Miss Langford?" Hale asked.

"Pretty much."

"Are you telling me," Vance chimed in, "that the woman with whom I've been trading insults for the past fifteen years now holds the future of Henderson in her hands?"

"No. I'm tellin' you that if you want the CC Dallas state-of-the-art learning center and dormitory situated prominently on your sports academy campus, you need to help me get Miss Langford to acknowledge that she's my wife."

"Your wife?" Josh whispered wide-eyed.

"Top secret," Crain told him pointedly. "At least for now."

"Okay. Whatever," Josh said. "As a teacher of computer science, as a football coach, and as someone who is also trying to get a girl from Henderson to be my wife, I am all over the academy idea. I say let's do this. Let's get Mr. Carraway hitched, or...acknowledged...or whatever and see how fast we can get other sponsors to jump on board."

"Hold on just a damn minute," Pinks said. "You can't buy Tansy with a dormitory and some fancy classrooms."

"Yes, he can," Vance said. "That's a darn bargain. For us."

"I'm not trying to buy *Tansy*," Crain insisted. "What I'm trying to do is leverage the cooperation of the men in this room. You got a problem with that, *Pinks*?"

"No—no, he doesn't," Vance insisted. "You just have to promise me when this is all over, you'll take her back to Dallas with you when you leave. That's all I ask."

Not for the first time Hale Evans asked his son, "What in the world do you have against Miss Langford?"

"Long story, Dad. Long story."

Brooks stood, looking down at his phone. "Y'all keep on negotiating this Tansy nonsense. I've got a call to make. Be back in five," he said before exiting the room.

CHAPTER SEVENTEEN

The women were all laughing over Dallas' Pretty Kitty Brazilian Wax Salon Tansy was describing when Brooks appeared in the foyer. She glanced up and immediately noticed how serious he looked.

"Brooks?"

"Sorry to interrupt," he said. The usual mega-watt smile he showered on Molly and Genevra seemed a little forced. "Tansy, if I could have a word with you? Promise it won't take more than five minutes."

"Okay," she hedged. First Pinks and now Brooks. Lord help me, she thought as her chickens continued to come home to roost. "Ladies, keep jotting down ideas," she directed.

Brooks pointed toward the front doors. "Outside," he said quietly, falling in behind her as she headed toward the door.

She turned right when she hit the sidewalk, slowly walking away from E&E. Books was quiet at first, matching her slow pace, sticking his hands in his pants pockets. When they had ventured down two vacant storefronts, he turned to her and stopped, running a hand through his bronze curls.

"I don't even know what to ask," he said. "Because Crain is claiming you were married in Vegas on May 12, and yet I distinctly remember you breaking into my house in early June suggesting we pick up where we left off. Tell me you didn't try to break up Lolly and me while you were married to Crain."

She opened her mouth to speak but could find no words.

"Tansy?"

She shrugged her shoulders.

"What the hell? What if I had dumped Lolly and taken back up with you?"

"You didn't."

"But what if I did? You were married, for Christ's sake."

Tansy leaned back against the building, folding her arms over her chest and studying her feet.

"Tansy."

"What do you want me to say?" she shouted, her head springing up, embarrassment taking the form of frustration. "Yes, yes, I was married to Crain. Technically. Technically, I was married and seeking an annulment. There. I said it. Are you happy now? Because truth be told, trying to break you and Lolly up is far from the worst thing I've done. So frankly, if you want an apology you're going to have to get in line."

"An apology? Yeah, that'd be nice. But what I'd settle for is an explanation."

Brooks looked incredulous. Like trying to break him and his little kindergartener up was the worst thing she could possibly do.

"I'm sorry," she said, pushing off the wall and spinning back toward the office.

"Hold on." He caught her by the shoulder and turned her back around. "Talk to me. Help me understand. Crain's in there trying to enlist our help in making you admit you're his wife. Now, he seems like an okay guy, but none of this makes any damn sense to me. If I'm gonna take somebody's side in this, I gotta know the facts."

"What do you mean, he's trying to enlist your help?"

"Tansy. The guy is not giving up without a fight. You gotta know that."

Part of her was elated to hear it. Another part was flat out scared to death.

"Tans?"

She turned in the opposite direction from E&E and started walking, mostly so she didn't have to look Brooks in the eye when she confessed. "I'm crazy about him," she said. "I went into that civil ceremony with stars in my eyes after Crain swept me off my feet in the short span of two dates and one private jet ride to Las Vegas. Who wouldn't have been? He's happy all the time. His manners are impeccable. He's kind to all his employees...and he thinks the world of me. Misguided as that may be. I was caught up in all that Crain Carraway magic and I didn't give anything or anybody else a thought. I just went with being happy and figured I'd work the details out later."

Brooks blew out a breath and after a few more steps halted their progress. "Okay, I get how a guy with a plane could sweep a woman off her feet. So what the hell did he do that caused you to run?"

"He called his momma. And I could tell she was upset by the news. That's when it hit me. My own mother had been planning my wedding for the past couple of years. My wedding to *you*. Which made me think about how we'd dated for two long years and how cruel it was that I'd left town without a word, and how my mother, and this entire town, was never gonna forgive me for dumping Henderson's Crowned Prince for a...ya know...big ol' Texan that I barely knew."

"I was already with Lolly then. It would have worked out fine."

"Maybe," she said, resuming their stroll. "But I didn't know about Lolly. And yeah, maybe if I'd had the sense to bring Crain home once or twice, easing everybody into the idea. Maybe if I'd made things right with you and *then* got engaged, had the parties, booked the church, and let my mother talk me into the wedding dress she wanted me to wear. But to just up and elope? Leaving my parents out of all that pomp and circumstance they've been plannin' on since the day I was born? I am Garland Langford's daughter, and that is not how things are done."

"Still. You married the man. You went ahead and did it. You should've had the guts to own up to it. Not come back here acting like you'd never left."

"Why are you shouting at me?" she shouted back.

"Because," he barked. "Because," Brooks said again, softening his voice, "for a moment, you coming back gave me pause. Made me hesitate moving forward with Lolly. It wasn't fair putting me in that position, and it certainly wasn't fair to Crain or Lolly."

"I was afraid," she mumbled.

"Afraid of what?" he snapped.

"Afraid I'd never be able to come home," she cried. "When I started thinking about how the news of me marrying Crain was going to upset my parents and upset this town, I was afraid I'd never be able to come home again. So I left Crain with no explanation, just like I'd done to you all those months before. I tried to rewind the nuptials, lied to everyone through omission, and simply pretended it didn't happen."

"And even though he's here now, you're still pretending."

"What choice do I have?"

Brooks halted her. "You can tell the damn truth."

"To whom? My parents? Yeah, okay, they'd have to get over it eventually. I mean, surely my mother would at least appreciate the private aviation side of me being married to CC Dallas. But tell Crain that I left him and ran back to try to patch things up with you? No, thank you. That part even I don't understand."

"I'm gonna do my best not to take that personally."

"Brooks," she sighed. "Let's face it. You and I were together because we lived in Henderson. Because you're tall and I'm tall. Because you're a Bennett and I'm a Langford. And yeah, we liked each other pretty good. But mostly, we both really liked the idea of you being mayor and running this town."

"You're gonna stand there and tell me that's all there was between us?"

"Are you gonna stand there and tell me I'm wrong?"

Silence.

"I didn't think so," she said, resuming their stroll.

"All right. Okay. Let's take my ego out of this equation for a minute and talk about Crain."

"There's nothing to talk about. I'm unwilling to subject the man to the wrath of my mother, or the rest of this town's wrath for that matter. And even if I were willing to sacrifice his mental health by going there, I've betrayed his trust coming and going. I'm unworthy by all accounts…so, let's just leave it at that."

"You don't love him."

"I do. That's the problem. I love him. But he's in love with Elizabeth."

"Yeah, I don't get all that."

"I know you don't. And you don't need to. Just trust me on this. Crain fell in love under false pretenses."

"How?"

She shook her head and spread her hands. "In Dallas, I was…different. I was calmer, less agitated, because all I had to do was think about myself. I didn't have to constantly think of living up to the Langford name and my parents' expectations. I just didn't worry about what people would think."

"So?"

"So? So, Crain thinks I'm sweet. Sweet! Like praline pie or something. No one who knows me thinks I'm sweet. *You* never thought I was sweet."

"Well what do I know?"

"You know me. The real me."

"Well, maybe around Crain you're different."

"Maybe around Crain I don't have the sense I was born with. Clearly, or I would have laughed at his suggestion of marriage after only two dates."

"Not if it's the real deal. Hell, if I thought I could get Lolly to marry me in Vegas, I'd be on a plane tonight. When it's right, it's right. The rest of the world be damned."

"Yeah. Well. Even if it was right, I have now managed to twist it into all wrong. And the best thing I can do for the man is to get him out of town before he realizes it."

"The best thing you can do for the man is tell him the truth. One way or another, it's gonna set you free."

Yeah. She'd be free. There was no doubt in her mind Crain would set her free. And didn't that just twist a knife in her gut.

When she and Brooks walked back into E&E, the place was flooded with women. Tiny little Piper with her pretty yellow curls had shown up just as Genevra had predicted. And now Evie Jackson, with her silver-gray updo and ever-present Confederate pearls, the grand dame of Henderson's social elite and Tansy's mother's own personal mentor, was shockingly laughing and carrying on with Molly DuVal. The same Molly DuVal Evie Jackson had single handedly gotten tossed out of town five years back after Molly had run off with Vance while still engaged to Evie's grandson. This was quite the turn of events.

When Evie spied Brooks and Tansy, she gave a little wave and finished up her conversation with Molly.

"Brooks," Evie called as he tried to bypass the group of females, apparently heading back to the big boys club meeting down the hall. "If I might have a word, please."

Tansy watched Brooks do what he always did. He turned toward Evie and poured on an expression that said nothing would make him happier.

"And you, too, Tansy. Please," Evie said, waving her hand for her to join them. "May the three of us speak in private?" she requested.

"Of course," Tansy said, leading them down the hallway past Hale's office. When Evie Jackson asked you to jump, in this town you simply smiled and asked, "How high?" So Tansy led them past the conference room and on toward Vance's office. She stopped and waited for Evie and Brooks to go in ahead of her. Then she followed suit, turned, and shut them all inside.

"Henderson Harvest Daze is almost upon us," Evie started without preamble. "And I have heard, Brooks, that you plan to be our town's next mayor."

"I plan to run against Mayor Stevens in the next election," Brooks confirmed.

"I see. Well, we all like the sound of that. Don't we, Tansy?"

"We do," Tansy agreed. She had no clue what this was about. Perhaps she was there simply to play the yes-man to whatever Evie had up her sleeve for Brooks. For Evie Jackson and the power she held in this town, Tansy would play yes-man. Crain's Elizabeth might find it a bit unsettling, being that she was so darn sweet. But Tansy—Tansy didn't feel one iota of compunction about yes-manning Brooks into whatever Evie wanted. Bring it on, she thought absently.

"I've also caught wind of this committee you've put together. What are you calling it? Team Henderson?"

"Correct. A group of us are actively researching ways to bring economic growth to Henderson and the surrounding area," Brooks explained.

"Which, I understand, will help to draw our young people back home and new families to Henderson."

"That is my hope," Brooks stated.

"Well, you must know that I have a stake in all this. Even though three out of my four children reside in Henderson, none of my grandchildren could find work here after graduating from college."

"That is exactly what we are hoping to change, Mrs. Jackson. I'm glad we can count on your support."

"But we need to come at this from all angles, wouldn't you agree?"

"What did you have in mind?" Brooks asked patiently.

"I want you and Miss Langford here to be the new faces of our Henderson Harvest Daze celebration."

"The two of us?" Brooks questioned. "To be the new faces? I'm not sure I understand."

"Consider this the changing of the guard. Our Harvest Daze committee is old and tired, and their ideas are old and tired. Henderson not only needs economic stimulus to thrive, we need an injection of young blood and fresh ideas to our waning traditions. Starting with this year's Harvest Daze. We need that tired old barbershop quartet to step aside for a band that can really get people moving. We need trendier food, more fun fundraisers, things that will bring family members from far and wide back to Henderson and keep the high schoolers there in attendance. And we need alcohol."

"Excuse me?" Brooks said, wide-eyed.

"We need a one-day permit to serve alcohol on the school grounds so we can have a wine-tasting booth, along with the beer truck. If the Catholic Church can do it for their fundraisers, Henderson ought to be able to. So I need you to get that done and get the police department behind this."

"Mrs. Jackson, that's just going to stir up a whole lot of trouble. That high school is supposed to be an alcohol-and-drug-free zone. I already have a problem with the city turning a blind eye to the beer truck year after year."

"Then you and Tansy figure out a more appropriate spot to hold the festivities. A fresh location would probably add to the new feel we need for this event. I want you to get your friends to help with social media. Put Harvest Daze online and twerk it out there or whatever you do. The Old Guard will always show up. That's what we do. What I'm enlisting the two of you for is to find a way to interest young people. Your crowd. All those who live within driving distance—we want them to drive in for the day. Then you two, as a couple, get up on stage and generate some excitement. Give the crowd something to chew on that promises the revitalization of this town. Something that gets people excited."

"As a couple? Mrs. Jackson, we're not a couple," Brooks insisted.

"Well, you were before, and you could be again," she suggested, the tone of her voice pitching higher. "The two of you are exemplary citizens. Both of you good looking, well known, with no scandalous issues to blemish your universal appeal. Brooks, as our local sports hero and rescuer of old people and dogs, not to mention this town's next mayor, and Tansy, following along in your dear mother's footsteps. You two are our shining examples of Henderson's future. So I want you to take on this event together."

"Take on the event together?" Brooks shouted in disbelief.

"Of course," Evie said as if it was the most natural idea in the world. "Brooks, it will give you the perfect platform to promote your candidacy and show this town you're more than ready to take on its challenges. While at the same time, it gives Tansy an opportunity to demonstrate that she is more than a pretty face and also gives her the perfect chance to soothe all those ruffled feathers she created when she left you for Dallas a year ago. Tansy, consider this your apology to the town who loves you."

"Apology?" Tansy erupted.

"You owe us an apology."

"I do?"

"Certainly. You don't grow up around here in a vacuum. When the two of you fell in love, the rest of us fell in love with you. The two of you. Together."

Both Tansy and Brooks started to object, but Evie held up her hand and closed her eyes.

"I don't care to hear it. Whether you are together romantically or not, you two still exemplify the new face of Henderson, and I want *that* face introduced during Harvest Daze."

When neither Tansy nor Brooks spoke, Evie said, "Have I made myself clear?"

"Yes, ma'am," Brooks said. "We'll see what we can do." The look he threw Tansy indicated he was beyond pissed at this turn of events.

"Mrs. Jackson," Tansy cajoled, "my mother hasn't put you up to this, has she?"

"Whatever do you mean?" Evie said, with too much sugar dripping off her words. "If I recall correctly, you recently had a friend in need. And now, all I ask is that you return the favor by overhauling one of this town's oldest traditions. Are we understanding each other?"

Ahhhh, so this is about Piper, Tansy realized. Piper and Vance and Hale and Genevra. Evie was blackmailing her with the juicy news about their shotgun weddings. Either Tansy works with Brooks on Harvest Daze and becomes the new face of Henderson, or the Evans clan goes down in the eyes of Henderson's social elite. She should have known it was never going to be as easy as donning a tiara and sash and going back to Ole Miss with her mother. She was beholden to Evie Jackson as well.

"Brooks? Hashtag Henderson Daze?" Tansy asked brightly. "I'll go see about opening a Twitter account."

As Evie Jackson strode past Tansy, not even bothering to hide her mission-accomplished grin, she strode out into the hall and bumped right into Crain and the rest of Team Henderson as they filed out of the conference room.

"Well, who do we have here?" Evie asked in a highly delighted and breathy voice as she looked Crain's tall body up and down.

Tansy had never heard Evie do breathy. She rolled her eyes.

Crain, of course, seeing that Tansy was standing behind Evie, turned on that big Texas hospitality he was so good at showing off.

"Well, now, darlin'," he said, leaning down and taking up Evie's hand. "I'm Crain Carraway. Just a good ol' boy from Dallas," he said looking right into her eyes like she was the most interesting person he'd met in Henderson. "And who might you be?"

Don't bother with the schmooze, Crain, Tansy thought. She's not my mother.

My mother!

Now that Evie Jackson had been introduced to good ol' boy, Crain Carraway, Tansy knew it was only a matter of time before her mother would hear about him. And she really didn't want her mother hearing about Crain. Ever.

"Excuse me, Evie," Tansy said, busting up the little tete-á-tete that was forming. "Mr. Carraway is on a tight schedule today. He's got a flight back to Dallas later this evening. I need to get him started on the tour of our business district right now, so he's back here in time for the lunch meeting. I'm sure you understand."

"Of course," Evie cooed at Crain. "Never let an old woman get in the way of progress."

"If I see an old woman, I'll be sure to steer clear," Crain teased.

Evie patted his hand, tittering. "My goodness, Mr. Carraway. I won't be forgetting *your* name."

Of course not, Tansy thought.

"It's Crain to you, Mrs. Jackson. Please call me Crain."

Yeah, just…tattoo it on her arm, why don't you?

Tansy broke in. "Are we done here?"

"Tansy Langford, my goodness," Evie said, startled. "Is that any way to treat a guest in our town? There's no reason to rush poor Mr. Carraway around like we are poorly bred Northerners. Where are your gentile southern manners? Your momma would be surprised."

"She would indeed," Tansy agreed. "I apologize, Mr. Carraway, but a schedule is a schedule."

"And truth be told, Mrs. Jackson, this is the part of the schedule I've been looking forward to," he said with a wink. "So if you'll excuse us?" Crain said, nodding and indicating Tansy should lead the way.

"All right, then," Evie said. "You go on and enjoy yourself."

"I believe I will," Crain responded.

He probably kissed the old bat's cheek for the love fest the two of them were putting on. Tansy didn't wait to find out. She headed into the lobby, pushing through all the socializing that was going on—when did this become the local hangout?—and down the stairs and out the door, hoping Crain would have the sense to follow.

Evie Jackson. Of all the people to have met Crain. Tansy sighed heavily, turning left and walking away from E&E.

Well, that was it. She had to git 'r done, as they say. Deal with him and get him back on his plane and off to Dallas. Evie Jackson was a complication Tansy couldn't afford.

CHAPTER EIGHTEEN

"Elizabeth," Crain shouted.

Tansy turned and shushed him as he came down the sidewalk toward her. "No one calls me Elizabeth."

"I do."

"And by shouting it out like that, you're gonna draw unwanted attention to us, so stop it."

Crain couldn't help himself. He just grinned.

"What?"

"Your lips."

"What about my lips," Tansy said, reaching up to touch them.

Crain jostled his head a bit, shaking the question off. "I just like 'em," he said, wondering what the hell was so special about her lips. There was something, but hell if he could put his finger on it.

"Stop looking at my lips. People will talk."

His gaze slid to her eyes. Pretty gold flecks danced around the center of her irises while bands of dark green circled the edges. "Let 'em talk."

"Crain, please," she said, hustling him down the sidewalk by grabbing at his hand and dragging him behind her.

He figured holding hands was a step in the right direction, so he followed along peacefully. But when he tried to entwine his fingers in between Tansy's, she shook him loose.

"Aww, come on," he said. "That was nice. If I'm holding your hand, I don't want to fidget with my darn ball or anything else."

"Get out your ball. This is a business meeting. I'm showing you Henderson's illustrious business district."

"It's far from illustrious, and I've already seen it. Vance gave me the tour this morning while we ran."

Tansy stopped and turned. "You run?"

"No, but Vance does, and he insisted I accompany him. Which required breaking into his damn Tenderfoot Boutique so he could sell me running shoes and attire. He's completely taking advantage of the fact that I did not pack for an extended stay. Of course, he's putting me up so, I can hardly complain."

"Then why would he insist that I drag you around the block?"

Crain stepped into her personal space and lowered his voice. "So I could kiss you."

"Kiss me?" She backed away.

"Yes, kiss you." He stalked right after her. "He saw us lip-locked yesterday. Thought we might want to try it again."

"We are not trying that again."

"Oh, but we are," he insisted, backing her into a little brick alcove carved out between two storefronts. For the moment, they were hidden from view. "We're gonna try it over," he said as he clasped both her hands and brought them up to his mouth. "And over," he said as he kissed each hand in turn. "And over," he said as he brought her hands up over her head against the wall and leaned in to place a kiss on the side of her throat. "And over," he whispered as he kissed her cheek.

"Crain," she said. Probably meant it as a deterrent, but he loved hearing his name come out of those lips. Her North Carolina accent was stronger now that she was back in her hometown, and it got him right in the nuts. So yeah, he wasn't deterred. Not at all. He leaned in and touched his lips to hers in the softest caress he could manage. Just focused all of his concentration on what it felt like to have his own lips up against those sweet ones he found so fascinating.

When she didn't start up with all the verbal nonsense, he slid his tongue across her bottom lip just soft and gentle-like, so he could memorize the line and scope of that full bottom lip. The one he'd had a hard time taking his eyes off.

Then some sort of magic occurred, and Elizabeth dropped that tempting bottom lip just a little bit from the sassy top one—the impish little bow-shaped upper lip his tongue longed to trace the contours of. So he touched his tongue to the bottom part of the bow and gently ran the tip of it from side to side.

Was that a little purr he heard coming from inside this wild Carolina hellcat? His tongue sneaked in for a bit of mating before he decided to ease her into something other than a make-out session on a public street at noon.

"Dinner tonight," he whispered against her lips. "Somewhere discreet."

She kissed him then; her tongue taking over for a moment. Sending all of his powers of concentration away from her lips and straight to his groin. Damn the woman was talented. Talented and distracting.

He pulled back and waited until she opened her eyes.

He raised his brows. "Dinner?"

She sighed and turned, shouldering him out of the way. She looked right and left before she ventured from their secluded alcove to resume their stroll.

Man, did he just learn the hard way. Next time he had his lips on Elizabeth, he was keepin' his damn mouth shut—so to speak. Still, he needed to get the two of them together privately so he'd get some answers.

"Elizabeth?" He maneuvered himself to the outer edge of the sidewalk and matched her pace. When there was no answer, he said, "Sweetheart, you do realize you're gonna have to talk to me, right? Now if you'd like to get on my plane, come back to Dallas, and have the chat about our four-month separation in front of my momma and daddy, we can do that. But if I had my druthers, we'd hash whatever issues you have out before my momma drags you out to buy a wedding dress."

That brought her up short.

"What are you talking about?"

"She's planned us a church wedding."

"Crain!"

'I know, darlin', but she was not happy about missing out on our nuptials, so she's gonna make us do it all again. She's also not gonna be happy if your parents don't show up. So, really, the best way to handle this is to do the whole *Guess Who's Coming to Dinner* thing tonight with your parents and then head on back to Dallas tomorrow."

She started to protest, but he interrupted.

"*Or*—we can have dinner tonight, just the two of us, your choice of destination, to discuss why you got cold feet in the first place. Your choice, sweetheart. I'm leavin' it all up to you."

"Crain," she sighed, turning down the walk and starting their stroll again. "You don't want to be married to me. You barely know me."

He thought about that for a moment.

"You're right about one of those. Not so much the other."

She turned her face toward him, those beautiful, classic features of hers catching the light in just the right way to make him weak in the knees. God, he had it bad.

That's when it hit him. How much this really meant. He may be making light of it at the moment, trying to tease her into going to dinner with him, but damn if he didn't feel like a man overboard, flailing around in the deep end of the ocean. This was a sink-or-swim issue if he'd ever faced one.

"Why?"

"Why what?" he answered, putting his hand in his pocket and gripping that rubber ball.

"Why do you want to be married to me? After I ran off, asked for an annulment, and hid out in my hometown so you wouldn't be able to find me—"

"I found you."

"Yes. You did," she said as she stopped. She turned toward him and looked him in the eye. "I can't imagine a man like you waiting four months on any woman. Why have you?"

"I'd told everybody I'd married Elizabeth Langford, Ole Miss's sweetest Hotty Toddy ever," he said. "And then you got cold feet. What was I gonna do?"

"Sign the annulment papers."

"And then what? Tell everybody I'd made a mistake? When I didn't? Elizabeth, you may have gotten cold feet, but let me assure you that I haven't changed my mind about us. I want you to be my wife. You're perfect for me. I've looked for my Mrs. Carraway for a long time. And yeah, I messed it up good by hustling you to the altar, so I'm willing to take responsibility for that. But you've got to help me out here by talking to me. Stop trying to get me on the next plane out of town, because darlin' you at least know me well enough to realize I'm not leaving Henderson until we've reached an understanding."

He glanced at his watch. "Now, unfortunately I'm due at The Tavern for lunch with Vance and the Surly Duo, so if you could point me in the direction I need to head—"

"Surly Duo?"

"Brooks and The Pink One. They might like what I'm bringing to the table, but they don't like me one little bit. At least not when your name comes up." He thought about that for a moment and then narrowed his eyes at the woman he craved. "Now why is that, do you suppose?"

The gaze from her pretty green-gold eyes dropped toward the ground. "I imagine they're just bein' protective. Unlike Vance who clearly wants to use this situation to his advantage. He thinks if I'm your wife, he can get you to drop your consulting fee for E&E."

"He's not wrong about that. After all, my wife's people are from Henderson," he said with a sly grin. "Why wouldn't I want to do what I could to help the town out?"

"You can't do that."

"Do what?"

"Combine me and Henderson. Help Henderson if you want to help Henderson. But don't do it because of me. You've got to keep whatever business dealings you have here separate from your personal relationship with me."

"Fine. As long as I have a personal relationship with you."

"That's not…exactly what I'm saying."

"I know what you're saying. But the truth is I would have come and gone yesterday if you hadn't been sitting in that office. And that's just a fact. Although…"

"Although what?"

"I can't go back to Dallas without you, so I may as well stick around and help out."

"What do you mean, you can't go back without me?"

"Elizabeth, your bout of cold feet created quite the little hiccup. When I say my friends and family have badgered me beyond what my somewhat robust physical endurance can take, I am not kidding you. Not one little bit."

"Yes, but since I *didn't* tell anyone that we got married, having *you* in Henderson is now a big hiccup for me."

"Welcome to my world."

"Crain," she ground out. "This is an impossible situation. You have no idea what it's like being me."

"Well that's for damn sure, since you haven't told me anything, *Tansy.* And yeah, I imagine a secret husband showin' up is a helluva predicament. But you're gonna have to saddle up and deal with it, darlin', because I'm here, in Henderson, and I will buy and sell the place before I hightail it back to Dallas empty-handed."

"What does that mean?"

"It means I want some time alone with my wife, so she can explain to me what the hell happened."

When she drew in a breath—her eyes getting all teary—his heart broke. He couldn't help it. He reached out and pulled her into his arms.

"I'm not tryin' to make your life miserable, Sweetheart," he said against her ear. "I'm just tryin' to figure out what I did wrong."

She sniffed. "You didn't do anything wrong."

"I did something to make you run out on me."

"No, you didn't." She pushed back from him and wiped at her eyes. "You didn't do a thing wrong, Crain. This is all on me. I know I owe you an explanation, but it's just too hard to put it in words."

"Try."

She looked up at him like he'd sentenced her to be tortured on the rack—clearly confused by his insistence. In fact, she started sputtering. "T-t-try?"

"Yes. Try your best to put it in words."

When she just stood there, mouth open, he decided to help her by starting the sentence for her. "Crain, I got cold feet after that amazing night in our wedding bed because…"

"Because…" She dragged out. And then her lips smacked shut, only to open again. "You know what," she said, her eyes narrowing. "It is your fault."

"Go on."

"You called your parents. That's what you did," she accused. "I heard you on the phone telling your parents we'd eloped. And then I heard your precious momma's reaction to our stupidity."

"Stupidity?"

"Nobody's parents want to be cut out of their child's wedding. What we did was thoughtless and unconscionable."

"No. What we did was spontaneous and awesome."

That startled her a bit, forcing her to crack a smile. "Okay, it was spontaneous and awesome at the time," she conceded with her cute little bad-girl grin. "And yet, once I saw it through your momma's eyes, I realized it was selfish."

"So you ran away because you were worried about the wrath of my momma?"

"Lord, no. I was worried about the wrath of my own momma."

"Ah. Now we're gettin' somewhere."

"Crain," she said, snuggling right into him, "the thought of telling my parents I had run off to Vegas and married someone whose name they'd never heard me mention was…well, it was just too much. It brought into focus how new our relationship was and what a dumb thing we did after only two dates. I mean, I hadn't even admitted to you I wasn't from Dallas."

"Yeah. About all that—"

"See, you don't know me. The real me. You know the Dallas me. The carefree working girl who didn't even bother to tell you I was from North Carolina. Face it. You married a girl under false pretenses, and I'm just trying to let you off easy."

"Easy? How is anything about this easy?"

"Well, if you'd just sign the papers, it would be like this never happened."

"Is that what you want? For us to have never happened?"

"No. No. That's not what I'm saying."

"Well, that's what I'm hearing. And it's pissing me off." He dropped his hands from rubbing up and down her arms and started poking her in her chest and backing her up. "Because whether you're known in these parts as Tansy Langford, the reality is that you are Elizabeth Carraway." Her back hit the wall. "The same Elizabeth who slid her hand onto my thigh during our dinner date and then practically gave me a lap dance at The Ice House the following evening. So, don't blame me for things moving along quickly. It might have taken a good month to convince you to go out with me, but once I got you there, you were as eager as I was to be on it."

"That was Dallas."

"What's so different about Dallas?"

"I can't act like that here. I can't *be* Elizabeth here. Too many people know me and expect me to be Tansy."

He got in real close and lowered his voice. "Yes, but even Tansy likes the way I kiss."

She gulped.

"I'm not denying it," she whispered. "I'm not denying any of it."

"You're denying that you're married to me."

"Not denying. I just haven't told the world."

"Same result."

He stepped away. Angry. Damn angry. "Fine," he finally said. He was done groveling. He pulled out his phone and pulled up Maps. Hell if he was going to ask her for anything else. Including directions.

"What are you doing?" she asked.

With his head hung down over his phone, he said, "Going to my business meeting."

"You're actually taking that seriously?"

"I've made a commitment," he said exasperated. "Not that you'd grasp the meaning of the word, but in the Lone Star State, a man stands by his commitments."

"So, you'll be staying? In town?" The high-pitched panic in her voice made him want to hit something.

"I don't know why Tansy Langford would have a problem with that. Since I don't know who she is or want anything to do with her."

"Crain, I'm sorry."

"We're done talking."

"Just," she pleaded. "Just…you know…keep a low profile, okay?"

"Done talking," he said to himself as he walked away.

CHAPTER NINETEEN

"She kicked you in your nuts."

"I see I forgot to put on my poker face," Crain responded to Vance as he flopped into the booth next to The Pink One.

The men around him chuckled.

"Y'all go right ahead and laugh," he said, rolling up his shirtsleeves and rubbing his hands through his hair. "My pride is already beat to a damn pulp."

"We've ordered some beer and wings guaranteed to restore whatever manhood Tansy stole from you."

"Well, that's a good thing I guess," he said, taking a long pull on the beer that was offered.

"So no CC Dallas state-of-the-art learning center for the new school yet?" Vance asked.

"And no dormitory either," Crain said.

"I imagine you're not a man used to having difficulties with women."

Crain shook his head. "Not generally, no. But I've never made the mistake of marrying one before either."

"Well, maybe it'll make you feel better to know you're sitting here in good company. Between the three of us, we've had plenty of women problems."

"Is that right?" Crain asked. "Your wife seems rather smitten with you."

"My wife of two weeks *is* smitten with me. However, she's also smitten with the idea of starting up some kind of pie plate business with Molly DuVal, the woman I lost my virginity to and later stole from her fiancé for nothing more than a weekend of hot sex." He pointed his longneck bottle across the table at Crain. "That, my Texas friend, has disaster written all over it."

Crain didn't disagree, and apparently neither did Brooks.

"Why does Piper want to go into a pie plate business with Molly? Piper's a lawyer," Brooks said.

"A lawyer and soon to be mother of Vance, Jr. Believe me, I've tried to derail this little project. But I'm getting off-topic, because Crain is gonna love this." He looked at Crain, his brows going big. "This one over here," Vance said, pointing the bottle toward Brooks, "finally landed the very young and very pretty love of his life— Lolly DuVal, Molly's cousin—who just happens to be the same girl who kicked this one over there," he pointed at Pinks," to the curb because he was too nice, safe, and boring."

"What?" Crain asked looking between the two men.

"It's true," Brooks grinned.

The Pink One was not grinning.

"And you're working with him?" Crain asked Pinks.

"Yeah, they're laughing now," Pinks said. "But what Vance neglected to share is that he, too, was in love with Lolly and got himself tangled up in a love triangle with his buddy Brooks here after she dumped my ass. So for the record, there were three of us in love with Lolly—all at the same time."

"And you're *all* working together? 'Cause I gotta tell ya, I'd put up a fuss havin' to eat lunch across from any man who has been with my woman."

Vance immediately choked on his beer. He pressed a napkin to his face until his eruption subsided. "You do know this is a small town, right?" he gasped, trying to get his airway clear. "You better get used to the fact that half the men our age dated Tansy at one time or another."

"You?" Crain pointed, his eyes wide.

Vance pulled back, his face screwed up in disgust. "No. Not me. Never me. That woman hates my guts. And I assure you the feeling is mutual."

"Brooks?" he eyed one of the Surly Duo, thinking that made things a little clearer.

"She and I dated for two years," Brooks said, looking him in the eye. "But as these two have told you, I'm in love with Lolly. And you won't be receiving an introduction to her any time soon."

"Why the hell would I want to meet Lolly? I've got my damn hands full with Elizabeth. Do not introduce me to this Lolly."

"At least you know Tansy—Elizabeth—is not after your money," Pinks said.

"Nope. Doesn't want my money and is claiming she doesn't want me. Although she doesn't mind me stealin' a kiss. Which is the tiny, little sliver of hope I'm clinging to. So I'm upping the stakes, gentlemen."

Crain paused as a heaping platter of wings was laid on the table, and dishes handed around.

"Picture this," he said as his dining companions filled their plates. "One state-of-the-art stadium—designed by the architectural firm Populous if you want it retro-style—able to convert from football to baseball, located dead center on your sports academy campus. I'll commit to gather the funding and pour money into it myself, if you all help me figure out a way to get Mrs. Carraway, a.k.a. *Tansy*, to give our marriage a shot."

"How long do we have?" Vance asked. "Are you talking a week, a month, first of the year?"

"Hell. I'm talking tomorrow—or as long as it takes. I don't know."

"Bring your parents into town and introduce her as your wife," Pinks said. "That oughta give you some quick results, one way or another."

"Well now, here's the thing, *Pinks*. I'm not really interested in a quick result if it's not gonna go my way, ya hear? But I can't be hanging around Henderson forever. So…that's not necessarily the worst idea. Let my wife take on some of the heat I've been dealing with."

"Why can't you hang around Henderson?" Vance asked. "You've been conducting your consulting business from here for two days. Obviously, you've got good people you rely on back in the Dallas office. You can travel from here to meet with clients just as well as you can travel from Dallas."

"Other than this little escapade, I do all my business in Texas."

"So why not go national? If we do manage to make Henderson the sports capital of North Carolina, the Crain Carraway name will mean something up and down the East Coast. You should take advantage of that. What's stopping you from hanging a CC Henderson shingle on a storefront right in the center of town?"

"Well, one thing that's stopping me is Elizabeth. She's asked me to be discreet while I'm fulfilling my obligation to y'all. Hanging a shingle would hardly be discreet."

"So there's your plan," Vance said as if it was the most obvious thing. He leaned in across the table and got serious. "You don't be discreet," he said. "You be larger than life. You move in here with a new business, bringing that Texas swagger with you, and in two weeks' time, everybody around here is going to know who you are."

"And what's that get me besides pissing Elizabeth off real good?"

"Think, my man. A good-looking guy like you in his thirties? Everyone is going to want to know about your marital status."

"That's the damn truth," Brooks piped in with a laugh.

"And if people think you're single, just as they believe Tansy is, you'll no doubt draw a lot of female attention," Vance went on. "Which, I'm just betting, Miss Langford may not appreciate. You'll be pressing the issue from all sides without you actually pressing the issue."

"Huh?"

"Trust me on this. It's a great plan," Vance said, biting into a wing.

Crain sat back and thought about it. No doubt, it had its merits, and he wasn't sure what else he could do, short of knocking on her parents' door and introducing himself. He looked over at Brooks, the future mayor of this place. "You want your stadium. Do you think it's a great plan?"

Brooks may have appeared to finish chewing and take time to carefully wipe his face with his napkin, but Crain could tell he was thinking—obviously choosing his next words carefully.

"Tansy cares for you," Brooks said quietly, his head bent low but his eyes zeroing in on Crain. "I'm not gonna betray a confidence, but I spoke to her this morning about all this, and you deserve to know at least this much. She's into you. She just believes she's not good enough for you. Which, by the way, is pure bullshit."

"You don't like me much, do you Brooks?"

"I like you fine. I like your stadium, learning center, and dormitory a lot. But my allegiance is to Tansy, and what I don't like is being in league with this secret of yours."

"It's not *my* secret. The whole dang city of Dallas is well aware I'm a married man—without a bride to show for it. And I've made no secret that I'm eager to have that resolved."

"Tansy's secret then," Brooks said. "Whatever. I don't like being a part of it."

"Then you'll be happy to help me resolve it quickly. What else did you two talk about?"

Brooks sat back, looking over at Pinks before his gaze drifted back to Crain. "She thinks you fell in love with her under false pretenses. And she's probably right. Because being Tansy Langford in this town is not easy. Her momma and daddy hold her to a high standard, and she walks the walk for them. Always has. She no doubt let her hair down a bit in Dallas because she could and probably needed to."

"So you're telling me that I fell for a fake?" Crain asked. *That is such bullshit.* "Which one do *you* think is the real Miss Langford?

Tansy, the one who has been jumpin' through hoops for her parents and this town all her life or Elizabeth, the one who showed up in Dallas and started living as she saw fit?" His gazed drifted to each of the men. "I'm probably the *only* one who knows the true Miss Langford. I just need a way to introduce Elizabeth to her own hometown."

"It's not easy being Tansy," The Pink One said. "I've played witness to what goes on between her and her mother. They're both beautiful women, but they're wound tight."

"You got any ideas?" Crain asked Pinks.

"I say bust it wide open. Sign her papers, annul the marriage, and then pursue her out in the open with all of Henderson as witness. If she has feelings for you, why stand on principal and let the elopement stand in the way of your future?"

"Because the day I married Elizabeth was my best day ever. In spite of her cold feet. I'm not about to erase that or pretend it didn't happen. I love her," he said, running his hands through his hair. "She knows how to handle me. How to soothe me. I need that in my life. I need her. I can't risk any of that by signing a bunch of legal papers."

"Hell," Vance said. "Just do what my father and I did. Get her pregnant. Then she'll be only too happy to confess the marriage."

Brooks laughed. "It has worked well for the Evans men."

"Don't get her pregnant," Pinks said, eyeing him seriously while the other side of the table sat in amusement.

Crain tilted his head and spread his hands. "It'd probably get the job done. And I'm not getting any younger. But I hear ya, and trust me, that one I'll keep deep in the arsenal."

"Here's another reason CC Dallas should go national and open a branch right here," Vance interrupted. "Rye Langford owns a lot of real estate on our little main street. Including the spot right across from E&E Investments. Certainly make doing business between us easy, and it's right in the center of town where nobody is going to miss it. Especially Tansy."

"Rye Langford? Elizabeth's father?" Crain asked.

"Correct. If you need office space in Henderson, you'd be making a deal with your very own father-in-law. Offer to buy the space rather than rent it, and I bet right now, with the way our economy is, he'd throw his oldest daughter in with the deal," Vance said through his laughter.

Crain leaned back. "Y'all have me venturing into dangerous territory. Setting up a meeting with Tansy's father. Committing to a new branch of CC Dallas that is not located in Houston, Austin, or even San Antonio. If I wasn't dangling that new stadium and dormitory out there, I might think y'all have it in for me."

"But you do have the stadium, the dormitory, and the state-of-the-art learning center dangling out there. Not to mention one beautiful bride," Vance said. "So that puts us all in this together. We all rise or fall on this marriage of yours, so you'd best get it straightened out quickly."

Crain's phone sounded as a text came in. He pulled it out of his pocket and read.

"Huh. Seems your father, Hale, has decided to join Team Carraway. He's letting me know that Miss Langford has stopped by the Evans Estate at your wife, Piper's request."

"Has she now?" Vance smiled. "A lot of stuff can happen when you drag a woman across that property line."

"No doubt. That place is like freaking Disney World. Speakin' of. I do not intend to overstay my welcome like The Pink One here."

"Dude," Davis protested. "I'm like the pool boy, errand runner, and handyman all built into one. Not to mention occasional bodyguard for all members of the ever-expanding Evans family. Trust me. I earn my keep."

"The Ninja is not lying," Vance agreed with a laugh.

"Well, since all those jobs are taken, and I'm a full grown adult, does Rye Langford deal in Henderson's housing market as well? I'm gonna need a place of my own for the time being."

"Rye does not," Vance said, "but you do need a love nest—somewhere to sweep Tansy off her feet and into without causing a lot of raised eyebrows. For her sake. And I've got an idea about that. Give me a day or two. I've got you covered."

Crain grunted. He was suddenly putting a whole lot of faith in three men he met yesterday.

Lord help him.

CHAPTER TWENTY

Tansy sat next to Piper on tall stools in the opulent Evans kitchen. Their heads close together, forks in hand, tasting two identical apple pies in identical mammoth green ceramic pie plates.

"This is good," Tansy said.

"Which one is good?"

"What do you mean which one? Aren't they both the same?"

"The recipe for both is exactly the same. Painstakingly the same. Everything is the same except for the pie plates they've been baked in. But I'm hoping they're actually the same, too."

"I'm not following."

"The results. I'm hoping both pie plates have produced the same results. So taste test them both again and focus on any differences. Anything at all."

Tansy took a big forkful from one pie and savored the flavors, paying attention to the delicious crust that was warm and buttery with a nice light crispness to it. Then she took a similar forkful of the second pie and closed her eyes so she could focus all her attention on the similarities or differences.

"These are good," she said. "And I'm not using the word good as in 'good apple pie.' I'm using the word good as in 'These pies are deliciously decadent and could be served in any one of Raleigh's top restaurants.' There's something special about them both. Because I can't tell any difference. No difference at all." She noticed Piper's face lighting up, but went on with her thoughts. "I think it's the crust. Something about the crust—the butteriness really comes through, and it feels good in my mouth. Really makes me want to have another bite. There's something about this pie. There's something about…"

"The pie plates. There is something about the pie plates that makes every recipe I put in them outstanding," Piper said. "And believe me, I've tried recipes that no one would ever have thought to put in pie plates while trying to figure this out."

"What exactly are you trying to figure out?"

Piper's smile lit up her pink cheeks and her beautiful blue eyes. "Molly DuVal made this enormous pie plate for Genevra and Hale's wedding gift. I fell in love with it as soon as Genevra unwrapped it, because pies are my specialty. Well sorta. I don't really have a specialty, but I know baking. I know the science behind baking, the interaction of ingredients, and I know how things work and how they're supposed to come out tasting. And my mother had an award-winning piecrust recipe. Really. The woman won awards."

Tansy grinned and dug her fork back into pie number one.

"Anyway," Piper went on, "of course I was dying to bake in this oversized pie plate ever since I saw it. So when I moved in here after our wedding, I put it to good use. With crazy good results. None of my recipes have ever come out tasting so…decadent, as you say. I knew it was the pie plate right away. I just needed a second opinion and was waiting until Genevra got back from her honeymoon in Europe to acknowledge it."

"Okay. So how did you get two pie plates?"

"I asked Molly to make me one. To see if it was lighting striking once and only once or if the magic could be reproduced. She brought it to me this morning. What do you think?'

"I think both pies are identically decadent."

"I do too," Piper grinned.

"So what's the big deal?"

Piper's brows pulled together. "You aren't a baker, are you?"

"No. I don't claim to be any sort of a cook at all."

"Obviously. Because if you were a baker, you'd be trying to think of ways to smuggle one of these out of the house without me noticing. You'd be begging for Molly's phone number and calling her up right this minute to get your order in. The big deal is that with Molly's pottery and my mother's award winning crust recipe, I am sitting on a gold mine. If I can market this correctly, bakers all over the country—all over the world—are gonna want one of these beauties in their kitchen."

"Really?"

"Really."

"Huh. I had no idea. I thought good pie was just good pie."

"Good pie is just good pie. But great pie can put Vance, Jr. through college."

Tansy looked around her. "I think from the looks of this place, Vance, Jr.'s college tuition is all locked up."

"Bah. This is all Hale and Genevra's. We're freeloaders," Piper said.

"Freeloaders?" Tansy smiled. "Vance has money. If he's telling you otherwise, he's trying to hide something."

"Oh, he's told me he's a millionaire. I just don't believe it."

"A millionaire?"

"So he says," Piper scoffed.

"Well," Tansy said while laughing and going for a little more pie, "why don't you believe him?"

"I did at first. That's the reason I didn't tell him about the baby right away. I figured he'd think I was trying to trap him—because he's a millionaire. But after we were married...so fast..." Piper rolled her eyes. "I realized he was pulling my leg."

"What?"

"He's not a millionaire. He might have a nice nest egg, but he's no millionaire. A millionaire would have made me sign a prenup." She shook her head as she looked at Tansy. "There was no prenup."

"Why would he need a prenup? You're obviously crazy about him."

"Prenups have nothing to do with love."

"That's the lawyer in you talking."

"That's the businesswoman in me talking. The businesswoman who is going to put this big pie plate on the map. Somehow."

"You sound like Brooks and Vance wanting to put Henderson on the map."

"I do, don't I…" Piper sort of drifted off, thinking. Tansy took the opportunity to steal another forkful.

"You know, if I could think of a way to market this pie plate and help raise awareness of Henderson all at the same time, it would be ideal. Because Molly is moving back to town and actively looking for a way to make her pottery business a contributing force in Henderson. She's apparently got a reputation she's trying to reinvent."

"Hmm. I am aware."

"Selling a lot of these would mean she'd have to hire people to work for her. So that would be good for Henderson. I hear she's working with your father, looking at places in the center of town to set up shop. Right now, she's overwhelmed at the thought of paying rent for a business and paying rent for an apartment."

"She should move in with Josh."

"She would love to. She just doesn't want to flaunt her unmarried status in front of Evie Jackson and…"

"My mother," Tansy finished for her.

"Yes," Piper conceded with a sigh. "Your mother and the rest of Henderson's moral majority. Who, by the way, have been very kind to Genevra and Hale. That wasn't what they were expecting."

"It's not how the old guard usually operates," Tansy acknowledged. "But it's about time they start to simmer down and allow all of us to live our lives. They get so upset when their kids and grandkids pull up roots and leave, but who wants their every move scrutinized? Who wants to be held to impossible standards? And why is it their business what anybody else is doing?"

"Aww, they're probably just bored. I mean, how many games of bridge or whatever can you play a week? Gossip is their recreation.

If you can think of a way to pull them in on Team Henderson, I'd bet they'd love it. They sure aren't shy about their opinions."

"You can say that again. Evie Jackson has roped Brooks and me into being the New Face of Henderson Harvest Daze. And she wouldn't take no for an answer."

"Harvest Daze?"

"A town festival. It's fun. Brings everyone back together for a big day and night. Most everyone comes back for it, sort of like New Year's and the Fourth of July. But like everything else around here, it's gotten stale, and the biggest draw is the beer truck. So, now it's generally referred to as The Daze."

"Pie-eating contest. Does it have one of those?"

"Probably did at some point, but not anymore as far as I know. What? You want to introduce Molly's big pie plate at a pie-eating contest?"

Piper's mind was spinning, Tansy could tell. Piper was not looking at her, but she was shaking a finger in her direction as she hopped off her stool and headed to get a large platter and a spatula.

"Look at this," she said as she cut and scooped the pie out of one of the big pie plates. She pushed crumbs out of the way to reveal a beautiful crest in the center of the pie plate. "Molly created a mold of the Evans family crest and then pressed it into the center of this pie plate. It really made it a showpiece. If it didn't bake so well, it could be displayed on the wall. Frankly, I think that's what Molly had in mind. But what if we have her create a coat of arms, or a seal, for the town of Henderson and press that into the center? Call it Henderson's Big Pie Plate. We could introduce it at the The Daze. We could recruit the rest of Genevra's nieces and sister-in-laws to help bake pies and sell pieces at the fair so people could taste the difference the big pie plate makes. And then The Henderson Pie Plate Company, or whatever we're going to call ourselves, can sponsor a pie-eating contest or a pie-baking contest and give away one of these as the prize."

"Or you could simply sell them there."

"Or we could sell them there," Piper agreed with glee. "I've got to get Molly on the phone. See what she thinks. When is this Daze?"

"The end of October. You've got about four weeks."

"Hmm, we'll need to work fast," Piper said.

"And it would certainly help me out. Evie wants Brooks and me to come up with better entertainment and give the whole event a facelift. She's right. It needs one. I just hadn't planned on it falling into my lap at this late date."

"Why you and Brooks?"

Tansy shot Piper a look out of the corner of her eye. "I'm guessing my mother has something to do with that. She's suggested I do my best to win Brooks back now that Lolly is back in grad school."

"Excuse me?" Piper's brows had shot clear into her forehead.

"Don't worry. I'm not interested in Brooks. But my mother is having a hard time letting the dream of me being the mayor's wife die."

"You and Brooks have a past?"

"We, um. We were fairly serious. Until about this time last year. The truth is he wasn't in love with me, and I wasn't in love with him. But the town of Henderson loved the two of us together. Especially our parents. So we just acted like we were on board with it. I got wind that he was planning to propose, and I didn't exactly not want to marry Brooks, I just wasn't ready to settle. So I left for Dallas."

"Dallas?"

"Yes. I'd done some internship work for Mrs. Bush during college and she remembered me when I applied for a job at George W.'s presidential library. I was hired and moved to Dallas to take the job. I didn't tell Brooks I was leaving. I just left. Which means he's not a big fan of mine right now, although he seems to be much happier with Lolly than he ever was with me. So, I think I've been forgiven."

"Oh my gosh. Have you met the hunky Dallas tycoon Vance and Hale have staying at the house right now?" Piper's eyes went wide. "He'd be perfect for you. Tall, gorgeous, crazy charming. Like…like he's made of manners, but they're just a little understated. Nothing frilly, yet still right there on the surface. He's actually sort of like Brooks, but without the dark underbelly."

Tansy burst out laughing. "Brooks has a dark underbelly?"

"Oh sure—you know what I mean. He's the Golden Boy, but he doesn't like it. It's the cross he thinks he has to bear. But this CC Dallas guy. Crain? He's like the spokesperson for all of Texas, and he's *volunteered* to do it. With a smile."

"Well, that's actually what I need to talk with you about." Tansy glanced at her watch. "But I could use a little wine and a place where we'll be assured some privacy."

"Can you drive an ATV?"

"Probably…"

Piper was already grabbing a previously opened bottle of red from the bar. "Follow me."

A dozen minutes later, they were shrieking and laughing as Tansy did her best to maneuver Vance's huge ATV out of the shed without taking down the side of it or scraping too much off the door. Eventually they were bumping slowly down the back side of the property with Piper clinging to Tansy's waist, laughing so hard she snorted, the bottle of wine clasped in one hand and banging Tansy on the thigh whenever they hit a big bump. Tansy could barely see through the tears in her eyes, which made her laugh all the harder. She followed Piper's directions as best she could without getting them tossed into a creek when she cut a turn too close, or getting them knocked off the thing altogether by low-lying pine branches. Finally, they came to rest in a spot of late afternoon shade by a charming little creek out in the middle of nowhere.

"You wanted privacy," Piper said, swinging a short leg over the machine and hopping off. "Here's your privacy. It's where my husband, *the millionaire*," she said in air quotes, "is going to build me a house."

"Wow," Tansy said. "I didn't know all this was back here."

Piper spread a blanket out on the softest grass she could find and then handed Tansy the bottle before she laid down flat on her back and closed her eyes. "Drink up and start talking."

Tansy looked at the wine bottle, wondering for a moment how she was supposed to drink it without a glass. Glancing over at Piper, she tugged the cork out and held the bottle high, giving it a once over. She brought it down to her lips, closed her eyes, and upended the bottle, taking a long swig. She wiped her mouth, saying, "My mother would be mortified."

"Your mother isn't here. Just us. So, spill. You know this Crain Carraway from Dallas?"

"I do," Tansy admitted, taking another sip and making herself comfortable on the big seat of the ATV.

"You two have an affair or something?"

"Two dates and a one-night stand," Tansy said.

Piper shot up to a sitting position, her blond curls flying. "Was it awesome?" she asked, pushing her hair out of her face. She was smiling from ear to ear, obviously hoping for juicy details. "What's he look like with his shirt off?"

Tansy couldn't help but laugh. "He looks amazing with his shirt off." She took another swig from the bottle. "With his pants off, too. He's everything you think he's gonna be and then some. Because he's…" she sighed, "you know, *Crain*. He's like the Big Pie Plate—only human. He makes everything better just because he wants it to be so."

"Yum."

"Yes, yum," Tansy said, raising both arms and the bottle above her head, stretching and luxuriating in the thought. "And he was mine, all mine. For a good, long night and a few minutes in the morning and then…" She brought her arms down and felt her shoulders droop. "Then I got cold feet and left before he came out of the bathroom. I snuck away like a chicken. Afraid of what people would think. Because we had gotten a little carried away the night before and decided to get married."

"He asked you to marry him? You were engaged? To CC Dallas?"

"Ah, no. I actually married CC Dallas. That night. Because we were in Vegas."

"You married him? CC Dallas with all that shucks-darlin' Texas swagger? That? You married that?"

"I know it's absurd, but yes. I married *that,* and now I'm doing my best to unwind it. But Crain's like a damn dog with a bone. He won't let it go and he's not signing the annulment papers because he opened his big Texas mouth and blabbed to everyone that he'd gotten married. To Elizabeth Langford of Dallas, Texas, because that's who he thought I was. Now I think he just wants to save face."

Piper's mouth hung open, her eyes aghast.

"I know!" Tansy agreed. "There are no words." She shook her head. "Don't tax yourself trying to come up with any."

"Was there a prenup?" Piper whispered.

Tansy tilted her head and gave Piper a "come-on-now" look. "It was a spur of the moment, impromptu, crazy Vegas moment. He didn't get down on one knee and whip out a prenup. He doesn't need a prenup—I'm not after his money."

"Obviously, or you wouldn't have run out of there so fast. So, why did you? Run out of there so fast?"

Tansy sat on that question, staring at her friend but not really seeing her. She took in a deep breath and sighed it out. "I was scared to tell my parents," she said. "Simple as that." She looked toward the trees. "I was scared to tell Brooks. I thought he'd be upset." She looked back at Piper. "I thought I'd be shunned by all the people I look up to in Henderson. I thought…I thought I wouldn't be able to come home."

When she saw the expression on Piper's face change, she went on. "Those thoughts crossed my mind in split seconds, and I panicked. I grabbed my clothes and purse and raced for the door before realizing how nonsensical they really were.

"Of course, after all these months of hiding from it, I see the truth now. My parents would have gotten over it eventually. They would have probably approved of Crain in the end. Because they love me, and I'm their daughter. But I didn't see it that way at the time. I just thought about how long my mother had been talking about my wedding to Brooks, and I imagined her disappointment.

"How could I explain that I wouldn't marry The Hero of Henderson after two years, but married a man I hardly knew after two dates? In my mind, at that moment, it didn't even make sense to me. I mean, if I was going to marry anyone, it should have been Brooks, right? So I bolted."

"And now you regret it. Bolting," Piper said.

"How can you tell?" Tansy said, letting a self-deprecating smile sneak out.

Piper patted the blanket next to her. Begrudgingly Tansy swung a leg over the ATV and drank another sip as she kicked off her shoes and joined Piper on the blanket. She secured the bottle upright on the grass and then lay down on her back looking up at the sky.

"I do regret running out on Crain. I should have given him the chance to talk me down. Mostly, I regret the spontaneous Vegas wedding that started it all. Not the Crain part, just the rush to the altar part. I should have insisted on an engagement period, brought him home to meet my parents. Smoothed things over with Brooks. I came back to Henderson and immediately wondered why I'd panicked. Wondered why I felt so strongly that it was my job to make my parents happy, to make Brooks happy, or even to make the rest of this town happy. Why me? Molly DuVal has it right. She does what she wants and…"

"People talk behind her back."

"Yeah," Tansy sighed. "I guess that's it. I'm afraid of what people say behind my back. In fact, I'm not just afraid of it. It dictates what I do. In my head, I hear their voices regarding every action I take or don't take."

"That's a hell of a way to live your life."

"I didn't even realize I was doing it."

"Is that why you asked your mother to go easy on Vance and me and the Evanses?"

Tansy looked over at Piper. "I don't know what you're talking about."

"Uh-huh. You're not just worried about what they're saying about you, you're worried about what they're saying about me."

"Maybe," Tansy hedged. "But I'm trying to get over it, because truly, I'm the only one suffering. My parents' lives go on. Brooks has moved on."

"So there's nothing stopping you from picking up with Crain. Especially if that's what he still wants."

Tansy sat up and drank another gulp of wine. She set the bottle down and laid back beside Piper.

"If he would just sign the annulment papers, then we could start fresh. Date like two normal people. I could introduce him to my parents without them being shocked that I'd been married for the past four months, secretly hiding from my husband. I mean, imagine trying to answer all those questions?"

"You're in a bit of pickle," Piper said.

"Ya think?" Tansy laughed, her sense of humor being distorted by the wine. "Brooks told me that the truth will set me free. And I suppose it will. It sure would give Henderson something to talk about other than your growing belly. But I'm scared the whole truth will cause me to lose Crain altogether."

There was a distant sound of a motor.

"What do you mean, the whole truth?" Piper asked. "Crain's not your only secret?"

"Crain's the only secret I'm keeping from Henderson. But I have a Henderson secret I'm keeping from Crain."

The sound was growing louder.

Piper turned on her side, bending her elbow and propping her head up on her hand to look down at Tansy. "Davis," she said.

"Vance told you."

"No. I was on the dance floor with you the night he played the drums at The Situation. I saw the way you two were looking at each other. You looked like you were gonna eat him alive, and he looked like he was going to let you."

"Oh, Lord," Tansy sighed. "We were that obvious?"

"Probably not to everybody. But I was standing right there."

"Vance knows about it. In fact, Vance knows about me being married to Crain. He also knows I tried to break up Lolly and Brooks while I was married to Crain. Which, ya know, means I definitely have to start being nicer to Vance. The guy could out me to everyone."

"So what about Davis?"

"I feel terrible about Davis. He's none too happy with me either. As he puts it, sleeping with a married woman was not on his bucket list. But the truth is I thought it was done. I'd been given the news that the annulment papers had come through that afternoon. And as much as I'd wanted the annulment, once I heard…I just…" Tansy felt the sorrow well up inside her chest.

"You were upset."

Tansy nodded briskly, unable to speak.

"Because you thought Crain had signed the papers."

Tansy nodded, wiping at her eyes.

"And even though you wanted the annulment, you were sad because it appeared Crain no longer wanted you."

Tansy nodded again.

"I get it."

Piper lay down and let the silence heal. Finally, she said, "So Davis. He was your rebound."

"Yeah," Tansy choked out. "He came by the pool that day and asked me to stop by The Situation if I was interested in a little fun. Later on, after I thought the annulment papers were returned, I figured it was either go home and cry myself to sleep or take Davis up on his offer."

"So he isn't aware that there were extenuating circumstances that led to you two hooking up?"

"He knows I thought I was no longer married. He doesn't know how sad I was about it."

"Ah."

"Yeah. Ah."

"So getting Crain to sign the annulment papers now…"

"Would alleviate my guilt. Would help me feel like I didn't cheat on my marriage. Would really give the two of us a fresh start."

Way down at the end of the stand of trees, a blur of red came into view. Turning the corner and heading right for them.

"Uh-oh," Piper said.

"What?" Tansy asked, squinting into the distance trying to see what it was.

"I'm not supposed to drive the ATV."

"You didn't drive it. I did."

Vance was heading right for them on another ATV. This one red.

"I'm not sure semantics are gonna matter much. I kinda wanted to sneak this in before he got home."

As they came cruising up, the girls could see Vance had Crain jammed on the back of the big four-wheeler.

"I can't believe both of them can fit on one of those," Tansy said.

"Yeah, maybe all that weight will make them spin out or something before they reach us."

"Piper!"

"I'm just saying this is probably not going to go well for either of us."

CHAPTER TWENTY-ONE

Vance throttled down and came to a stop with his eyes trained solely on Piper. He looked her up and down, assessing her health as best he could from a distance while Crain unwrapped himself and got off the ATV behind him. Once he got off the vehicle, he stood next to Crain, hands on hips and said, "I now see exactly where this whole thing has gone wrong for us, Carraway."

"Is that right?" Crain responded, not taking his eyes off Tansy.

"Uh-huh. Because if the two of us had a lick of sense, we'd have insisted that the vow to *obey* be reinstated into the marriage ceremony before taking on these two. Imagine what life would be like right now if we'd had the forethought."

"Hindsight's 20/20, compadre. Where were you with your big ideas four months ago?"

"And Piper, who has been told she's too damn tiny to safely drive one of these machines, would not have put herself or Vance, Jr. in harm's way, giving me a heart attack in the process."

"Oh Lord," Piper said, rolling her eyes and face toward Tansy. "Do you believe this?"

"He is a control freak," Tansy said.

"Clearly not a very effective one," Vance said, stomping up to his wife and inspecting her from head to toe. His hands slid over her bare arms and legs, admiring the way her yellow cotton dress hugged her breasts and tummy. The pounding of his heart was easing just because she'd smiled and winked at him as he started his rampage. And now his blood was heating up just a bit in spite of his anger over what she'd done.

"Vance, I drove the ATV. We were fine. She was in good hands," Tansy soothed.

"Oh, so you have your own Kawasaki, do you?" he asked without taking his eyes off Piper. "Or is your machine a Yamaha?"

"Well, I don't exactly have one—"

"Yeah—didn't think so," Vance said as he pushed the curls back from Piper's face. "Your sneaky friend here is going to get turned over my knee." He smiled down into Piper's eyes. "'Cause she is well aware that I don't want her...Dammit!" he said, stepping back from Piper, letting his hands drop from her face. "I can't even stay mad at you," he said with a laugh. He turned to Crain and said, "Run, buddy. Before you get in any deeper I say sign the damn annulment papers and save your sanity. Because this little one right here"—he pointed at Piper—"she's got me over a damn barrel. She defies me at every turn, and I'm so crazy about her I can't even get fired up over any of it."

He pulled Piper to him and kissed her like he meant it, letting the rest of his fear for her safety ease out of him and into the kiss.

Damn woman.

"What the hell was so dang important you couldn't wait for me to get home and drive you out here?"

"Tansy wanted to tell me about Crain, so we needed a private place to talk. Besides," she said, pressing her lips back against his, "you know this is one of my favorite spots."

"'Cause this is where I'm going to build your big-ass kitchen," he said, smiling down at her, with his arms clasped loosely around her back.

"Yeah, right," Piper said.

"I am. Of course, I am. What's that supposed to mean?"

"Nothing," she said. "In fact, I was telling Tansy about 'our house.'"

"What's with the air quotes?"

Piper shook her head and smiled. "Not a thing. I'm just playin'."

Vance wasn't sure what was going on, but he was damn sure something was. He let his hands swing down and pick up one of hers, pulling her behind him.

"If you two will excuse us," he said to Crain and Tansy as he helped Piper onto the red ATV. "It seems my wife and I have a few things to discuss." He threw his leg over the seat and sat himself behind her, swatting her hands off the handles. "Oh, by the way— Piper and I have moved into the big house. A cleaning service is finishing up at the pool house now, so Crain, I want you to use that as your own for the rest of the week and into next if you need it. Tansy, Annabelle Devine would like you to house sit her parents' home for the next couple of months while they're in Florida. They'll be back the week before Thanksgiving, and you'd be doing them a favor. I took the liberty of telling her you'd do it. Figured it would get you out from under your parents and into your own place for a while." He looked between Crain and Tansy before starting up the four-wheeler. "Y'all can thank me later."

He revved up the ATV and kicked up some dirt as he pulled away, turning and going back the way he came. Piper had to grab on tight to the sides of his thighs. He took his left hand off the handlebar and slid it across her midsection, pulling her back against him as he gunned it, heading up the steep slope. He put a quick peck on her neck, and she turned her face, the wind blowing her curls all over the place, and smiled up at him like he'd hung the moon and stars.

And for her, he would have.

They coasted into the shed, stopping inches from the back wall. Then he picked her up and spun her around, so she was facing him on the seat. She squirmed up close, throwing her arms around his neck and tossing her shapely legs over his thighs, hoisting herself into his lap. This was a position that really worked for them. It gave her a boost, so her lips were just about level with his. He took full advantage of the situation by pressing in and taking her mouth.

He still couldn't believe Piper Beaumont was his. All the sweetness and light he'd been missing for so many years, and now he had it every morning when he woke up and every night before he fell asleep. And then there were moments like right now, when there was so much joy shoved into one moment it stole his breath away.

"I love you," he said, between eager kisses. He couldn't tell her enough. Couldn't imagine being able to say it so easily. And yet, with Piper he couldn't hold it in.

"I love you, too," she cooed, smiling against his mouth.

When her fingers found their way into his hair, all he could think was *Ahhhh.*

"How was your day?" she asked as they kissed. "Tansy told me about Crain," she said as she lightly scraped her nails against his scalp. "She loves him, by the way."

Vance pulled back and looked at her. "You think so?"

"I know so. When she says his name she adds about seven more vowels, pronouncing it 'Craaaiiin,' all breathy like."

"Well, that's good news. We need her all breathy for Crain."

"There are issues though."

"I am well aware," Vance said as he went back to kissing her lips.

"You think giving up our honeymoon cottage for a week is going to help move things along with them?"

"Can't hurt," he said, pulling at the hem of her dress. "You and I've got a lot of good mojo happening in there."

"So what bedroom did you move us into?" she said, as his hands toyed with the little bows tying up the sides of her lingerie.

"The blue one," he said against her lips. "Figured we needed at least one room between us and Pinks. What in the world do you have on under here?" he wondered.

"Mmm," she said, "something I hope to tempt you with."

Oh, he was tempted.

He pulled back and smiled a wicked grin. "You gonna show me?"

"Maybe," she said. "If you'll agree to taste test two pies for me later on, and then help me brainstorm the best way to introduce Molly's Big Pie Plate at Henderson Harvest Daze."

"Done," he said, his mouth back on hers.

"That was easy," she said against him.

"Because I'm hard," he retorted.

She snuggled in closer, hooking her ankles together behind his hips. "Mmm," she said.

"Yes, mmm, indeed." He leaned back and slid his hands under her ass, pulling her against his boner. "God, that feels good."

"Should we take this up to the blue bedroom?" she whispered against his throat.

"Probably a good idea," he eked out as Piper rocked herself against him. "Can't take care of Naughty Piper in the shed with the other ATV still out there. Come on, baby doll," he said, sliding his leg over the seat and bringing her entire body with him. He copped a feel before pushing her toward the door. "Straight to the blue bedroom. Do not pass Go. Do not collect two hundred dollars."

He pressed himself up against her back as she walked, kissing her neck and making her squeal and race forward a bit.

"It's only Tuesday," she said.

"So?" He walked alongside her now, picking up her hand and swinging it between them. His mind was wandering to what was under her dress.

"Well, it's early for you to be finished for the day."

"Yeah, well, E&E has a lot riding on this Crain and Tansy thing. Actually, *Henderson* has a lot riding on this Crain and Tansy thing, so I figured getting them together is part of the job right now." He looked down at Piper and licked his lips, rubbing his fingers around the back of her neck. "The fact that I caught you stealing a ride on the monster ATV is just pure luck." He lowered his voice and leaned down to whisper in her ear. "You will be servicing me for that."

Piper stuttered a laugh and looked at him, appalled.

"You and your little bows are going to be very, very naughty." He grabbed her ass, and as they approached the French doors, they could see Vance's elegantly clad grandmother, Emelina, in the kitchen. "We say hello. I will stop to kiss her cheek but you are to keep going right to the stairs, up to the blue bedroom. Do you understand?"

She nodded, the back of her head bobbing with curls.

He leaned down and said right against her ear as he opened the door. "You like it when I get bossy."

"I do," she said at full volume, drifting a smile his way before his little wife turned her attention to Emelina.

"How is the Garden Club?" Piper asked his grandmother as she moved through the kitchen.

"Same old, same old," Emelina said in her heavy Spanish accent. "They're planning the same old end-of-year luncheon in the same old room at the same old club. I'm tired of old," she said, "but I'm too old to come up with something new. Piper, perhaps you'll help me."

"I would love to, Em," she said, continuing to move through the kitchen while Vance kissed his grandmother on the cheek. "How 'bout we do some brainstorming over dinner. Genevra will help us."

"Genevra's from Henderson. I want out-of-town ideas."

"I'll have them for you," Piper shouted, now completely out of the kitchen and starting up the stairs.

Emelina looked at her grandson. "Why is she heading upstairs?"

"We've temporarily moved into the blue bedroom so the man from Texas can have some privacy."

"Oh," Emelina exclaimed, looking out the windows across the pool. "So he's staying?"

"Abuela, the longer he stays, the better it is for you, me, and everybody else around here. So," he said, heading after Piper, "I'm counting on you to use all of those Sophia Loren charms of yours to get CC Dallas to set down some roots here in Henderson."

"I am on the job," his grandmother said, pulling open a few cupboards as Vance turned his attention to the legs disappearing at the top of the stairs.

He took the steps two at a time.

The blue room was hardly ever used, as the house had five guest bedrooms and this one was the furthest from the stairs. It probably could stand to be updated, as it was overloaded with heavy fabric window treatments with tasseled trim, French silk wallpaper, and beautiful but stuffy antiques. The bedding might have been outdated, but it was still lush and inviting with all sorts of pillows and throws tossed on the thick satin bedspread. He started pulling the decorative pillows off and piling them in a corner of the room when Piper caught his eye as she came out of the en-suite bathroom.

He stopped dead and felt drool pool in his mouth. *This marriage thing just gets better and better. Dear God.*

He dropped the pillows where he stood, sat heavily on the bed and crooked his finger at his bride. "Come here," he whispered.

Her hair was pulled up on top of her head in one sexy mess—it drove him crazy when she did that because it left her neck all bare and inviting. Of course, he wasn't going to have time to worry much with her neck, because her stretchy lace camisole was cut down to there, exposing more of her voluptuous breasts than it covered. Her midsection was left bare and there was no evidence of pregnancy in her tiny waistline that he could tell. His gaze dropped down to those saucy hips of hers tied up like a birthday gift with pretty blue bows his fingers were itching to untie.

He didn't need it, but his Johnson sure enjoyed the lingerie show Naughty Piper kept putting on night after night. It was like he'd hand-picked the hottest model and was treated to his own personal fashion show without all the wings and nonsense. And this little number was his favorite so far.

He felt his head swim a little bit as she stopped before him— her orange-blossom scent always driving him mad. His voice came out a little like he'd been drinking when he told her to take off her top.

She didn't hesitate, his Naughty Piper.

It was an embarrassment of riches, it really was. Because as beautiful and perfect as her breasts were, rounder than a tiny body had the right to claim with their pale pink nipples, he was an ass man, and man did she have one fine ass.

"Turn around."

She did as she was told, clasping her hands together underneath her chin and looking back over her shoulder at him as he ogled her sweet little derrière. But it was the whole picture that had him throbbing in his trousers. Her blond curls, those tiny shoulders, the curvy silhouette of her back along with the creamy luster of her skin. And knowing that skin was far softer than his rough fingertips should ever be allowed to touch.

He reached out and drew his index finger down the length of her spine, watching goose bumps appear. He tucked that finger into the top of her little tiny panties and carefully pulled her back against him between his thighs. His hands slid over her ass and up and down the side of her hips over the ribbons tied there. He kissed her neck and whispered that she was making it darn easy for him to get used to being a married man.

"Mmm, I'm spoiling you," she purred.

"You are indeed," he said into her shoulder. He was tempted to take a bite—to leave some sort of mark.

"So you'll have plenty of fantasies of me looking like this to relive when Vance, Jr. starts making an appearance."

"You think that's going to slow me down?"

"Mmm," she hummed. "You like my body the way it is now."

"I do," he whispered between her shoulder blades. His fingers toying with the ends of the ribbons.

"So, I'm just using this opportunity to show it off a little."

"I like it," he said as he kissed his way across her shoulders. "A lot."

She turned within his arms and pressed her gorgeous breasts up against his chest. "I think you're gonna like this a lot too," she said quietly.

Just the sultriness of her voice had his eyelids drooping to half-mast. But thank God he hadn't closed them, or he would have missed that pink tongue of hers take its time wetting her lips. He watched as it skimmed in between her upper and lower lips, getting both of them moist. And then he watched as her tongue licked over her bottom lip a few times. Then she stroked along the top one, slowly, one side to the other, and his balls started to ache. Piper leaned in and used that tongue of hers on his own lips. Tickling them open, pushing its way through until his own tongue joined the dance and a contented sigh escaped.

Her hands went to work on his shirt, starting with the buttons at the top. He started at the bottom, unbuttoning button after button until his hands met hers in the middle, all while their tongues played.

He pulled his shirt off, causing them to lose contact for a moment. A moment Piper took advantage of by looking down and unleashing his belt. Vance stood briefly to rid himself of his pants. Piper followed his hands with her own, pushing his boxer briefs down his thighs and over his knees. He sat back down and kicked everything off. Piper kicked all of it out of the way as well. Then she kissed his nose, the dimple in his chin, his Adam's apple, his collarbone. Her hands cupped his chest, pressed against the muscle there, and drifted over the six-pack abs she loved on him so much. Her lips, those sexy wet lips, trailed after her fingers down the center of him, causing him to groan in anticipation of where this might be heading.

He felt her hands against his thighs, felt the pressure as she used his legs to support her weight as she went down to her knees. He felt her breath on his balls. *Jesus.*

"Did you lock the door?" she managed to say as her tongue slid up his cock. He hadn't. Unworthy son of a bitch that he was. But he wasn't going to tell her that. He just gave a "mmm" sound.

"You can't be loud," she whispered before her mouth circled the tip of what felt like the biggest boner he'd ever sprouted. "Even though I kinda like it when you get loud," she said, making him groan. Her mouth slid down one side of him, slowly. She cupped his balls with her hand as she warned, "But we're not alone here." The tone of her voice conveyed she was well aware she was teasing him in more ways than he could count. Her tongue moved back up, and she tantalized the head with some fancy licks. "So, you're going to have to control yourself."

Not likely.

When she took him into her mouth and started some kind of magical lick, twist, and suck combination, his eyes shot open because he was afraid he was going to lose it right then. He took a deep breath, and focused on her sexy head of hair right there between his thighs. He reached out and started taking out the tiny clips holding it all up out of her face, sucking in a breath when it got to the point he couldn't handle anymore.

"Baby doll," he eked out. "Come on up here, now. I can't take much more of that. I mean it. You...you shatter me...and I, I really want..." He sucked in a deep breath, unable to finish his thought as Piper continued to use her talented tongue and mouth in more and more provocative ways.

It felt too good. Instead of pushing her from him, he spread his legs further apart. And then she did something she'd never done before. She went lower and used that talented tongue and mouth on his balls. *Holy Christ, is that good.*

He must have let out a sound indicating just how he felt, because he felt her giggle. Right between his legs, he felt his cute little wife giggle at him. Well, damn. He started giggling too. His eyes might be shut, but he knew he was grinning from ear to ear, even as he flinched, trying not to come. Trying to make it last longer. Lord, Naughty Piper was hot. And so very, very naughty.

He couldn't take it anymore. Vance pulled her up off the floor and tossed her on the bed. "You're trying to kill me," he accused, crawling over her, watching her lick those naughty lips. He rolled the both of them, causing Piper to shriek. She landed on top, right where he wanted her, her chest smashed to his and her legs along both sides of his hips. "Now," he whispered, narrowing his eyes. "I'm gonna watch you untie those tempting little bows and slide yourself onto me."

Piper pressed her hands against his chest as she lifted up to a sitting position, smiling all the while, blond curls in mad disarray. "Bossy, bossy, bossy," she teased. "Are you sure you don't want me to do all that facing the other way?"

He felt his eyes go wide. *Oh, hell yes.*

He started to sweat. Wasn't sure why the idea of this was so hot, other than the fact that he was an ass man and loved looking at her ass, but it was heating the hell out of him. His prick was springing itself around like a joystick on remote control.

Piper bent toward him, kissing him senseless as she eased one knee over him. Then she sat up and turned, straddling him so that he could now admire her beautiful back and mighty fine backside. Her fingers wrote a sonnet with the act of untying one side of her dainty little panties, and then the other. His hands reached up to coast over her flesh as the material drifted away.

"Dear God, Piper," he breathed, watching as she eased down onto him, his length disappearing as the feel of her wrapped around him, the sensations spreading throughout his body, tightening his chest and the muscles along his shoulders. He tried to relax, but he was juiced. He had visions of pushing her forward, getting on his knees and taking her from behind, fast. But this gift she was giving him was too erotic to give in to his escalating desires. He was going to lay back and enjoy this—even if it killed him.

CHAPTER TWENTY-TWO

Tansy held her breath so long she began to feel her pulse pound increasingly within her temples. She couldn't believe Piper and Vance just up and left her here—practically in the wilderness—alone with...her husband, who stood there looking all dreamy and tall.

Wow, her heart sighed. She really liked how he wore his hair and the way his clothes fit his body. Those damn cowboy boots he had on were like an aphrodisiac. She felt herself lick her lips as she eyed them, her gaze traveling back up his dark blue jeans, undressing those strong, well-formed legs that had tangled her up good. Once playfully as they'd danced together after the wedding ceremony and several times less playfully that night in their honeymoon bed. She'd found the hair on his legs sexy and the hair on his chest even more so. Groomed, but so he still looked like the male of the species.

He was all male, this one. Narrow hips, trim waist, gorgeous chest, broad shoulders with a capital B. From the top of his cowboy hat which she hadn't seen much of while he'd been in Henderson to the tip of the boots he made fit in wherever he went, Crain Carraway was everything a girl could want physically. But to Tansy, he was so much more.

Because Crain treated the world like every bit of it was good. Like every person he interacted with was worthy. She'd never heard him talk behind someone's back, and she'd never heard him say a cruel or unkind word to anyone. Even when it may have been justified.

Oh, heavens, she thought. What in the world was he not saying about her?

She watched him move to the ATV she and Piper had ridden. He took the key out of the ignition and pocketed it.

Smart man.

CC Dallas, Inc. wouldn't be what it was today if the man left everything to chance. Crain was a take-control guy, but unlike Vance, he did it subtly, with a smile and a genuine concern for the people around him. His clients loved him because he saw what needed to be done, and he had a team ready to do it. He was a catalyst for progress and thought it should happen fast. He was the springboard for making deals happen and putting goals in motion. He loved building a business that supported good ideas. One that supported other people's dreams.

And right now, probably because of the half bottle of wine Tansy had drunk, her dream was to let him whisk her back to Dallas. Leaving behind a town of people who loved her but controlled her every move. All she had to do was ask, and he'd do it. She knew he would. From that look he was shooting her way, he hadn't given up on her yet. No indeed. He was still aiming to git 'r done.

The beauty queen in her relished that knowledge. The beauty queen still believed in fairy-tale endings. Tansy, on the other hand, felt a foreboding. Because she knew she didn't deserve Crain Carraway, didn't know a woman alive who did. But he was hers for the taking. If she stopped being so afraid and just told him the truth.

"Mind if I sit," he asked, pointing at the blanket she stood on.

"Crain—"

"Please," he interrupted, holding up a hand. "Just ten minutes. Just give me ten minutes with Elizabeth while nobody's lookin', so I can stop worrying that I'm going insane. So I can stop worrying that Elizabeth Langford of Dallas is nothing but a figment of my imagination. Please, darlin', have a little mercy."

Tansy had decided to tell him about her night with Pinks, but Crain wanted ten minutes with Elizabeth, and Elizabeth loved Crain, so… Elizabeth also loved the way he said *darlin'*."

"All right," she said, feeling happy for the reprieve. She sat cross-legged on the blanket, pulling her short linen skirt down as far as she could.

"All right?" he questioned.

Tansy gave him a smile, not blaming him for being suspicious. She patted the blanket beside her, resolved to give Crain ten minutes of what he needed.

"You're not going insane," she assured him as he knelt beside her. He sprawled out and laid on his side, bending his arm and cupping his head in his hand, looking at her. "I think we both know this is an issue involving my mental health," Tansy said. She gave him a small consolatory smile. "And I'm sorry I've got you knee-deep in my...stuff. I truly am. I shouldn't have run out on you, and I regret that."

"Thank God," he said as he rolled to his back and stared up at the sky. He bent his arms up at the elbows and tapped his fingertips against his chest.

"But we shouldn't have eloped either."

Crain remained silent.

She was making herself crazy with the same old argument, and it was obvious from Crain's silence he was tired of hearing it too. "Okay," she soothed. "I'll stop. I'll be Elizabeth for ten minutes."

Propping an arm under his neck, he turned his head in her direction and studied her. After a long pause he said, "So, Elizabeth, tell me about yourself."

Tansy looked into his handsome face, his somber expression so unlike what she was used to from him. "I'm from a little town in North Carolina where the people are lovely, but everybody is in your business. Which is why I left, moved to Dallas, and worked for The George W. Bush Presidential Library and Museum."

"Mm-hmm," he said, turning his face back toward the sky. "Why change your name?"

Tansy lay down beside him and settled in with her hands clasped together on top of her midsection. "Elizabeth is my given name, though no one has ever called me that. I rather like it." She sighed. "I'm named for my grandmother, who I'm quite fond of. No one calls her Elizabeth either. She's Betty."

Crain smiled up at the sky. "You're definitely not a Betty."

"No. Not a Betty. And once they read my full name off my job application and called me Elizabeth, I really liked the sound of it. I also liked the clean-slate feeling it inspired within me. So I didn't bother correcting them, and voilà—I became Elizabeth in Dallas."

"My Elizabeth," he said, taking her hand and holding it between them.

"Yes," she whispered, because suddenly lying on her back and thinking about being his Elizabeth had her all choked up. "Your Elizabeth."

"How come—" But Crain stopped himself and cleared his throat. He let a bit of silence slip into the air before he said, "You told me you went to Ole Miss. Is that true?"

Tansy turned her head and looked at him. "Everything I told you was true."

"I was convinced you were from Texas. I assumed you were from Dallas. Is that my bad or yours?"

She shook her head. "I figured a man who named his business after his hometown might be a little fanatical about the place. And everyone in Texas thinks their state is the be-all and end-all. I was not mentioning North Carolina until I had to."

"First of all," Crain said as he rolled to his side, "I named the firm CC Dallas because it's located in Dallas, not because it's my hometown."

Yeah, right. But Tansy nodded while trying to hide her smile.

"And second of all, it's not like you were gonna be any less appealing had I known you were from North Carolina."

"Hmm," she said, stifling a laugh. "Your nose is growing."

"What? It's not like I'm a separatist. It wouldn't have mattered to me that you were raised in an inferior environment," he said, starting to laugh as she leaned over and swatted at him. "People can't help where they're born."

"See," she said, rolling back flat. "I know who you are Crain Carraway."

"So you refrained from telling me you weren't from Texas because you believed me to be some sort of Texas elitist."

"That right," she sang.

"Well, what about the killer suits and those smart-girl glasses?"

She turned her head, smiling. "You like the glasses?"

He moved closer, rolling onto his stomach. Their sides touched and she felt the heat of him everywhere. "I love the glasses," he said, looking into her eyes. "I mean, in a business setting they're very sexy. They sort of mesmerized me. Had me longing to take them off of you, you know. And after I did that, I imagined pulling that pencil thing out of your hair. So, yeah, I liked the glasses. I miss the glasses."

"Hmm. Maybe I'll put them back on tomorrow."

"Judas Priest," he whispered under his breath. "Do you even need them?"

"I need them when I'm not wearing my contact lenses."

"So my question stands. Killer suits and smart-girl glasses in Dallas, but not here. Why?"

"My mother is a beautiful woman," she explained. "She won the title of Miss North Carolina and went on to compete in the Miss America Pageant back when she was twenty-one. She enjoyed being Miss North Carolina and, I swear to you, would put that crown and sash on every day if she could get away with it. People in Henderson continue to fawn over her because of that title. And she prides herself on all of it. To her, appearance is everything."

"Right. Got it."

"So, too, are the appearances of her daughters. If I've been told to pull my shoulders back and suck in my stomach once, I've been told a thousand times."

"You do have nice posture."

"Because if I don't, I will disappoint my mother, and when I disappoint my mother, she turns on the silent treatment and everyone in the house suffers. *No one* wants to disappoint my mother. Least of all me. So even though I actually see better with my glasses, my mother insists on the contact lenses. She's actually recited the rhyme, 'Boys don't make passes at girls who wear glasses' to me many times."

"I keep telling you it's time she met me. The glasses kinda slay me."

"Well, she loves the suits just as you apparently do. But here in Henderson, they're my mother's uniform, and I don't want to be my mother, so…"

"You dress like you're living on Nantucket."

She turned her face toward him. "I see you've been talking to Davis."

"The Pink One seems to know you well. Says you wear navy, white and gold. Occasionally red."

"The Pink One knows a lot about everything."

"It's true. I've tried to hire him away from E&E."

Tansy tried not to react to that. Having Pinks work for Crain was the last thing she needed. She changed the subject. "Any other questions for Elizabeth?"

"Just one. Why'd you say no three times before you said yes?"

"You mean, why didn't I go out with you the first time you asked?"

"Or the second, or the third?"

She stared at him, evaluating her answer. "This could open a can of worms."

"Okay," he said cautiously. "If it does, we'll…just…go fishin'."

"Oh, ah, okay," she hedged, wondering if this was going to affect whatever work he was doing for the next mayor. "Crain, the truth is that when I left Henderson, I was dating Brooks Bennett. And I didn't really end things with Brooks before I moved. I just sort of left. Which, in my mind—"

"Whoa, whoa, whoa," he interrupted. "You just left? As in left without a word? Like you did to me? Or you left after an adult discussion about you moving to Dallas and what that would mean to your relationship?"

She blinked. Twice.

"You did this to Brooks, too, didn't you? Oh my God," Crain exclaimed as he rose up to a sitting position. "Are you married to Brooks? Is that what this is about? Is that why Brooks looks at me like I stole his woman?"

Tansy sat up. "Of course I'm not married to Brooks."

"There is no 'of course' to it. You ran out on me, and now I'm finding out you ran out on Brooks. You're a serial runaway bride for all I know."

"I'm not. I'm really not," she defended, although she realized that the evidence was proving otherwise. "Look," she said as she moved behind Crain and started rubbing his shoulders. "Give me a minute to explain, and I think you'll understand," she said, digging her thumbs into the bottoms of his shoulder blades. "Let me back up at bit."

She felt the tension ease off his muscles just a little. But when she peered around him she noticed he was working that red ball of his with both hands.

She took a breath and willed herself to slow down, to let the explanation ease out of her, to soften her voice and talk as if she was singing a lullaby.

"When my mother," she started slowly, "the beauty queen," she pointed out, "could no longer compete in pageants, she did the next best thing. She entered her firstborn daughter into pageants."

"You?"

"Yes, me. Now, I was eager at first, because I liked the attention she was giving me, and I wanted to please her, and I liked the fancy little dresses. But after competing in two pageants, I sort of became neutral to the whole thing. I didn't not like them, I just didn't particularly like them. I didn't mind going to dance class, but thought I might like to try gymnastics instead. Of course, my mother pointed out how tall I was compared to the other girls and strongly suggested that dancing was a better choice for a talent. I wasn't necessarily thinking about a talent. I was just thinking about what I liked."

Tansy's hands started working up and down Crain's neck. He leaned his head forward, his thumb and his index finger slowly rotating the ball in one hand.

"Ever since I was in third grade, I was encouraged to read the newspaper at the breakfast table every morning, and my father was encouraged to quiz me on the week's current events every Friday night at dinner. I didn't mind reading about current events, or being quizzed by my father, but I was more interested in the style section, the advice columns, and of course, the funnies. My mother said reading the rest of the paper was fine, as long as I did it on my own time after I finished all my homework."

Tansy smiled to herself as she ran her fingers up Crain's scalp. She really did like his hair.

"On your own time?" Crain asked.

"Yes," she laughed. "As if I was on the clock from breakfast to dinner. I'm telling you. Being me is a full-time job. It always has been."

"Go on."

"So, that was my life. My mother wanted me to participate in pageants, I participated. She wanted me to take dance, I danced. I did what she wanted me to do, and eventually I stopped considering what I might want to do. I stopped even having an idea about what I wanted to do."

Tansy scraped her fingernails gently through Crain's thick hair.

The red ball dropped from his fingertips.

"I went to Ole Miss because my mother went to Ole Miss. Now, I loved it—but I never gave myself a choice. I never looked at another school because she wanted me to attend her alma mater."

Her hands drifted back to his neck. "My whole life has been lovely. It's just been my mother's shade of lovely. Even my relationship with Brooks. His parents and my parents really liked the idea of the two of us together. So we went out. And then the whole town really liked the idea of Brooks and me together, because he's the Golden Boy and I was Miss North Carolina's daughter, and didn't we make a handsome couple? And I just went along with it because Brooks is Brooks, and what woman in her right mind would object to Brooks? I mean, aside from Vance being his best friend, he's pretty perfect. At least my mother thought so."

Her hands drifted down Crain's back, massaging as they went.

"I had been lulled into this life that was going along pretty well, except it had nothing to do with me. And it took realizing that Brooks was getting ready to propose to snap me out of it. I didn't know if I wanted to be Brooks Bennett's wife. I didn't have a clue about what I wanted at all. I figured getting out of town, away from my parents, away from the rest of the well-meaning people who all thought they knew what I wanted, was the only way to figure things out.

"I couldn't risk talking to Brooks and having him talk me out of it. So I took the easy way out. And when I got to Dallas and my employer started calling me Elizabeth, I figured that was perfect. I decided I liked that name a whole lot better anyway, and no one was around to tell me I didn't.

"And then I found out I liked steak over chicken. Glasses over contacts. The exact same designer suits as my mother, which is actually weird, but they fit well, so whatever. And big, happy business tycoons over local sports stars with mayoral aspirations."

"Hey. I happen to be a local sports star too, ya know."

She leaned over and kissed his cheek. "You have Brooks beat by two sports."

"Damn right."

"So if you want to know why I didn't jump at the chance to go out with the CC of CC Dallas the first chance I got...it was because you caught me off guard. I didn't move to Dallas to find love. I left here to find myself. But once you asked me out, I felt sort of obligated to Brooks. Nothing between us had been settled, which was my fault. But the thought of coming home and dealing with Brooks and my mother and the fallout from the breakup...I liked being Elizabeth too much. And I liked Dallas. And all that was still too fragile to chance having it messed up by flying back to Henderson even for a weekend. So I just let you wear me down."

"Huh," he grunted. "Took me a damn month."

"I found your persistence endearing."

"Endearing?"

"Endearing at first. Then I found it rather sexy."

"Sexy?"

She leaned over his shoulder and whispered against his ear. "It got to the point you couldn't take your eyes off me when I was in your office. I swear to God it was like foreplay."

"No wonder you put your hand on my thigh during dinner."

"I needed to make it clear."

"You needed to make what clear?"

"That I was interested."

Silence.

"Elizabeth?"

"Yes?"

"Are you interested now?"

CHAPTER TWENTY-THREE

Vance came out of the bathroom drying his hair after a brisk shower, only to find his precious wife curled up in bed, sound asleep. Sex usually jacked Piper up, but she'd been collapsing into a nap every afternoon since she'd been released from the hospital. Something about fatigue during the first trimester the doctor had told him. Genevra suffered with it too, and lately dinner preparations had once again fallen to his grandmother. Maybe it was time for him and his father to hire a chef. At least for the evening meals. With the ever-expanding population at the Evans Estate, it wasn't cool to expect his grandmother, or their wives, to provide for everyone. Tonight, he'd see what he could do to help out in the kitchen. Tomorrow, he'd look into a chef. Or put Pinks on it.

Speaking of, he went and knocked on The Ninja's door.

"Come in."

Vance opened the door, stuck his head in and caught Pinks pulling on a turquoise polo shirt over a pair of loose jeans. "Hey."

"What's up?" Pinks said. "The meeting with the surveyors at the old Myers farm went well. At first glance, they didn't see anything overtly problematic with the property."

"Carraway's right. It's the best spot for the Academy. I just wish it were a little closer to the center of town. But giving ourselves room to grow is the right move."

"We'll know more when they're done."

"Right. Thanks for taking care of that. Okay, so—just giving you a heads up." Vance pointed with his thumb down the hall. "Piper and I will be down the hall for a couple weeks in the blue room. I'm giving Carraway the pool house."

Pinks' jaw dropped, his eyes bugged out, and he gasped in exasperation. "Carraway gets the pool house?"

"Carraway needs the pool house."

"That's crap. I need the pool house."

"Carraway needs the pool house to entertain his estranged wife."

Pinks turned toward his dresser, pushed in the drawer and grumbled, "I wouldn't mind entertaining his estranged wife in the pool house."

Vance lowered his voice and implored Pinks with an urgent whisper. "You're done with Tansy. You know that, right?" he said, coming all the way into the room and closing the door. "Under no circumstances can you have Tansy."

"I know, I know," Pinks said, his face all pinched up like he was in excruciating pain. "I know I can't have Tansy."

"You don't even *want* Tansy," Vance told him, thoroughly disgusted. "Tansy is old…tall…hideous even, and you're half her damn age. What you do need is to get out more. You need to head to Raleigh and blow off some steam. Pick up a few girls your own age, for Christ's sake."

Grunt.

"Seriously, man. You're twenty-three. You've got a whole lot of cute little fannies to back into walls before you even think about getting stuck on any of them." Vance stared hard at Pinks, trying to figure him out. "I don't get it. I really don't. You, Crain, even Brooks a while back, all tied up in knots over Tansy Langford. I do not see what all the fuss is about."

"Well, you're the only man around here who doesn't. She's got a tongue on her for sure, but she's also beautiful, savvy, and competent. And if you *ever* tell her I said that, I will kick your ass."

"I couldn't get those words across my lips if I tried. But I have to admit, the woman's definitely become more appealing. Now when I look at Tansy, I see a big, fancy stadium, a plush, new dormitory, and a bunch of state-of-the-art classrooms that we don't have to raise funds for. And you will not be messin' that up, ya hear?"

"I hear," Pinks said. "And if you say it one more time, I'm going to toss your lazy ass in your own damn pool. I know the stakes, and I'm dealing with it, all right?"

"All right. Just so we're clear. Come on. Piper's out cold. Let's round up Dad and see what we can scramble up for dinner."

They found Hale in his study behind his desk. "What's up?" he asked as Pinks followed Vance into the room.

"Might need to hire a chef," Vance said.

Hale looked around his son. "Davis, you seem to be able to do everything else around here. You want the job?"

Without missing a beat, Pinks responded, "What's it pay?"

"Pinks the Wonder Ninja is doing enough," Vance interjected. "In fact, Pinks the Wonder Ninja needs a weekend off so he can go get laid."

"Jesus!" Pinks said.

Hale just smiled and continued to clean up his desk. "How are you dealing with all this, Davis?"

"Doing fine, sir. Happy to help where I can."

Hale looked up. "I mean about Miss Langford's unlikely marriage."

"Ah…"

Vance patted him on the back. "He thinks Tansy and Crain are a match made in heaven."

Hale's gaze shot between his son and Pinks. "Since when?"

"Man, is it that obvious?" Pinks sighed, sounding a bit mortified.

"It's not obvious unless you're a fifty-year-old watching the dynamics of the next generation playing out at your conference table. Have I mentioned how much fun I'm having working with you all?"

"Oh, God," Davis said.

"Miss Langford's a good-looking woman," Hale told Pinks appreciatively. "I can't blame you a bit."

"Listen," Vance said, stepping in between Pinks and his father. "Miss Langford is a pristine, state-of-the-art, very, very expensive stadium that is going to be the draw for turning Henderson into the Sports Capital of North Carolina. That is what she is to you, and you, and me," he declared, pointing at all of them. "So I suggest Romeo and his fan club start putting their heads together and figure out a way to get Tansy to fall in love with the man from Dallas all over again. Because without Crain, we've got nothing."

"We've still got a good idea," Pinks protested. But when Vance turned to get in his face, he held up his hand and said, "I know. I know. I'm on board. Let's…git 'r done."

"Wine," Hale said, "and candlelight. Let's force the issue by having a mandatory business meeting with all E&E employees over dinner tonight. We'll pull out some of our best bottles and see if we can't set the mood."

"I can grill steaks," Vance said.

"And I can throw potatoes in the oven," Pinks added.

"And I bet I can manage a salad," Hale said, picking up his phone. "I'll text everybody so it sounds like official business."

CHAPTER TWENTY-FOUR

"Elizabeth?"

"Yes?"

"Are you interested now?"

Crain reached up and captured her hand as it rested on his shoulder. He turned it and pulled it forward so he could kiss the inside of her palm. Her other hand drifted into his hair, and he closed his eyes, relishing the feel of her fingertips gently stroking his scalp. The world always eased up when Elizabeth touched him.

She wasn't answering his question with words, but he could feel it in her touch. He'd seen it in her smile. Had heard it in her laugh. It was fine she wasn't talkin'. Hadn't he declared he was done talkin'?

"Come here," he whispered, compelled to kiss the very lips that drove him insane. Maybe he was a little surprised she complied, leaning over his shoulder, angling her head just right so their lips could meet. It had been so hard to get her to do anything he requested in the last day and a half—hell, the last four months—but this seemed simple. One girl, one boy, all alone as the afternoon eased into evening. In a grassy spot, hidden from the rest of the world by Carolina pine trees, on a really exceptional Indian summer day in September.

He shifted his body, his hands stroking through her hair and capturing her face as he enjoyed their kiss and the way it made him feel. He wasn't trying to seduce her, he was simply enjoying the first quiet moment he had with his wife. The thought had him pulling back and opening his eyes.

"You're my wife," he said calmly. "That wasn't a game we played in Vegas. We said the vows, we promised to love and honor one another."

Elizabeth slid her tongue over those beautiful lips. "I haven't lived up to my part," she whispered.

"You've dug us a hole, but I'm wagering we'll find a way to climb ourselves out."

A grin popped through her serious countenance before her gaze dropped toward the ground.

"What?" he asked.

"Your Texas vernacular." She looked back at him, stroked her fingers over his cheek. "I do love it," she said, laughter in her eyes.

He closed his eyes for a moment, loving having her this close. Gathering his courage, he asked cautiously, "And what about the rest of me?"

She leaned in and kissed him again. "Elizabeth loves Crain," she said against his lips. "Don't doubt that. But Tansy…"

"Let's keep Tansy out of this a little while longer," he said, pushing her down onto the blanket, their lips still connected. "I'm sure her baggage is all fine matching pieces," he said as he stretched out beside her, his chest lying across hers, his weight propped up just a bit by his elbows on either side, "but she's got a ton of it."

"Fair enough," she said, letting him get lost in her lips.

This was probably a mistake, his mind grunted, as his body made moves like it was on autopilot. His willy was headed toward hard and long, and his hands itched to cop a good feel. Her lips felt too good underneath his, and when he slipped his tongue in her mouth, things started getting hot all over. Yeah, making love right now might not be the smartest thing the two of them could do, he thought as he pushed her tiny, little cardigan down her arms, but it sure beat the hell out of another circular conversation.

When there was only a sexy little cotton tank top and bra between him and those killer tits, he started kissing his way down her throat. Maybe gettin' her pregnant was the answer. It would pretty much guarantee him an introduction as her husband somewhere within the next nine months. His hand snuck underneath the end of her top, touching all that gloriously soft skin of her belly. His body scrambled down so he could put his mouth on her belly button, both hands now working their way up, shoving her tiny shirt all the way up and over her head. Then he looked his fill, feasting his eyes on a treasure he'd about given up on ever unearthing again.

"God, you're beautiful," he said to her chest.

"I like that you think so," she said softly, her hand coming up to caress his face.

He turned his head and bit at her fingertips at the same time he used his right hand to pull the cup of her bra down, exposing one full breast. His hand was on her in a flash, molding and rubbing. He moaned at the feel of his woman, the delicacy of her skin, the plump pliability, the sounds that she made at skin-to-skin contact.

His mouth dropped onto her flesh, his tongue following his fingertips, leading him right to the protruding tip of her breast. When he latched on and sucked, both of them felt the vibrations of lust course through their bodies. Elizabeth's pelvis bucked, and Crain threw a leg over, snuggling it in between the two of hers, He purposely laid his thigh heavy, right up against the juncture of her thighs, and shimmied that tiny skirt of hers up and out of the way, so his pants were flat against her panties. He moved enough to get her going, sucked enough to satisfy his own eager longings for the moment. Wondered in the back of his mind, how far she was going to let this go?

And then he remembered. They were married. And whether anybody else knew it or not, this wasn't anything that needed to stop.

Unless Tansy got in their way.

He reached behind her and unhooked her bra, sliding it down her outstretched arms.

Whomever he had underneath him now was definitely standing in line for the rodeo he was selling. He just needed to make sure she bought a ticket. He started pulling at his shirt, and even though it was all buttoned up, with her help he somehow managed to pull it over his head. Without wasting too much time, he settled himself, chest against chest, letting the world melt away, everything gone except the feel of her beneath him.

He kissed her long and hard, eagerly and seductively. He stroked her wherever his hand could feel naked flesh, and he kept moving against her, stimulating her need.

When his need reached a level that could no longer be toyed with, he rolled onto his back, desperate to be out of his pants. He was struggling with the belt buckle when his phone went off, playing the Aggie War Hymn for a ringtone. He pulled the damn thing out of his front pocket, hit the decline button and threw it to the side, looking back down at his waist, his hands working swiftly trying to free himself of his pants.

Elizabeth rolled into him, kissing his face while he couldn't get the cursed button of his jeans undone. Finally, it came lose as he reached for her lips, straining his neck while kissing her, sucking her tongue into his mouth as he unzipped his fly. He pulled her on top of him, skimpy skirt all bunched up around her waist, his pants open but still in place. She spread her legs to either side of his hips, and he jackknifed up to a sitting position, using one hand behind him to add leverage as he ground his erection against her.

Her breath caught. He squeezed his eyes shut and did it again. His bare chest against hers. Her arms around his neck. Her tongue in his mouth. One arm around her waist pulling her in tight. And he was about to lose it.

He had the urge to call her every dirty name he could think of, because she was making him lose all control. He ground against her again, grunting. She completely shifted, sliding herself against his torso, against his pelvis, so that when he rocked again, she came, her mouth pressed open against his. Her breath caught, an eek of sound escaped, and then she shuddered, and moved, and moaned against him—all over him. He just went with it, rode it out, and when the Aggie War Hymn started up again, he let it come and come hard.

Truth be told, the War Hymn just made it that much better.

And it reminded him of something. Something he'd have to put some thought to later.

Right now—right now, he just wanted to enjoy this. This mess he'd made of himself, his woman limp in his arms.

He'd get to the other mess eventually. The one they'd gotten themselves into with their folks and he'd deal with it.

They both would.

But for the moment, he took his time, gently caressing the voluptuous beauty in his arms, grateful that after four months he'd finally found her, sending up a prayer to the man upstairs that they'd find a way to make this impromptu marriage of theirs work. 'Cause the good Lord knew he needed Elizabeth in his life. From the first time she'd reached out and touched his hand during an office meeting, immediately easing his jumpy nature, he knew his life would go a whole lot easier if she was by his side.

He kissed her temple, thinking he hadn't exactly imagined the lengths he'd have to go to secure their future, but as he held her now, he still felt as certain as he did when the thought first struck him. Elizabeth Langford was the one for him.

When he felt like moving again, he rolled Tansy onto her back, pulled out a bandana from his back pocket, and did his best to clean himself up before zipping up his britches. Then, leaning over Elizabeth's soft, sweet body, he kissed her lips briefly as he reached for his phone lying at the edge of the blanket.

His momma. Of course it was.

Not a good time to be bringing that up if that was what had scared Elizabeth off in the first place. He'd call her back. Later. A text came in and Crain read it.

"You got your phone with you?"

"No," she said. "I left it in the kitchen, in my purse."

"Looks like E&E is having a business dinner tonight up by the pool. All hands on deck it says, including me."

Elizabeth shook her head and began to sit up. "I doubt they mean me. I'm not included in much."

"Well, why is that? A woman with your abilities should be running the damn show."

That made her smile. At least he could do that. Make her smile. And watching her get dressed was definitely making him smile. The woman knew how to wear lingerie.

"They're going to need me more and more as the business gets going," she said, fastening that sexy bra behind her back. "And as Brooks' campaign heats up," she said, pulling her tank top over her head and settling it into place. When she pulled her hair out and fluffed it up, all streaky blond, ends curly and falling well past her shoulders, he remembered how beautiful she looked the night they got hitched.

But if he'd learned anything this afternoon, it was that beating that horse was not getting him where he wanted to go—so he switched tactics.

"How 'bout you work for me?"

"Work for you?" She stopped pulling on her itty-bitty cardigan and looked at him like he was crazy.

"Sure. It's not like I can stick around Henderson forever. If I go into business with E&E and this town on the sports academy, I'll need someone here working on my behalf when I'm in Dallas. You can be my man in Henderson."

"Your *man* in Henderson?"

"Sure," he said, like it was the best idea ever—knowing damn well it was not what she was expecting after their erotic little skin-on-skin interlude. And if he was any kind of a judge, by the look on her face, she was not appreciating his big idea.

Well, good then. Maybe he'd make some headway coming at her from another direction.

"What do you say?" he went on as if encouraged by the idea. "I'll find office space in town; hang a shingle outside just like Evans & Evans. I think CC Henderson has a nice ring to it, don't you?"

"CC Henderson," she said, deadpan.

"Ah-huh. Maybe it's time I take my business national."

"And you're going to start by expanding to the booming metropolis of Henderson, North Carolina?"

"Why not?"

"Why not? You know why not." She stood and straightened her skirt looking around for her shoes.

"You don't think it's a good idea?" he asked as he stood and began putting himself back together.

"You know, I don't think you setting foot in Henderson is a good idea, much less starting up a business here."

"Who am I talking to?"

"What?"

"Who am I talking to right now? Who doesn't think CC Henderson is a good idea? Elizabeth or Tansy?"

"I am one and the same."

"No. Not really."

She started to say something. Opened her mouth real wide, too. Then just snapped it shut. He pulled his shirt over his head as she let out a big sigh.

"It's okay, darlin'," he said. "I'm seriously hooked on my sweet Elizabeth, but I might be starting to dig on Tansy the badass too, so…"

"So?" The green in her eyes shot out a challenge.

He liked a challenge.

Stepping forward, he grabbed her around the middle with both hands, pulling her tight against him. "So, when I'm in town," he said low and quiet, looking down at her upturned face, "count on me keeping my bride sexually satisfied. And at the same time, trust that I'll be romancing the shit out of her alter-ego, Tansy."

She blinked a couple times. "I'm not sure how I feel about that."

"Really?" he said, taking a step back and smiling. "'Cause I'm kinda lookin' forward to it. Like datin' two women at the same time. Which I've never done, by the way. Not my style. But this. Best of all worlds. It'll be like cheatin'—legally. I can romance Tansy out in the open for all of Henderson to see, while my wife and I sneak around having back-alley sex. A little crazy, but I'm up for it. That is, unless I can convince you to do this the easy way and simply admit to your folks and the rest of Henderson that we're already hitched.

"The easy way would be if you'd sign the papers."

"I'm not signing any papers."

"Why not?"

"Because it's the only damn hold I have on you," he scowled. "Now, I can see my ten minutes with Elizabeth is up, so how 'bout you set Tansy's ass on the seat of that machine and let's go see about this dinner."

"When did you become so bossy?"

"Oh, Sweetheart, that's not bossy? *This*," he said, twirling her around, picking her up, and throwing her over his shoulder before stalking toward the ATV, "is bossy."

"Aa—" The air whooshed out of Tansy's lungs as her diaphragm landed on Crain's shoulder. And as she tried to sputter out words and wiggle off, he landed a gentle swat to her sweet, little backside and told her to settle.

He brought her down and placed said backside into the seat of the ATV. Then he leaned in, kissed her lips, and whispered, "Sit here and be still," before he headed back to collect the blanket, his rubber ball, and the empty wine bottle they'd left behind.

Sit here and be still. The same words his momma issued time after time while he was growing up. Man, his momma might just get a kick out of what his bride was putting him through right now. Might even suggest he deserved it after he'd been such a handful to raise.

Lord, his momma.

Maybe Elizabeth was right. Having one momma worked up at a time was proving more than he could handle. He needed to settle his own momma down before he started working on Miss North Carolina.

"Okay," he said as he straddled the seat behind Elizabeth and turned the key in the ignition. She grabbed the handlebars and he was content to let her do the driving as long as he could wrap his arms around her and cop a feel as she drove.

"Okay, what?" she asked before they took off.

"Okay. We'll do it your way a little while longer."

"So you'll sign the papers?"

"No. But I'm willing to keep our marriage from your parents for the time being."

She turned and searched his face.

"A short reprieve," he warned. "Now start driving before I change my mind."

CHAPTER TWENTY-FIVE

Tansy was all hot and bothered by the time she pulled the ATV into the shed. Somehow, Crain had managed to slide himself underneath her, leaving her bottom to bounce about on top of his lap. Whether intentionally or due to all of the bumping around on the ride back up to the Evans mansion, Crain's hands and growing erection had managed to put her back in the mood. Big time.

She turned off the ignition and sat there in the quiet. Not moving. Sitting on top of what felt like a smoldering powder keg. Wondering how they could get it done in this unventilated shed without looking like they'd taken a sauna when they eventually emerged.

Wondering when she'd started thinking of sex in terms like "getting it done." Tansy sighed. That was not her. And it definitely wasn't Elizabeth.

Of course, she'd never pretended not to be married before. Or to be two people at the same time. If she hadn't run out on him in Las Vegas, she and Crain would've probably had a nice, long honeymoon period and then settled into sex with a reasonable amount of time in between. At least more than fifteen minutes.

When she felt him lean down and suck on her neck, she nearly came undone.

"Apparently I have an all-access pass to the pool house," he whispered against her skin.

At least the two of them were on the same page on this subject, Tansy thought. Only…"I'm not setting foot in that pool house."

"Why not?" he whispered as he kissed his way up toward her ear.

"Because it's Vance's pool house. And until Piper showed up, Vance Evans was a dog with a capital D. There's probably a revolving back door, and some sort of version of the red room of pain behind that tame pool house exterior."

"Perfect. Because you deserve a good, sound spanking for what you've put me through."

"Mmm," she hummed as his hands landed on the bare flesh under her tank top. "And yet you remain undaunted."

"True that," he coaxed, ever so lightly caressing her breasts, causing her nipples to peak. "As long as your body keeps responding in ways that twist me up, I'm gonna keep comin' and comin' hard."

"Figuratively or literally?" she said on a sigh as she leaned her head back to rest against his shoulder.

"Both. Damn straight on both."

He wrapped her up firm and secure in his arms, squeezing her around the middle and back against his chest, conveying more than simple sexual desire. It felt like an endearment. And as much as it made her heart leap, it also sank a proportionate amount too.

Her emotions bounced around inside her chest. Everything from elation to dread. She should have told him about Pinks back there on the blanket when she had a chance. While the two of them were alone, away from the rest of the world. The thought caused her to go real still. Get real quiet.

Finally she whispered. "Maybe we should go see about this dinner situation."

She felt Crain relax his hold, his arms unwinding from her midsection, his fingers trailing over her body before securing her at the waist and helping her move off the ATV. She stood in the center of the shed, her feet rooted to the ground. She either had to tell him now and let the chips fall where they may, or she needed to keep this from him forever and deal with the guilt on her own. Find a way to forgive herself.

She felt him come up behind her. Quiet. He stood behind her a moment, then kissed the top of her head. "I'm sorry this isn't easier on you," he said as if reading her mind.

"I shouldn't have run off," she whispered into the quiet. "I wished I'd stayed."

"Well, there's something."

It came out happy. Like Crain himself. She couldn't make herself turn to see it, but she imagined he had that cute grin on his face. How could she possibly tell him the truth about what she'd done and risk never hearing that smile in his voice again?

She turned abruptly into his arms and hugged him tight, burying her head against his chest.

"I'm sorry," she whispered, guilt shredding her insides.

"Aw, Sweetheart. You got cold feet," he said, pulling her off him and looking her in the eye.

Yeah, there was that cute, little smirk.

He plucked a kiss off her lips, turned her around and gently swatted her derrière as he pushed her toward the door. "I get it. I do. Calling my momma and everybody else all on my own was a bonehead move. We should have made a plan to tell the world together. I just…well, you know me. I got fidgety and couldn't sleep because I was so excited. Truly darlin', my enthusiasm got the better of me," he explained as they stepped into the evening air and headed up the steps toward the pool. He took her hand in his. "Tell me you'll give me a chance to work this out for us. 'Cause you know there's just something between us worth making a big fuss over."

What had Piper called it? Crain's big aww-shucks Texas swagger? Whatever it was, Tansy thought, looking up into his handsome, over-the-top, way-too-happy face, she was hooked. Hooked and reeled in, and now she just needed to stop flopping around the boat and accept the inevitable. She was done for.

In that moment, Elizabeth Tansy Langford made her decision. She wasn't going to tell Crain about her night with Pinks. Ever. He didn't deserve the potential pain it would cause. She wasn't willing to hurt him just so she could have a guilt-free conscious. No. She'd suck it up, put her big girl panties on, and let this big, happy Texan be just that.

Still. If she could get him to sign the annulment papers somehow, she wouldn't feel so guilty about the Pinks incident for the rest of her life or worry that this top-secret marriage of theirs was doomed.

"I'll tell you what," she said, throwing out her own little come-and-get-me grin. "You tell me you'll reconsider signing those annulment papers, and I will reconsider stepping into Vance's den of iniquity."

They'd just about reached the kitchen door when Crain pulled her into his arms asking, "Sweetheart, why are you so dang set on erasing one of my best days ever?" He kissed her then, intently, purring over her lips. "I mean, I wouldn't mind another wedding night as soon as you're willing to give me one," he said, squeezing her backside with one strong hand, "but I see no good reason to set you free now that I've got my hands on you again." He leaned in and kissed her neck, causing her to squirm and squeal over the tickling it caused.

Vance burst through those beautiful French doors holding a large platter of steaks. "You two do understand the concept of windows, right?" He pointed back through the doors.

Still all clinched in one another's arms, Tansy and Crain turned their heads to find Emelina, Hale, and Davis watching them with undisguised interest.

"Ooops. I do believe our cover is blown," Crain said without a drop of remorse as he released Tansy from his hold and followed Vance. "Whatcha doin' with those sirloins there, Slick?" he hollered. "Might want to rub those bad boys down with some salt, pepper, and spices. Perhaps a little…"

Tansy stumbled to find her footing after being released so abruptly. Hale helped her stabilize herself saying, "Sounds like a barbecue war is about to commence. Last night there was a lively discussion over Southern BBQ versus Texas BBQ."

"You should have heard the man wax poetic over brisket and jalapeño sausage," Emelina added, following Hale out the door. She leaned in toward Tansy's ear confessing, "That big cowboy gets so riled up he starts flexing his muscles without even knowing. A sight I do not want to miss," she said before she took off after Hale.

Tansy looked across the pool to where Vance and Crain came to stand at the built-in grill, indeed in heated discussion.

She sighed at the thought that her self-proclaimed husband had literally just dropped her to run after a few pieces of meat. "I don't know what I'm so worried about," she mumbled to herself, brushing at her skirt and turning to head indoors. "Trying to spare his feelings while he's more interested in a good steak."

Her head came up abruptly as she stepped through the French doors, remembering there'd been one other person in the room.

Yeah. Pinks.

There he stood, young and handsome, arms folded over his chest, staring her down like she had some 'splaining to do.

"Just when I think this cannot get any more awkward…" he started.

"I know it. I know. Look, I'll just get my handbag and go. Don't let me ruin your…steak," she said sarcastically with a shake of her head.

In her peripheral vision, she saw his arms release. Then she heard Pinks sigh as she moved across the kitchen.

"What do you mean go? You can't go," he said doggedly. "There's a…you know…meeting. Mandatory meeting. Called by Hale. So, you know…you kinda have to be here."

"I do?"

"Yeah. Ya do. Don't let me scare you off. I'm…I'm gonna figure out a way to get used to this."

"I'm required at the meeting?"

"Of course you are. Why wouldn't you be?"

"Because I'm the office manager. Not a member of the boys' club."

"Stop it. You know you're on the team. And with things like that list of businesses you're coming up with for us to work on drawing to Henderson, you're becoming more and more essential."

That brought her up short and she turned to face Pinks fully. She mimicked his original pose by crossing her arms over her chest and eyeing him up and down. "Exactly what are you trying to pull?" she asked.

"Pull?" Pinks feigned that he was taken aback by her accusation. It was such complete bullshit acting that she cut him off before he had a chance to perjure himself further.

"Yes, pull. With the 'becoming more and more essential' crap. You may not be trying to get in my pants, but you're trying to pull something off here, and we both know it. So, spill."

"I have no idea what you're talking about," he said, holding up his hands and backing away.

"You don't think I'm essential. You think you could do my job in addition to yours with one hand tied behind your back."

"I never said that." He pointed his finger at her, coming back on the offensive.

"Maybe not in those exact words, but you've said it in one form or another every day since we've met."

"Because you're a pain in the ass," he shouted, stalking forward and getting in her face. "If I said the sky was blue, you'd argue it was more of an indigo-grey splattered with streaks of linen. You're always trying to one-up me. And why the hell is that? Huh? I'll tell you why it is. I'm the one person in this whole damn town whom you don't feel the need to please. So while you smile and pose and 'yes, ma'am' and 'yes, sir' everybody else around here, with me you're a bossy, mean pit bull that takes a bite out of my ass every time she can."

"You are so wrong," she said as they stood toe-to-toe.

"I am dead-on right," he scowled.

"No, you're not," she said lightly. "I don't feel the need to please Vance either."

She started to turn away, but he grabbed her arm, holding her in place. "Maybe before he started signing your paychecks, but not now. Now you're all 'yes, sir' with Vance too."

She wanted to deny it. Tell him the sky was indeed an indigo-grey or whatever he said. But she couldn't think of a comeback because…*she sighed*…because it was true. Too true.

"I'm sorry," Davis said, dropping her arm.

"Sorry?" That had her head snapping up in surprise.

"I did not mean to go all Incredible Hulk on you. Whether I think you're essential to the team or not, Hale's called an all-hands-on-deck E&E meeting over dinner tonight. He wants you to be here."

She waved him off, heading over to pick up her handbag. "Make my excuses. I'm sure you'll fill me in tomorrow and as you said…it will just make things more awkward if I stay. I'm not essential. I know I'm not."

"Tansy. Stop and think about this a minute. You're the only employee who doesn't reside here at the moment. If Hale didn't want you here, he wouldn't have had to call a meeting. The rest of us were going to be eating together anyway. I think you should stay."

She stopped to consider that. Then she glanced out the window, making sure she and Pinks were still alone. She looked back at Pinks, mentally sighing over what a nice kid he was, and vacillated a moment before she dove in.

"I'm not going to tell Crain about the two of us," she stated.

There. She said it.

Pinks stepped in closer, his brows furrowed. "Why the hell would you even consider telling him about us? You can't tell him about us."

That was not the reaction she anticipated.

"That would be suicide," Pinks went on. "If not for you, then for me. For Henderson. CC Dallas would not take that well at all. No. No, you can never tell Crain Carraway about the two of us."

"Well, if I did, he could hardly blame *you*, now could he? You didn't even know about him at the time. And what do you mean it would be suicide for Henderson?"

"He's a man, with an ego, and a business Henderson and E&E need right now. You cannot make me responsible for busting that up. You don't want to own up to marrying the guy, that's your decision. But either way, you've got to keep me out of it. He can never know. It would ruin everything."

"I'm not sure it would ruin everything," she said dramatically. "It may ruin my personal relationship with him. But he's got integrity. He wouldn't let that stand in the way of whatever he's doing with E&E."

"Tansy. I am begging you to trust me on this one thing," Davis pleaded. "Absolutely no good can come from Crain finding out about us."

"What did I miss?" Piper said as she entered the kitchen looking all bright and refreshed.

"Hopefully a very, very awkward situation," Pinks said as he eyed Tansy. Then he turned his Super-Hero-In-Training smile on Piper. "How 'bout an alcohol-free cocktail before dinner, Mrs. Evans?"

CHAPTER TWENTY-SIX

After Crain wrestled Vance into adding chili powder and paprika along with a pinch of brown sugar to his regular steak seasoning, he asked Hale if Elizabeth was included in the dinner meeting. Hale and Vance looked at one another before answering. Emelina spoke up and with her lovely Spanish accent and said, "Dear Boy, is it not obvious? We're serving red meat for virility, and my son's best wines have been decanted to literally sway Miss Langford into your arms. I trust any Texan worth his salt could drag her from the table into the pool house. The rest we leave up to you." She patted his behind suggestively.

Crain turned an eye toward Vance. "You've pulled your gorgeous granny in on this covert mission?"

"Gorgeous Granny lives for this stuff," Vance said with a sly smile toward his grandmother. "Plus, there's a lot at stake." He got serious as he prodded the raw meat with a fork. "You want Tansy, and I want that stadium full of bells and whistles. The dormitory and learning center too. Now, if wine and candlelight doesn't have the desired effect, our next move is to drug you both and toss the two of you into Tansy's bed back at her parents'."

"You wouldn't."

"Hey, the stakes are high. I aim to get this job done one way or another."

Crain cleared his throat and stepped in closer to Vance, Hale, and Emelina. "I think it's important to keep the specific details of my little incentive program to ourselves. As much as I appreciate the help in getting Elizabeth—I mean, Tansy—to accept our marriage, I'm sure she wouldn't appreciate me putting a price on her head in order to have that happen. Nor will she appreciate the fact that y'all are selling her out for brick and mortar even if it comes in the shape of a fancy new stadium."

"We understand," Hale said in all seriousness. "Take it from two men who were willing to misfile old police records to protect my bride's past from becoming fodder for the Henderson gossips. If the Evans family tries to be anything at all, it tries to be discreet."

"Bah! Like bulls in a china shop, these two," Emelina said. "They don't know the meaning of the word discreet, as I'm sure you're finding. But both of them do understand money." She nodded to her son and grandson. "For which I am grateful. And they want to see a whole lot of yours invested in Henderson. So I believe your secret is safe, Mr. Carraway. At least with the three of us."

"Pinks has been lectured," Vance assured Crain, "and Brooks won't mention it to anyone. Especially Lolly. Certainly no good could come from that.

"Genevra and Piper don't know the specifics, they're just enamored with all your Texas…" he waved a hand up and down Crain, "brawniness and have been the crux of big scandals themselves, so they're willing to help us—ah, you—get Tansy back. Truth be told, it's rather a fine team you've managed to gather on your side in the matter of two short days."

"I have no complaints," Crain said, twisting the grill fork out of Vance's hand. "I like mine rare, if you don't mind," he said, flipping the largest steak on the grill and then handing the long utensil back. He turned and winked at Emelina. "And in return, I'm offering this gorgeous granny of yours my Texas help in the kitchen.

They entered to find an irritatingly young and handsome Pinks sitting between Piper and Tansy at the counter. Crain grunted at the sight of both women mooning over The Pink One as he shared a very animated tale about some ninja competition or fraternity party brawl. Crain figured there wasn't much of a difference one way or another.

"You're like a damn fox in a hen house, aren'tcha there, Pinks?" Crain boomed as he came on the scene.

"Jealous?" Pinks smiled.

"Little bit. Maybe," Crain conceded, eyeing Elizabeth, noticing the fancy looking drinks in front of all of them. "From where I stand, it looks like you think you're living in a co-ed dormitory back in college."

"Oh, we hope we're having that much fun," Genevra said, entering the kitchen. "I never had the chance to go to college because I was pregnant with Lolly, so I enjoy all the young people coming in and hanging out." She looked over at Crain with a delightful amount of curiosity. "Did you know there is actually a shot called a Blow Job?"

Crain wasn't sure he heard the woman right. "Excuse me?" he said squinting.

Genevra clasped a hand over her mouth, eyeing all the startled looks in the kitchen. "Forgive me," she whispered through her fingers. "Clearly over the summer I've grown immune to Pinks and The Outlaw's attempts to make me blush. Now I'm making our guest from Texas uncomfortable. And, oh my, Tansy, please don't go and repeat what I just said to your mother."

Tansy looked at Crain and laughed, promising she wouldn't ever repeat anything that happened at the Evans mansion to her mother if Genevra could do one thing.

"What's that?" Genevra asked.

"Tell me exactly what a blow job is."

Complete…silence.

It started with a snicker from Pinks, and then everybody burst out laughing.

"I mean," Tansy clarified through her mirth, "what are the actual ingredients in the shot named Blow Job."

"Oh, way too easy," Genevra retorted. "I'm not a Blow-Job virgin you know."

As the words came out of her mouth, Hale was walking in through the French doors, and unfortunately taking a sip of wine, which he then spewed outward on a choke/inhale/*what?* combination that almost killed him.

"What the hell?" he said, grabbing for dishtowels to clean up himself and the floor in front of him.

No one could explain as they were all laughing too hard. Crain used it as an excuse to step close to Tansy and put his hand on her back. When she looked up at him, glowing with mirth, he kissed her quickly before turning his full-blown smile and attention back to the Evans Family Comedy Players.

"What'd I miss?" Vance asked, stepping through the doors with a platter of sizzling steaks in hand.

"We'll explain at the table," Emelina said, herding everyone into a buffet line and then ushering them out onto the pool patio and toward the oblong, umbrellaed table. All eight of them seated there made it cozy.

They filled Vance and Hale in on the Blow Job shot challenge and the antics grew from there. Genevra did, in fact, know the ingredients: a quarter ounce of Bailey's Irish Cream and a half ounce amaretto almond liqueur topped with whipped cream. She also demonstrated how you were to do the shot, leaving your hands behind your back and using your lips to pick up the glass and drink it down.

Crain felt his face flush watching Genevra talk about it. But when Elizabeth's hand landed on his thigh, he started feeling hot a lot further down.

Hale refreshed Tansy's wine.

Crain enjoyed Vance and Pinks bantering back and forth sharing their N.C. State and Phi Delta traditions. He noticed his Elizabeth was quiet through the exchange but had a smile on her face, enjoying it along with the rest of them. It made him wonder why she held such a grudge against Vance.

Vance was the one who filled her wine glass the next time.

Crain was eventually encouraged to share a few of his Texas Aggie traditions. His Elizabeth wasn't surprised that Texas

A&M had five male Yell Leaders instead of the traditional SEC cheerleaders, or that the students were considered the 12th Man and stood during the football games in readiness to go in and play if the team required it. What she didn't know was the term "mug down," so he demonstrated it to the whole table by describing one of the great Johnny Football touchdowns like a local sports commentator and then pulling her over for one long, hard smooch.

"You had the excuse to kiss your date every time they scored?" Hale asked, as Tansy shoved him back playfully. Crain dragged his eyes off her adorable, albeit embarrassed, smile.

"Nah. Not me," he said. "Never had a date to kiss because I was out there on the field."

"You should hear his ringtone," Elizabeth said, tossing him a cute little smirk. "The Aggie War Hymn."

"What else would it be?" he asked the table at large while filling her wine glass himself.

"What'd they do at Ole Miss, Tansy?" Hale asked.

"Oh," she said, sitting up taller and putting a serious face on. "At Ole Miss, we have a saying. 'We may not win every game, but we've never lost a party.' At Ole Miss, it's all about The Grove."

"The Grove?"

"Ten acres in the center of campus adorned by oaks, elms, and magnolias. On game day, there are party tents as far as the eye can see and tailgate set-ups you can only dream of here in North Carolina. My mother may be a lot of things, but I tell you this, no one throws a tailgate at The Grove quite like my mother. She is the queen of The Grove. Last weekend, she decked out a tent with a chandelier and served a signature cocktail called The Hot Flash to the other past homecoming queens."

"How was your trip back?" Hale inquired. "In all the excitement of Crain's arrival, we forgot to ask."

"More fun than I anticipated." She sent him a grateful smile. "My mother, well, you saw what she was wearing. But she was in her element, surrounded by all her old cronies. They all fawned over my father, so he ended up having a good time, too. I hadn't been back in years. It was good to see what was new and what has stayed exactly the same. It was great to catch up with the handful of my sorority sisters who showed up. And then, my sister introduced me to her crowd. I had never met her roommate, so that was fun. I'm glad I let my mother talk me into it. Oh, and we won the game," she said brightly. "That didn't happen much while I was a student. But they've got a new coach ushering in a whole new era for the Rebels."

"Isn't there an Ole Miss chant of some sort?" Vance asked The Pink One.

"No, no. We're not going there." Tansy held up her hand.

"That's right," Pinks said back to Vance with a sly-dog grin. "How's that start again? If we've heard it in the office once, we've heard it five or ten times."

"I'm not doing it. Not here," Tansy protested.

"You don't have to do it," Vance insisted with an evil grin. "We're just trying to remember how it started."

"Stop," Tansy implored.

"Hmm..." Pinks said. "I believe it starts with someone yelling..."

"Please don't—"

"Are...You...Ready?" Pinks yelled.

"Helllll Yeah! Daaamn Right!" Tansy yelled sort of sheepishly, but then got into it as she clapped her hands reciting, "Hotty Toddy, Gosh Almighty, Who The Hell Are We, Hey! Flim Flam, Bim Bam, Ole Miss By Damn."

She fell back into her seat, laughing and beaming at the lively round of applause. "Well now, that's some team spirit," Crain said as he put his arm around her and pulled her close. "I'm starting to like this tiger of a Tansy y'all been hiding here in Henderson. My goodness darlin', I believe I should take you to an Aggie game and let you loose. You can yell with the best of them."

Piper and Genevra immediately wanted to learn the words, and eventually Tansy had the whole table repeating the Ole Miss chant. When Emelina excused herself to see about dessert, Piper sang the Carolina fight song complete with the infamous last line,

"Go to Hell, State," which her husband promptly took offense to. Especially since she didn't actually attend Carolina until law school.

"Did Miami University in the great state of Ohio even have a football team?" he teased.

"Oh! Oh!" she stammered in outrage. "Does two-time Super Bowl champion Q.B. Ben Roethlisberger ring a bell? Y'all can just simmer down because Big Ben hails from good old Miami U. And don't even get me started on ice hockey."

"You know ice hockey?" Crain asked.

"Pfft. Who doesn't know ice hockey?" Piper responded, but then sent him a look that pleaded, "Please don't challenge me on that with questions."

He smiled back and chuckled softly. He noticed Pinks spring up and run back into the mansion. When The Pink One returned, he was holding the biggest pie plate Crain had ever seen.

"What in tarnation?"

"It's Molly's Big Pie Plate," Piper explained in total glee. As Emelina put a second pie gently on the table, Piper just beamed as she looked over both pies. "I need everyone to try a bit of each to confirm what I already know."

"Baby Doll, if you already have the answer to your test question, why not just let us enjoy the pie without your inquisition," said Vance.

"Clearly you've been her test dummy before," Tansy sympathized with Vance. "She peppered me with questions in a taste test this afternoon."

"I just want to be sure," Piper said, dishing out the pies. "And then I want all of you business tycoons to tell me how I can best market this Big Pie Plate to Henderson and beyond. And Crain, I want your best advice too, pro bono. You like the pie, you give me advice for free."

"Deal," Crain said as he dug in.

"Tansy suggested introducing it at Harvest Daze, and since she's running that with Brooks now, I don't need to jump through hoops to get the idea passed."

"Whoa, whoa, whoa. Time out," Crain said as he sat back and made a T with his hands. "You're running something with Brooks?" Crain asked as nonchalantly as he could while internally shouting, *Not gonna happen.*

"Ugh," Tansy said, slumping down into herself. "Evie Jackson dug her hooks into Brooks and me at the office this morning. Wants the two of us to be the New Faces of Henderson. Wants us to revitalize the Harvest Daze events by bringing in a band and a liquor license and then getting on stage and making some grand announcement that's going to turn this town around and send it skyrocketing into the 21st century. Something so big all her grandchildren are going to want to move back to Henderson."

"Hmm," Vance said.

"What do you mean, she wants the two of you to be the New Faces of Henderson?" Crain grumbled. That hand of hers rubbing up and down his thigh was not going to soothe him. Okay, maybe it was a little. Still… "Why you and Brooks? Why not pretty little Piper and that guy?" he asked, gesturing toward Vance.

"That guy?" Vance was incredulous.

"Crain, it's fine. It's nothing really. She heard Brooks is ready to run for office and thought she could guilt him into it—which she did—and she wants me to do it because…well, because I'm pretty sure my mother put her up to it."

"Why in the Sam Hill would your mother put her up to it?"

"Who the hell is Sam Hill?" Vance asked.

"It's an expression," Crain barked across the table before returning his attention to Tansy.

"Well, obviously, my mother isn't aware of *you*," Tansy soothed with a gentle caress to Crain's face. "So she…you know, is still trying to play matchmaker."

"With Brooks?" Vance shouted from his end of the table. "That is not happening."

"Of course, it's not happening." Tansy snapped, shooting daggers at Vance. "Brooks is with Lolly. I'm married to Crain. What part of this aren't you following?"

"The part where your mother thinks it's okay to bust up Brooks and Lolly. Nobody is busting up Brooks and Lolly," Vance declared.

"I'm not trying to bust up Brooks and Lolly," Tansy shouted.

"Well, you did once," Vance shouted back.

There was a collective intake of breath and then complete and utter silence. Forks hung suspended in midair. Nobody moved.

"Really?" Tansy said to Vance.

"Really?" Crain asked Tansy.

"Really?" Piper asked the table at large, all curious and bright-eyed.

The Pink One made a grand show of taking Vance's wine glass and moving it way out of his reach. "Loose lips," he said quietly.

Tansy whipped her head around toward Vance. "Is Piper aware that you also tried to bust up Lolly and Brooks?"

"Really?" Piper asked Vance, still overly amused.

"I did not try to bust them up," Vance denied.

"Yeah, ya did," Genevra said.

"A little bit," Hale agreed.

"I even heard about it in Raleigh," Pinks said. He was the only one who had returned to eating his pie. "Which is how I ended up in this sweet deal of a job and kick-ass place to live, so…"—he hit Vance on the back—"I have no issues."

Crain whispered in Tansy's ear. "You just told me you didn't speak to Brooks the entire time you were in Dallas."

"I didn't," Tansy said quietly.

"So why is Vance accusing you of trying to bust them up?"

Tansy sighed. "Because to the uneducated bystander, that may have appeared to be the case. And let's face it, Vance is clearly uneducated."

"What the hell do you two have against each other?" Crain asked.

"I've been trying to get to the bottom of that myself," Hale chimed in.

"Nothing. Nothing," Tansy insisted. "We've just known each other way too long—"

"Since fourth grade," Piper added.

"And there's a lot of water under that bridge. It's childish, and I'm attempting to get over it. That is until *he* starts in on ridiculous accusations about me busting up Brooks and his little kindergartner. Oops." Tansy eyed Genevra. "Nothing against Lolly. She's just… young."

"Yes, she is," Genevra kindly agreed.

"Same age as Pinks," Vance said to the table at large. "Tell me, *Tansy*, do you think my man, Pinks, is too young to be lured into a sexual encounter by a woman your age?"

Abruptly Pinks stood, tossing his hands in the air. "Whoa, whoa. Let's hold on here one cotton-picking minute. Where I may not have objected to the conversations about Blow Jobs or male cheerleaders over dinner, I am firmly putting my foot down when it comes to my love life. *That*…is totally off-limits."

Everyone chuckled and went back to eating Piper's pies. Crain leaned in to Tansy and whispered, "Something's going on, and I plan to get to the bottom of it."

She rubbed her hand over his thigh. "Nothing's going on. Relax and enjoy yourself."

"I'm not a dumb jock, Elizabeth. I can add two and two."

Tansy looked up, startled. "Crain," she whispered as pie comparisons were being offered around them. "I've never thought of you as a dumb jock." He could see her frantically searching his eyes. Her expression was confused and full of concern, socking him right in the solar plexus. "Where did that even come from?"

He was suddenly emotional. Every latent vulnerability he'd ever possessed surged forth and swamped him.

Elizabeth had never treated him like a dumb jock, but sitting here, surrounded by nice-enough people whom he barely knew, after four months of heartache, frustration, and being down-right outraged over the fact that she wanted him to sign annulment papers without the courtesy of a conversation between them…and the fact that he'd done nothing but eat out of her hand ever since he found her…sure made him feel like one.

Maybe he did rush her down the aisle. And maybe he did let the world in on their secret a little too fast. Maybe he was completely to blame for this debacle they found themselves in.

Then again maybe, just maybe, Elizabeth Tansy Langford Carraway wasn't the girl for him after all.

CHAPTER TWENTY-SEVEN

Tansy paced the lobby area of Evans & Evans Investments, Inc. dressed in her favorite designer suit with her hair up in a messy bun and the smart-girl glasses—as Crain liked to call them—perched on her nose. Last night Crain had stood up from the Evans' table, taken her hand, and led her into the house. She knew she was in big trouble when he called a cab and tucked her safely inside, sending her on her way home to her parents.

Big Trouble.

It became evident as the wine wore off and her headache started up that she was once again in deep when it came to Crain Carraway. Having him push her out the door instead of pulling her into Vance's disgusting pool house was a huge sign that something had gone terribly wrong.

Before she had fallen into a fitful sleep, she vowed to do whatever she needed to do to win Crain back. So this morning, she dressed the way he liked, planned to let him call her Elizabeth all he wanted, and was even considering telling her parents that she'd been married to someone they'd never met for the last four months.

Right up until her mother gushed a little too much about the suit she'd "finally had the sense to wear" and began listing a myriad of techniques she should employ to win Brooks back.

Brooks.

Was that what set Crain off? Vance leaking that she'd tried to break them up when she'd come home from Texas?

She'd already told Crain about her relationship with Brooks. If she had to confess that she was trying to rewind her life due to the fear she had of never being allowed to come home, then she'd do it. She'd tell the truth and figure out a way to make him understand that she was temporarily insane at the time. She didn't want Brooks. She wanted Crain. Crain was the man for her.

She was wringing her hands, worried about everything, when Pinks came in from the back door and made his way to the lobby area.

"What the hell have we got here?" he asked, giving her a very thorough head-to-toe once-over. "Looks like Crain's elusive Elizabeth has decided to make an appearance."

"Is he with you?" she whispered.

He shook his head. "Haven't seen him." He held out her car keys. "Drove it in for you," he said, lifting a paper bag into her line of sight. "And these are for you."

She took the bag and pulled out a black box that said Magnum Ecstasy. She blinked a couple times. "Condoms?"

Davis shrugged. "Someone suggested Crain should try the Evans method to marital bliss."

When she didn't understand, he went on. "Get you pregnant."

"Oh!"

"Figured you might want a heads up about that approach."

"Yes. Yes, um. Thank you," she said, stuffing the box of condoms back in the bag. "I'll keep that in mind." She scurried around her desk and stuffed the bag into her tote. She sat down and eventually looked up at Davis.

He was staring at her, his expression solemn.

"That was kind of you," she said quietly.

"Yeah. I'm a fucking prince," he said, turning and walking off down the hall.

Tansy dropped her head to her desk. She'd done nothing but wreak havoc over the last four months. Stuff she couldn't defend or explain. At least not well enough that it would make any sense to those who mattered. Maybe she should leave Henderson for good. Stop trying to be a part of something nobody wanted her to be a part of anyway. Go back and face Crain's family on her hands and knees, begging for forgiveness for being so cruel to their son. Send her parents an email announcing her marriage and then let them deal with it as they saw fit. She felt worn out. Exhausted by the pressure of the last four months. Exhausted trying to pretend, trying to unwind, trying not to love a man who was kind and happy and thought she was as sweet as praline pie.

The bells above the front door jingled, causing her head to spring up in anticipation. Hale and his good looks came up the steps slowly, a comforting smile on his lips.

Tansy held her breath. It was obvious he had bad news.

"Good morning," he said.

"What's happened?" she asked as she stood.

Hale shook his head. "Nothing much. Just…ah, our colleague from Dallas has…*temporarily* gone home."

Tansy swallowed. "Temporarily."

"I believe so."

When she couldn't get words to form with her lips, Hale took pity and went on. "He left a note this morning explaining he had business to attend to in Dallas and would be in touch."

"In touch?"

"Yes." Hale drew the note from his pocket and handed it to her.

She took it and read it. It was just as Hale had said. Nothing more.

All she could do was blink. And breathe. She did remember to breathe.

"There are flights to Dallas twice a day out of Raleigh."

Tansy's head popped up. "What?"

"E&E could send you to Dallas. If that's what you want."

She looked down at the note. Crain would have flown her back with him if that were what *he'd* wanted.

"That's a kind offer," she acknowledged with as much of a smile as she was able to force, folding the note but holding on to it. "But Crain Carraway is a man of his word. I'm sure he'll be in touch."

CHAPTER TWENTY-EIGHT

Crain stood facing his dear daddy, his sweet momma, and his pain-in-the-ass brother, scraping his hands through his hair, going through the same story a third time. No, he'd never bothered to ask where she was from. No, he had no idea she went by another name. No, she hadn't told her parents or anyone else they'd gotten hitched, and yes, his brilliant plan for eloping had turned into a clusterfuck of epic proportions. Well, that part he'd tamed down for the sake of his momma. Lord knew the woman was riled up enough.

"I simply don't understand," she said. "She got cold feet because you called us? Of course you would call us. We're your family."

"She didn't get cold feet because I called my family," he said patiently. "She got scared because she could tell you weren't crazy about missin' our nuptials—"

"That's putting it mildly."

"And she knew her momma was gonna be just as upset. Maybe even worse."

"Well, what's wrong with her momma, not wanting her daughter to be married to my boy?"

"Momma, she hasn't even met me. Just like you haven't met Elizabeth—Tansy—Elizabeth."

"Well, which is it son?" his papa asked. "You sound about as confused as I am right now."

"She's Elizabeth. My Elizabeth. She just thinks she's Tansy."

"So she's got amnesia?"

"No," he sighed. "She doesn't have amnesia, Pop. She just acts differently in her hometown than she did here in Dallas. So I have four unaccounted months where she was up there in Henderson and I was here in Dallas—looking for her—going out of my mind—and I have no idea what she was doing other than sending me those damn annulment papers every time I turned around."

"Sign them."

"What?"

"Sign the papers," his momma said. "You don't need that kind of trouble in your life. Marriage is hard enough without involving an unwilling bride. She's turned you into a man who has lied to his friends and family, telling us she couldn't wait to meet us but was stuck taking care of a sick out-of-town relative. Sneaky, heartless, shrew if you ask me. No. You don't need a woman like that in your life."

"See now. This is exactly why I lied." Crain shook his finger at his momma. "Because you're judging her on this mess alone. And this mess is not who she is. It's just who I forced her to be by rushing her down the aisle. She happens to agree with you. She keeps tellin' me it was irresponsible of us to get married without our parents present. But you know what? I still think it was awesome. Because it was the one damn thing I've done for me and me alone. Marry the girl I was certain I'd enjoy building a big life with. And now…"

"Now?" his father prompted.

"Now," he faltered. "Now, I'm not certain of anything."

There was a good long bit of quiet. Then his brother stood, looked around at his parents, and settled his gaze on Crain. "What is this exactly? Is this like halftime during one of your Aggie games? Are we supposed to circle up and put our heads together to come up with a game plan? 'Cause I got one, Bro," he said, slapping Crain on the back. "Let's you and me head back up to this Hendersonville—"

"Henderson," Crain corrected.

"Right. Way up there in Kentucky—"

"North Carolina."

"Right. I figure between my award-winning Team Roping skills and your big jet, no doubt we can have this Elizabeth Tansy Elizabeth back in Dallas by nightfall. Then…we set her ass down right here and let Momma talk some sense into her."

"Don't think I won't do it," his momma said.

"What do ya say? If you're lookin' for backup—I'm your man."

Crain was hard-pressed not to smile. "I appreciate that, Cash. I'll keep it in mind."

"Won't be the first time I've kidnapped a woman. Not likely to be the last."

"I hear ya. If she needs kidnapping, you're my man."

"And don't you forget it. Now, I'm gonna head out and see a man about a horse. You need me, call my cell. Momma," Cash said, going over to kiss her cheek. "I want you to sit here and continue to talk Crain's ear off about this, ya hear. Just go on and on and make sure he really knows how you feel about him eloping in Vegas. And don't leave anything out about your feelings for his bride either, 'cause that's sure to help." His mom swatted his backside. Cash turned to his father. "And Daddy, after she's done all the damage she can possibly do, I want you to take this city boy out and make him shoot something. Just make sure it's not Momma. Okay?" he asked the room at large. "All right, then," he said, putting his cowboy hat back on his head, "My work here is done. Keep me in the loop."

It was the most words his brother had uttered at one time in the thirty years since he'd been born.

CHAPTER TWENTY-NINE

By Friday morning, Tansy figured she'd make herself crazy worrying about exactly when Crain Carraway was going to "be in touch." She'd stopped herself from texting him so many times over the last two days—because what did she have to say really? *I'm ready to tell my parents?* Because she wasn't. Not really. Not if he wanted out and was in the process of signing the annulment papers. *I miss you?* It was true. It was also totally lame. *Are you coming back? Are we through?* The questions she really wanted to ask but wasn't sure she could handle the answers. And she didn't think coming clean in a text about trying to get back with Brooks or get over Crain by spending a night with Pinks would help her case at all. So she locked her cellphone in her father's safe and went to work without it.

Once there, she started making plans for Harvest Daze, not bothering to try to form a committee of her peers at this point, but using anyone who walked in the door for ideas and insight. When Josh McCourt stopped by, she grilled him about his high school football team and ways they could contribute. He said they'd volunteer for set-up and clean up if she'd sign off on their service-hour requirements. She agreed. She also asked him to see what the team would think about taking turns manning an old-school kissing booth throughout the day while wearing their jerseys.

And since their little band really got the town whipped into a dance frenzy last summer, she asked Davis to call Jesse James, a.k.a.

The Outlaw, to see if he'd be willing to leave college for a weekend to play a set with Davis at The Daze.

She followed that up by calling the music director at the high school to inquire if there was a student rock band that would be appropriate to play their own set. And while she was at it, she booked the small but proud Henderson High Marching Band. She pictured them starting off the Harvest Daze festivities with a rousing march through Henderson's streets, bringing out the crowds and leading them to wherever this function was going to take place.

Huh.

"Vance!" she yelled, getting up from her desk and heading back to talk with him.

"You bellowed?" he said, not bothering to look up from a mountain of paperwork.

She squinted, not really believing what she was seeing. "Are you actually doing real work?"

"Are you actually asking me that question?" he countered, looking up and spreading his hands. "I work nonstop. I'm always working, no matter where I am."

"Your wife's belly is starting to prove otherwise."

"You don't think that's work? Let me tell you something. Keeping Naughty Piper satisfied is long, hard work. The woman keeps throwing my past in my face, telling me I should have the stamina of Ulysses."

"Serves you right."

"Says the woman with the most scandalous past to date. Speaking of, have you heard from Tex?"

She shook her head. "Have you?"

"No, but he's on the job. Or his team is. I've been getting email updates from CC Dallas about the questionnaires they've already started sending IMG Academy graduates, along with a list of potential donors, contributors, and partners. We're going to need to start setting up meetings very soon. On top of that, we need to start interviewing local land developers and architects."

"Have you decided on the location?"

"Not really. We're going to need to get some funding together before we can bid on any of it. We like the old Myers farm though. We like it a lot."

"Do you think it'd be possible to move Harvest Daze out there? To the Myers farm? Brooks doesn't want any alcohol served on the grounds of the high school, so we're looking for a new place. The Myers farm wouldn't be as centrally located, but I've come up with this idea to have the marching band lead a parade from the old location to the new location. Maybe we entice Mr. Grissom to use his Classic Car Club of America's Raleigh connections to transport all our prominent senior citizens out there in style. Make a car show part of the new Daze."

"I like it," Vance said. "I'd like it a whole lot more if we were sure that's where this academy was going to be built, or even if we knew for sure we were going to get this off the ground. That would be some announcement for you and Brooks to make on stage."

"You don't think there's any way we'd be able to do that? Make the announcement at the Daze?"

Vance shook his head. "I'd be thrilled if we're able to announce it at next year's Daze. This kind of thing takes time and planning," he said, indicating the paperwork. "Lots of planning and lots of money." He stopped for a minute, rubbing a pencil between his fingers, looking Tansy over. "Have you done something to yourself?"

"What do you mean?" she asked. Every defense mechanism she had stood on guard.

Vance tilted his head, eyeing her. "I don't know. You look... different."

"I'm wearing pink."

"You are, aren't you?" he said, smiling as if the puzzle was being solved.

"My hair is up," she said.

His eyes darted to her hair. "So it is. I like it."

"I'm wearing glasses."

Vance's gaze drifted to her glasses, and he started nodding his head. After a moment, he asked slowly, very quietly, "Should I start calling you Elizabeth?"

She shrugged.

"All right then, Elizabeth," he said. "I'll see what I can do about borrowing the Myers land for Harvest Daze and push hard for some sort of collaboration that would enable us to make an announcement. Or at least put out a teaser. Maybe. We'll see."

"There's a motto at CC Dallas," she said. "Why wait?"

"So that's what Crain Carraway thought when he took one look at you dressed like that? Why wait?"

She never thought about it like that. "Maybe."

"Listen," Vance said, "I'm sorry the Brooks thing came up the other night. It's just that I am sensitive about Brooks and Lolly."

"I know you are, and I appreciate you not telling anyone about me and Pinks. I was gonna come clean with Crain, but I don't see the need to hurt him any more than I already have. So, you know. Thanks."

"Well, thank you for not talking Piper into annulling our marriage."

"I couldn't if I tried. I heard you told her you were a millionaire."

"I am a millionaire."

"She doesn't believe you."

"She believes me."

"Well, she did. Believe you. At first. But now she doesn't."

"Well, why the hell not?"

"Because you didn't make her sign a prenup. She's convinced any real millionaire would make her sign a prenup."

"Did Crain make you sign a prenup?"

"Crain doesn't need a prenup."

"But I do?"

"The lawyer in Piper thinks both you and Crain need prenups."

"Hold on a second." Vance picked up his desk phone and called his buddy Duncan James. "Duncan, I need a favor. I need you to draw up a retroactive prenup for me to give Piper. Yes, I know it's not your field, but that doesn't matter. I'm just trying to make a point. I want it full of lawyer mumbo-jumbo, and I want it outrageous. In fact, I want you to research the worst, messed-up crap ever thrown in a prenup, and I want all of it in there, ironclad, and I want it fast."

Vance hung up the phone, smiling. "If Piper wants a prenup, Piper's going to get a prenup. And don't you dare tell her."

"Wouldn't want to ruin your fun," Tansy said before turning and heading back up the hall.

When Tansy walked into the office lobby, there was a cowboy standing in the center of it. Not just some dude dressed up for Halloween. No. Standing before her was the genuine article. The poster boy for Ft. Worth, Texas, if you will. Hell, for the Stockyards Championship Rodeo, from the looks of it.

Rugged, fit, glorious to look at from the white straw hat in his hand to the worn buckled boots on his feet. His jeans rode low, his shirt was tight, and his perfectly unkempt hair would make grown women weep for younger days. No doubt he was causing trouble from coast to coast, and for the first time, Tansy was grateful to be a married woman.

He spoke so quietly, she almost didn't hear him when he uttered, "Now doesn't this clear a few things up?"

"May I help you?" she asked, feeling confused, like she couldn't figure out exactly how he'd been beamed in from the old West. "Are you looking for Vance?"

"Vance?"

"Vance Evans? Or Hale? The owners?"

"No," he said, standing his ground, hands tucked partially into his front pockets. "I'm lookin' for my sister-in-law."

"Your sister-in-law?"

"One Elizabeth Carraway."

"Elizabeth Carra—Oh." Tansy blinked a couple times, the fog inside her brain clearing. "Cash?" she whispered.

"Look at that. Almost like we've been properly introduced."

"Crain has your picture in his office," she said absently, taking a good look at his handsome face. "Although, it doesn't...do you justice."

"I've heard that a time or two." He gave her a broad, slightly lopsided grin.

Suuuuuch trouble.

Tansy shook her head to clear her mind. "How did you find me?"

"Crain called a meeting. Came clean about what's really going on between you two."

"In a meeting?"

"A family meeting."

"Oh. Wow. So your parents…"

"Know everything. How you ran off on Crain. How you used a fake name."

"I didn't use a fake name," she protested.

"How you told him you were from Dallas—"

"I never said I was from Dallas."

"And then scampered off to the backwoods of Mayberry and repeatedly sent him annulment papers through your lawyer."

"Twice. I sent them twice."

"And how he *accidentally*," he said, adding air quotes, "found you."

Wow. It suddenly occurred to her that there would be no safe haven in Dallas. She would never be able to live all that down. She felt herself deflate and let out a big sigh. "I suppose y'all hate me."

"I can't speak for the rest of them, but rest assured, I do not hate you. Do you have any idea what it's like to be Crain Carraway's brother?"

Tansy shook her head.

"Suffice it to say that I could never keep up, so I quit tryin'. Crain may argue the facts, but a case could be made that everything he touches turns to gold. And with women? Well, let me just say you are the first one to *ever* tell him no."

"I didn't tell him no. I said yes."

"Well, maybe at first you said yes. But baby, you woke up the next morning and ran out on the poor son of a bitch. It was like he won the lottery and then lost the winning ticket."

"And you're happy about this?"

"I wouldn't say happy. More like amused. And curious. I had to come meet the one woman who has proven that all men are indeed created equal. I needed to come find the one bucking bronc who was capable of throwing my big brother."

"I didn't throw him."

"Oh—he's thrown. Landed flat on his ass and can hardly sit down."

"And you're gloating about it."

Cash separated his thumb and forefinger about two inches. "Little bit. But, hey, I've been thrown a time or two myself."

"Hmph. I seriously doubt that," Tansy said as Pinks came through the door.

He took in Cash, eyed the cowboy hat and boots, and then looked over at Tansy. "Another secret husband from the Lone Star State?"

"Just a secret brother-in-law," she said as if it were no big deal. "Cash Carraway, meet Davis Williams." The men shook hands.

"Should I bother to ask what brings you to Henderson?" Pinks said.

"Just passing through. Wanted to see what all the hubbub was about."

They both eyed Tansy.

"Yeah, well," Pinks said, "She's a cross between a pit bull and a beauty queen. I guess you don't see much of that in Dallas."

"Not regularly, no."

"Sort of an acquired taste."

"Exotic. Definitely tempting."

"I'm standing right here," Tansy said.

Pinks went on as if she hadn't spoken. "Crain given up?"

"Don't rightly know."

"You gonna report back?"

"As soon as I walk out the door."

"Huh."

After a few heartbeats, Pinks asked. "She pass inspection?"

"With flying colors."

"You sure? I mentioned the pit bull thing, right?"

"About time my brother got a bite taken out of his ass."

"Okay, then," Pinks said. He shook Cash's hand again and took his leave down the hall. "I'm gonna go get to work."

Cash didn't take his eyes off Tansy as he placed his hat on his head and then tipped it to her. He turned without a word, heading for the door.

"Wait," she called out. "Will you do me just one favor?" At his nod, she smiled. "Tell him what I was wearing."

CHAPTER THIRTY

The following Monday, Tansy stood chewing on her fingernail in front of the big picture window, watching the scene unfold directly across the street from E&E Investments.

Crain was back.

In a big way.

She'd been working at her desk, excited about the new Harvest Daze ideas Brooks and the police department had come up with over the weekend. They were going to set up a makeshift jail in the middle of the festivities. If you got thrown in, you had to raise money to get yourself bailed out. All fun and games, and all to fund the new Henderson Helping Henderson campaign to polish up their city.

The rumble of an engine caused Tansy to stop what she was doing and lift her head. When the front window of the office started vibrating, she stepped from behind her desk to look outside. A huge, red, jacked-up, monster Denali HD 4X4 the likes of which had yet to be seen in Henderson. Mostly because anyone who'd actually want to drive something like that—teenagers and total rednecks—couldn't afford it. In Tansy's opinion, it was flashy and ridiculous, even if it was shiny and new and sort of heart-thumping exciting. How the hell would someone even climb up into that thing, she wondered as the driver door popped open, and a big, broad, ex-Aggie football player hopped out.

Her body sighed. *Craaaain.*

She smiled and held up a hand to wave, but he didn't toss one glance in her direction. Didn't even bother to look over at E&E, didn't bother to set a foot toward her office. Instead, he moved around that crazy truck to the opposite sidewalk and stood, hands on hips, looking at an identical storefront directly across the street.

Huh?

She stood there, admiring his back, feeling a sexual flush bloom throughout her body as her eyes trailed down over his backside and checked out his rear end and muscular legs in his casual business pants. It had been a week since she'd been in his arms, but every night he'd managed to come back in her dreams. She woke up hot and bothered, and right now, she felt nervous on top of it. A little hurt that he wasn't racing in to see her. A little worried about what she'd do if he did. A little—

What the…?

Evie Jackson, with her stylishly coiffed grey hair and her ever-present three strands of pearls was walking up to Crain and greeting him like he was one of Henderson's own. She hugged on him like he was one of her long-lost grandchildren come back from foreign soil, and he pulled her right in to him, greeting her back like he knew who the hell she was.

What?

Evie turned and held out an arm indicating something down the street, causing Tansy's eye to follow along, and—holy crap—there was her own daddy hurrying up the sidewalk with a big smile on his face and his right hand stretched out. Stretched out in greeting to Crain Carraway his own—albeit secret—son-in-law.

Kill me now.

Tansy felt sick. Felt heat swamp her chest and flow right on up her neck and face. Everything went into slow motion as she watched the queen of Henderson and her own father fraternize with the one man who could rip apart the facade she'd been working on all her life.

Panic had her wishing she'd told her parents about the wedding. If not right away, then first thing when Crain showed up in town. Because now, oh Lordy, now she didn't know what was happening across the street, but she sure saw the writing on the wall. And it spelled disaster.

She stood there, watching. Couldn't move a muscle. Probably wasn't breathing. Watching the three of them exchange pleasantries or something, until all three turned to the storefront across from E&E, looking it over like it had magically appeared beside them. She watched her father gesture down one side of the street, and then the other, probably pointing out other vacant stores in their tiny business district. Then he took something out of his pocket, must be a key, and proceeded to open the front door and march them all inside.

Closing her out.

"Pinks!" she yelled.

God love him, he came running.

"Wow," he said, skidding to a halt beside her. "Those are some kick-ass wheels."

"Would you mind going over there and finding out what is going on?"

"Over where?"

"Across the street. I just saw Crain, Evie Jackson, and my father head in."

"Your father?"

She nodded.

"And Crain?"

She bit her lip.

"Uh-oh."

She couldn't help it. She teared up.

"Okay, all right. Don't…you know, get all emotional on me. I'm on it. I'll just go over there and play dumb. You know. Like I don't know anything. I'll…be right back." He turned and bolted out the door.

He really is a Super-Hero-In-Training.

It took for-eeevvver.

Tansy paced. She sat. She checked her watch. She paced again. She stared at the door across the street, trying to see into the window, but it was hopeless. From her vantage point, she couldn't see inside at all. Finally, she saw the door open.

Nothing.

Nothing, nothing, nothing, and then out came Evie, laughing like Tansy's life didn't hang in the balance. Followed by her father, and then Pinks, and then Crain.

Craaaain.

Oh, stop it, she told herself. Get a grip. The man just went behind your back and had a meeting with your father, and you're all *Craaaain*?

"What's so interesting?"

Tansy jumped at Vance's voice. "Mmm Humm Mmm," she said, pointing out the window. Apparently, she had no words.

"Ooooh. Wow. Ooooh."

Yeah. Vance couldn't come up with any either.

That didn't make her feel any better.

They watched as Pinks dashed across the street, heading toward them. Watched as Crain and Rye Langford shook hands. Watched as Rye led Evie down the street to her car. And watched as Crain took one short glance across the street and then headed back into the building behind him.

Pinks came through the front door.

"Well?" Tansy asked.

"Well," Pinks said, shooting a look over her head toward Vance before settling his gaze on her. "He's back, and it sounds like he's considering expanding CC Dallas. Apparently, he remembered meeting Evie last week and, I don't know, called her to find out whom he needed to meet with to look at possible office space in Henderson. She put him in touch with your dad."

"He called Evie? Why wouldn't he call me? Or one of you? Why did he have to call Evie?"

Pinks didn't say anything. He just stared her down.

"What!"

"I'm guessing he's tired of playing your game."

"What's that supposed to mean?"

"It means, stop playing with the man's affections, and either fish or cut bait. Then again, maybe I'm wrong. Maybe this has become just about business for Crain, and he's already done what I don't seem able to do. Get over your sorry ass and move on."

"Davis—"

"Save it. I'm not interested. I'm really not interested." Pinks headed back toward his office. "I'll be heading to Raleigh for the weekend," he told Vance.

"About damn time," Vance said, nodding in affirmation.

Tansy looked to Vance for help where Pinks was concerned.

"Let it go," he offered. "Let him work through it. He'll get there."

"Should I offer to quit?"

"It's a small town. The two of you aren't going to be able to get away from each other, even if you try. Quitting doesn't buy either of you much, and frankly, we are starting to get real busy. E&E needs you."

Tansy turned her attention back out the window. At the big red truck. At the storefront in the dead center of town right across the street. Remembering how Crain had kissed Evie's cheek and shaken her father's hand.

"I asked him to be low-key and discreet."

"Probably not in his wheelhouse." Vance said. "He's Crain Carraway. Being larger than life is who he is. You can't ask a man to be less than who he is. He tried it your way, and it didn't work for him." Then he added before walking away, "It wouldn't have worked for me either."

Tansy harumphed.

Men.

From the looks of things, Crain now had her sworn enemy, Vance (although that was starting to feel like such an old story), her precocious one-night stand, Pinks, and her very own father standing on his side of all this. Or he'd done what Pinks had suggested and moved on. Gotten over her and come back to Henderson strictly on business.

Ouch.

That might solve her problems, but her heart didn't seem to like the thought one little bit.

Her feet felt rooted to the floor for a few more seconds, until she couldn't help but give into the urge to find out. She had to know where things stood between her and Crain. Needed to know what he was thinking and when the anxiety she'd been feeling for months now was going to end. And, most importantly, how it would end. She left her purse, her jacket, and her pride and headed across the road.

The knob was loose for turning, the door unlocked. The place was relatively dark as she entered, only daylight coming through the large front window to light the dim interior. Wood floors, wood paneled walls. She glanced around, noticing the layout was the same as E&E's, only in reverse. She walked up the three steps into the foyer and called for Crain.

An arm darted out from the right, pulling her into the little alcove where her desk would sit across the street. Her back hit the wall, her breath forced out in a whoosh, and then her mouth fell under attack. Crain grunted as he kissed her, one hand on her breast, his other hand tangling up in her hair. Just when she was about to close her eyes and give in to all of it, he pulled back and growled, "I'm so furious with you."

She'd never seen him furious before, and she sure didn't like that it was directed at her. Worse, her body wasn't going to be able to function properly, or at all, if she didn't figure out a way to get his hands and lips back on her.

She threw her arms around him, pressed her lips to his, and banged right up against his immobile frame. That, apparently, created the desired effect. All of a sudden, she was stumbling backward, her back bouncing against the wall once again, Crain's mouth, Crain's hands, Crain's body taking control.

He was pressed hard against her. She had a little trouble drawing a breath, but that didn't stop her hands from clawing at his shirt, searching for flesh. While his chest pinned her to the wall, his hands reached under her skirt and ripped her panties apart in three good tugs. Then one hand went to her breast while the other stroked between her legs, making both of them moan at how ready she was, how good it felt.

As her need for him skyrocketed, she worked her fingers over his belt buckle and unzipped his pants, reaching in to release his hard-on, cupping it with one hand and pushing his pants down off his hips with the other. He groaned against her mouth, moved both of his hands to the backs of her legs and picked her up, stepping into her sweet spot.

"You don't deserve this," he said, his voice rough and harsh. He worked himself along her flesh, stroking himself between her folds. He lined himself up with the center of her core, and she wrapped her legs around his waist.

All of a sudden, he stopped.

With his forehead against her shoulder, he panted a few times, his breath heating her breasts, her body desperately aching for what he held back. He stretched his neck, pulling his head up and looked into her eyes.

"You don't deserve this," he rasped, dragging in a couple deep breaths. "None of it." She could feel his heart pounding, saw the tense muscles pulling at his mouth and jaw. "Aahh," he cried, pounding a fist against the wall by her head, struggling with some internal demon. He took her chin in his hand, squeezed firmly, and said it again. "You don't deserve to feel good," he pressed his lips to her mouth and ripped off a kiss, "but hell if I'm denying myself any longer," he said, pushing himself in long and deep. He squeezed his eyes shut, turned his head to the side as if he were being tortured and held himself inside her. "Jesus Christ."

He slid partially out, adjusted his hands, hiked her body up higher and then did it again…and then again…and then again.

"Crain," she panted.

"No talking," he said.

He bent his knees and then impaled her hard. She threw her head back, and it slammed against the wall. "Ouch."

He eyed her face as she let go of him to rub the back of her head while he continued his rhythm. "You okay?"

"I'm...ouch...I'm fine. Don't stop."

"Not even an option," he said, pumping her hard again.

He was breathing heavy and starting to really increase his pace when she realized, "You're not wearing a condom."

"Nope. But I'm not planning to finish in you either."

"Where..." Bump.

"Are...you..." Bump, bump.

"Oh God..." Big, deep bump.

"Planning..." Bump.

"To finish?" she managed just as the mother of all orgasms crept up and rocked her world. At that moment, she didn't care where Crain finished, just as long as he finished her. Just as long as he kept going, and going, and Oh My God going. Right there. Right like that. Hitting all the right places. Oh, please. Oh, God. Oh yeeessssssssssss...yes...yes...yes.

Yes.

Ahhh.

Yes.

She slumped against him, putty in his hands.

Her legs fell from his waist. He pulled himself loose and spun her around, guiding her hands to the wall in front of her. Then she felt his cock rub against her bottom, heard him grunt, felt his body jerk against her, heard an obscene whisper, and then felt a sensation of wetness as anger and frustration, along with a whole lot of passion, left Crain's body.

Lord, she was mad for him.

He turned her around and kissed her lips. Not with near the same urgency, but not with a whole lot of tenderness either. His rage wasn't spent, just simmered down. In the middle of the kiss, she realized he was cleaning her up and putting her back together, so to speak. He cleaned himself up, too as he fastened his pants and tucked in his shirt as well. A proficient multitasker.

She wasn't crazy about that.

"Crain," she said. But he pulled her lips back under his and kept doing what he was doing. Eventually, they were decent, and the kiss ended.

"Crain," she started, but he touched a finger to her lips, silencing her.

"I'm not interested in talking right now."

"Yes, but—"

"No buts. It would be dangerous to try to have a discussion. Trust me."

"What do you mean danger—"

He grabbed her up in his arms and crushed his lips to hers. This time, he twirled them so his back was against the wall. Open-mouthed, he kissed her speechless. She was just about punch drunk when he finally stopped.

"Wanna go again?" He held her face in his hands, looking deep into her eyes. "Because I sure don't mind shuttin' you up."

He kissed her again just to prove it.

Finally, he deliberately set her from him. "It's not near quitting time, and I assume you're still employed across the street?"

She nodded lamely.

"Probably should be getting back."

She nodded again, felt him push her toward the door. Heard it slam behind her. She stood there, getting her bearings, wondering what in the world had just happened.

CHAPTER THIRTY-ONE

Pinks and Vance stood side-by-side looking out the front window. They watched as Tansy stood on the sidewalk outside of the office space across the street, swaying like she'd had one too many shots of tequila.

Swaying, for Christ's sake.

"What the fuck do you think went on in there?" Pinks spat.

"You know exactly what went on in there."

"I haven't got a clue. I've never left any woman, including that one, sex-drugged before. And here I thought it was the man's money and good looks that had her picking him over me. But right now, it seems fairly obvious it's his bedroom skills."

"You forget. I was the one who found Tansy at her desk the morning after your little 'let's fool around on Vance's brand-new conference table' escapade. Trust me. You did your job, and then some."

"Yeah, well that was all about me getting mine and her getting hers. A sexual battle of wills. And God it was hot."

"You need to let it go."

"I'm working on it. It's just…at the moment, I feel like I want to hit something."

"Well, it's not going to be Crain. I don't care how good your double ninja skills are, that guy's got a hundred pounds on you. Isn't there some sort of competition you and all your black-belt buddies can partake in without you landing your ass in jail? You know, one of those free-for-alls where use your heads to bust up wood or concrete or something?"

"Concrete?"

"Okay. Maybe not concrete."

The bells above the door jingled as Tansy walked through. All Pinks could see was her messed-up hair, her half-tucked, barely there camisole, and the creases across her skirt that hadn't been there thirty minutes ago.

Jesus. He really did want to hit something.

But it was her dreamy, little smile that threw the punch to his gut.

Too nice, safe, and boring for Lolly, and apparently too young for Henderson's prodigal daughter to take seriously. Oh yeah, and the fact that she was a married woman was a helluva problem. He was cursed when it came to the women of Henderson.

He turned and stalked back to his office.

Vance was right. He needed to take his lovin' out of town.

And he'd find himself something to hit while he was at it.

CHAPTER THIRTY-TWO

Monday afternoon, Crain entered the office and didn't give Tansy so much as a nod in her direction. He just marched past stoically, heading toward the conference room.

She got the same treatment when he left.

On Tuesday morning, she found Crain and his big, sexy body shower fresh, dressed in jeans and a drool-inducing fitted T-shirt sitting in the chair behind her desk. His expression was unreadable.

She wanted to take a bite out of him.

Instead, she dragged her tongue back into her mouth and said, "Morning," setting her Marc Jacobs tote—red with gold trim— primly on top of the desk. She had on the white summer suit she'd purchased in Dallas right before they'd eloped. The flimsy, navy V-neck blouse she had under it was a little see-through to show off her pretty, lace, navy-colored bra.

She took off her suit jacket in a slow, exaggerated motion to make sure Crain noticed. She was rewarded by a long intake of breath, as he pulled out his rubber ball and began fisting it in his palm.

Yeah. He noticed.

Finally, his gaze drifted to her eyes. "You've got your hair up, I see."

"I do."

"And you're wearing your glasses."

"I am."

"Think that's gonna help clean this mess up?"

"Maybe."

He looked away with a grunt.

She came around and got in his lap. "You ready to talk to me? Tell me what's going on?"

"No."

"You planning to shut me up again?" she said with a wicked smile, clasping her hands at the back of his neck.

He seemed reluctant to look at her, but he let the ball drop and spread his hands around her waist. His large, warm, capable hands. He smelled smooth, like amaretto, and husky, like pine, so good the desire to bite him crept up all over again. Tansy snuck her nose right against his neck and breathed deep. "I like the way you smell," she whispered. Then she nipped him.

"Jesus," he said, tilting his head back and speaking to the ceiling.

"If you didn't want to talk to me, why'd you show up here so early?"

He reached an arm down, pulled at the lever on the chair, and released it so it tilted back. She slid further against him.

"Couldn't sleep," he mumbled.

"Mmm. Me, either," she cooed against him. She kicked her heels off and heard them clatter to the floor.

He took one finger, just one finger, and dragged it slowly around her knee. "You don't go in for pantyhose much," he said. "Not even in the office."

"Nope."

He traced his finger over her thigh, following the hem of her skirt. "I noticed that before I noticed how much you like to show off your lingerie." He lifted his head and looked her in the eye.

"Sue me." It came out a little breathy because she was thinking about his fingers.

"And you don't wear fancy perfume," he said, his nose and lips precariously close to her neck. "Just a scented soap. Or maybe it's your shampoo. Flowery," he whispered. "Enticing," he said as his lips landed on her clavicle.

His tongue caused heat to drip and puddle at the edges of all of her most sensitive body parts. Her thighs clenched inadvertently, shifting her bottom against him. She felt the evidence of his body responding in kind, swelling beneath her as her need for him grew.

She pulled his hand from her knee and pressed his palm against her breast. His reaction was that of a cannon ball being fired—big, swift, and hitting its mark. He groaned against her mouth, his tongue tangling with hers, his fingers sinking into the plushness of her breast, all causing her desire to soar. She wanted him desperately. Felt like she'd been starved for weeks.

Only they were in the office, and the last thing she wanted was for—

"Pinks," Crain nearly shouted, breaking their kiss and springing the chair upright so fast Tansy flew off his lap and landed stomach first against her desk.

Yeah. This was it. The last thing she wanted. "Ouch," she grimaced, standing up gingerly and pulling her skirt down over her thighs.

"Really?" Pinks said. Staring at them like their impropriety was the most offensive thing he'd ever seen. "What the hell do you need the pool house for if you're gonna treat the office like this?" he shouted at Crain. "Take it across the street, the two of you. We've got serious work going on here. Serious work. We're trying to stop the damn town from collapsing around us and E&E sure doesn't need this kind of nonsense threatening the firm's reputation."

"The firm's reputation?" Tansy shouted in disbelief. "What the fu—"

Crain clapped a hand over her mouth.

"You're right. We're sorry. It won't happen again," Crain offered. "Now, can I talk to you about the latest land surveys when you have a minute?"

"Got 'em right here," Pinks said, patting his satchel with long rolls of paper sticking out of the top.

"Great," Crain said, releasing her like she was busy work. He moved around the desk and was buddy-buddying up to Pinks, the two of them leaving her in the dust so fast she'd like to choke on it. "I was up all night thinking about how cool a pool would look at the entrance to the campus. Not just any pool, but one that…" His words trailed off as the two of them headed down the hall, turned into Pinks' office, and shut the door.

Leaving her on the outside.

She slouched into her chair. Was that why Crain couldn't sleep? Because he was thinking about the sports academy all night?

Her head lolled back, honestly wondering if the big Texas tycoon from CC Dallas was done with her. Or, at least done with trying to get her to admit she was his wife. He certainly had responded to her, but hell, he was a man. Probably would have responded to any female crawling into his lap and shoving her backside into his crotch. She laid her head on her desk in a state of turned-on frustration, curtailed only by a bit of heartache.

This…sucked.

She closed her eyes and forced herself to breathe deep and remain calm. Maybe she should go ahead and tell her parents. Force Crain to come up to scratch, if you will.

Or maybe that was his game, she thought feeling a sprinkle of hope, pushing herself upright.

Or maybe he was just as he said. Furious with her. And, really, who could blame him?

On Wednesday, Tansy took the opportunity to spy out the front window every chance she could, because there was more activity happening across the street than she was lining up for Harvest Daze. A crew of painters arrived early that morning and left at noon. A plumber she knew, an electrician she'd never heard of, and somebody with a pad of paper, a pen, and a tape measure attached to his belt came and went. Crain stood outside a long time with the guy with the tape measure gesturing at the window. When he turned and pointed in her direction, she darted behind her alcove, peeking her head around the corner and watching as he pointed to something. The sign Pinks had the foresight to have made, she guessed.

She sighed and headed back to her desk, knowing she needed to pay attention to her own work and stop worrying about what was going on across the street. Crain would tell her when he was ready.

Hopefully.

She'd just gotten her head back in the game when Hale came out of his office and gestured across the street. "Tansy…are those your *parents*?"

She bolted around her desk and skidded to a halt next to him. She caught what appeared to be her father introducing Crain to her mother.

Her mother!

Her hand flew to her open mouth, and she just stared, wondering what was going to happen now that her mother had met Crain.

"This is…" she stammered, *my worst fear? The end of life as I've known it?* "…comical," she spouted on the beginnings of a horrified laugh.

Hale looked at her like she'd gone mad. And maybe she had. She couldn't help it. Nervous laughter just took over, and she went with it, her hands collapsing at her sides. "And I deserve it," she said. "Coming back here, pretending my life in Dallas never existed, when clearly my life in Dallas—" she pointed at Crain—"was worth hanging on to."

She sobered then on a sigh.

"Why don't you just go out and make it right?" Hale suggested.

She could, couldn't she? She could walk out there right now and blow all three of their minds by admitting the truth. Go out and just make it right.

But then her eye caught sight of Pinks as he came up the sidewalk, watched as he waved to Crain and her parents across the street and then ventured through E&E's front door. He nodded to Hale and then to her, he said, "Looks like your days are numbered."

Yeah. She might be able to go out there and admit some of the truth. But she knew deep down in the pit of her stomach there was just no way she could ever make it right.

Wednesday afternoon—late afternoon—late enough that Tansy had ingested two Tums and taken some Alka Seltzer in an attempt to mellow her totally stressed-out stomach, Crain finally came in and made his way to her desk. He stood there, tall and imposing, hands clasped in front of him, perfect posture, his athletic form enhanced by the casual attire. She could tell he'd been involved in a lot of physical activity, probably working right along with everyone else going in and out of his new office—or whatever it was he was creating over there. He might have remained silent, but his expression spoke volumes. He was now the one with the big secret, and she was at his mercy. He looked her over, his eyes dilating as he took in her suit. One she'd worn in Dallas.

He cleared his throat, a smirk on his lips. "Elizabeth."

It was the first time she'd heard him say her name in over a week.

"How 'bout penciling me in for a private meeting?"

Oh, she thought as she deflated, this was business.

"With whom?" she asked, pulling the calendar toward her.

"With you."

Her head popped up in surprise. His unreadable expression had her suddenly feeling very, very nervous.

"Maybe you have time now," he suggested.

She looked around, feeling disoriented. She wasn't sure she was ready for whatever was going to happen next. "Do you...do you just want to pull up a chair?"

"No," he said, looking around and then bringing his gaze back to her, "I'd prefer if we did this behind a closed door."

"Oh. All right." Crap. This had bad news written all over it. Tansy got up slowly and moved around the desk, leading him down the hall. Hale had left—he liked to work from home—but she didn't feel comfortable using his office. Vance's office came up next. He was on the phone and gave them a brief wave as they walked by. Pinks was in his office and got up, assuming they were coming to speak with him, but Tansy just kept going. She opened the conference room door and then waited for Crain to enter first.

She shut the door in Pinks' face.

Crain was smiling when she looked at him. Actually smiling. Smiling like the old Crain. Like the original CC of Dallas. The happy tycoon and ex-athlete she'd fallen for so fast. The one she married on a whim and then ran out on in a panic.

For the first time in over a week, she was able to draw a full breath. Couldn't help but smile back at all that happiness. He made smiling contagious. "What?" she asked on a short laugh.

"Your parents. They've invited me to dinner Friday night."

"What?"

"They want me to meet their daughter."

"I don't understand."

"Your dad—funny guy by the way. Apparently, he and I have hit it off over this real estate transaction. I mean, he must like me okay, because this morning he brought your mother over to meet me."

"I saw that."

"Yeah, I was wondering if you got a glimpse of that little meet and greet. Caught me totally off guard, I tell you. I wasn't… you know, counting on that. But Miss Evie must have told your mother—"

"Evie? You call her Miss Evie?"

"Sure. What do you call her?"

"I call her Mrs. Jackson. Everyone calls her Mrs. Jackson. Maybe we refer to her as Evie behind her back, but it's always been Mrs. Jackson to her face."

"Hmm. Told me to call her Evie. Anyway, she must have told your mother about 'The Man from Dallas'—your mom said that's what she called me—and it piqued her interest, so she came on by with your dad to check out the renovations I'm doing to the office space."

Tansy felt herself standing there, arms tightly folded over her chest, rapidly tapping her foot. *What the hell?*

Crain must have noticed, because he stepped forward and started rubbing his big hands up and down her arms. "Now before you go gettin' all mad at me for contacting your daddy, just think about this for a second. Your parents appear to like me. They've actually invited me to dinner so they can introduce me to *you.*"

When she failed to lighten up, he said, "Come on. This has got to be a step in the right direction."

"What direction is that Crain? You shoved me in a cab over a week ago and went radio silent for five days. Then you show back up in Henderson, making a whole lot of noise by driving a ridiculous truck and doing business with my father behind my back. And you've refused to talk with me about any of it, claiming you're too furious to speak."

"Well, I was," he said, backing away. "I was furious with you. Still am. You left me. You left me hanging for four long months. And from all accounts, while I was pining away for you, doing my best to find you, *lying my ass off* to protect your reputation, you were here pretending that I didn't exist. I'm not an idiot, darlin'. I can put pieces of conversations together. You left me, ran back here, and tried to patch things up with Brooks. Why wouldn't I be furious with you?"

"So your leaving without any explanation was your way of getting back at me?"

"Hell, no," he spat, closing in on her with his big, imposing body. "Leaving without explanation was my way of staying out of jail. Thoughts of strangling that pretty neck of yours have kept me up more nights than I care to admit."

Tansy dropped her defensive position and sighed, knowing he had every right to be furious. She placed a hand on his cheek to try to soothe him and admitted, "I was worried you weren't coming back."

"You should have been. When I left, honest to God, I didn't know which way the wind was gonna blow. I just knew I had to get out of the enemy camp and back to familiar territory."

"Enemy camp?" Tansy dropped her hand and turned to hoist herself up on the conference table. She let her legs swing beneath her. "Everyone who knows about us—they're all pulling for you. I'm getting very little support in all this."

"Well," he said, coming to lean against the table beside her, "that's because everybody in the know wants what CC Dallas can offer Henderson. On top of the fact they know you're totally in the wrong." He turned his head, his eyes looking over her face. "You know something? There hasn't been one time I've tried to kiss you that you've pulled away. Not once. You want me to kiss you, among other things."

She did. She wanted him to kiss her and other things. Lots of other things.

"So when I got home and rehashed it all with my parents—"

"I can't believe you did that, by the way."

"Oh, hell. I realized I was no better than you with how I finagled the truth. And I didn't see any reason to tangle with your momma until I'd done right by my own. So I came clean. Told 'em you ran off on me and told 'em why. Told 'em it was my fault, rushing things the way I did. I let the damn chips fall, and I dealt with it, just like you're gonna have to do," he said, reaching down and squeezing her hand. "Because Elizabeth has already admitted she loves me, and Tansy's practically admitted she's just a chickenshit—afraid of living her own damn life. I couldn't wait to tell the world that we were married, and you still refuse to acknowledge it to anyone. Me included."

"I concede that we're technically married. I admit I should have never run out on you in a moment of panic. I totally shouldn't have gone into a state of denial over it. And I know the Brooks thing looks bad—"

"He's assured me that trying to get back together with him was a knee-jerk reaction to the thought of your parents finding out about our wedding."

"You talked to Brooks?"

"Of course I talked to Brooks. I needed to know the truth. The whole truth."

Hmm.

"He told me what happened, but he also told me what you said about your relationship with him—that it was one of convenience—which matched up real good with what you'd already led me to believe. And he told me something else."

"What?"

"He said that you love me. But you think I've fallen for you under false pretenses. That I love Elizabeth, but I don't know Tansy. Oh, and that you didn't want to subject me to your mother. Which, darlin', I don't understand because she was just as sweet to me as my Elizabeth is."

"Crain," she sighed.

"Just tell me the truth about something, okay?"

She was weary. Felt downright browbeaten. Just wanted his big, strong arms to hold her up, so she hopped off the table and turned into him, wrapping her arms around his waist.

"Tell you the truth about what?" she said into his chest. She couldn't look at him. Afraid of what he was going to ask.

"Do you really think my truck is ridiculous?"

She laughed, hugging him harder. "It's loud. And obnoxious. And it broke my heart you didn't race over to give me a ride."

"So how 'bout we stop fighting each other and create a united front? Figure out how the two of us can work together to ease your parents into the idea of our marriage. Especially now that the perfect opportunity has presented itself."

"Perfect?"

"As perfect as it's bound to get."

"So you plan to just walk in, let them introduce us, and then what? Mention over dessert that we just so happen to be married?"

"If you'd like. *Or* once we meet Friday night, we can pretend to start dating, out in the open, so your parents and this whole town can see us together before we eventually tell them that we've been keeping a secret. Sort of ease them all into it. Ease them all out of Tansy Langford and into Elizabeth Carraway."

She couldn't help but smile. She liked the idea. A lot. She wanted to date Crain, she liked being Elizabeth. She also wanted to bring up the annulment papers again but was afraid to mess with the mood they'd created. One of cooperation, anticipation, togetherness. Just like it had been back in Dallas.

She took up the front of his shirt in two fists and pulled at him so his lips hovered over hers. "Is your momma ever gonna forgive me?"

"I've got people working on that."

"Cash?" she whispered against his lips.

"And my daddy," he said, before he took her breath away.

CHAPTER THIRTY-THREE

Two days later, Crain eagerly walked into Henderson Country Club. The kid inside of him felt like skipping because today was the day things were finally going to get turned around for him and his bride. Four long months of pain, anguish, and heartache were finally coming to an end. He hated perpetrating a lie but whatever it took to get his Elizabeth back in his arms, back to Dallas, and into his bed he'd come to realize he was willing to do. He was like a damn dog left outside on a leash and near starved to death. He was gonna sit up and beg to whoever had the food in their hand. And right now, that was Mr. and Mrs. Langford, who were waiting for him at the top of the foyer stairs.

His in-laws.

Only they didn't know it yet.

He tried to swallow that and put on his best "looking forward to meeting your daughter for the first time" face.

It had occurred to him and Elizabeth that her parents were overlooking the simple fact that the two of them should have already met considering his work with E&E, Inc. But hey, if they hadn't thought that one through, maybe pretending this was the first time the two of them were meeting would be a breeze. At least he hoped as much. He hated this lying business, but he'd been lying to them inadvertently for four long months, and at least now he felt considerable hope that he and Elizabeth were on their way to a resolution of this very awkward, very unsatisfying situation.

Now that he'd found her and they'd managed to put all that murky four months of water under the bridge, he was desperate to get his hands on his wife again. Even if he had to woo Tansy Langford and her clan to do it.

"Mr. Langford," he said in greeting, holding out his hand.

"Call me Rye," Tansy's father said.

"Rye," Crain nodded. "Mrs. Langford," he said, smiling at the former beauty queen as he handed her an enormous bouquet of long-stem roses tied up with a big red bow. Garland's eyes lit up like she was reliving every moment of her glory days, accepting the bouquet and cradling it in her arms just as she must have when she'd won the crown of Miss North Carolina.

"Oh, Crain. These are just—well, they're just beautiful, aren't they, Rye?" she said, sniffing the bouquet.

"They are indeed," Rye said, nodding to Crain, silently letting him know that he'd just worked some magic.

Garland snuck her arm under his and led him into the club's mixed grill. "Let's show you off a bit, shall we? I can introduce you to a few of the prominent people in our little town while we wait for our daughter to arrive."

Maybe her mother was unaware that Elizabeth had arrived, but Crain's eyes were drawn to the tall, curvaceous babe in the long, sexy dress across the room. A vision with her gorgeous blond streaks curling down over her shoulders. She was definitely dressed for a night out. There was no suit, or glasses, but she made his heart race and loins ache just the same. Yes, Elizabeth Tansy Langford had definitely arrived.

"Of course, you know our Tansy," Garland said as they approached the table where she stood.

Crain did a double take at Garland's words. "I…I," he stuttered, unsure of what part he was supposed to play now. Was he supposed to know Tansy? Or pretend this was their first meeting as originally planned?

"Crain," Tansy said with a nod. She wasn't smiling. Not at all. Her hands clenched the back of a chair, and the tight grip sent muscles contracting all the way to her bunched-up shoulders.

"A pleasure," he offered, meeting her eyes, trying to send a "what the hell is going on" with mental telepathy. "You're as pretty as your momma," he went on with his original plan. "I was sure happy to be invited to dinner so I could get to know you better."

"Oh—" Garland laughed, practically tittered at Crain. "I'm sorry, Crain, but Tansy's off the market, as they say."

"She is?" For one brief second, he was hopeful.

"Afraid so. She's practically engaged to our next mayor and local sports hero, Brooks Bennett. Have you met Brooks?"

Crain eyed Tansy. *Not this again.* He was more than done with having Brooks and Tansy's relationship shoved in his face—*again*. He struggled to keep the ire out of his voice when he answered her momma slowly and patiently. "I have met Brooks and was under the distinct impression he is dating Mrs. Evans' daughter."

"Oh, that. No. No, no, no. That's just a…*thing*," Garland said, waving it off as if none of it mattered. "Tansy and I've collaborated, and I'm confident she and Brooks will work it all out very shortly."

"Is that so? You've *collaborated*?" He threw a look at Tansy that said he was not happy about that bit of information or about how any of this was going down.

"Mother—" Tansy tried to interrupt.

"Oh, here she is now, Crain. Take a look. That's our daughter, Scarlett. The one we want you to meet."

Crain glanced over at the young beauty coming through the double doors, stopping to say hello to an older couple at a nearby table. Her hair might not actually *be* scarlet, but it was a pretty shade of dark red. It was pulled back in an elaborate collection of twists and swirls into a fancy ponytail, thick as a horse's mane, twisting fat and plump all the way back over her shoulder and beyond. Her skin was a pretty shade of alabaster, her cheeks rosy, and her lips painted a dead-on red. Her eyes looked smoky with a double set of long black lashes. She was slightly built, like her mother, with long legs that went to hell and back, and a short, short dress meant to show them off. She appeared much taller than she actually was due to the heart-stopping platform heels that would make Elizabeth his height if she ever decided to wear them. Maybe he could get her to borrow them from Scarlett. He wouldn't mind staring eye to eye with Elizabeth every once in a while.

Mrs. Langford whispered, "She's just arriving back in Henderson for a long weekend. Her fall break from my alma mater, Ole Miss."

The dawning might have been slow in coming on his unconventional brain, but it came, and when it arrived, it hit him right in his solar plexus.

Crain leaned his head down next to Tansy's mother's and whispered. "You invited me here to meet Scarlett?" *Of course, they did. Why would anything about his relationship with Elizabeth be easy?* He was thinking about what kind of screwed-up mess he'd now gotten himself into. Being set up to date his own sister-in-law. Well, he was nipping this one in the bud. "Mrs. Langford, are you aware that I'm thirty-five?'

"Don't you worry about that," she assured him, leaning her head back toward Crain. "Our Scarlett is a handful. Needs a man in her life who knows how to take control. Rye and I think the two of you might be perfect for one another. You being a hard worker and established, her being sweet and young and ready to show you a good time. Balance the both of you out, if you will. Now Scarlett's only home for a long weekend right now, but there are Thanksgiving and Christmas and, good Lord willing, she'll graduate in May. Since you're new to town, we just thought an introduction over dinner would be appropriate. Give the two of you something to think about."

Crain turned his head all the way around toward Tansy, his eyes as big as he could make them.

Her stare was blunt and heated. He could read the words, "See what I'm up against" as clearly as if she'd spoken them.

Yes, he could see. But Garland Langford was about to find out she was no match for The Man From Dallas. He wanted her daughter, but he wanted the grown one. The beautiful, sweet, business professional, and if he had to take on Brooks and all this Henderson bullshit that came with her, so be it. In for a penny, he thought as Rye Langford brought his very young, very self-possessed daughter forward to meet him.

"You're the owner of that big, red truck?" Scarlett asked him as they shook hands.

"If you're talking about the Denali, then yes, that's mine."

"Hmm," she said, looking him up and down like he wasn't a decade too old for her.

So not going to happen.

"How 'bout you walk with me over to the bar," Crain said, eager to set this thing straight.

"I'd like that," Scarlett said as she threw him a wink.

Dear God.

He didn't touch her, just pointed the way and followed her over to where Harry the Bartender stood wiping a glass and staring down Crain with a big-ass smirk on his face. He couldn't remember if Harry was in on this whole charade or not, but it was obvious Harry knew something. Knew Crain was up to his ears in trouble at the moment. In fact, Harry started making Crain's old-fashioned before they'd even made it to the bar.

"What do you drink?" he asked Scarlett, determined not to look at her.

"Twelve-year-old tequila. On ice."

"She'll have a Coke," he told Harry.

"Tequila," she said around Crain.

"You got a license on you?" Crain asked.

"I'm twenty-two."

"Bullshit. You're sixteen, if you're a day."

Scarlett laughed at him. "Tequila, Harry. Make it a double."

Crain eyed Harry, lifting one finger so Scarlett couldn't see. Harry nodded his understanding. Then Crain turned and leaned an elbow against the bar. "How can I put this to you delicately?" he pondered, looking down into red hair, green eyes, and a whole lot of sass. "It appears your parents have invited me here so that you and I could get to know each other. However, as pretty as you are, your sister Elizabeth is the one I'd like to get to know."

"Her name is Tansy."

"Her name is Elizabeth," he said, making the decision to be part of the solution instead of the problem. "And I don't give a good goddamn that your mother thinks she's about to run out and marry the illustrious Mr. Bennett."

"Brooks is big time," Scarlett said as she took her cocktail from Harry.

"I'm big time," Crain said, pointing to himself. "Brooks is small potatoes. And I'm willing to give you just about anything if you'll make an excuse and hightail it out of here early so I can get this night headed in the direction I want."

"Fine. Give me your keys."

He eyed her up because this girl was definitely crazy. "I know you didn't just ask for my truck."

"Tansy has her Camry. You two can take that."

"Do I look like I'd fit in a Camry?"

She gave him a once over. "Fine. I want one hundred dollars. If I'm getting out of here early, then I'm heading to Raleigh for a night on the town. It's gonna cost you."

He was pulling out his wallet before she finished yammering. "If only it were this easy with your sister," he said under his breath. He pulled out three one-hundred-dollar bills and snuck them into her hand, looking over his shoulder to make sure no one saw. "Now you have enough money to buy your own uptown drinks, you hear me? A guy buys a pretty girl a drink, he's expecting something in return. You don't need that kind of trouble while you're supposed to be home visiting your family. Especially not while I'm footing the bill."

She batted her green eyes up at him, proving that she was no stranger to manipulating men.

"Shit. You're nothin' but trouble aren'tcha? And here I thought your sister was bad." He turned and led her back to the table. "Play this up. Make it good. And do it fast," he ordered.

CHAPTER THIRTY-FOUR

The roundhouse kick came out of nowhere, and "Shit!" Pinks thought as he took a fucking heel to his cheekbone. *This*, he thought as he shuffled back, fighting to regain his equilibrium, *was a bad idea*. He had no business participating in the North Carolina Open Taekwondo Championship. It'd been months since he'd been in training. "Damn!" came a blow to his thigh. He might have to physically get his head examined if he didn't get his shit together fast. Snorting up a deep breath, he stood his ground and glared at his asshole opponent. He didn't know the guy, but he was determined to label him with all the pent-up feelings he wanted to rid himself of by hitting something. And that something was a third-degree bullshit black belt who, for all intents and purposes, looked just like himself. Six foot. Brown hair. Athletic build. Solid 170 pounds of muscle. Only this guy didn't have an ax to grind.

That was gonna be his downfall.

As Pinks quickly slid his feet together, he thought of Lolly's affections turned toward Brooks and jumped into a sidekick, nailing "Brooks" with his heel right at hip level.

"Chww" his breath came out as he made contact.

He backed up, his arms held defensively, and thought of Vance and all the bullshit he'd put him through over the summer to prove himself. He whirled in, his hips turning, power resonating up his spine, and landed an open-handed strike to his opponent's chin.

"Chww" the sound came from him again.

Now that felt good, he thought, bouncing on his toes, letting the son of a bitch absorb that shock and come at him again. *Damn good.* Hitting something had never been the answer to much before, but right now as he was warming up to this sparring match—he blocked a sloppy punch—it sure felt like a way to get back his mojo. The mojo Tansy had sucked right out of him on that fateful night he'd made the mistake of laying claim to all those curves. So different from Lolly with her thin, athletic body, Tansy was all woman, all the time and Pinks was just—"Fuck!"—being beat to hell every time he looked at her. He wanted her. He couldn't have her. And tonight, he was going to find a way to get over her or die trying.

He spun, kicked, and took that sucker down before he knew what hit him. The damn wimp was tapping out before Pinks even started to bring on the pain.

Pinks hopped up like he hadn't been clocked twice in the head—adrenaline was like that—and immediately blocked a punch, catching his opponent's arm. He used the guy's forward momentum to his advantage by stepping in and grabbing his arm with both hands. He twisted, lowered his center of gravity, and threw the guy forward to the mat. He followed him right down, tossed him over, and buried his shoulders into the mat.

Point scored for him.

At the end of three periods, Davis was beat to hell but had come out victorious. The beating felt good in a way, made him stop wallowing in self-pity for a moment and narrowed his focus. The victory helped him remember who he was.

He showered, changed clothes, and threw his duffle into the back of Hale's red Aston Martin One-77 he'd been driving since he'd started working for the man. There were perks to being an E&E employee, and this was a big one.

A hot car attracted hot girls, and originally that had been the next thing on his agenda. Hit the pickup spots in Raleigh and nail something pretty. He checked his watch, ten o'clock. Funny how as a college student that time signified the beginning of the night. And now, as a working man, it marked when he'd start heading to bed.

Right now, he wasn't so much longing for a good tangle with the weaker sex as much as he was a bag of ice pressed to the side of his face. And a cold beer. Still, he'd gotten some of his confidence back; he felt that for sure. And since he was to be in town for the whole weekend, there was still a Saturday night in Raleigh to work on his mojo.

He pulled out of the Lee Brothers Martial Arts School parking lot and headed through town. Spanky's wasn't fancy, but he'd be able to get the ice he needed and could sit on a bar stool unnoticed, licking his wounds. Let the Friday night partiers rage around him while he enjoyed a beer, nursed the swelling he felt on the rise, and—

What the…?

Yeah, he was doing a U-turn.

A Couple Hours Earlier

Crain watched Scarlett leave the table, trying hard not to chuckle under his breath. The lovely and manipulative Garland Langford had met her match in daughter number two. And as Crain wished that Elizabeth maybe had a little of Scarlett's spunk when it came to dealing with her mother, at the same time he was feeling real sorry for any son of a bitch whose heart Scarlett managed to ensnare. He pictured the grounds of Ole Miss littered with her broken and battered castoffs.

Scarlett had done what he'd asked and more. They weren't even through the salad course before she asked Crain his age and then proceeded to spit her tequila all over the table.

"Thirty-five?" she said, clearly horrified by that number, dabbing her napkin at the mess. The look she threw her mother made Crain wonder if she wasn't a drama major.

"You think that's a little old for you?" Crain asked, leaning in like he was for real.

"I think old for me would be…like twenty-seven," she shouted.

"Scarlett, please," her mother said.

"You…" Scarlett went on, flicking her hand at him like he was of no further interest, "you are downright ancient."

Crain held his hands up and looked over at Garland. "I tried to warn you," he said. "I'm downright ancient in this one's eyes." He tossed his thumb toward Scarlett. "Now your Elizabeth, I'm hoping she might see me in a different way."

Tansy continued to eat her salad like chaos wasn't erupting at the table. "I think you're handsome…charming," Tansy said between bites. "The perfect age for settling down. Did I mention that I loved living in Dallas?" she added.

"Well, there you have it," Scarlett said. "A match made in heaven. And I might add that, frankly, Mr. Carraway makes Brooks Bennett look like small potatoes."

You said it.

"Brooks is going to be mayor," Garland insisted.

"Of Hen-der-son," Scarlett articulated. "This one could be gov-ern-or of the entire state of Texas."

Well, that's a stretch. Though Crain definitely appreciated Scarlett's enthusiasm. And he definitely appreciated the way Garland Langford was now looking at him. The girl had just earned her three hundred dollars.

"Mother, did you know that CC Dallas has its own private jet?" Elizabeth added casually.

Garland Langford looked at Elizabeth, looked back at Crain, and then smiled her beauty-queen smile before her eyes landed on Scarlett. "Sweetheart, you are dismissed."

"Thank heavens," Scarlett sighed like a woebegotten teenager. She placed her napkin on her plate and stood.

The men stood as Scarlett said her goodbyes. Harry was there in a flash, removing any remnants of Scarlett from the table. When she got to her daddy, she snuggled right into him and cooed, "I love you, Daddy" real sweet-like. And then Crain heard her ask, "Can I have a fifty?"

Crain cleared his throat and threw her a warning look. She just smiled up at him brightly as Rye counted off two fifties and handed them to her with a kiss. "Have fun darlin'. Stay at Molly's and be home in time for the game tomorrow. We'll spend some time together then."

"I can't wait," she said as her long legs and way-too-short dress headed out the door.

Crain sat down and got to work on his campaign for governor.

Davis did a U-turn, illegal by all accounts, and pulled into the parking lot of The Charlie Horse—a fancy club instead of his intended college bar—where the source of his distraction, a pretty girl in a party dress with a pair of long, shapely legs, stood checking her phone.

Well, look at that, he thought. His mojo was making a resurgence.

It might have been ten o'clock at night, but Davis pulled on his sunglasses to cover up his swollen and soon-to-be black eye. He parked right up front where the One-77 could make an impression and have an eye kept on it. He flashed a twenty at the bouncer who started in his direction and got a quick nod of approval. While he backed off, Davis approached the girl.

"Whatcha doin'?" he asked, real casual-like, even though he was a half-step into her personal space, and his posture was far more imposing.

Lean and Mean stood her ground, giving him the once-over. Even with the glasses on, he probably looked a little banged up. At least his nose wasn't bleeding, and he smelled pretty good.

Finally she broke into a thin, sexy smile. "Sugar, I'm just killin' time, waiting for my friends to show up."

"Is that right?" he said, pulling his wallet from his back pocket and making a grand show of handing it to her. "Well then, how 'bout we wait together? I'm buyin'."

Her smile blossomed then, accompanied by a tiny little laugh as she rubbed her painted fingertips against the leather of his wallet. Her fingers were long, like her legs, and pretty, like her smile. Her teeth were real white. He noticed that even through his shades. And her lips reminded him of Tansy's. Which wasn't necessarily a bad thing. Tansy had great lips.

He watched as she tilted her head to the side and licked those lips in a sassy invitation that went straight to his nuts. She turned toward The Charlie Horse, and Davis fell in behind, letting his eyes drink up the curve of her waist shown off so well in that fancy little bell-shaped dress. Maybe she'd come from a wedding all dressed up the way she was, he thought absently as they both stepped inside. Those killer flesh-colored heels made her legs look that much longer. No wonder he'd noticed them while driving down the road.

"That your car?" she asked as she led him toward the bar.

"You want a ride?" he asked in response. He'd be happy to let the car do all the work for him.

She seated herself on a barstool and opened her little clutch purse, depositing his wallet inside. He took his eyes off her for half a moment while he sat on the stool beside her, turning his body so it faced her completely. She was giving the bartender some fancy sign language and when she finished and looked back at him, he nearly burst out laughing. The wicked little temptress had taken out her own sunglasses and put them on. He sat there with a full-on grin, falling in love.

"What are we drinking?" he asked while they stared at each other through dark lenses.

"Boilermakers," she answered.

"Where you coming from?" he asked, curious.

"Family reunion," she said.

He nodded, reaching out to touch her cheek. It was an impulse. An impulse he followed, figuring she could simply swat his hand away and give him back his wallet if she didn't want him touching her.

She did him one better. She reached out and gingerly touched the side of his face, right where that roundhouse kick had landed, her lips forming into a sexy, little O.

"I'm guessing there's a story here," she said.

"Not a very interesting one," he responded. Suddenly, her lips were all he could see. Red as red could be underneath those dark shades. Serious ambrosia to a starving man.

"Probably better get a little ice on that," she whispered to him, those lips of hers making the prettiest of pouts. "Wouldn't want to spoil those good looks."

That made him grin.

When the bartender brought their beers and shots, she asked him for a bag of ice, indicating the bruise on his face. Then she took the pint glass in her hand and very gently held it up against his cheek. He didn't flinch a bit, but she did, giving away that she was less of a badass than she wanted him to believe.

Hmm. Going for it.

"You like me," he said with his big, wide grin.

"You gave me your wallet," she countered.

"You're nursing me back to health."

"Your eye swells too much, you won't be any good to me."

"Hell, you've already got my wallet. What else could you possibly be hoping for?"

She tilted her head and gave him a look. He wished she'd have removed her glasses first so he could get the full impact of that look. Decipher that look.

"You think a swollen eye's going to get in our way?" he went on, undaunted.

"I'm not going to give it a chance," she sassed back as she took the bag of ice wrapped in a clean towel from the bartender, thanked him, and then handed it to Davis.

She reached over with two hands and carefully removed his sunglasses. Slowly. Dramatically. She was studying him, he could tell. Assessing his injury. Checking out the rest of his face. The color of his eyes. He couldn't see her behind those dark shades she wore, but he felt her scrutiny.

"Fuck this," he mumbled before putting the ice on the counter and reaching up, mimicking her movements exactly. He took off her glasses with two hands. Slowly. Deliberately. Revealing what he'd only managed a glimpse of outside in the dim sidewalk lighting.

Forest green eyes, deep as a river, blinked at him under rows and rows of long dark lashes. Sultry eyes. Passionate. Intense. A stark contrast to her pretty-pale nose, narrow and sprinkled with freckles. Putting those voluptuous lips with these come-on eyes, she was striking. Way past pretty. Downright beautiful.

She tucked her chin, setting his sunglasses on the counter. Then she took his hand, turned it palm up, and placed the ice in the center. She lifted his hand slowly to the side of his face so that the ice covered his cheek and eye. She fixed his elbow so it was propped up on the bar and then took both hands and physically tilted his head so he was leaning into the ice, keeping it in place without a whole lot of effort. Her fingers trailed down the other side of his face and he wanted to groan at the contrast. She made him as comfortable as he could be under the circumstances.

She handed him his beer, reached back for a shot glass and dropped it in. "Drink up, pretty boy That bruise has gotta hurt."

He smirked at that. At the pretty boy thing.

"Are you generally a glutton for punishment?" she asked before taking a dainty sip of her whiskey.

"Not usually, no."

"The other guy look worse?"

"A little."

When she held silent for a few seconds, he capitulated. "It was a Taekwondo tournament just down the street. I've been in the mood to hit something for a while, so I signed up. Turned out to be a significant lack of judgment since I haven't been training regularly for a few months now. The side of my face is evidence I was not in top form."

"So you lost."

"Actually, I won," he said after his first sip. "The roundhouse kick to the eye knocked some sense into me, and I started to pay attention."

She knocked her shot glass against his pint. "Congratulations," she said, before taking another sip of her shot, following it up with a sip of beer.

"Thank you."

"So Taekwondo is…?"

"A form of martial arts. Similar to karate. Originated in Korea."

"And the color of your belt is…?"

"Black."

Her eyes went wide, and she looked toward the ice. "Then what color was his belt?"

"Black. Third degree. Which was bullshit. If I'd been on my game at all, he never would have touched me. Totally pissed me off."

"So is this Taekwondo your thing? Your passion?" she asked.

"It was for a while. One of them anyway."

"And the others?"

He thought for a moment, looking her over, and then he laid out the truth. "Lacrosse. The Wolfpack. Making money. Playing the drums in front of a lot of screaming women."

"You play the drums?"

"Occasionally. It's just a hobby," he admitted. "What about you? What's your passion?"

"Hmm," she said around a sip. "Ahh, let's see. Skipping out on dates."

"Good thing this isn't a date," Davis said.

"No. That happened earlier. Let's see, oh, stealing wallets."

"I guess I made that one too easy for you, didn't I?"

"I'll live."

"What else?"

"Kissing. I'm a good kisser."

"Now that I find hard to believe," he said.

"Seriously," she said. "I've got a black belt in kissing. Which is a real shame for you, because a black belt kissing a black belt…" She shuddered in distaste. "It would sort of be like tongue wrestling, and really, we don't want to go there."

Oh, we're definitely going there.

"Since I'm actually a double black belt I might be able to teach you a thing or two."

"Huh," she scoffed. "That's what they all say."

He laughed. Really laughed. Enjoying himself. He set his beer on the bar and took hold of one of her long-tapered fingers. "So Miss Black Belt in Kissing, what's your name?"

She jerked her head a bit, causing her lush ponytail to fall forward over her shoulder. "My friends call me Red."

"Ah, because of your hair," he said, making his move by holding on to her whole hand.

"Something like that."

"Then we have more than a black belt in common. *My* friends call me Pinks."

"Pinks?" It was her turn to laugh.

He laughed with her. "It's true. I'm sure it didn't start out as an endearment. Just the opposite. But it stuck, so I run with it."

"Red and Pinks, killing time together."

"You can't make this stuff up," he said, smiling into her pretty smile, liking the fact she was holding his hand back. Unfortunately she shook him loose when her phone buzzed and she went to dig it out of her clutch needing both of her hands.

He watched her read a text and begin to text back.

"Your friends?" he inquired.

Red nodded. "They're heading to The Oxford." Her head snapped up. "Would you mind if I took your picture? I'm telling them I'm busy nursing a patient back to health."

"You're a nurse?"

"Oh God, no. I'm just, you know, blowing them off."

"You're not going to follow them over to The Oxford?"

"And leave you in your hour of need? Smile," she ordered, holding up her phone and snapping it, leaving him temporarily blinded by the flash.

"Cute," she said, looking at the photo.

"With an ice pack covering half my face?"

She looked him over, assessing. "Maybe your right side is your best side," she offered.

He pulled the ice pack away from his head. "How's the left side look?"

She surveyed the damage. "Cold."

He smiled.

"I think you'll live to fight another day," she went on.

"No doubt," he said, placing the ice on the bar and taking a long guzzle of his beer. He licked his lips and then patted them with the tiny cocktail napkin. "Since you're staying, you want to dance?"

"Oh. That's…that's a really bad idea," she said before tossing back the rest of her shot.

"And why is that?" he asked.

"Because I'm a black belt on the dance floor too, and you've had the shit beat out of you enough for one day."

He chuckled. Finished the last of his beer and took the shot glass out, setting it on the bar. "I'll take my chances," he said, sliding off the stool. "How 'bout you let your buddy behind the bar hold on to that little clutch of yours. Make that the prize for whichever one of us comes off the dance floor victorious."

There was going to be no skipping out on him. He was making sure of it.

Red handed the clutch containing his wallet to the bartender and let him help her off the stool. In those crazy heels, she was just a couple inches shorter than he was.

"That oughta work," he mumbled, letting her lead the way.

Crain made his intentions known loud and clear to his unbeknown past, present, and future in-laws that their daughter Elizabeth—as he continued to address her throughout dinner—was his sole romantic interest. He even mentioned that he believed their paths might have crossed in Dallas, and how delighted he was to find her hiding herself here in Henderson when he'd arrived. He let them know he was eager to spend more time with Elizabeth now that

Mrs. Langford seemed willing to put the *Brooks Bennett for Mayor* thing aside, and how much he looked forward to getting to know the whole family as he and Elizabeth became better acquainted. He even suggested they all might want to take a trip to Dallas, on his plane, so that Elizabeth could introduce them to George W. and Mrs. Bush, and he could introduce them to his folks as well.

"You might have been pushing it with that one," Tansy laughed when he'd finally managed to get her alone in his truck after a very long, but very productive, evening.

He started the heavy machine up and revved the engine. "I was on a roll, darlin'. Once I saw saliva dripping out of your momma's mouth at the words private jet, well, I knew she was going to be putty in my hands. I was laying it on thick. Brooks Bennett, my ass."

"I think Scarlett had the Brooks issue beat to death with the word governor. How did you manage to get her on your side so fast?"

"I told your sister I was interested in you and gave her three hundred dollars to get out of my way."

"Three hundred dollars?"

"Best return on an investment in a long time. Now where are we going so that the two of us can celebrate?"

"I don't know," Tansy said as if she were bewildered. "Maybe you'd like to give me a *ride* in your truck."

He looked at her through the darkness. Saw that sexy smile. His voice came out low and quiet. "Nothing I'd like better than to give you a *ride* in this truck." He threw it in gear.

Davis had done his best to keep his growing intentions from bumping up against Red as they danced. But when she turned around and rubbed her plump, little ass up against him for the third time that night, he figured she needed to know exactly what she was up against. Literally. So he pulled her back into him, kissed her neck, and asked against her ear if she was ready to leave with him.

He about choked when she turned and said yes.

Yes?

Just like that?

"Bullshit."

"Come on," she said, fingering her hair, shooting him a come-on look, and holding out her hand.

He couldn't speak. Apparently didn't have to. Because she took him by the hand, retrieved her clutch, and paid their bill without touching his wallet. Before he knew it, he was seating her in the One-77 and telling her to buckle up.

He was trying to figure out the closest hotel when she dangled a key in front of him. "I have the place to myself," she said. "Turn right."

He followed her directions, his adrenaline pumping like a mad son of a bitch. He ran around the car to help her out of her side and followed her up the stairs to a small but well-maintained apartment. She struggled with the key a little bit and then pushed the door open and searched for the light switch.

"Not your place?" he surmised, glancing around at the tiny one-bedroom apartment.

"A friend's. She's letting me borrow it."

Davis made a careful study. Three steps forward, about twelve to the right and boom, there was the bed. "You aren't from around here?"

"No. Just here for the night."

Davis hit the light switch, casting them into darkness. He swung her around, backing her up against the door, his hands at her waist, his hips right up against hers, and his voice in her ear. "Then I'd better show you a helluva good time."

He leaned in and nipped her bottom lip. She pressed a hand against his chest, and he stopped immediately, looking into those deep green eyes. Her breath was coming fast and hard, and she panted the words, "The name Pinks doesn't seem to fit you all of a sudden."

He leaned in and kissed her good and long, tossing Pinks and his nice, safe, boring reputation behind him. Instead, he tucked his knee between her legs and ran his hands through her hair, letting pins and hair ties drop to the floor. "I have another nickname," he whispered as he pulled her from the door, bent down, and scooped her up into his arms, counting the steps forward and to the right before he tossed her on the bed. "The Ninja."

His shirt was over his head, his shoes toed off, and his pants unzipped quicker than he'd taken that first hit tonight. He noticed Red had sat up and scooted toward the headboard. He reached down and removed one of her heels, tossing it over his shoulder, hearing it clatter around the floor.

"You nervous?" he asked, reaching over with both hands and removing the other one. He tossed that one behind him as well.

"Those shoes cost me four hundred dollars."

"Those shoes…are worth every penny," he said, placing one knee on the bed. "Those shoes…got you a ride in a One-77," he went on, crawling up over her, encasing her within his arms and legs. "Those shoes…guarantee you at least three hardcore, black belt, ninja-fied orgasms." He snuck one arm underneath her and flipped them both so she lay sprawled out on his chest. Her dress was unzipped before she could protest.

"And if you let me stay the whole night," he said, divesting her of her party dress by pulling it unceremoniously over her head, "there'll be two more just like them in the morning," he grunted, flipping them both back over so he was now on top, noticing that the creamy color of her lacy bra was almost the exact color of her skin. His new favorite color. "And if that happens…" he trailed off, more interested in kissing those ruby red lips."

She twisted her mouth from under his. "If that happens… what?"

He grinned down into those smokin' hot eyes, knowing now he had her right where he wanted her. "If that happens," he soothed, stroking her hair, touching her cheek, "then we'll have smashed my own personal record and *you* will tell me your real name."

"Not gonna happen," she said, pulling his lips back to hers.

"Oh, it's gonna happen," he said against them as he reached into the pocket of his jeans and pulled out a short string of condom packets. He tucked those under her pillow for safekeeping and got busy kissing her lips. And man, she was not kidding when she said she was a black belt at kissing. She was turning him inside out. He groaned, needing to think of something other than how hot this was, how engorged he felt, how much he wanted to be inside of her, and demonstrate his stamina. Which he was starting to worry was not going to be all it was cracked up to be.

So he sucked on her tongue and gradually pulled his mouth away, beginning a slow, concerted effort of kissing his way over her chin…down her neck…past her collar bone…and beyond.

Crain had driven Tansy out to the old Myers farm so he could show off his new 4X4 and all it could handle. They were bumping over an outlying field when Tansy realized there were no lights around them, anywhere. But overhead, through his open sunroof, she saw a clear sky full of stars. She reached her hand over to Crain's thigh and squeezed. The man downshifted and spun the wheel, throwing her against him. They came to an abrupt stop.

"You got something on your mind, Mrs. Carraway?" he said as he turned off the motor.

"I might," she said through a smile.

"How 'bout meeting me around front, and I'll show you what's under the hood."

"Okay," she said. Not exactly what she had in mind, but if he wanted to show her what was under the hood, she'd bite.

He cut the headlights but kept the running lights on so Tansy could at least see a little bit as she picked her way along the uneven ground in her long dress and heels. Leaving one hand on the truck for balance, she followed it around to the hood, meeting Crain in the middle.

"I think we're finally on the right path," he said, taking off his sports coat and laying it down on the top of his truck. "I mean, my parents are up to speed," he said, hoisting her up, causing her to squeal a bit as he sat her on top of the huge hood. The surface beneath her was warm and felt good combined with the night air.

"I'm not gonna need but a few weeks before I take your daddy out to dinner and ask him for your hand."

"You're gonna do that?"

"Would we be in this mess if I'd done it right the first time?"

"Probably not."

Crain put one booted foot up on the big fender. He leaned in and kissed her sweetly. "So I'm gonna pretend what we've been pretending, and I'll ask him for your hand—do my damnedest to get his blessing—and then, once we pop the champagne while we're showing your momma your big-ass engagement ring —"

"I'm getting a ring?" she said with glee.

He stopped and looked her square in the eye. "Again, would we be in this mess if I'd done this right the first time?"

"You don't need to get me a ring."

"Like hell," he said, leaning in to kiss her. He pulled her closer to him, moving her fanny to the edge of the hood. "You're getting a ring. A big one. One that will not go unnoticed by anyone between here and Dallas."

"Wow."

"My wife deserves it," he said against her lips. Crain's big hands skimmed up and down her sides. "She deserves a lot of things." She felt his fingers slide all the way down the thin silk over her hips, down her legs, reaching her ankles. He gripped them tight before starting a slow, steady glide up the front of her calves pushing the hem of her dress up as he went. His fingers trailed over her knees, and—*oh God*—splayed and laid claim to her thighs. Everything inside her went tight.

"I've been neglectful since we've been married. So from now on…" he insisted as he kissed across her cheek, as he pulled her dress out from under her and bunched it up around her waist, "you're either going to be snuggled up in that pool house with me, or I'll be helping you pass the hours house-sitting at the Devine's. But for now," he said, coaxing her to lie back on top of his sports coat, "I'm going to shut the hell up and use my mouth to try to make you forget just how neglectful I've been."

"Craaaain," she breathed as his lips touched down in the center of her tummy. His tongue swirled around her naval, and she scraped the tips of her fingernails through his hair. His fingers caught in the sides of her thong, pulling it down her legs, off and discarded. And then all she felt was pleasure. Such divine, exquisite pleasure as Crain made love to her with his lips, and his tongue, and his fingers, and his mouth.

❦

"Fuck," Davis exclaimed as his hand flew to protect the hurt side of his face.

"I'm sorry…sorry…so, oh shit, I'm…you know…"

"Yeah, you're sorry," he said, plowing into Red, not stopping for anything, even if it was the second time she'd inadvertently whacked him. This little dynamo was a powder keg, and when she went off, she went off hard. Hard and fast, and—oh, man—he couldn't get enough. He trapped her hands over her head and leaned down into her face. "Hit me again, and you're on your knees."

He let go, and she immediately slapped his good side.

"You have got to be kidding me," he spit as he pulled out, flipped her onto her stomach, pulled her hips up, slapped her beautiful, bare ass and plowed right back into her.

"Ah!!" Her arms sought something to hold on to or push against as the top of her head hit the headboard. "I didn't think you'd really do it," she cried. Which had him practically laughing as he sucked in a deep breath and sat back on his haunches, pulling her up with him, still locked in tight.

"You knew I'd do it," he said, pulling the soft, silky skin of her back up against his chest, starting to pump slow and deep from this sitting position. He kissed her cheek and neck and then squeezed and rubbed her breasts with one hand while he got busy with his other, bringing the redheaded minx to her twenty-third climax. Or something. He'd lost count hours ago.

There was absolutely nothing nice, safe, or boring about the last four hours they'd spent in bed, on the floor, half in the bed and half on the floor. In positions he'd only read about. Davis knew he was never gonna forget this night—if it didn't kill him first.

He had run out of condoms long ago, but thank God for the stash of all shapes, sizes, and colors they'd found under the bathroom sink. He had surpassed his personal best the third time he came, and Red over here had come silently, come quietly, come moaning, come crying, come yelling, come screaming, and one time had come while she bit the shit out of his shoulder. He loved it. Either she was Aphrodite come to earth to give his beat-up ego a boost, or the two of them were the world's most compatible, albeit combative, lovers.

He didn't care which it was as his balls pulled up, and he came, growling in her ear that she was the best night he'd ever had.

"Water," he gasped through parched and sore lips as he lay next to Red, trying to catch his breath. "Water, Advil, ice for my face," he went on. "Then a shower. We'll clean each other up. Then fresh sheets, if we can find them. Then sleep."

He rolled over and tugged Red out of bed. "Come on. You gotta stay hydrated or this shit's gonna kill you."

She laughed, her head lolling backward, her body exhausted as he tried to sit her up. He took both her hands and pulled her to her feet. "Come on," he coaxed, "I'll help you."

"You go," she said. "I need to use the bathroom. Bring me a glass of water. You can come in when you hear the shower running." She started drifting toward the bathroom. "Don't forget ice for your face," she said, shutting the door behind her.

Davis smiled.

Then he turned on the light, took one look at the bed, and went into sheer panic.

CHAPTER THIRTY-FIVE

There was blood everywhere.

Maybe not a lot of it. But they'd manage to smudge the wealth of it around pretty good with all their black-belt antics. It wasn't bright red, and it was dry. Probably happened about four hours ago, the first time he'd felt the extreme pleasure of penetration.

He sank down on the edge of the bed, stunned. His shoulders slumped, his back curved forward, and suddenly, he felt every bit as tired as he probably should. He eyed the closed bathroom door.

This turn of events was a complete surprise. Downright shocking. Little sassy-sass Red in there was a virgin. "Was" being the operative word. Thanks to him, she "was" no more. In fact, she was now not a virgin five or six times over.

"Shit," he said, holding his head in his hands. He'd had no idea. None. And now, he didn't even know how he was supposed to feel about it. If he was honest, he'd have to say he felt relieved he didn't know any better, because he'd just had his all-time best night ever, which may not have happened had he known she wasn't…as sassy as she pretended to be.

How the hell did she feel about it was the important question, and one that hit hard in the center of his very sturdy solar plexus. He took another look at the sheets and panicked. He had them off, bound up inside one of the pillowcases and by the front door before a minute ticked off the clock. Then he searched for and found, thank God, another set of sheets and had the bed made up as best he could by the time he heard the shower turning off. He hit the lights, dashed into the kitchen for two glasses of water, and was holding out his hand offering her one as she opened the bathroom door. She stood there dripping wet, wrapped loosely in a towel.

How his dick sprung to life after all this, he hadn't a clue. Except that she was just as beautiful dripping wet and a helluva lot hotter.

"I thought you were going to join me," she said, taking the glass from his hand and drinking the water down in one long chug.

He took the empty from her and handed her his full glass. "Drink that. I'll get a refill." He left the room. "I changed the sheets," he said over his shoulder.

"Did you get some ice for yourself?" she asked as he came back to the bedroom. He stumbled. Literally stumbled over his own two ninja feet. She was standing in the middle of the room completely naked, using the towel to dry her hair, and all praise to Benjamin Franklin and his magic of electricity, the light shining in from the bathroom left nothing to his imagination.

Nada.

He would have placed a bet against it, but this night just got better.

He went up, took hold of her elbow, and kissed her for being the best damn night he was ever gonna have.

"What was that for?" she asked softly, smiling, looking as if he'd managed to reach her on some deeper level.

"For being you," he said quietly. "I'm gonna take a quick shower. Drink your water down, and I'll be right out."

He showered fast, wondering how to broach the subject, because let's face it, he had to broach the subject. He wasn't falling that far off of the nice, safe, boring path. He still wanted to be able to look his mom in the eye.

And she didn't have to talk about it if she didn't want to. Didn't need to give him an explanation, didn't need to do anything. He just needed to acknowledge it. Acknowledging that she just gave him her virginity had to be the right thing to do.

She was sitting in the bed, covers pulled up to her chin, drinking her water when he came out. He turned the light off in the bathroom, but turned on the one atop the bedside table, so he could see her face. He took her water, set it aside, and then crawled in, pulling her down underneath him, so he'd be sure to have her undivided attention.

He kissed her sassy little mouth because he couldn't help himself. The memory of those lips was going to drive him crazy.

"So. You got something you want to tell me?"

She quirked a brow. "I don't owe you my name unless we smash your personal record. In the morning."

"Trust me. My personal record was blown right along with my mind several hours ago. And your name," he said, kissing her in the center of her chest, "will be cared for like a rare and precious jewel. Locked away inside for safekeeping. God, you smell good," he said, getting distracted, giving into his instincts and licking her from sternum to collar bone.

"Hmm," she smiled, tilting her lips down to kiss the top of his head. When he looked up, she ran her fingers through his damp hair, perhaps trying to style it. "I like your hair. You've got great hair."

"I haven't found a part of you that I'm not wild about, and I've been searching pretty hard, in case you haven't noticed."

She smiled.

He really liked her smile.

Davis rolled to his side, pulling her into a modified wrestling hold by wrapping his arms around her torso, digging his upper leg in between hers, and tucking his foot underneath the shin of her lower one. In competition, it was a way to apply pressure to an opponent's knee so that they'd tap out. Right now, he was just trying to pin her in place while he kissed her senseless.

"Baby," he whispered as he loosened up his hold so he could stroke her hair back off her face. "When I changed the sheets, there was evidence that I may have hurt you." He kissed her temple and then pulled back, placing his head on the pillow they shared so he could look at her. "Did I?"

She shook her head no.

"Was this your first time?"

Those heavily lashed eyes blinked a few times and then she gave him a little smile and said, "And my second, and my third, and my fourth, and my—"

They both started to laugh.

Davis rolled to his back, bringing his free hand up to run it down his face. Embarrassed happiness bubbled inside him from head to toe. He tried to cover his grin with his hand as he looked at her but then thought, what the hell. "I can't even feign a protest," he admitted. "I just hope you'll remember this night fondly, because there is no way I'm ever going to forget it."

"Pinks," she whispered. "If you untangle my leg, I'll do my best to demonstrate my gratitude and maybe give you one more memory."

He unwrapped himself from her and settled on his back. He reached up, shut off the light, spread his legs as she snuggled herself in between, and watched her head disappear under the covers. He laid his head back, took one last glance at the ceiling, and then let himself die and float off to heaven.

That was the last time he came, though he made sure the hot-blooded orgasmatron in his arms got hers another three or four times. She was so quick to please, so multi-orgasmic, that he'd lost count on whether she was coming or going until she collapsed on top of him, begging for him to stop—for good, she said—and let her sleep. He was pretty sure she was crying from sheer exhaustion when she said it.

Fine.

He'd done his job, and she wasn't kicking him out. She even let him cuddle her in close. Of course, she might have been passed out at that point. Still, he fell asleep feeling more satiated and contented than he ever had before.

Morning never came. It was mid-afternoon when the two of them woke up. Baby Red's hair was in corkscrews spread out everywhere, and she moaned when he told her the time.

She moaned again when he had her all cleaned up in the shower and repeated her most vocal orgasm with his tongue on her clit and her back against the wall. She tried to reciprocate, but Davis grabbed her hand and told her he didn't know which hurt worse, his face or his cock. She kissed them both tenderly.

On the way out the door, Davis grabbed the soiled sheets, and Baby Red wrote a note to her friend, leaving a hundred-dollar-bill so she could buy new sheets for herself.

And condoms.

They got in the One-77 and headed back to The Charlie Horse where Red told him to just drop her at the front walk. He noticed there were three cars in the parking lot. Obviously, she didn't want him to know which one was hers.

He grabbed her wrist before she could get out the door. "You got a secret?"

She blinked those green eyes several times but remained silent.

"I know you're not married," he said. "But what? Engaged? A senator's daughter?"

She ducked her chin and smiled, shaking her head before looking at him again. "You have a very vivid imagination."

"Not so vivid, I assure you."

"Although I do have family here, I reside outside of North Carolina. So, it's probably best if we just…"

"Keep things simple," he finished.

She nodded.

"No names. No numbers. No sexting across state lines."

She laughed.

Davis released her wrist and made quick moves to get out of the car. She met him as he came around to her side. Without hesitation, he snuck an arm around her waist and pulled her in tight against him. "I'm Davis," he whispered, smiling down into all that glory as he ran his fingers through the hair that fell over her forehead. "I left my card for you when I retrieved my wallet. When you're back in North Carolina, look me up." Then he kissed her. Like he meant it. Like she was the best night he'd ever had, and he was never gonna forget it.

Red staggered against the One-77 when he released her. For as long as he lived, Davis would never forget the picture she made. Hair mussed up, dress a bit askew, tottering on her tall heels. She touched her long, pretty fingers to her lips. Lips swollen from their night together. Lips swollen from their very last kiss. And then those same lips formed the prettiest sound he was ever gonna hear.

"I'm Scarlett."

CHAPTER THIRTY-SIX

Things had begun to move at the pace Crain Carraway liked 'em.

Saturday morning, he held Elizabeth's hand as she called Harry and Jody Devine. The Henderson couple who she was housesitting for had three grown daughters: Tess, Grace, and Annabelle, all off living elsewhere. Tansy had known them all her life. She'd told Crain that the Devines were the least likely Hendersonians to participate in gossip, and she trusted Mr. and Mrs. Devine not to give them away, especially since they'd be in Florida until Thanksgiving. So he listened to her tell their story, asked if it would be all right if her *husband* moved into their home with her while she house sat, and asked if they would keep her secret.

Jody Devine immediately told them to take over the master bedroom and then offered to throw them a reception in place of their annual New Year's Eve Ball. Harry Devine seemed to get a real kick out of the details from their brief courtship and impromptu wedding. Crain couldn't decide which one was more of a romantic. In any case, he was delighted by their generosity and heartened by their enthusiasm. May the rest of Henderson be so obliging.

He moved out of Vance's pool house that same day.

On Monday, Crain set the stage for serious work. He gathered Hale, Vance, Brooks, The Pink One, who had his face all beat to hell—Crain didn't ask—and the computer-geek football coach, Josh McCourt, in the conference room.

"I'm in," he said, standing at the head of the table. "With both feet. For all intents and purposes, Elizabeth and I are dating, her parents approve, and it's just a matter of time before we become engaged."

"Engaged?" Vance joked.

"Yes, engaged," Crain stressed. "Immediately after which, we'll tell her folks about our not-so-secret elopement."

"Well, at that point, why bother to tell them at all?"

"Because my parents know the truth. All of Dallas knows the truth. The Langfords need to know the truth as well. Then Elizabeth and I, plus all of you yahoos, will go along with however the Langfords want to play it from there. Understood?"

Brooks had that megawatt grin on his face when he asked, "How'd ya manage all that, Tex?"

Crain cleared his throat and mirrored that grin on his own face. He put his hands in his pockets and said, "I simply explained to Garland Langford that Brooks Bennett was small potatoes. Then I pulled out a picture of AirDallas, and she practically pushed Elizabeth into my lap."

"Mrs. Langford does like to fly private," Brooks acknowledged with a laugh. "Nice move."

"You've got to bring something to the table," Crain said before moving on. "Now, at Team Henderson's suggestion, CC Dallas has gone national, and CC Henderson is located across the street. During this honeymoon period with the Langfords, I plan to be here most of the week. I was hoping Elizabeth and I could fly out after office hours Tuesday, spend Wednesdays at my office in Dallas, and fly back before E&E opens Thursday mornings. Elizabeth will be working for E&E on the sports academy project while in Dallas. I just need to…" his words trailed off.

"Need to get her acclimated back into Dallas," Hale offered.

Crain looked down at the conference table, tapped it with his finger, and nodded his head.

"You aren't planning to stick around?" Vance asked. The disappointment in his voice was obvious.

"Fellas, I'm from the Lone Star State. That's my home. But I'm committed to this project and to Henderson. That office across the street will be fully staffed and operational, and my plan is to simply reverse the schedule once I'm able. Be here every Wednesday in the office, bring Elizabeth home to see her friends and family."

"It's a good plan," Hale said. "It's a good plan for your company and a good plan for Henderson. E&E will help any way we can."

"So where do we stand on the dormitory, learning center, and kick-ass, retro, baseball-to-football, situated right-in-the-center-of-campus CC Dallas & Henderson Sports Academy Stadium?" Vance asked.

"I said I'm in, didn't I?" Crain smiled at Vance. "You got 'em. All three. We might want to rethink the stadium name a bit. Seems a little unwieldy. But I'm putting people on all three as soon as I get back to Dallas."

"Crain, I'm glad this is working out for you. Really I am, because beyond all this Tansy nonsense—"

"Elizabeth. My wife prefers to be called Elizabeth."

Vance looked up, somewhat startled. Then a slow grin split his face. "I believe she does," he said. "From now on we'll do our best to remember it."

Even the Surly Duo nodded, both looking noticeably less surly. Crain took a deep breath as Vance continued.

"Beyond the circumstances that have led CC Dallas to branch out into Henderson, having your company here is a real boon to our struggling little town. We need to be able to rely on what you're promising."

"In Texas, a man's word means something. But if you boys from the Tar Heel State need me to sign something, I'll sign something."

"Pinks, get Duncan James on the phone."

It was the first time since Crain had met the kid that The Pink One didn't jump up to get the job done. In fact, he didn't raise his head at all, apparently deeply engrossed in his phone.

The entire table noticed and stared.

"Pinks?" Vance called again.

Nothing.

"Pinks, pull your damn head out of that cellphone and get it back in the game."

The Pink One looked up, startled.

"Shit," he said, looking around the table at all the eyes on him. "What'd I miss?"

"What the hell happened to your face?" Brooks asked.

"Never mind that," Vance countered. "I need you to get Duncan James on the phone. You think you can handle that?"

"And then some." He jumped up and was dialing before he'd gotten out the door.

"What happened to his face?" Brooks asked again.

"Some Karate Kid tournament," Vance answered. "It'll heal. But this phone business. I think he met someone. I swear to God the kid's got a habit of falling fast and falling hard."

"So tell me about this Duncan James," Crain said, bringing the room back on task. He had a nagging feeling that The Pink One's love life was not something he wanted to discuss. Ever.

"He's a buddy of ours. Smart business attorney in Raleigh. In love with Annabelle Devine. Same Devine family Tansy's house sitting for. This may be a good opportunity for E&E to hire Duncan away from the Raleigh firm and get him to work for us exclusively. Get his sorry ass moved into town. Make him bring Annabelle with him."

"I'd rather him open his own firm here," Brooks said. "Will CC Henderson be needing legal counsel?"

"I've got people in Dallas for whatever needs to be drawn up between me and E&E. But if your buddy's good, I could use him here, sure."

"Business brings business," Brooks said.

"So is it your goal, as mayor, to promote Henderson businesses or to attract outside businesses to Henderson? Because there's a big difference."

"It's my goal to support the growth of the businesses already in place. But ultimately, we need to attract larger companies to

Henderson, or this town is not going to survive another generation. Henderson Helping Henderson has an underlying goal. We need our citizens to do a few things for themselves and willingly contribute to the overall state of our town. It's crucial we bring the cost of operations down, so we can provide overly attractive incentives to new businesses."

"Like lower tax rates?"

"Like zero tax rates for the first number of years. Low or no rent for our main street storefronts in exchange for upgrading and maintaining the properties. Free marketing to the local area and beyond. We want this to be a win, win, win situation. We want to put Henderson and its proud heritage back on the map."

"Free marketing? No rent? How are you gonna manage that?" Crain asked.

Josh McCourt piped in for the first time. "Molly, Piper, and Tansy—I mean Elizabeth—are putting Evie Jackson on it. All of it."

That was news to Crain. "What the hell is Evie going to do?"

"Rally the old guard. Piper thinks they like to mess in all the young people's lives because they're bored playing bridge all day. Too much time on their hands. She wants to give them a place on Team Henderson. Get them involved in encouraging growth instead of chasing people out of town. I think they've even spoken to your grandmother about it, Vance. She complained that the Garden Club had gotten stale. That she wanted out-of-town ideas. She's on board too."

"Why is this the first I'm hearing about it?" Vance asked.

"Because when you're home, you and Piper are holed up in the blue room," The Pink One said as he came back in the room. "And I hear a lot of things coming from that room, but not much of it sounds like conversation."

"That's it," Vance said to Pinks. "We're moving your ass to the pool house."

"Fine by me."

Crain noticed The Pink One tried to hide his grin and that Vance was now kicking him under the table, getting a chuckle out of him. Those two were close. Probably good to keep that in mind.

"Henderson needs attractive and affordable lodging," Crain offered. "So that the Evans family does not have to supply housing to its employees or business associates on a regular basis."

"It's on the list," Brooks said. "And it's a long list. My motto has to be 'One Thing at a Time.'"

Crain's motto was "Why Wait?" so on Tuesday, when his sweet Elizabeth asked him to meet with Piper and Molly about their Big Pie Plate, he ushered them into his brand-new conference room and had them take a seat.

"It's not just a big pie plate," Piper said. "It's revolutionary. Everything tastes better baked in the Big Pie Plate."

"There's your tagline," Crain said.

"I like it," Molly chimed in.

"And we've got a big idea to go with it," Piper continued.

"We want to be rich," Molly interjected.

"And help put Henderson on the map," Piper added.

"But mostly the rich part," Molly said, beaming ear to ear. She pulled back just a bit before saying, "So Vance Jr. can attend college…among other things."

Crain felt like he was jumping around in a Moon Bounce with these two. He cleared his throat. "Okay, so you've got a revolutionary pie plate, and you want to put Henderson on the map while at the same time making yourselves rich. So what's your big idea?"

"We want to link the pie plate with Henderson, North Carolina. So if it hits big, the town of Henderson will become a household name. We plan to put the town crest right in the center of the Big Pie Plate, so that everyone knows where it came from, where they're manufactured. We plan to open the Big Pie Plate Store right here in the center of town and make it an old-school storefront, real cute, to attract visitors from other areas. Our ideas include a tasting room, cooking classes, recipe books, other ceramic pieces by Molly, and anything else we can come up with to draw women, bakers, and foodies alike.

"Now, we have a couple of aces up our sleeve," Piper said moving on.

"And what are those?" Crain asked.

"The recipe to my mother's award-winning piecrust and the fact that Evie Jackson's best friend Thelma Gibson's daughter-in-law has a big in at QVC."

"The shopping network?"

"Yes, and we have prematurely managed to get an appointment way up North in West Chester, Pennsylvania to show off what our Big Pie Plate can do."

"Wow."

"Yes," Piper repeated wide-eyed, "Wow."

"But here's our problem," Molly said. "In order to introduce the Big Pie Plate on QVC or any shopping channel, we have to be able to manufacture thousands of pie plates. Quickly. It is our understanding that officials from the shopping network will want to visit our factory, and…you know, there is no factory. I make each one by hand."

"Hmm," Crain said.

The two women sat staring at him as if he had all the answers.

"Is the appeal of the Big Pie Plate the fact that it's made by hand?" Crain asked.

"Of course," Molly responded, at the same time Piper said, "Absolutely not."

The two turned and looked at one another.

Yup. A Moon Bounce.

"Think big, Molly," was all Piper had to say before turning back to Crain. "It is our belief that the specific ingredients in Molly's ceramics are what makes it cook so well. I submitted a patent for the particular chemical makeup and the size and shape. Which won't mean a thing if this takes off, because everyone will be trying to reproduce the Big Pie Plate."

"But they won't be able to," Molly said. "Being big has nothing to do with the cooking results."

"Is there any reason that you believe your Big Pie Plate can't be machine-made and create the same baking results?" Crain asked Molly.

"Probably not."

"Would you like to spend all your time making Big Pie Plates, or do you like the idea of freeing yourself up to do other things as well?"

"Well, when you put it that way."

"Here's what I suggest you do. Keep your appointment with QVC. If they like your product, tell them you'll be in touch and come back to see me. Evie Jackson isn't the only one with connections. I'll donate $10,000 pin money and put you in touch with some top-notch manufacturing facilities."

"We want to do it in Henderson," Piper insisted.

"I know. I know you do, but you're going to need someone to make the manufacturing equipment to be used here in Henderson, and you're going to want it fast. At the same time I want you to put a strong business plan together and start doing your own fundraising on Kickstarter. You'll still need other investors, but they'll look at your business plan a whole lot closer if you're doing what you can to raise funds on your own."

"And if we have QVC in our pocket."

"Especially if you have QVC in your pocket," Crain agreed. "Then you hit up ol' Team Henderson across the street for one of the plethora of abandoned buildings you can't help but trip over around here. Demand free rent and a storefront. Then you market your Big Pie Plate on the Internet with YouTube videos and online cooking shows."

"Online cooking shows?" Piper's eyes lit up.

"I'm assuming they have them," Crain said. "They have everything else."

"We could do an online cooking show," Piper said to Molly, practically breathless with excitement. "Our own online cooking show. Sell the Big Pie Plate ourselves. Genevra can help."

"You and Genevra can do an online cooking show. I will be creating the pie plates off camera."

"Oh, come on," Piper said rolling her eyes. "If we make it a naked online cooking show, you'd be right in front of the camera."

"If we make it a naked online cooking show, we won't need QVC."

On Wednesday, when Crain found himself back in Dallas without his sweet Elizabeth—because Henderson's Harvest Daze Queen Tansy had too much on her plate to join him—he became the surly one. He rubbed the damn red right off his ball thinking of ways to force his wife into submission. He was not working himself to death for her hometown and the crazy people in it if he wasn't getting any fringe benefits. So he flew his ass back to Henderson early, forgoing a night in his own damn bed, crawled in next to Tansy at the Devine's, and told her what was what.

Or he meant to.

It didn't occur to him until he was at his desk Thursday morning that nothing had been settled except his pent-up sexual frustration. That had been settled good.

Clearly, he was no match for his wife's feminine wiles, but he knew someone who was in the same boat, so he marched himself over to Vance Evans' office, ready for a little powwow.

"I'm investing in your wife's company," Crain said as he took a seat in front of Vance's desk.

"What company?"

Crain smiled. When he was right, he was right.

"Henderson's Big Pie Plate. I think it's going to be big."

"Henderson's Big…oh," Vance stopped himself. "That thing does make good pie. I don't even like pie, but I find myself looking in the warming drawer every time I walk in the kitchen."

"She and Molly DuVal met with me Tuesday. Wanted my opinion."

"Your opinion about what?" Vance asked, immediately becoming part of the Surly Team.

"See I thought that might be your response." He sat up in his seat, clasped his fingers together, and lowered his voice. "It appears the women around here are as ambitious as the men and probably twice as capable. Elizabeth refused to take time away from her Harvest Daze planning to accompany me to Dallas for all of thirty-six hours. And your pretty, little Piper has a lot of big ideas about the Big Pie Plate because she wants to put Vance Jr. through college."

"I'm putting Vance Jr. through college."

"I thought that's what you'd say."

"Why does my wife think I'm incapable of putting our children through college?"

"I didn't ask."

"I don't understand."

"I didn't think you would."

"No. I mean, I seriously don't understand. Women. Piper included. You may not know this, Crain, but before you arrived in town, I had a real issue with women. Apparently, I don't even like them."

"This is not news to me."

"Molly DuVal and I go way back—infamously—so I'm pretty certain that my wife's passion for Molly's pie plate is the Universe's way of paying me back. And apparently keeping Perfect Piper barefoot and pregnant is not keeping her out of trouble."

"I think we need to band together. I can help you out, and you do the same for me."

"Whatcha got in mind?"

"A conspiracy."

"I'm in."

"You tell Elizabeth that part of her job is to be in Dallas once a week, and I keep you informed of the shenanigans Piper is whipping up behind the scenes. For instance, I'm pretty sure she's gonna be starring in her own online cooking show."

"Yeah, I'm not gonna be down with that."

"And there was a naked version of it being bandied about as well."

"Molly!"

"See there, you do know women."

CHAPTER THIRTY-SEVEN

Friday evening, Vance knocked on the pool-house door and waited until he heard a muffled shout before entering. It was amusing to stand on the threshold and look around the place through the eyes of a married man. This truly was the quintessential bachelor pad, and since Pinks was now the only bachelor on campus, it was right that it be bequeathed to him.

"How's it going in here?" Vance shouted without taking another step inside. The kid hadn't had a place of his own since he'd arrived in town. Vance felt the need to respect his privacy—a changing of the guard if you will.

Pinks poked his wet head out of the double doors of the bedroom, rubbing a towel across it. His body was naked down to his waist, where he'd pulled on a pair of jeans. A broad smile split his lips as he noticed where Vance stood. "Come on in," he said. "Let me throw on a shirt." Then he disappeared around the corner.

Vance stood his ground. "I need you to witness something for me. I'm gonna give Piper a post-ceremony prenup, and it requires a witness's signature."

It did Vance's heart good to see Pinks storm around the corner looking like he was going to take a swing at him. If it were anyone else threatening Piper, he'd want Pinks to look just like this. Right up in the perpetrator's face. "You're not giving Piper a prenup," Pink's growled.

"Hang on there, Rocky Balboa, and hear me out. How's that face of yours, by the way? Looks like it's healing up okay. You ever get in to see a doctor?"

"Quit stalling. What the hell's going on?"

"Apparently, my wife doesn't believe I have the means or ability to pay for our child's college tuition."

"What?" Pinks exclaimed, stepping back and squinting his eyes.

"Yeah, that one hit me out of the blue, too."

Pinks started to laugh. "You told her you're made of money, right?"

"I did. But what I understand from Tansy, or ah, Elizabeth, is that because I didn't make Piper sign a prenup—while she was in the hospital, severely dehydrated due to the fact that I knocked her up—Piper doesn't believe I'm made of money. The Lawyer Beaumont is convinced that any businessperson with assets would have had the sense to draw up a prenuptial agreement and have it signed before the wedding. Apparently Perfect Piper believes she's married to a delusional loser."

"So you're planning to teach her a lesson."

"Don't you think she deserves one?"

"Damn straight."

"Good. Loyalty back where it belongs. Now." He held the papers up. "This is a fake. Total fake. I mean, maybe it's real—I had Duncan write it up because Piper's a lawyer, and she's going to read every word. But, you know…"

"You're not really making her sign a prenup."

"Ever. But in order to make a point, I told him to throw in every lousy, devious, underhanded prenup bullshit he could come up with. So keep a straight face and plan on some fireworks."

"I will enjoy playing along."

"I can always count on you for the really important stuff," Vance said as the two men left the pool house and crossed the distance to the main house kitchen. "My father has promised to keep Genevra out of the kitchen for a while. I don't want her to see this."

"What about your grandmother?"

"She's on board."

Pinks was outright giggling like a damn girl at that when they stepped through the French doors and into the kitchen.

"What's so funny?" Piper and her bouncy curls asked, her head popping up over a large mixing bowl as they came in. She kept stirring as if her life depended on it.

"Nothin'," Vance said. "I think Pinks met someone," he continued nonchalantly.

"What?" Pinks shouted, horrified.

"I know," Piper responded, all big-eyed and excited. "He told me."

"What!" Vance roared, turning on his buddy.

"He inadvertently stole her virginity and can't decide how guilty he should feel about it," Piper said.

"Piper!" Pinks exclaimed.

"I told you, you need to talk to Vance about this," she said sincerely. "I'm sure he's deflowered dozens of young women. He can coach you through this."

"Holy shit," Vance whirled on Piper. "I have not deflowered anybody. *Anybody*, do you hear me?"

Piper stopped her stirring and rolled her eyes. "Oh, come on. With your reputation? Please."

"Piper," he said quietly, moving in for the kill. "I thought we had an agreement. No. You know what?" He stopped, placed the prenup on the island, and found himself a pen. "I'm adding an addendum." He spoke as he wrote. "Throwing Vance's misspent youth in his face—"

Piper looked around him to Pinks. "That's what he likes to call it now."

"—will result in vast and various penalties to be doled out as Vance feels appropriate. No ifs, ands, or buts." He paused. "Scratch that. There will definitely be a butt involved," he said glaring at his uppity bride. "Initial here please."

"What is this?"

"A prenup," he said, eyebrows raised.

"You got me a prenup?" she said, awed.

"I didn't get you a prenup, Piper. Nobody *gets* their bride a prenup. I'm handing you a prenup and demanding you sign it post-nuptially."

She literally launched herself into his arms, wrapped her legs around his waist, and kissed him all over his face. Vance turned them both around to face Pinks. He held her with one arm and pointed to her back with the other. "I swear to God, this was not the reaction I was going for, Piper," he said, pulling her off him, making her stand on her own two feet. "Why in the world are you happy about this?"

"Because, if you're making me sign a prenup then maybe you do have enough money for my lava stone countertops."

"Baby doll, if I didn't have the cash for your lava stone countertops I assure you I would find a way to earn it and then some. Whatever you want, you are going to get. Although I'm not paying for Vance, Jr.'s college tuition. You're on your own with that." When she blinked a couple times, he said, "Kidding. Kidding. I can afford to send the kid anywhere he gets in. Although, he'll be going to State. On a baseball scholarship. After he graduates from the sports academy we're building. But if he has a sister," he said, "she gets to go anywhere she wants."

"You need to forget about baseball. Uncle Pinks will be coaching the kid in lacrosse as soon as he can hold a stick," Davis said.

"Vance, Jr. so much as utters that foul word, I am running your ass out of town."

"I'll own this town by then. Just watch me."

Vance didn't have a comeback. Because that was a highly probable possibility.

Piper reached over, picked up the prenup, and clasped it to her heart like it was a treasured teddy bear from childhood. She sauntered toward him, all playmate-of-the-month, intent on thanking him with a kiss. "You better read those," he warned.

"Of course I'm going to read them. I'm not ridiculous."

"You're a little ridiculous. Not believing I'm a millionaire. Pinks. How much money did I donate to the Phi Delts when you were a freshman?"

"One million dollars," Pinks said, imitating Dr. Evil.

Piper stopped dead in her tracks. "Now *that* is truly ridiculous."

⚭

"So to what do I owe the pleasure?" Brooks managed to ask after he got over the initial shock of finding a sullen Vance Evans sitting in the shotgun seat of his squad car.

"Mind if I ride along?" Vance asked. "Piper has locked me out of the bedroom."

Brooks burst out laughing. "I told you that prenup was a bad idea," he said, putting the car in gear. "I bet she took one look at the thing and told you what you could do with it."

"You would think, wouldn't you? Not Piper. She took one look at it and leapt, into my arms kissing the shit out of me. It was like I had just made all her dreams come true."

"I don't get it."

"It's a lawyer thing. Nobody gets it."

"So what happened?"

"She starts reading the damn thing, and I'm watching her nod her head, agreeing with everything like the standard run-of-the-mill prenup she was expecting. And then she turns the page and starts reading the clauses I asked Duncan to throw in there, and after a minute or so, she starts throwing a damn fit. Not because of the pudgy clause, where if she gains more than fifteen pounds of excess baby weight I can leave her and she gets nothing. Not the minimum six-times-a-week sex with thirty minutes of fellatio on every third Sunday."

"I cannot believe Duncan put that in there."

"Not the four-boys-and-a-girl-or-there's-a-penalty clause. No, Piper doesn't get mad at any of that. Because the woman knows she has me over a barrel. Fully. She knows, damn well, the only thing I will not tolerate is her leaving me. *That* I would not live through. So, she gets pissed because it's obvious to her that I'm bullshitting her about the whole thing. And *that's* what got me locked out of the bedroom."

Brooks looked over at him, stared at him for a second, and then shook his head. "I love you, man, but you really, really, really don't deserve Piper."

"I am completely aware," he sighed. "Hey…is that Finn McIntyre's truck again? Look at that. Look at that. He's doing exactly what he was doing the last time we pulled him over. Driving slow and wobbly. What do ya bet he's got Ashley McCauley in there putting her hand all over his…knee. I told her to keep herself buckled up while one of my ballplayers was driving. Pull them over. I need to handle this."

"You can't handle this," Brooks said, turning on the lights. "You don't have a badge anymore."

"I'm still the damn coach."

"It's not baseball season."

"Whose side are you on here?"

"I'm on the side of the law. If something goes down, I need to be doing things by the book."

"You really are the fucking good cop, aren't you?" Vance said as he opened the door and stormed out of the car. "Leave it to me. I'll make a citizen's arrest."

"You're not arresting anybody," Brooks shouted after him.

"I'm the bad cop, remember? I'll arrest whoever I damn well please," Vance shouted back. He banged his knuckles on Finn's door, yelling, "Open up." Then just for the hell of it, he threw a big grin back at Brooks and added, "You're under arrest."

"Don't tell me what I can't do," he whispered as Brooks joined him.

"Finn," Brooks yelled. "You in there? Let's get this window down, son."

The window came down and there was Vance's star sophomore—nice, cute, and *tall*—according to Ashley. His shirt was askew, and if Vance wasn't mistaken, there was a fresh hickey on the right side of his neck.

But when the beam from Brooks' flashlight hit the inside of the car, Ashley was not the one snuggled up next to Finn. Ashley had been replaced by a little blonde with a helluva rack. One look at her put the fear of God, or at least the fear of JB DuVal, the girl's father, into the hearts of both good cop and bad.

"Yeah, I'm gonna need you on this," Brooks said to Vance.

Blond, bodacious Tinley DuVal happened to be Genevra's niece and Lolly's cousin. Which posed a problem for both Brooks and Vance, considering she was now sort of extended family. Vance had already caught her flirting her ass off in the boys' locker room after football practice a few months back, and although she wasn't coming off as bold as Ashley McCauley when they'd pulled her over with Finn, Vance knew big trouble when he saw it. And right now, he figured he, Finn, and Brooks were all standing in about a foot of it.

"Finn, why don't you step outside and show me how you can touch your nose and walk a straight line. You remember the drill," Brooks ordered.

Finn was all, "Yes, sir," very respectful and businesslike, and when he hopped out of the truck, Vance shut Little Miss Tinley inside and followed Finn and Brooks down the road a fair pace.

"I'm not drinking," Finn started, looking at them both like a deer caught in the headlights. "I swear I'm not. It's just…every time I get a girl in my truck…all hell breaks loose."

"What happened to Ashley?" Vance wanted to know.

"I couldn't handle her. She was all over me," Finn said. "It was like being in a truck with an octopus. More hands coming at me than I had time to swat away. And this one," he said emphatically, pointing at the truck, "she's like a damn vampire. When I told her to stop kissing me while I was driving, she went after my neck and practically sucked the blood out of me."

Both Brooks and Vance took a good look at his neck.

"Yeah. You're not gonna want your momma to see that," Brooks said.

"Look. Don't get me wrong," Finn said. "I like girls. I mean, I like 'em more and more every day. Not like I like baseball or anything, but you know, they're cool sometimes."

"They are cool sometimes," Vance said, biting back his grin. "Maybe you oughta stick to the ones your own age."

"Only they're not the ones asking me out."

"Tinley asked you out?"

"You're kidding, right? Do I look like I have the balls to ask Tinley DuVal out? I've never asked anybody out. All these girls just keep asking me for rides. The next thing you know, they're trying to crawl in my lap. While I'm driving."

"Okay, all right. We're definitely getting the big picture here," Vance said looking over at Brooks. "We can do one of two things. One, we can take your license away. That'll give you the excuse you need not to be caught in a chokehold by some super-hot upperclassman while you're driving, making yourself a menace on the road. Or two, you can meet me in my gym office Monday after school for a little coaching on how to handle yourself around women."

"I'm not sure that's appropriate," Brooks started to object.

"The kid is sixteen. He's one of our players, and we don't want him running into any problems. And this problem," Vance said, indicating Tinley waiting in the truck, "is not going away. You got a better idea?"

After a moment, Brooks shook his head. "I guess I don't. So what's it gonna be Finn?"

"I'd like to hear what Coach Evans has to say. If I don't like it, I'll hand over my license."

"Fair enough," Brooks said, clapping the kid on the back.

"All right, now walk with me back to the truck," Vance said, holding up his hand so Brooks wouldn't follow. "Look, if you're gonna be the pitcher on my mound, you're gonna need to learn to control the game. When you're on the mound, you're in charge of the pace of play, the pitches you throw, even how close the batter can stand next to the plate. He's inching in too close, what are you gonna do?"

"Throw an inside pitch to back him off."

"Exactly. Now, what kind of an inside pitch are you gonna throw Miss Tinley right now?"

"I'm gonna tell her that y'all are ready to take away my license, and that if she ever wants another ride in my truck, she'd better sit in her seat with her seatbelt buckled."

"Perfect. You got this. See you Monday after school."

CHAPTER THIRTY-EIGHT

As far as Crain could tell, things were moving along very nicely in the win-friends-and-influence-Henderson part of his life. After a couple weeks in his new office, where he figured half of Henderson had poked their head in the door at one time or another, he was recognized around town, and lots of people called him by name. Since no news about the sports academy plans had been made public, Crain assumed it was Evie Jackson and Garland Langford spreading the word about him.

One or the other of them was in his office two or three times a day. Bringing him lunch. A potted plant. An invitation to something at Henderson Country Club. They liked him. They liked the idea of him and Elizabeth. And that was making all the difference with his bride.

Tansy Langford of Henderson had finally turned back into his sweet, darling Elizabeth from Dallas. He just hoped handing her the package in his hand was not going to set the whole process back a step.

"What's that?" she asked as he joined her in the Devine's kitchen one evening.

"A peace offering. From my momma."

It wasn't a peace offering. It was a strong-armed request. But Crain was in the business of marketing, so he was spinning this the best way he knew how. Still, he could tell just the mention of his momma continued to strike fear into the heart of his bride.

"What is it?" she whispered, horrified.

"It's addressed to you. I'm going to let you do the honors." He set it on the kitchen table, figuring she'd get to it when she'd get to it.

He watched her get to it quick.

"Bridal magazines?" she questioned, dumping a good half dozen of the things onto the table. She picked up the note as she sat and read aloud. "Elizabeth, it would honor and delight me to gift you with the gown of your choosing. I very much look forward to meeting you and your lovely parents." Elizabeth's head halted. "Lovely parents? How does she know my parents are lovely?"

Crain leaned down and kissed her nose. "Because I've told her they're lovely. That's how."

"She wants to buy me a wedding dress."

"She has since I called to tell them we'd eloped. I don't think she's still insisting on the church service, but she would like us to have a wedding reception in Dallas to introduce you to all of their friends, and ours."

"Ours?"

"Yes, ours. Your friends from the presidential library, my business associates and friends, some of whom you've already met."

Elizabeth went very, very quiet.

"Sweetheart? What's going on inside that pretty head of yours?"

"We were right to elope."

Crain's brows shot up.

"This is going to get very complicated."

"Yes, but apparently that's what we do. We do complicated." He pulled a chair out and sat down next to her.

"Suppose my parents want to have a wedding and reception here?"

"A full-blown wedding?"

"You have met my mother, right?"

"Yeah, well, as long as they are aware of the truth, I don't care. We can't have two sets of parents thinking two different things."

"Yes, and we can't have two separate weddings."

"Why not? I deprived you of the first one. I'll make it up to you twice over. Bring on the weddings."

"Crain, be serious. With the work I'm doing on Harvest Daze and the two of us killing ourselves for the sports academy, not to mention Brooks' campaign, when would we find time to plan a wedding?"

"You have met your mother, right?"

"Oh, yeah." Elizabeth's eyes lit up. "She'd be the one planning the wedding."

"Correct. And with Bridezilla in Dallas," he said, casting his hand over all the magazines, "she'd forgive you for running out on her favorite son in a minute if you gave her carte blanche there."

Elizabeth leaned in, grinning all cheekily. "Are you her favorite son? Because I have met Cash, and I'm pretty sure there's not a female between here and Dallas that he can't rope around his finger."

"Even you?" He said, pulling her onto his lap.

"Oh, no. Not me. I've got my hands full right here," she said, working at the buttons on his shirt.

"You know what would be fun about two weddings?" he said.

"Two wedding nights?"

"And two honeymoons."

"Ha. As if the CC in CC Dallas/Henderson could get away for two honeymoons. Maybe one nice long one in between each wedding would work," she said, lifting a brow. "Where shall we go?"

"Hawaii. They have topless beaches in Hawaii, right?"

"You want your bride exposed on a topless beach?"

"Yes," he said, nuzzling into her cleavage. "As long as none of our Henderson business associates are there, I'd be okay with that. In fact, imagining you on a topless beach is a fantasy that keeps me up nights."

She stopped unbuttoning his shirt. After a moment, she started unbuttoning her own. "What about topless kitchens?"

"Topless...? Oh, man," he said, watching her strip out of her sheer navy blouse. "Is this what married life is going to be like?"

he asked, licking his lips as she stood and walked over to pick up an apron. She tied it around her waist and then wiggled out of her pencil skirt.

Dear God.

She stood before him—hair in his favorite business bun on top of her head—in navy blue heels, a very 1950's retro, ruffly apron, her navy blue bra, and her panties. Panties she immediately pulled down from underneath the apron and shimmied out of, kicking them free from her heels.

Ho-ly Fu—

Then she reached behind her, unclasped her bra, and made a great show of sliding off the straps and letting the bra drip from one finger before it fell to the floor.

"Now. What can I get you for dinner?" she asked, posing before him.

Crain was stunned speechless, unable to move. His eyes were trained on her gorgeous full breasts, the salmon color of her areolae, and the stiff peaks of her nipples. In all likelihood, drool was dripping out of his mouth. He was starting to sweat. His throat was dry, and his voice was hoarse when he found it and forced it through parched lips.

"Whiskey."

"You want whiskey. For dinner."

He licked his lips, his eyes drifting to the hem of her apron and stopping to feast on her lean, soft, shapely thighs. "I want whiskey while I sit here and watch you make dinner."

"Coming right up." She turned and headed into the butler's pantry. Her ample bottom winked at him underneath the apron's big bow as she walked, one cheek exposed and then the other.

Jesus.

She came back with a bottle of his favorite label and a large shot glass. Stood before him a moment until he was able to drag his eyes off her incredible tits and up to those golden orbs flashing green lightning at him. She poured him a shot, and when he was unable to reach for it because his dick was literally getting in the way of every other function, she sat both the bottle and the shot on the table.

"Elizabeth." It came out raspy. Barely audible. And the emotion that welled up in that moment hit his eyes before he could stop it. All the anguish she'd put him through, all the misery and heartache, it all meant nothing. He loved her from the moment he laid eyes on her, but he never imagined it was gonna be like this.

"Sit back," she said, gently running the back of her hand down his cheek. "Enjoy your whiskey. Let me be your wife."

He grabbed the shot and downed it, because if he didn't, he'd likely start bawling like a baby. He swiped the back of his hand over his lips, over his eyes. She poured him another before she turned and strutted away to open the refrigerator door.

All of a sudden, his worst fears started pouring from his mouth. "You know I have issues," he said quietly, cautiously, watching her backside as she pulled things out of the refrigerator. He swallowed hard. "I know, you know I have issues because you started to soothe them the first time I got close to you."

She turned her pretty face in his direction. "You get antsy," she said.

He cleared his throat. "That's a nice way of putting it." His eyes trailed over her naked back, so goddamn sexy. From her beautifully sculpted shoulders down to the indentation of her waist, her skin was fresh and creamy. If he could move, he'd go over there and lick his way up her long, regal spine.

He licked his lips instead.

"I actually suffer from dyslexia, from ADHD, and probably some other unique cognitive shit as well."

"Hmm," she said thoughtfully as she placed ingredients on the counter and set a frying pan over a gas flame. "Probably why you haven't been able to achieve much success," she said, right before she kicked up a heel, leaned back and threw him a poster-girl smile.

"Humph," he grunted, watching as she went back to work. His whole body stilled, wrapped in stalwart attention as he watched her back, her legs, her sweet ass jiggling as she spread butter on bread.

She layered paper towels over slices of bacon and put them in the microwave. He watched as she sliced a tomato.

It was now or never.

"I, ah, am concerned that one of the reasons I rushed you to the altar was that if you thought too much about it, you wouldn't want to marry me."

She spun, her beautiful tits swinging into view.

Dirty bastard. You do not deserve this.

She blinked a couple times, turned off the flame, and came towards him, taking his face softly between her hands, setting his chin against her sternum, and raising his eyes to hers. "Crain. You are the kindest, most ingenious, hardworking man I've ever met. Of course, I wanted to soothe you. You deserve to be soothed."

"Do you want children?" he asked quietly.

She stoked her fingers through his hair, and he closed his eyes to focus on that luxury.

"Yes," she said quietly.

"I'd like children," he said, his eyes remaining closed. He opened them and looked her in the eye. "I was a hard kid to raise. One of the reasons I love my momma so much is because I know it wasn't easy for her." He felt his eyes well up again.

Christ.

"Some say…" he started. He stopped. Swallowed. Too full of emotion to go on.

"You're worried about passing your brilliant and unique brain on to our offspring," she said, giving voice to his worst fear.

He didn't have the ability to speak, so afraid he'd burst out crying like a baby. All he could do was turn his head and kiss her palm.

"I love you, Crain. And together we'll love our kids right on through whatever life throws at them. You've figured it out. Our kids will too. Your mother will help us. And my mother? Well, we'll keep her away from them as much as possible."

He laughed at that. As always, she found a way to soothe him.

"Your mother's just fine," he said, wiping at his eyes. "She brought you into the world, didn't she?"

"Oh, don't hold that against her," Elizabeth quipped. "She's not gonna be happy when she finds out what I've done to you. In fact, I believe she's forgotten Brooks Bennett ever existed. She's going to be simply mortified that I ran out on CC Dallas and his big jumbo jet."

"That jet is turning out to be worth every penny," he said, wrapping his arms around her naked waist. He laid his head in his favorite place—right on her chest—and felt her stroke his hair. "We need this," he said, and for the first time he meant it. "We need the fancy wedding. We need your daddy walking you down the aisle and me standing at the end of it, willing to take you off his hands."

She laughed at that.

"We need all our people witnessing our promises," he continued. "We need to do this right. Not just for our parents, but for us. We deserve it. But probably even more, you need to know that I want to show you off on nude beaches and that our kids might be more than a handful. We need to have the discussions we're a little afraid of. Clear the air."

He felt her stiffen.

"What?" he asked.

"Nothing," she said, breaking into a forced smile before she kissed the top of his head.

"Sweetheart, if you've got something on your mind, now is the time to start dealing with it." He blinked up at her.

She met his gaze and was about to confess something, he was sure of it.

"What is it?'

"I love you, Crain. That's all it is," she said, pulling away from him. Turning back to the stove.

"I can handle it," he said, eyeing her sumptuous naked body. "Whatever it is."

She stopped, her hand on the knob of the stovetop, staring at nothing. Then she said quietly and firmly. "I want you to sign the annulment papers."

"Why?"

"Because."

"Because why?"

"Because it erases everything I did to you while in a state of total panic. That's why. I don't like that I ran off on you, hid from the truth, and was afraid to tell everyone that we were married. I'm ashamed of my behavior."

"Ashamed of your behavior? Why? Because of the Brooks thing?"

"Yes, because of the Brooks thing, and because of…everything else."

Crain stood, feeling like he was finally getting his turn to soothe his wife. He crossed the kitchen floor slowly, loving the sight of her in all her naked, high-heeled, skimpy-apron glory. They were so not going to be able to work in the same office after this. This was an image he was never gonna get out of his mind.

He took her in his arms and kissed her good, letting their tongues get all tangled up. "I'm over the Brooks thing," he said against her lips, rubbing his hands over her backside, pulling her up against his aching desire. "And the moment you took your panties off in this kitchen, I forgave you everything else," he said, one hand sliding up to get itself full of her luscious breast. "And when you took off that sexy, lace thing you like to call a bra, after I admitted I'm one kinky bastard, well, then, darlin', there's nothing I wouldn't forgive you for. You want to soothe me? Strip yourself naked like you just did. All my synapses stop their foolishness and just sit up and beg.

"Now we're gonna take this conversation into the bedroom, where I will feast on what I really want for dinner."

"All right." She feigned a heavy sigh. "If you want to. But I mean, you can hardly call yourself kinky, if we've got to take this to the bedroom."

Crain dropped his hands and staggered back a step. "Sweetheart, you did not just call my bluff."

She shrugged.

"Outside. Now."

"What do you mean, outside? What about the kitchen table like normal kinky people?"

He backed her and her practically naked body up, right out of the kitchen and he didn't stop until he hit the screen door with his palm and pushed her naked backside out onto the patio ahead of him.

It wasn't even dark yet.

"Crain," she breathed, huddling into his chest. "What the hell are you doing?"

"Improvising. Practicing. For the nude beach." His hands worked fast to twist the apron around her waist so that her bottom was covered from any prying eyes. The Devine's backyard was large and well landscaped. Still the slight possibility existed that they'd be seen, which had his big body humming and humming hard.

"I honestly didn't know this about myself," he said, feeling up her tits with both his hands. His boner raging. His eyes canvassing the territory around them. "But you have brought out the kinky bastard in me. And throwing down a challenge like that? Sweetheart, I'm a Texas Aggie. You really ought to know better."

He slid his thumb over that bottom lip of hers, the one that could make him hard simply by staring at it.

"Now I'm pretty sure no one's gonna watch you blow me, but I promise you, just the possibility of it is such a turn on it's gonna have me coming fast."

"Crain."

"On your knees, baby."

"Crain!"

He kissed her hard. "On your knees."

She complied.

Good Lord, she complied.

His mouth fell open in utter shock, and he almost convulsed with an orgasm right then and there as his beautiful wife did what she'd done the night they eloped. Sank to her knees, ran her hands down to his belt, and then slowly unzipped his fly.

He closed his eyes and felt her breath, heavy and fast, through his boxer briefs. His fingers wove their way into her glorious hair, pulling out the stick that held it on the top of her head. He focused on the feel of those soft tresses sliding through his fingers. His body struggled not to squander this opportunity, determined to make it last. Combing through her hair, he let it cascade down her bare back, imagining what she'd look like if he were the one watching.

His nuts grew tight at the thought.

"Baby," he breathed in appreciation. Her hands were freeing him, his pants still bound by the belt, but she and her talented, little fingers managed to get his cock loose. Once it sprung forth, her sexy, warm mouth was on him, rocking his world.

Hot damn.

He sucked in a breath and then let out his praise, rough and quiet. "Baby, you are so good." He opened his eyes and looked out at the landscape, committing everything to memory as she sucked him into nirvana.

He waited until it was painful. Until he couldn't wait any longer. Then he pulled his bride from her knees and picked her up by her sweet, little ass so she'd wrap her legs around him. He swung them both around and braced his arms around her back, protecting her as best he could from the red brick wall he was going to use as leverage to pound his way to a climax, making sure she got hers.

It was hot, it was frantic, and it was more than he'd ever dared to let himself dream. He'd marry her four times over if that's what it took to make her his. She was more than his greedy soul needed, and everything it could ever want. And when he felt her internal muscles convulse and grip him, he let out the breath he'd been holding in a gasp and then a groan as he spilled his life into his woman.

"You okay?" he asked, panting. His heart was pounding against hers, his breathing was out of control against her neck, and his cock was still buried deep inside. *Fuck, that was good.*

She nodded.

"Talk to me."

She mumbled something into his hair.

"What?" he snapped.

She lifted her head, limp-eyed and drugged. A few strands of hair were stuck to her lips. "I said, I think I must be a little kinky too."

He grinned. Big and happy. "Well, look at that. We really ought to have these tough conversations more often."

CHAPTER THIRTY-NINE

Crain actually started to enjoy Henderson. Now that his place with his bride was secure, he started paying attention to the dynamics surrounding him. And it came as a happy shock that he actually liked his business associates.

Hale Evans, Crain found out, could buy and sell CC Dallas, and yet deferred to Crain on every occasion, listening intently to what he and his research team had to offer. Crain noticed Hale's constant smile during his brief forays into the office. The man was used to working alone and generally was only in the office for meetings. But while there, he sure seemed to enjoy the camaraderie, and his pride was obvious as Hale watched his take-charge son, Vance, do what Vance did best—boss everyone around—and how Pinks never said no to any of it.

Crain had to admit The Pink One was growing on him. Once The Ninja came back with his face all beat to hell, he somehow seemed less irritated with Crain. The kid was smarter than the rest of them put together, way the hell smarter than Crain. And he had abilities far beyond his years to get the job—any job—done. Crain envied Vance, thinking that if Crain had The Pink One constantly by his side, the two of them could move mountains together. Then he realized that that's exactly what Vance and Pinks were doing here in Henderson. And he felt a sense of calm envelop him, realizing his dream of the sports academy was in good hands. Real good hands.

Brooks Bennett had the best reputation and worst disposition of anybody in town. Crain couldn't understand it. He'd seen it with his own eyes. Brooks outside the office raining sunshine on everybody he'd meet. Then he'd set one foot behind the closed doors of the conference room and turn as surly as Crain's damn brother, Cash.

What the hell?

Eventually, he started figuring it out. Brooks was all sunshine and light on Mondays. He was loving life and everyone in it on Mondays. On Tuesday, he was all business. By Wednesday, he was griping about small stuff, and that's when Vance and The Pink One started piling it on. Relentlessly. Giving him shit coming and going about how three days without laying eyes on this Lolly person reduced Brooks' ass to one sorry state of affairs. And on Thursdays—well, they just stopped calling meetings on Thursdays.

But whether Brooks knew it or not, it had become obvious to Crain that Brooks was the one calling all the shots. Vance was in business to make Brooks' dream of revitalizing Henderson come true. While Brooks' heart and soul was Henderson, Vance's heart and soul was Brooks. And Piper. Only Vance could handle Brooks, and had been doing it half his life. Vance in no way, shape, or form had a handle on his wife, which was pretty much what he and Crain ended up bonding over.

And that was all about to come to a head.

Crain and his moderately kinky wife were now very much into public sex. At lunchtime. In his office. Behind his office. On the floor in front of the damn picture window in his office. They were on borrowed time before it all blew up in their faces, and he knew it. So as he was pulling out of her and helping her off the couch in his reception area, he came up with a great idea.

"Tonight," he panted, pulling himself back together. "On the plane…we're going to join the mile high club."

"Ooooh," she groaned, wiggling into her panties. "Tempting. But I'm not going to Dallas."

He'd been ready for it. It had happened every damn week, so why would this one be any different? He finished tucking in his shirt and securing his belt in silence. Then he turned and left her in his office. He hightailed it across the street, marched across E&E's

foyer, and slammed his palm up against Vance Evans' office door. It bounced open, startling Vance in the process.

Crain stepped in and slammed the door shut behind him.

"If my wife is not on that plane with me tonight, I swear to God I will have an investor making Piper an offer for her own cooking show so fast your head's gonna spin. And don't think I can't do it. One look at those blue eyes, blond curls, and that come-to-daddy figure and there will be a bidding war." He leaned over the desk and into Vance's face. "Have we reached an understanding?"

"Tansy's just scared she's going to have to meet your mother."

"Which is why she needs to be on that plane. I cannot show up without my bride one more time, or my momma is going to go ape shit. And I can't be the bad guy on this. Which is why the two of us have an agreement. You do my dirty work, and I do yours."

Vance pushed back from his desk, irritated. "Why the hell do I always have to be the bad guy?"

"You're her employer. You've got leverage. Make it clear that part of her job is to be in Dallas once a week."

"She's married to a millionaire. My measly paycheck no longer has the hold it once did."

"Well, you better think of something, because I need her in Dallas."

"Fine, fine," Vance said, getting up from his desk and grabbing his cellphone. "Where is she?"

When Crain didn't respond right away, Vance looked up, curious.

"Ah, she may be over at my place. We, ah, just had lunch."

"Oh, you mean the sex palace across the street?" Vance pushed by Crain to get out the door. "You know the two of you aren't fooling anybody with your afternoon delight shit. Stay here," he threw over his shoulder.

Crain let the man go. When he heard the front door jingle, he stepped out of the office and moseyed down the hall, catching the scene unfolding through the front windows.

Elizabeth had been coming across the street when Vance got to her in the middle and pulled her back toward CC Henderson. Crain watched as the two of them talked on the sidewalk, Elizabeth shaking her head no and folding her arms over her chest, resigned to give his momma another fit by keeping her feet firmly in Henderson. He watched as Vance tried to reason with her, cajole her, but Elizabeth was having none of it. Not even bothering to look at him. She just kept shaking her head no and staring at her feet. And then he saw Vance mouth the word "fine" and hold up two hands like he was done.

Shit. Now I'm going to have to be the bad guy.

But Elizabeth's head snapped up as Vance pulled out his cellphone and started sliding his finger over it time and time again until he located what he wanted and planted that in front of Elizabeth's face.

Well, now. That's got her attention.

Crain's eyes narrowed, his focus more intent on the scene as he watched his Elizabeth make a grab for the phone and Vance pull it back, protecting it against his chest. He watched as Elizabeth turned into Tansy and started poking the guy in the chest, moving him backward down the sidewalk as she apparently laid into him about whatever he'd showed her.

Vance held up both hands like he was surrendering, then sort of offered her the phone, shaking his head like this was going to be the easiest thing in the world.

Crain saw Tansy hesitate before she finally relented and reached for the phone. Vance pulled it away, wiggling a finger in her face and getting a sharp nod before he handed the phone to her. With deliberate haste, Elizabeth's hands worked over Vance's phone, sliding a finger over the top and then working it again. She then swiped a finger one way a few times and then back the other way until she seemed satisfied and gave him back his phone.

She was not happy.

Vance was delighted.

He put his phone back in his pocket and swiped his hands in front of him like an umpire calling a runner safe. Like the slate between the two of them had been wiped clean. Elizabeth said a few words and twirled, moving down the sidewalk out of Crain's view as she dug for something in her tote.

Vance jogged across the street and into the office.

"Hey, man," he said, patting Crain on his arm. "I gave her the rest of the day off to pack. You are good to go." Vance kept walking, heading back to his office.

Crain turned and yelled. "How'd you manage that?"

"Women, Tex. I'm good with women," he yelled behind him.

"Good with women, my ass," Crain muttered, pulling out his own phone. "Are you sure she's gonna show?" he yelled.

"I'm sure," came Vance's response.

Crain texted Elizabeth.

Wheels up at 5:45.

Then he texted his momma.

Nick & Sam's. Reservations at 8:00.

His pretty wife was heading for another showdown.

Tansy armed herself as best she could. Meeting Crain's momma was her worst fear. Well, her second worst fear. Telling her own momma she'd eloped was still high on her list. But ultimately, Crain finding out she slept with Davis while they were married was her ultimate worst fear. And that fear was what Vance had held over her head to get her on the plane—for her own good, he had said. If she went to Dallas and met Crain's mother tonight, she'd get that behind her and be able to move forward, he'd said. Then Vance promised to forget any knowledge of the morning he'd found Tansy half-dressed and passed out on her desk. He even let her delete the photos he'd taken, so he would no longer have physical evidence.

A stabbing pang of fear and regret washed over Tansy as she thought about all that, and not for the first time did she wish she'd told Crain about Davis immediately when Crain had shown up in Henderson. It would have either ended everything right there, or they'd have it well behind them by now.

Tansy sighed.

Really? If she had to do it all again, would she have risked losing Crain? Risked hurting him? Risked that big, happy smile? No. He didn't deserve to feel that hurt. Never needed to know about it. It was a fear she had decided to live with. The rest of her fears she'd have to face eventually, she knew.

Bring it, she thought as she continued to tear pages from six bridal magazines. She laid them all neatly in a pretty, floral-printed file and stuffed that into her tote. Then she fired up her iPad and her Pinterest account, which held only one board, aptly titled "Dallas Reception." She texted Crain asking for his mother's email address, and received an immediate text back.

I love you. MellyCarraway@gmail.com

Remember that when the shit hits the fan, she texted back, adding *I will see you on the plane*. Then she shut her phone off, so he couldn't distract her from her mission.

She was irritated with him anyway.

Through Pinterest she invited her mother-in-law—*holy shit*— to join her Dallas Reception Board, giving Melinda Carraway the ability to add to and edit it. Then she did a Texas Weddings search and pinned whatever she halfway liked onto the board, making it look like she'd been giving this reception idea some thought.

Then she took the bull by the horns, remembering the old adage "the best defense is a good offense", and wrote out an email to Crain's momma.

> *Dear Mrs. Carraway,*
>
> *Thank you for the beautiful bride magazines and your very generous wedding gown offer. I don't deserve it, I know. Yet your olive branch is more than welcome, as is your generosity and willingness to give me a chance to make up my past behavior to you and your son. I'm very much looking forward to finally meeting Crain's momma and daddy.*
>
> *I hope it won't be too much of an imposition if Crain and I beg your help planning our Dallas wedding and reception. Your knowledge and expertise will be invaluable to us, and*

I look forward to hearing your thoughts on the subject over dinner tonight.

See you soon,

Elizabeth

It was probably a little much, but Tansy was pretty sure that much was needed to truly smooth over four months of abandoning Melly Carraway's "Baby Bear." Giving his mother carte blanche over the entire Dallas affair was one of the best ideas out of CC Dallas yet, Tansy was sure.

She hit the send button and then hit the shower.

ॐ

Crain boarded the plane at 5:40, literally crossing his fingers like a school kid. He stuck his head in and breathed a sigh of relief as his eyes landed on his beautiful bride.

Elizabeth was there, all tucked in for takeoff, looking prim and proper in an elegant, pale pink cocktail suit. She was as fine and sophisticated as he'd ever seen her. He noticed her hair had been curled more than usual, then left long, allowing soft waves to cascade past her shoulders. Her nails were freshly painted in a pink slightly darker than her suit. Her face was artistically made up, as if she was going for a cover shoot. Her jewelry, he noticed, was understated, except for the large Seaman Schepps bracelet she must have borrowed from her momma.

His wife apparently wanted his people to know she was no pauper.

Interesting.

Her lips were a distraction immediately. He looked closely, trying to see what she managed to do to them that got his nuts sprung and roaring to go every time he saw her. He noticed in fascination that one lip—the bottom one—was painted a shade darker than the top one. Just a subtle, little difference that had him wanting to grab that bottom lip with his teeth and chew on it a bit.

His big smiled vanished as a thought occurred to him.

"You aren't gonna let me touch you, are you?"

"Nope."

He sat himself in the seat across from her, knowing that staring at her for the next three hours was not gonna be easy. "I'm guessing you did not get your pretty self all fixed up for me, did you?"

"I did not."

"Hmm. Well, my mother is bound to approve, and you'll have my daddy eating out of your hand before the introductions are complete." He moved to buckle his seatbelt. "Thank you, by the way, for showing up. I wasn't convinced this was ever going to happen."

"Yes, well, *my boss* believes that getting this meeting behind me will improve my concentration at work. He required it."

Total bullshit.

Crain leaned forward and picked up her hand in his. "How is it exactly that Vance could get you to do the one thing I couldn't?"

"He threatened me."

"With what?"

"My job, what else?"

What else indeed?

"All right," he said, sitting back as the plane started down the runway. "I'll play your game. I'm just happy you're here, Sweetheart. Truly, I am. This dinner's been a long time coming and one I have mostly been looking forward to."

"This dinner is going to be a disaster," she grumbled, gripping the sides of her seat like she always did when they took off.

Crain already knew differently, but was willing to let her stew. After all, paybacks were supposed to be a bitch.

Melinda Carraway fell all over herself trying to make her new daughter-in-law comfortable. It was downright sickening, Crain mused as he silently nursed his second old-fashioned while he continued to watch his parents—chairs all scooted in right next to his bride—hanging on her every word. He watched them fawn over her, laugh uproariously with her, and shine their delighted smile upon her as if they had just witnessed her hang the moon and the stars and then turn around and shit a pot of gold out of her ass.

He was disgusted.

He watched it go on a few more minutes before he leaned forward, tapped his hand on the table, and growled, "What exactly is happening here?"

The three of them, all with their bright-eyed smiles, turned their heads in his direction as if they were surprised by his presence.

"Crain?" his mother asked.

"I mean, I'm glad y'all are getting along, I really am. But don'tcha think a little restraint is called for?"

"Restraint?"

"Yeah, restraint. You are aware this is the woman who caused me nothing but pain, heartache, and embarrassment over the last several months, right?"

"Oh, Crain." His mother waved him off like all that was incidental. "You're over it. We're over it."

Apparently, he wasn't over it.

"Momma, wouldn't you like to go ahead and give Elizabeth that good talkin'-to you had in mind a few weeks ago?"

"Crain. Darling boy," his mother soothed. "We're happy to see you too," she assured him. "Now why don't you pick us out a good bottle of Cabernet to go with our steak dinner," she suggested, shoving the heavy wine list across the table to him and turning back to Elizabeth.

"You know they call her Tansy back in Henderson," he grumbled as he flipped the thing open. "Wears flip-flops to work," he trailed off. Nobody was listening to him anyway.

A good steak dinner soothed him better than the traitorous women seated across from him had. The two who had their heads together with their nonstop yammering all night. He and his daddy got bored watching them scheme up wedding reception scenarios and took themselves into the bar for a scotch and a good cigar. Sitting there, enjoying the comfortable silence of men, Crain noticed he felt exhausted. Whether from stress, or relief—probably both—he was drained. His crazy bride had run him through the mill and back since their fateful trip to Vegas, and he was surely grateful to be able to see the light at the end of the tunnel now. He was eager for his old life back. Well, his new life as a married man in Dallas. There were ten days between now and Harvest Daze, where Elizabeth's obligation to Evie Jackson and the Henderson community would finally be complete. He figured he'd call her daddy tomorrow, arrange an evening this week to take him to dinner and ask for his daughter's hand. Then he'd officially propose to Elizabeth Saturday night—he'd ask Hale where to take her—and the two of them would have a heart-to-heart with her folks on Sunday, which would hopefully end in a celebration with a good bottle of champagne.

It might not be the announcement they were looking for, but come hell or high water, Henderson was going to be made aware of either Elizabeth Tansy Langford's engagement or her marital status during Harvest Daze.

CHAPTER FORTY

One week before Harvest Daze, Tansy and Crain stood in front of Garland and Rye Langford, showing off her dazzling yellow-diamond engagement ring.

And then they dropped the bomb.

"There's something Crain and I need to share with you now that you both approve of Crain and me getting married," Tansy said tentatively while her mother was still so enamored with her ring. "We eloped," she said, keeping her focus on her whopper of a diamond instead of the faces of her beloved parents.

"When was this?" her mother laughed, unable to take her eyes off her daughter's ring as she turned Tansy's hand this way and that, admiring the way the stone caught the light. "Last night? After dinner? Right after Crain proposed?" she jested.

"No, no, it was a while back," Tansy said as if this were an everyday conversation.

"We actually met in Dallas," Crain chimed in. "It was what you might call love at first sight—on my part anyway. You see, Elizabeth had come to my office representing the Bush Library, and I was smitten. It took me a while to convince her to go out with me, but once I did, it didn't take long for us to realize how compatible we were. I had business in Vegas and invited her to join me. I was inspired to get down on one knee and ask her to be my bride right there and then. Completely blew me away when she said yes."

"I don't understand," Garland said, still holding Tansy's hand and turning to her father. "Rye? What are they saying?" she asked her husband. "Are you saying you've been engaged since before you came back from Dallas?" she said, bringing her attention back to her daughter and Crain. "Why wouldn't you tell us?"

"Mother," Tansy said, "we weren't just engaged when I came home. We had actually gotten married. In Vegas. The two of us have been married now for over five months."

Garland Langford blinked. Then blinked again. "How is this possible?" she whispered, stricken.

"We eloped," Tansy said gently.

"Eloped?" her father shouted.

"Yes, sir. Eloped," Crain said. "It was a spur-of-the-moment decision after a whirlwind romance, but it was indeed legal and binding, as my bride found out after she ran out on me."

"Ran out on you?" both Garland and Rye repeated together.

"Mother, Daddy, let's sit down, and Crain and I will tell you everything. And once we do, the four of us will figure out the best way to handle this from here."

"Oh, Lord, what's Evie going to say?" her mother muttered. "And your grandmother?" she gasped, horrified.

"I see this runs in the family," Crain said next to Tansy's ear.

"I've already booked The Club," Garland said taking a seat on the couch. "Tansy. What have you done?"

"Mother, fear not. Crain and I have this all worked out. Now sit down, breathe, and let us explain how you are going to get to order our wedding cake and enjoy eating it too."

It hadn't taken long for Tansy's mother to perk up at the idea that she was being given carte blanche to plan her daughter's wedding any way she saw fit. As predicted, Garland insisted that the elopement be kept top secret but agreed to fast-track the wedding as much as humanly possible without raising eyebrows.

And the thought of another reception in Dallas where the Langfords would meet Crain's family and friends was just icing on her cake, although initially Garland was not happy that she'd have no say in that affair whatsoever. "Mother, Mrs. Carraway was as unhappy as you were that we eloped. Allowing our mothers to plan whatever events they choose to celebrate our nuptials is our apology for making a rash and thoughtless decision."

Tansy reached for Crain's hand and squeezed it. She no longer felt that it was a rash and thoughtless decision. She was feeling more and more as Crain had. Happy they'd done what they'd done now that their mommas were heavily involved. They'd managed to have their own wedding—would always have their own wedding to look back on, no matter what kind of future dog and pony show they would have to endure. And Tansy was determined to make the first four months of their married life up to Crain by going topless whenever she could.

He laughed out loud when she told him that and then stripped her shirt from her on the stage which had been set up for Harvest Daze late the night before the big event. They made love, laughing and imagining it was broad daylight and the entire town of Henderson was roaming the fields around them.

"Oh my God, are we exhibitionists?" Tansy asked in mock horror as they righted their clothes and jested about where and when they could meet during the actual festival for a conjugal interlude.

"Maybe not exhibitionists," Crain said, helping her off the stage. "More like danger junkies, or thrill addicts. Clearly the idea of being seen or caught appeals to us newly wedded Carraways."

"This is all you," she admonished. "I have never fantasized about anything like this."

"Maybe uptight and pit bull-mean Tansy didn't. But my sweet Elizabeth sure gets off good when there's a little danger lurking."

She couldn't deny it. When The Man from Dallas was right, he was right.

The morning of Henderson Harvest Daze broke bright with promise. The weather was a little nippy at first light, but with no clouds in the sky, the sun promised to do its job and keep everyone comfortable all day and into the night. The low temperature was supposed to be sixty-five degrees near midnight, and with any luck, Pinks and The Outlaw's band would have everybody dancing in the glorious night air well past then.

Tansy was excited. Relieved and excited. Relieved that the day was finally here, and she'd have this event and Evie Jackson off her back once and for all. Relieved that she was no longer blatantly lying to her parents and that she had met and made amends with her in-laws. Excited that she and Crain could announce their engagement to Henderson tonight but establish themselves as a married couple in Dallas by the following week's end.

Six more people had been brought into their confidence the night before. The Devine's house where Crain and Tansy were house sitting was now bursting at the seams with all the Devine sisters home for The Daze. Tess, who had gone through school with Tansy, had come home with one of Henderson's war heroes, Johnny Wilder, for a long weekend. Grace had brought her boyfriend and FBI spy guy home to partake in The Daze. And of course, Annabelle, the youngest Devine daughter, came in from Raleigh with Vance and Brooks' best buddy Duncan James on her arm. The four couples sat around until early morning catching up and exchanging stories. Tansy's new ring was not something the Devine sisters would miss, so they were the first people to whom Tansy and Crain announced their "engagement."

Brooks and the Henderson Police Department had worked alongside the Henderson High Varsity and JV football teams to set up tents, food stalls, carnival games, tables, chairs, and the big stage out on the old Myers farm after a full acre had been plowed and rolled. Vance's grandmother along with Evie Jackson, Tansy's mother, Garland, and the rest of the Garden Club had decorated the area with hay bales, mums, pumpkins, squash, and wild flowers. Vendors arrived early to set up their wares all the way from Raleigh, thanks to Molly DuVal and Piper. The high school's marching band was ready to lead the town toward the Harvest Daze grounds, along with the twenty or so antique cars that would transport Henderson's most prestigious citizens. The cars would then congregate in a field so that everyone could enjoy a close-up look and a chat with their proud owners.

There were pony rides and games for the youngest Hendersonians and lawn chairs set up for the oldest. It seemed everyone in between had been called upon to put in a few hours manning a game or selling refreshments. The kissing booth was already sparking controversy, but Tansy was okay with that. It got people talking and would get them to show up. In fact, Josh McCourt had heard that the high school girls from neighboring Oxford were going to make an appearance because of the Henderson football players who were scheduled to man the booth. Bring it, Tansy thought. Maybe next year they'd get Oxford to join forces with them and create one big festival to benefit both towns.

The makeshift jail in the center of everything was also controversial but not because random citizens could be thrown in for any trumped-up reason. That seemed to be an idea everybody liked and was scheming about. The controversy stemmed from who would benefit from the proceeds raised in order to get out of jail. It became a great opportunity for Brooks and the police department, the library, and the mayor's office to promote Henderson Helping Henderson. Brooks made sure his most personable rookie officers manned the jail, armed with information to explain H[3] in detail. He also came up with an alternative plan should you find yourself incarcerated. Instead of having to use your cellphone and raise pledges from inside the jail, you could simply sign up to clean up, paint, refurbish, or re-landscape any number of public buildings or areas in town using your own resources. Anything from public benches to vacant storefronts to the main streets around town. Brooks was thrilled about being able to get his message out and had baited just about everybody into making sure their best friends were thrown in jail at some point during The Daze.

Evie Jackson couldn't stop fawning over Crain after he'd managed to get distributors representing six different vineyards in the Napa area to provide wine tastings. There was also a cigar-rolling table, a guy who could make anything out of balloons, face painters, caricature artists, and a Make-Your-Own-Caramel-Apple-on-a-Stick booth, complete with a selection of mouthwatering toppings.

Piper's very-well-placed, lemon-yellow party tent featuring Molly's Big Pie Plate drew a lot of attention. The entire DuVal clan was on hand giving out samples of various fruit pies baked in the Big Pie Plate, which now sported Henderson's town crest. Piper and Genevra extolled the praises of the Big Pie Plate while taking orders and selling the stock they had on hand. Molly demonstrated how she made the pie plate, letting kids and adults alike get their own fingers into her clay.

The old Barbershop Quartet took to the stage in the beginning of the afternoon and didn't seem to care that nobody was paying attention. They were just happy to be there, singing their hearts out. The marching band drew a crowd with their drumming solos and more upbeat sound. The pompom girls doing a dance routine along with them didn't hurt. Things were running smoothly, and the attendance was already beyond Tansy's expectations.

Crain finally got to meet Lolly DuVal, who showed up at The Daze in one of her latest dress designs and patent red cowgirl boots. Back in July, Lolly and Tansy had bonded over Harry the Bartender's tequila shots. And now, out of the blue, here was Harry, offering each of them another shot the first time they got close to one another.

"What's that about?" Crain asked.

"I'm guessing Harry's just trying to keep the peace," Tansy laughed as she held out her ring toward Harry.

"Very nice, Mr. Carraway. Congratulations."

"Thanks, Harry. Remember, I've got a job for you in Dallas," he said.

"I'll keep that in mind," Harry said before moving off.

"Seriously. How am I going to entice Harry to come to Dallas? And Pinks. I really wouldn't mind bringing Pinks along as well."

"Leave Pinks and Harry here," she said, kissing him with tequila on her lips. "It'll be easier for me to get you to visit Henderson if they're here keeping things running."

"I suppose so," he grumbled. "Still, I feel like if I could harness the git-'r-done power in the two of them, I could rule the world."

"That's exactly how Vance feels," Tansy assured him. "He's not letting either one of them go."

"Smart man, that Vance."

"He's okay. But he's no CC Dallas."

Crain smiled down into his bride's beautiful face. Leaned in and kissed her again. "I'm glad you think so. Now I'm going to run over and check out those fancy-schmancy portable toilets you had dragged in here," he said, pointing to the long, white trailers with flushable johns and running water.

"I wasn't going to be stuck out here all day using a Johnny on the Spot," she said to him. "And neither was my mother. Make sure they're keeping them clean," she yelled as Crain headed off, waving in acquiescence.

Tansy watched his tall, handsome, happy form walk off and felt giddy with relief that after all she'd put him through, Crain Carraway ended up still being hers.

The two of them had finally leapt all of their giant hurdles.

CHAPTER FORTY-ONE

While Crain was in the fancy bathroom trailer designated for men, he thought to check the stalls and clean up a little, helping Elizabeth out where he could. Not that she'd be in here cleaning them herself, he chuckled. He knew that wasn't happening. He smiled big at the thought of either Garland or Elizabeth Langford with long rubber gloves on, cowering as they tried to clean up a public toilet in their fancy designer suits. No, he couldn't see that ever being part of either of their job descriptions.

He heard voices enter the trailer while he was back in the handicapped stall trying to rewind a long trail of paper towels and mopping up around the sink. He recognized The Pink One's voice immediately. He didn't have a clue who the other voice belonged to.

There was a lot of laughing and snickering between the two as the unidentified voice talked about Vance giving him the eye and keeping Piper out of arm's reach.

"Yeah, well you can't really blame him. You had your arms around her and your tongue down her throat after our gig at The Situation," Pinks said.

That little tidbit captured Crain's attention. He stood still and listened, amused.

"Had no idea she was his," the unidentified voice defended. "Tiny little thing with a great rack like that? I just kept thinking while we played our gig that if I was going for it, I was going for the one in the yellow dress. Big mistake. Ended up with a bag of ice on my jaw instead of your sexcapades on the new conference table."

"Yeah, well, that escapade turned out to be more than I bargained for."

"You told me it was off the charts."

"Yeah, well, it was. Until it wasn't."

"I'm not following."

"Turns out she's married."

"Married?"

"Yeah, and that is not public knowledge, although everyone at E&E knows it. So don't mention it to anybody, and definitely don't mention that she and I slept together."

"Vance knows."

"Yeah, well, he's the one who found us. Apparently used it to blackmail Tansy into helping him with Piper. And that's before Vance found out she was married. Which is a long story and has gotten itself all sorted out now. Still, trust me. No good can come from this information ever getting out. We all have too much to lose if it does. Besides, there were extenuating…" Pink's voice trailed off as the two men walked out and the trailer door closed behind him.

Crain found himself staring at the wad of paper towels in his hand wondering what the hell he'd just heard.

Tansy?

Did he say Tansy?

My Tansy?

With The Pink One?

Nah.

As he tossed the paper towels and started washing his hands, his dyslexic brain started firing off data—memories—and putting puzzle pieces together before he could stop it. Tansy still wanting him to sign the annulment papers. Pinks, part of the Surly Duo. Tansy saying she was ashamed of what she'd done.

Holy fuck. Had she done *Pinks?*

Perspiration broke out on Crain's forehead as his heartbeat quickened.

Nah. Definitely nah, he reassured himself. But as Crain slowly lifted his head and stared into his own reflection, the words he'd just heard and the pieces he already knew aligned themselves and churned up his gut. His reflection had one word for him.

Sucker.

"Fuck!" he spat, catching himself before throwing a punch and shattering the mirror. He threw the paper towels into the trash bin and busted out of the stall, crashing out of the trailer like a bull harnessed with a bucking strap.

Asshole Pinks and his punk friend were at the bottom of the ramp, and Pinks took one look at Crain coming at him and mouthed the word, "Shit." Crain grabbed hold of the back of Davis' collar, paying little attention to the horror on his face. "Where's Evans?" Crain demanded, pushing Pinks in front of him, searching for Vance amidst the carnival atmosphere.

"Crain, hear me out."

"Say one word and I'll lay you out in public. We're finding Evans. Now."

As always, The Pink One knew exactly where Vance was and what he was doing. When Vance saw them coming, his smile dropped, and he knew. *He knew.*

A little part of Crain died.

Vance left the crowd around him, and the three of them headed off behind the tents selling food and sundries and kept on walking, further from the crowd, until they were behind a couple of trailers.

Crain's teeth were clenched tight, his whole body in fight mode. He tried to snort up some air through his nose, tried to calm himself down so he made sure he didn't jump to conclusions. But all he could think about was how these guys must have been laughing behind his back, taking his pledge for the new stadium and everything else, knowing all along that the bait for his interest had betrayed him in the worst possible way.

Crain pushed Pinks in front of him and then stalked after him, bumping chest against chest. "Tell me you didn't fuck my wife and then let me throw blood, sweat, and tears into a town I don't give a shit about while I was trying to win her back."

Pinks didn't respond. Just stood his ground and stared him straight in the eye.

Vance pushed his way into the middle and backed Pinks away, reaching a hand out to keep Crain at bay. "He wasn't aware of her marital status. None of us were. You know that."

"Apparently, I don't know shit. When the fuck did this happen?"

"July. It was the night—" Pinks started but was cut off by a growl and an attempt to rip his damn head off.

"I'm gonna kill him," Crain growled into Vance's face as Vance tried to keep him arm's distance from Pinks.

"No, you're not," Vance grunted, giving Crain one big shove. "It's not his fault he's stuck in the middle of your nightmare, so just simmer down and let's talk this out."

"Look—" Pinks said, but Vance cut him off again.

"Not now. Just give him a minute," Vance cautioned.

Crain stood seething, trying to make the pain go away. Trying to understand what had just happened. Trying with all his might not to know the things he now had to acknowledge. His gaze darted between the two men whom he'd recently come to admire and appreciate. Who he claimed not only as business partners but as friends. The truth that had been hidden from him now put it all in a different light, and he felt the pain of that loss. The loss of what he thought he had.

He saw his dream of building the sports academy evaporate right before his eyes. The feeling that came along with that loss was excruciating. And then there was the panic he was holding at bay, panic that threatened to engulf him when he thought about a life without Elizabeth.

He reached for his rubber ball, but it was nowhere to be found. Yeah. He needed to get the hell out of here. Fast.

"Tell *Tansy*," he said with a sneer, "that ring of hers should be used as a down payment on the stadium. Because that's the only investment this town will ever see from me. You can consider our partnership dissolved. Please give Hale my apologies. This is not the way I usually do business. Then again, I'm not usually doing business with a bunch of miserable liars."

"No one ever lied to you," Vance claimed.

"Failure to disclose, gentlemen. Two sides of the same coin," Crain said as he turned away.

"At least talk to Elizabeth," Pinks yelled. "She'll explain."

Crain shook his head and kept walking. The truth finally sinking in to his thick skull.

There had never really been an Elizabeth.

There had only ever been Tansy.

CHAPTER FORTY-TWO

Tansy had been so busy herding the marching band off the stage and directing the set up for the high school rock band which was to play next that she hadn't thought too much about Crain's whereabouts. Everything seemed to be going so smoothly that when she was escorted to the makeshift jail by Evie Jackson for not racing over to show off her engagement ring, she laughed in delight and used the opportunity to sit down and rest.

Turns out she was sharing the cell with Lolly, whom Brooks had tossed in for "withholding affection," Lolly claimed as she rolled her eyes. "I'm a businesswoman trying to finish my masters. I can't race back to Henderson and service him every time he pouts."

Tansy laughed in mock horror, desperately wanting to change the subject. "And how is the House of DuVal coming along?" she asked.

"Good. Too good," Lolly said as she sat. "If my mother's good money wasn't tangled up in tuition, I'd quit school. Not that I'm not still learning, it's just that…"

"Experience is the best teacher," Tansy finished.

"Yes, and I'm getting a lot of experience designing and creating Brooks' sister Darcy's bridesmaid dresses along with a few special-order holiday gowns. I don't know which way is up half the time, so Brooks demanding my, ah, undivided attention makes things dicey."

"Just make it up to him tonight. I remember what happened the last time Pinks and The Outlaw played," she said, laughing. "Brooks had to cart you out of the bar."

"Yeah." Lolly chuckled. "I don't know why I like taking my clothes off in public when I'm letting off steam. Brooks pretends he doesn't like it." Lolly leaned in conspiratorially. "But truth be told, it kinda gets him going."

"I'll bet." Tansy laughed, thinking of her own kinky bastard who didn't mind her taking off her clothes in public. "I might have to try that along with you tonight."

Hale and Genevra showed up at the jail, Genevra clasping on to the bars and giving her daughter a soft smile. "We've come to bail you out," she said.

Lolly jumped up and said goodbye to Tansy as she squeezed through the door the officer unlocked. Once free, she hugged Hale tightly and said, "I'm glad Mom married a guy with deep pockets. The House of DuVal is not operating in the black just yet."

Hale offered to bail out Tansy, but she declined, saying she had her own deep pockets. Now that she was alone and somewhat rested, she pulled out her cellphone and dialed up Crain.

There was no answer.

When she called again, it immediately went to voice mail. And when she stood up to glance around the festival grounds to see if she could spot him, her heart stopped beating and dread filled her from toes to scalp.

Vance and Davis were coming for her, and she could tell by the expressions on their faces they had bad news. Tansy blinked a few times and waited for them to get closer before she asked the inevitable question.

"Who died?"

CHAPTER FORTY-THREE

Tansy walked into the office Monday morning and found the papers on her desk. The annulment papers. All signed neat and tidy by one Crain Lucius Carraway.

Hmm, she thought mildly. Lucius. For his father. And then she burst into tears.

She sobbed like she hadn't yet allowed herself to sob since being told Crain was gone. She'd been too busy calling him. Too busy chasing him down at the airport only to have missed him by minutes. Too busy trying to explain to her parents the unexplainable. Too busy questioning Davis and Vance, looking for a loophole. Too busy wishing she'd told Crain about Davis from the start. Too busy wishing she'd never met Davis Williams. Too busy hating herself for ever walking out on Crain Carraway in the first place.

When all the wishing and hoping and hating had run its course, all that was left was her stark, painful reality. So she sobbed. Like a woman burying a precious loved one. Sobbed like her own heart had fallen into the grave.

She sobbed for Crain and the pain he must have felt when he'd heard of her betrayal. She sobbed for him having to tell his parents after all they'd already been through. She sobbed for her own parents who were dealing with a world of gossip all centered around their daughter, the adulterous slut who had run off and gotten married and then carried on like she didn't know what that meant. She sobbed for all the work she'd done to prevent her secrets from coming out. For all the times she'd set aside her own happiness and how hard she'd worked to be what everyone wanted her to be. She sobbed for how it had all come to this.

Disgrace. Heartache. Emptiness.

She felt herself being pulled into Vance's arms, and she sobbed even harder. Sobbed for how nice Vance had been to her and for the toll losing CC Dallas was going to take on his business and his dreams for Henderson.

While she buried her face against Vance's shoulder, she heard Davis whip by, cursing under his breath and then slamming his way out of the office. And that's when she sobbed for Pinks. Because he was a Super-Hero-In-Training and none of this had ever been his fault.

She wiped at her eyes, pulling back from Vance. "I'm sorry I'm upsetting Davis. He doesn't have to leave," she said. "I'll stay away until I can get my act together. I'll…I'll work from the Devine's. Go get him. Tell him I didn't mean any of the things I said. He's not to blame. Not at all. And I know it. Deep down inside, I know it."

"Don't you worry about Pinks," Vance said, trying to help her wipe her tears. "He's a ninja. He can handle it."

Tansy went around her desk and pulled out a package of tissues, using them to mop her face and blow her nose.

"Are those the annulment papers?" Vance asked.

Tansy could only nod, afraid she might start with the wailing again. She sniffed and tried to find her voice. "Be careful." Sniff. "Be careful what you wish for," she said.

"You didn't wish for this, Tans. We know it. And we all couldn't be sorrier. Genevra. My father. Brooks and Lolly. Crain's a great guy, and I'm sure if we just give him a little time—"

"No," she said. "He's done. His cellphone's been replaced. They know not to put my call through at his office in Dallas. I was going to call his momma and then I thought, why? They'd already given me a second chance. And any woman worthy of a guy like Crain wouldn't have needed even that."

"Yeah. But he loves you."

Her breath hitched, and new tears started to flow. "He did," she whispered as waves of sorrow flowed from her. "He really did."

CHAPTER FORTY-FOUR

Crain sat at his big Texas-sized desk in his big Texas-sized office and didn't feel the least bit fidgety. The part of his brain which wasn't busy staring off into space right now noticed that his hands were laid flat on the desk, and his feet were planted firmly on the floor. For the first time in his life, he was grounded.

Probably too damn sad to fidget, he thought.

He had plans. Big plans for this week. He was going to meet up with every possible investor he could find to establish his own sports academy right here in his hometown. He'd make Dallas the sports capital of Texas, as if it wasn't already with Jerry's World and America's Team located just a half-hour away. Still, he liked the idea of giving athletes a place to learn competitive skills along with all the academic bullshit they needed to know. Most of all, he really liked the idea of providing dyslexic students an alternative to struggling in school. It was going to be a big week, because while he was busy floating his sports academy idea out there and gobbling up investors, he would be keeping Team Henderson from doing the same—keep them from gathering up assets to get the job done.

It had felt real good at the time he'd decided to do it. About thirty minutes after his plane had taken off from North Carolina. He'd take back the best idea he had given them and run with it. Do it himself, and do it better. It was no more than E&E and the rest deserved. Their just reward for wasting his time and duping him like they had.

Yep. He had a lot to do. A really busy week to get to. As soon as, you know, he felt like moving.

"Shiiiiit," he said out loud.

"Mr. Carraway. Your mother would like a minute of your time," came the voice of his executive assistant over the intercom.

"Perfect," Crain muttered, standing up to greet his momma as she came through the door. What was it about seeing your momma that brought all your damn emotions to the surface, he wondered, while trying his best to shower her with a smile.

His mother took one look at him and stopped short. "What's wrong?" she breathed, scurrying the rest of the way to him, laying her palms against his cheeks and looking deep into his eyes.

God, if he held it together through this, they should give him a damn Oscar. "Just stewing over a business dilemma," he said.

"Oh, thank goodness. For a moment there I wondered if Elizabeth was all right."

When Crain couldn't bring himself to comment, his momma did a double take and got herself all concerned again. "Well, is it an important business decision?"

He nodded. Probably the most important decision of his life.

"Well, I won't bother you with trivial wedding stuff then. When your father told me you were back early this week, I thought I'd stop by and get your opinion on a few things. But they can wait until Elizabeth is back on Wednesday. Let's have dinner at our place. I have a lot to show you."

"Momma, there's something I need to tell you. Why don't the two of us sit down," he said, showing her over to his couch. The two of them sat in silence for a bit. Crain wasn't sure how to say what he had to say. And then his distracted brain went right ahead without him. "Can I ask you a couple questions?"

"Sure," she said, looking real curious.

"How'd Daddy propose marriage to you?"

"How?" she asked, her brow knitting together.

"Yes. Was it spontaneous? Or did he plan it out?"

"He planned it. Not that I wasn't aware of his intentions. We talked about it enough. He'd even asked about my ring preferences. Still, he wanted to do it right, you know? Set the mood. Pick the perfect setting."

"And did he?"

"He took me to the place that had meant the most to him growing up. The Texas Highland Lakes where his family used to vacation two weeks every summer. He rented a boat and took me out with a picnic basket filled with food and wine. At the very bottom was my ring."

Crain reflected his mother's smile back to her. "Did you feel like you had to say yes? Since he had you out there in the middle of a lake?"

Melinda Carraway laughed. "A little. The thought did cross my mind that it was a good thing I was prepared to say yes."

"Hmm," Crain said, thinking. "I didn't do that for Elizabeth," he admitted. "I didn't ease her into the idea of marrying me. I didn't plan anything out. Didn't consider taking her to a place that meant something to me. I just sort of asked her. In the middle of Vegas. Without a ring, but with a wedding chapel right down the street."

"You wanted to make her yours."

"I did," he acknowledged. "I truly did."

"And you've suffered a bit for it," she said gently.

"You have no idea."

"But that's all behind the two of you now, right?" his mother coaxed, trying to pull him out of his melancholy.

"I thought so. But as it turns out, Tansy had not only tried to get back with her ex-boyfriend while we were married, she—"

There was a knock on the door. A firm, no-nonsense rap that was immediately followed by the knob turning and an unwelcome sight barging into the room.

The Pink One, in a suit and tie, took one look at Crain's mother and moved in like he'd been invited. Like he wasn't the thorn in his side. No, check that. The dagger in his heart.

"You must be Mrs. Carraway," Pinks said, turning on his Brooks-Bennett-Wannabe charm. "Crain's told us so much about you and Mr. Carraway," he said as he took her outstretched hand. "We're all looking forward to your visit to our little town of Henderson when Tansy—I mean Elizabeth—and Crain tie the knot." He shot a wary look at Crain.

"And you are?" his momma asked The Pink One, looking slightly dazzled.

Oh, come on, Momma. He's just a kid.

"I'm Davis Williams. Friend and colleague of your son, Crain. I'm here representing E&E Investments, Inc. and the town of Henderson. Here to get a few things straightened out."

Oh, no. You did not just throw me a look like I'm the bad guy here.

"Well, Davis, I'm sure pleased to meetcha. I'll get out of your way." She picked up her purse.

"No need," Davis insisted. "Stay. I'm sure you'll be interested in hearing this too." The slimy bastard put a hand on her shoulder, keeping her on the couch, while he sent Crain a warning look.

What the fuck? Two could play at this game.

"That's right. Sit, Momma. Make yourself comfortable. This one plans to own the town of Henderson someday and everybody in it. He's already staked his claim on everyone I know there, Elizabeth included. So whatever he thinks he can straighten out ought to be fascinating."

"Well, then. I can't wait to hear it," Melinda said, beaming. She turned her entire body toward Davis.

"Mind if I sit?" he asked Crain.

"As a matter of fact, I do," Crain spat.

"Oh, Crain, stop it," his momma scolded. "Of course, you can sit," she oozed up at Davis. "How 'bout something to drink?" she suggested. "Crain, get us all a Coke, why don't you? It'll be more friendly that way."

"Momma, I'm not interested in being friendly at the moment," he scowled.

"Don't embarrass your mother, darling boy. Go get the Cokes."

"Yes. We wouldn't want to embarrass *your* mother," The Pink One threatened.

This is a pissing contest, Crain thought, surprised. Right here in front of his mother. The Pink Ninja was swinging his dick around like he could have Tansy and the sports academy too.

"Why are you here?" Crain finally relented, getting up and going to the mini fridge to get the damn Cokes.

"Well, when you and I had our little altercation the other night, I never did get my say. Like I said, I'm here to set things right."

"An altercation," his momma said, her voice rising like it was the most exciting word she'd heard in a long time.

"Yes, Mrs. Carraway, you see—"

"Call me Melinda," his mother begged The Pink One.

"Momma," Crain turned and scolded. "He's a kid. He'll call you Mrs. Carraway, and he'll remember to be respectful." He eyed Pinks darkly.

Pinks wasn't biting. Neither was his mother.

"He's a handsome man," Melinda said as she reached for her Coke. "I'd prefer he called me Melinda, Crain. My goodness when did you get so stuffy?" she complained.

"Dear God," Crain muttered under his breath.

"Melinda," The Pink One soothed, talking directly to his momma.

So help him, Crain wanted to rip the guy's throat apart.

"You've met your daughter-in-law, Elizabeth, correct?"

"Yes. Finally." She eyed Crain like the holdup was all his fault. "Just two weeks ago."

"And I'm sure you noticed how beautiful she is," Davis went on treading into dangerous territory.

"She's as lovely as Crain said. Sweet too. We're very proud to have her as part of our family."

"And she was just as crazy about you and your husband. But there's recently been a glitch," Pinks said.

"A glitch?" his momma repeated.

"A glitch." Crain scoffed under his breath.

"Yes." The Pink One stared at Crain, "A *terrible* glitch. And it's all…my…fault," Pinks said deliberately.

"How terrible a glitch?" his momma asked. "I just ordered Save-the-Date cards this morning. We cannot change the date."

"No. No date changing," Pinks said. "That's why I'm here. To smooth things over so there will be no delay of any kind."

"If you think you're getting a stadium out of me, you aren't as smart as you think you are."

"I'm not here about a stadium," Davis said honestly, looking at Crain dead on. "I'm not here about dormitories or learning centers. I'm here for one reason only. To apologize. For taking advantage of *your* Elizabeth."

The two men glared at each other, Melinda Carraway's head swiveling between the two. When Crain didn't say anything, The Pink One turned his attention back to Crain's momma, showering her with his frat-boy smile.

"Melinda, when you meet Elizabeth's mother, I'm sure you'll find her delightful. She's beautiful, like her daughter, and she's used to getting her own way. Elizabeth, like some of us," he said, nodding in Crain's direction, "lives to please her parents, and in particular, her mother. Having worked with Elizabeth for a while now, I've seen Garland Langford in action, and I can tell you, growing up as Elizabeth Tansy Langford was not easy. Which, as you may or may not be aware, caused this whole problem to begin with."

"Yes." Melinda leaned in closer to Pinks. "I understand that poor Elizabeth was afraid to confess that she'd eloped with a man her parents had never met. Frankly, I can't blame her."

"Momma, did you just throw an eyeball at me?" Crain was incredulous.

"Eloping." She huffed the word at him like it was the most ridiculous idea he'd ever had.

"It was awesome," Crain defended.

"Yes," The Pink One said in agreement. He looked Crain right in the eye and threw his own words back at him. "It was awesome."

Then he turned his attention back to Crain's momma. "But I can certainly understand how you and Mrs. Langford would be upset by it, and why Tansy—I mean, Elizabeth panicked. A momentary panic, which she has confessed to me more than a few times she deeply regrets." Pinks turned his attention back to Crain, "She wishes she would have stayed...let him talk her down from her emotional turmoil. Let him help her solve the problem the two of them put into motion. Take responsibility for all of it and work it out, together."

"Are you about done?" Crain asked irritated.

Pinks ignored him and went back to talking to his mother.

"Anyway, Elizabeth came home to Henderson, as you are aware, and didn't tell anyone she was married, too afraid of upsetting Garland and Rye, her parents. And in an effort to make things right with Crain, she had an attorney in Dallas draw up annulment papers so that Crain could not be held responsible or beholden to Elizabeth, since she was the one with the serious bout of cold feet. She mistakenly anticipated that Crain would've reconsidered their quick elopement and signed the papers. Since she didn't want any correspondence to fall into the wrong hands, she rented a post office box in Raleigh and had a friend check the box periodically."

Crain's momma was nodding right along, thoroughly involved in the story.

"In the meantime, Tansy and I—I mean Elizabeth and I— started working together for the newly formed company, Evans & Evans Investments, Inc." The Pink One smiled at Crain's mother like he was about to share the best secret of all. "You should have seen us. Tansy and I butted heads from the first time we met moving furniture into the office. We were like oil and water from the get-go. I didn't like her, and she didn't like me. And it was a power struggle to see which one of us was going to come out on top in the eyes of our employers. I'm telling you, we fussed and feuded, but all the while, Elizabeth's beauty was not lost on me. I might have been competing with her on the job, but I can't deny I was rather attracted to her. I mean, can you blame me?"

Crain's mother said, "Good Lord, no. She's a lovely girl."

"And she's smart too. She could do her job and mine with one hand tied behind her back. I know it. Everybody knows it. So, maybe I was a little worried about that. Maybe I kept antagonizing her just because I liked her paying attention to me, even if it was just to put me in my place. Your son over here refers to me as a kid, and I guess, compared to his thirty-five years, I am. And kids are bound to do dumb things when they are new to the business world and just learning the ropes. Your son had the confidence to ask Elizabeth out. I had no such confidence, having just been tossed out of a yearlong relationship in college. So, I took advantage of the situation at a time when Elizabeth was at her most vulnerable."

"When was that?" Melinda asked.

"As I understand it now, Elizabeth had received word that the annulment papers she'd sent Crain had been delivered to her post office box in Raleigh." Davis looked over at Crain directly. "She didn't know that you had scribbled over each page with her preferred red sharpie that you'd sign them when she had the guts to face you in person. She was under the impression that you had signed them, and that the lawyer had filed them and then sent her a copy. She *thought*," Pinks stressed, "that her marriage had been terminated. She thought that she had lost you forever. And that thought sent her to our one and only bar in town to drown her sorrows."

Pinks let that bit of news hang there. In the room. Between them.

Crain felt sick.

Pinks turned back to Melinda and quietly said, "I'm ashamed to tell you that without being aware of the extenuating circumstances, I took advantage of Elizabeth when she was not only under the influence of alcohol, but, as it turns out, was utterly heartbroken as well."

Crain didn't know how his momma reacted to that little tidbit, because he had his head down, staring at the floor. Gut churning, fingers twitching, rage burning through his system. "I sent those papers back unsigned to make a goddamn point," he argued.

"And she got it. As soon as she drove into Raleigh to pick them up, she got your point. She realized right away that she was still married. But what you need to wrap your Texas-sized head around is that for a very crucial twenty-four hours, she believed she was no longer married. And worse than that, she believed that you didn't want her."

What Crain didn't want was to deal with this. He wanted to yell bullshit and throw the home-wrecking asshole out of his office. He looked over at his momma, who'd gone white as a ghost. "You okay over there, Momma?"

"Crain," she whispered. "What's happened? Is this why you're home early this week? Have you…done something with Tansy?"

"You mean have I strangled her like I should have a month ago? Not yet. And her name's Elizabeth, Ma. And good Lord, did you not just hear what The Pink One said? Whose side are you on, for Christ sake?"

"Yours, darling boy, always yours. But you can't blame the poor girl if she thought you'd dumped her. I mean, look at him." She pointed at Pinks. "Young, virile, gorgeous. Any woman would have wanted to cry on his shoulder."

"You think I'm gorgeous?" Pinks piped up.

"Enough! That's enough from the both of you. This is my life. This is not some damn daytime soap opera we're dealing with."

"Well, then, stop treating it like one," his momma ordered. "For goodness sakes. Either you're married or you're not. Either you love her or you don't. And if you're married, and if you love her, then forgive her. Immediately. Before I send her a whole lot of stones to throw back at your glass house."

"Excuse me?"

"Oh, darling boy. I will never forget the three separate pregnancy scares you made me live through." Before he could stop her, his momma turned toward the bane of his existence and elaborated. "Two in high school and one in college. He drags me in on them all and has me convinced I'm gonna be a grandma way before my time. False alarms, all three. You would have thought the man had never heard of a condom."

"I wore 'em," Crain defended, "and this conversation stays in this office," he threatened Pinks.

"What else ya got?" The Pink One asked his mother.

"No. Absolutely not. We are done here." Crain stood abruptly, cutting off the "Rake Crain Over The Coals" fest they had brewing. "Both of you. Out," he ordered. "Ma, you first. I don't trust the two of you together. Goodbye," he said, kissing her cheek. "Leave the building immediately."

"Will Elizabeth be at dinner Wednesday?" she asked sweetly.

"I'll let you know," he answered.

"Davis." She waved back at him as she headed for the door. "Thank you for calling me."

"My pleasure, Mrs. Carraway. I look forward to seeing you in Henderson."

Once the door closed behind his mother, Crain stared at The Pink One. "My mother? You involved my mother in this? Why would you do that?"

The Pink One shrugged. "One, I figured the odds were in my favor you wouldn't hit me in front of your mother. And two, if it was truly the mothers behind this mess, then maybe the mothers needed to help fix it. Look man, Tansy is despondent over this thing. She loves you. You know she loves you. You wouldn't sign the annulment papers until she faced you in person. You cannot cut her loose without giving her the same opportunity."

"I swear to God, if you're bullshitting me about any of this—"

"I'm not. Deep down, you know I'm not. You know me. You know Tansy. You know Hale and Vance. Not one of us wanted to hurt you. Okay, maybe I wanted to hurt you at first, but I'm over it. I'm over Tansy. I'm on your side. Clearly, as I'm standing here with my feet planted in Dallas."

"All right. All right. Whatever. Just…it's gonna take me a while to get over you being with my wife."

"I understand perfectly. Brooks was like that too. Didn't like Lolly's ex hanging around Henderson. But just like Brooks, you're the one who ended up with the girl." Pinks hit him affectionately on the back. "Once again, you're the top dog, my friend, and I continue to find myself the underdog.

"Underdog, my ass. Look, just keep your eyes and hands and everything else off my Elizabeth from now on, and I will endeavor to be as magnanimous as Brooks. But you're not off the hook. Not by a long shot. I need you to help solve this mystery for me. There's no way my stumbling into Elizabeth in Henderson was a coincidence. Who knew about me? About us?" Crain asked. "Who got me to Henderson so I could find Elizabeth?"

Pinks smiled. "It was Genevra."

"Genevra? How's that exactly?"

"She came into the office late one afternoon after all of us were gone and heard Tansy on the phone with that lawyer she hired. Apparently, she was having second thoughts about the annulment."

"Second thoughts?"

"Told the lawyer to hold off on delivering the papers to you. But he must have told her it had already been done. Genevra said Tansy sat for a long time in silence. She said it was a silence so heavy and sad she didn't feel she had the right to interrupt it. So she stayed hidden and slipped back out the door. The next day, she had the bells hooked up to the same door so no one could overhear Tansy's business again. Of course, that didn't stop her from snooping around and finding the lawyer's business card in her desk. Right on top of one of yours."

"Genevra," Crain said, trying to take it all in.

"Yeah, Genevra. And Hale. Of course, she told Hale all about it, and those two think everybody should be as happy as they are, so they played the rest of us, so we'd think it was our bright idea to call CC Dallas."

"So you, Vance, Brooks?"

"Were all kept in the dark. Knew nothing about any of it. Hale did keep badgering Brooks about getting you into town for the minor league stadium idea. I took it upon myself to get the job done when Brooks couldn't."

"You like one-upping Brooks, don'tcha?"

"I did mention he's dating my ex, right? So listen," Pinks went on, checking his watch. "There's this girl who was crying her eyes out when I left the office this morning. If you'd heard it, I guarantee it would have broken your heart. I know it did mine. If we can fire that big jet of yours up within the hour, I bet the two of us can be back there, begging her forgiveness before dinner."

"The two of us?"

"Damn right. I would never send a buddy into battle alone," he said, reaching out and offering up his hand.

Crain stared down at it a moment before he reached out and shook it. "Thanks," he mumbled.

"What's that?" Pinks feigned lack of hearing.

"Don't push it," Crain growled. "Now there's one other thing I need you to do for me."

"Lay it on me."

Crain eyed The Pink One, not believing he was actually gonna trust him with this. "I need you to get Elizabeth to The Century Tree."

"The Century what?"

"Come on. I'll explain on the way."

CHAPTER FORTY-FIVE

"I'm not going anywhere with you," Tansy told Pinks. "Ever."

Pinks looked over to Vance for help.

"If I were her, I wouldn't go anywhere with you either, dude. Not after the latest fiasco."

Pinks gritted his teeth and spoke through them. "Crain. Asked me. To escort you. You have to believe me."

"Oh, I believe you. I believe that Crain wants both of us on his jet, so he can remotely blow it up over some ocean. No, thank you."

Davis squeezed his eyes shut, rubbing a hand over his brow like he was in pain. "Fine. I give up. You don't want to go to Crain's alma mater, I'm not going to force you."

"Crain's alma mater? Texas A&M?"

"Look at that. Her attention is piqued," Vance teased.

"Shove it, Evans."

"Annnd everything is back to normal," Vance said, smiling his cheeky grin at Tansy.

"Why's he want me to go to Texas A&M?" she asked Pinks.

"I don't know. Maybe he's gonna get the Corps of Cadets together for a firing squad and finish us off that way."

"Don't think he won't do it. In Texas, you can get away with that sort of thing," Tansy said.

"Look," Vance said," do you want Big Tex back or not? Because my boy Pinks and I have a business to run. Now either get the hell on that plane or get back to work. Both of you."

"Fine," Tansy relented. "Boy, suddenly I have an awful lot of bossy men in my life telling me where to go."

"Yeah, well The Ninja and I are about to bow out," Vance said. "I have it under good authority that your resignation from E&E is going to be part of the prenup agreement."

"Prenup agreement?" Tansy asked wide-eyed.

"Piper's been in touch with Crain. Now that your first marriage is dissolved, she's sticking her nose in it. As if the woman doesn't have enough to worry about with force feeding me pie and cooking up Vance, Jr. in her belly every day."

"Fine," Tansy sighed. "If the man is fool enough to take me back after all of this, I guess I'm happy to know he's not fool enough to do it without a prenup."

"Who said anything about taking you back?" Pinks said, holding his hand out toward the door. "I'm still kinda nervous about that firing squad."

Pinks didn't get off the plane. He told Tansy that Crain had made it clear that his job stopped once they landed in College Station. There was a limo waiting to take her to campus.

Tansy looked at him a little teary eyed. "I don't know what you did to fix this. I certainly don't deserve your kindness after I put you in the middle of it. Every bit of my frustration since I left Crain was taken out on you. And yet, here you are, acting as the hero."

"I'll take that as a thank you. For putting up with your mouth all these many months and for getting Mr. and Mrs. Crain Carraway back together. And once you two name your first born after me, we'll be square."

"As if," Tansy laughed.

"Yeah, I know. And don't take it personally when I avoid you for a while. Crain has come around faster than I would have on this. I'm not going to be pushing my luck."

"I understand," she said.

"Go get your man," he told her.

She bit her bottom lip, feeling a whole lot of nerves mixed in with a little bit of glee. Then she grabbed her tote and started down the stairs of the plane.

"You be good to him," Davis called. "I still have your bra, and I'm not afraid of running it up the flagpole."

Tansy flipped him the bird.

❧

Elizabeth Tansy Langford Carraway had never set foot on the campus of her husband's alma mater before. It was overwhelming, more a city than a college campus, in her opinion. More buildings than Henderson could ever hope to build. Enormous in scope and busy, bustling with energy, everyone saying "Howdy" as they passed each other. The limo driver was sweet and determined to give her a tour of all 5,200 acres, pointing out Research Park, the *other* George Bush Presidential library, the polo fields, golf course, and various other athletic facilities. Any other time, she would have relished the tour, but right now, she couldn't enjoy it. She was too eager to lay eyes on her own tall, sexy Dallas-born Aggie.

Finally, the limo meandered around to an older, more academic part of campus and pulled to the curb. The driver pointed down a concrete path and told Tansy to head in that direction, assuring her the car would be waiting right here whenever she came back. Tansy left her tote in the automobile and exited.

She didn't own much white and maroon, but her lone pair of cowgirl boots was more maroon than Hotty Toddy Red, so she'd worn them. She'd paired them with a white suit, because Crain loved her suits, but this one had a frilly ruffle at the hem, which made it fun and a little flirty. She left the jacket in the car and walked down the lonely path in her body-hugging, scoop-neck tank top. She showed a whole lot of cleavage because she had carnal knowledge of the man and knew what he liked. She pulled her hair up into a messy knot and stuck the Aggie pencil she'd stolen from his desk through it. She'd learned a lot of things from her momma, and dressing for a campus showdown was one of them, tiara notwithstanding.

Lost in thought, and getting increasingly nervous about seeing Crain again, she was startled—practically fell into a faint—when hundreds of what looked like uniformed boy scouts with riding boots and musical instruments suddenly swarmed her. They took up ranks and began to play the Aggie War Hymn. When they started to march, she had no option but to march right with them. When they yelled, "Sounds like hell" in the middle of it, she tripped over her own boots, but gratefully found herself caught by the cadets on either side. They held tight to each of her arms and continued to march along as one.

The Fightin' Texas Aggie Band was forced to close ranks and squeeze between two buildings, which they managed in effortless precision. When they stepped clear, the horizontal lines merged with a flourish into two straight lines flanking both sides of the path ahead of them. Tansy was halted by the cadets at her side as the rest of the band members—numbers and numbers and numbers of them—filed past. When the last of the band, the drum line, stood facing the path in front of Tansy, their invigorating beat pounding a heady rhythm, the cadets moved her forward, down the center of the path, through the entire marching band as they continued to play.

It was overwhelming. It was fantastic. It was the best day ever, especially when she finally spied Crain at the end of it all. There he stood, tall and gorgeous, his big, happy grin shining over casual business attire, holding a fistful of roses. There was a glorious oak tree just beyond him, so big and wild some of its enormous branches cascaded to the ground.

The cadets marched her right up to Crain, drew their swords and formed an arch for her to walk under as she took Crain's outstretched hand.

"I'm sorry I didn't do this back in May," Crain said, gifting her with the flowers and taking her hand, leading her toward a bench situated on the path that ran right under the bowed branches of the big oak tree. "It's a tradition for Aggies to propose under the

Century Tree. The legend has expanded in recent years. Now whoever you walk under the tree with, well, you're basically stuck with for life. So, had I followed tradition…" he trailed off, leading her to sit on the bench.

Then Crain Carraway got down on one knee.

For the third time.

In front of the same girl.

Best day ever.

The Heroes of Henderson Series continues with
UnderDog

UNDER **DOG**

HEROES OF HENDERSON ~ BOOK 4

LIZ KELLY

Thanks so much for reading *Top Dog*.
Reviews help other readers find books.
I appreciate all reviews, whether positive or negative.

All of my Heroes of Henderson novels and novellas are complete romances in and of themselves and do not need to be read in any particular order. However, it's a little more fun that way.

Heroes of Henderson full-length Novels

Good Cop
Bad Cop
Top Dog
Tempting Vivi
UnderDog

Heroes of Henderson Novellas

Playin' Cop
Taming Molly
Kissing Cooper

Listed in order

Countdown To A Kiss
A New Year's Eve Anthology

Playin' Cop
Heroes of Henderson ~ Prequel
Previously published as
The Keeper of the Debutantes in
Countdown to A Kiss

Good Cop
Heroes of Henderson ~ Book 1

Bad Cop
Heroes of Henderson ~ Book 2

Taming Molly
Heroes of Henderson ~ Book 2.5
A DuVal Cousins Quickie

Top Dog
Heroes of Henderson ~ Book 3

Tempting Vivi
Heroes of Henderson ~ Book 3.5
A DuVal Cousins Novel

Kissing Cooper
Heroes of Henderson ~ A Christmas Quickie

UnderDog
Heroes of Henderson ~ Book 4

Sign up at www.*LizKellyBooks.com*
to be alerted when new books are released.

About the Author

Growing up every summer in a place where *dancing and romancing* are literally part of its theme song, Liz Kelly can't help but be a romantic at heart. And since her favorite author, Kathleen E. Woodiwiss wrote some of the world's greatest romances, she's just trying to give the world a little more of that. (Okay, maybe a little sexier *that*, but we are now in a new millennium after all.)

A graduate of Wake Forest University, where she met her handsome golf-addicted husband, (who is now sporting dark glasses everywhere he goes) Liz is a mother of two grown sons (also sporting dark glasses) and a miniature Labradoodle named Isabelle. They split their time between *The Windy City* of Chicago and the *Fountain of Youth,* a.k.a. Naples, FL where dancing and romancing continues on ad infinitum.